The Gospel in
George MacDonald

The Gospel in George MacDonald

Selections from His Novels, Fairy Tales, and Spiritual Writings

Edited by Marianne Wright

With Artwork by Arthur Hughes

From the Gospel in Great Writers Series

PLOUGH PUBLISHING HOUSE

Published by Plough Publishing House
Walden, New York
Robertsbridge, England
Elsmore, Australia
www.plough.com

Plough produces books, a quarterly magazine, and Plough.com to encourage people and help them put their faith into action. We believe Jesus can transform the world and that his teachings and example apply to all aspects of life. At the same time, we seek common ground with all people regardless of their creed.

Plough is the publishing house of the Bruderhof, an international Christian community. The Bruderhof is a fellowship of families and singles practicing radical discipleship in the spirit of the first church in Jerusalem (Acts 2 and 4). Members devote their entire lives to serving God, one another, and their neighbors, renouncing private property and sharing everything. To learn more about the Bruderhof's faith, history, and daily life, see Bruderhof.com. (Views expressed by Plough authors are their own and do not necessarily reflect the position of the Bruderhof.)

ISBN: 978-0-87486-766-4
19 18 17 16   2 3 4 5 6 7

Cover portrait by Edward Hughes, 1886. All other illustrations are by Arthur Hughes from early editions of MacDonald's works in the public domain.

Quotations from Scripture are from the King James Version of the Bible.

A catalog record for this book is available from the British Library.
Library of Congress Cataloging-in-Publication Data
Names: MacDonald, George, 1824-1905, author.
Title: The Gospel in George MacDonald : selections from his novels, fairy tales, and spiritual writings / George MacDonald ; Marianne Wright, editor ; appreciations by C. S. Lewis and G. K. Chesterton.
Description: Walden, New York : Plough Publishing House, 2016. | Series: The Gospel in great writers
Identifiers: LCCN 2016030353 (print) | LCCN 2016039298 (ebook) | ISBN 9780874867664 (pbk.) | ISBN 9780874867671 (epub) | ISBN 9780874867688 (mobi) | ISBN 9780874867695 (pdf)
Subjects: LCSH: Christian literature, English. | English literature--Scottish authors.
Classification: LCC PR4966 .W75 2016 (print) | LCC PR4966 (ebook) | DDC 823/.8--dc23
LC record available at https://lccn.loc.gov/2016030353

Printed in the USA

Contents

Introduction   *vii*

FINDING GOD

  1. Seeking   3

  2. Repentance   13

  3. Redemption   27

  4. Jesus   43

  5. God's Glory   57

  6. The Divine Plan   65

  7. The Boundlessness of Love   81

THE WAY OF DISCIPLESHIP

  8. Faith   93

  9. Obedience   115

 10. Growth of Character   127

 11. Conscience   141

 12. Work   147

 13. Prayer   161

GOD IN OUR MIDST

 14. Love of Neighbor   171

 15. Creation   193

16. Our Father in Heaven   203
17. Love and Marriage   209
18. Fatherhood and Motherhood   219
19. Education   229
20. Money   237
21. Moralism   249

ETERNAL LIFE

22. Death   261
23. Resurrection   287

APPRECIATIONS

    G. K. Chesterton   305
    C. S. Lewis   315

    Notes   327
    Bibliography   338

Introduction

In a widely reproduced photograph from an 1876 book titled *English Celebrities of the Nineteenth Century,* George MacDonald appears among a group of nine British literary giants. Charles Dickens is there, of course, as well as Anthony Trollope, Wilkie Collins, and W. M. Thackeray. The photograph—a montage created by a commercial publisher—is a visual monument to Victorian eminence: big black-cloaked men with big beards who wrote big famous books.

When this picture was first published, it was apparently uncontroversial to rank George MacDonald among the great writers of his age. Not so today. It has been at least a century since MacDonald has been widely read, and scholars outside his small fan base tend to approach his works as period pieces rather than as literature. So it is reasonable to ask: can we truly consider MacDonald a great writer?

C. S. Lewis, like many of MacDonald's admirers, had his doubts, writing that "MacDonald has no place in [literature's] first rank—perhaps not even in its second." Today's reader, when first confronted with MacDonald's writing, may well be tempted to agree. His books are long, his nineteenth-century mannerisms do not all age well, and several of his novels include patches of intimidating Scots dialect (more on that below).

All this. Yet mention MacDonald's name, and it will not be long before you find yourself speaking with someone who, like C. S. Lewis, has found MacDonald's books "beyond price" despite their literary deficiencies. Lewis goes on:

> I dare not say that he is never in error; but to speak plainly I know hardly any other writer who seems to be closer, or more continually close, to the Spirit of Christ Himself. Hence his Christ-like union of tenderness and severity. Nowhere else outside the New Testament have I found terror and comfort so intertwined.

✦ ✦ ✦

I was introduced to George MacDonald early in life by my grandfather. He could read aloud better than anyone in the world, and among the dozens of books he read to me and my siblings were MacDonald's *At the Back of the North Wind, The Princess and the Goblin,* and *The Princess and Curdie.* My grandparents' house was full of books, but it was obvious even to a child that George MacDonald meant something special to Grandpa. At a time when most of MacDonald's books were out of print and difficult to find, he would spend long weekend afternoons combing the catalogs of secondhand booksellers for titles he hadn't read. The books, when they came, were generally in poor condition. He mended and rebound them with loving precision, letting us help paint on the stiff bindery glue and select ribbons to bind in as markers. Into the back of each book he pasted a glossary of Scottish terms, and in the front he placed a photocopied overview of MacDonald's life along with a list of his works. The list was annotated in Grandpa's decisive handwriting to save future readers from wasting time on titles he considered inferior. There are marks of A+ for his favorites *(Robert Falconer, Sir Gibbie, Warlock o' Glenwarlock). Lilith,* which he could never see the point of, rates a D–. Like many people who love

MacDonald's writings, he made collections of extracts. It was from one of these—ninety-one short selections manually typed on a vintage Smith Corona and bound into a little volume he gave my father for his birthday—that I first discovered, at a time when I badly needed it, MacDonald's great-hearted, practical, but uncompromising account of the New Testament message. I read that collection numerous times before I read MacDonald's novels for myself, and although I have since read almost all his published work, I still return to that little book for inspiration and reflection.

✦ ✦ ✦

MacDonald dedicated his life to spreading the gospel; writing books was his main means of doing this. He once said, "People find great fault with me—that I turn my stories into sermons. They forget that I have a Master to serve before I can wait upon the public." In his work he returns frequently to themes of discipleship, conscience, and faith. And yes, he is sometimes—actually, often—preachy. But we forgive him because so many of his novels are terrifically entertaining in unexpected ways; when they were published they sold in the hundreds of thousands in both England and the United States. His 1875 novel *Malcolm,* for instance, was reprinted more than a dozen times after being serialized in a magazine. MacDonald's imaginative stories for children and adults are peerless in their invention, humor, and insight. As W. H. Auden wrote, "In that style of writing which is called visionary or mythic, MacDonald has never been surpassed." His explicitly religious works, meanwhile, are rich in wisdom, beauty, and generosity. The aim of this book is to bring together those passages from MacDonald's writings—novels, works of fantasy, children's stories, sermons, devotional writings, and personal correspondence—that best illuminate the good news of Jesus, which was the constant theme and the joy of his life.

The selections in this book have been arranged to follow the path of a life of discipleship (and to address some of the challenges to such a life: moralism and mammon). This organization is necessarily arbitrary at times—a passage about worship will inevitably be about prayer as well—and some passages have been split between chapters because they speak to different ideas. Arranging the material this way allows readers to explore MacDonald's insights on key themes in various literary forms and shows the consistency and largeness of vision with which he returned to the gospel's first principles. (Because this message is the focus of this book, no scholarly inquiry into MacDonald's theology or literary influences has been attempted.) All of Mac-Donald's published works were considered in selecting passages, but for the purpose of this collection some books proved more useful than others. The organization of the material into thematic sections forced some of the passages to be out of narrative order. Anyone wanting to find out more about the stories—which are by turns realistic, gothic, fantastic, romantic, and comic—should treat themselves to the original novels. Readers will notice that some names are repeated in different selections. This is because MacDonald revisited some of his favorite characters in several novels: Robert Falconer, who shows God's love to the people around him simply by being present with them; Donal Grant, whose serenely courageous faith is the result of weathering an early disappointment; Malcolm, the fisherman who combines childlike discipleship with iron integrity.

A handful of characters in MacDonald's novels speak a lowland Scots dialect. Because the remarks of these characters sound glib or contrived if "translated" into standard English (and because MacDonald himself resisted such simplifications), the selections in this book containing dialect have not been modernized. Readers are of course free to skip these passages, but most people will find them easy to understand if they are read slowly and sounded out phonetically; the meanings of those words and phrases that are less easily understood are given at the foot of the page.

✦ ✦ ✦

MacDonald believed that God makes use of the ordinary events of each day—the "holy present" as he called it—to lead and teach his people. He was convinced that the kingdom of God can be a reality in the here and now, and that it requires daily acts of obedient discipleship to bring it about. As a character in *Thomas Wingfold* says, "I begin to suspect . . . that the common transactions of life are the most sacred channels for the spread of the heavenly leaven." Some of these channels recur in MacDonald's books (and in this collection): the conversation with a parent or wise teacher; the delight in the created world and the everyday pleasures of life; the lengthy sickness that stirs the conscience; the experience of love between man and woman; the contemplation of death and life eternal.

There is an autobiographical element to several of these themes, so that some knowledge of MacDonald's life is instructive. (MacDonald himself had no interest in publishing the details of his history: he wrote in 1893 to a friend who had asked to interview him, "I never have and never will consent to be interviewed. I will do nothing to bring my personality before the public in any way farther than my work in itself necessitates.") George MacDonald was born in 1824 in a village in Aberdeenshire, Scotland, and was raised in a loving and happy home on his father's farm. He later said that his relationship with his father taught him that fatherhood must be the core of the universe. George MacDonald's early education in country schools emphasized stories—of Scotland's history and heroes, classical mythology, and the Old Testament—giving him experience in the power of stories to transform and illuminate everyday life. He left home to study at King's College in Aberdeen, receiving a master's degree in chemistry and physics in 1845.

Around this time, he decided to devote his life to serving God by spreading his word, both from the pulpit and through writing. He traveled to London to seek ordination as a Congregationalist minister, and when he was twenty-six, he was appointed minister of a church in Arundel, East Sussex. He left this position after three years because some of his views were considered heretical by the church deacons: he believed that God's love extends even to the heathen, and held out hope that God would eventually reconcile all creation to himself. (His belief that animals would also enter heaven was another point of disagreement.)

In 1851 he married Louisa Powell. Their fifty-one-year marriage was a partnership of deep love, mutual respect, and happy collaboration on the project of raising eleven children ("the wrong side of a dozen," MacDonald liked to say). He relied on his wife's literary opinions as well as the cheerful reliability with which she managed the affairs of their large household. Louisa was by all accounts a spirited woman. A typical anecdote tells how, during the bedlam of an earthquake that struck during a church service, she reacted by making for the organ and playing Handel's Hallelujah chorus while the rest of the congregation hid under the pews.

Even in the years of MacDonald's greatest popularity as a writer, the family was never financially secure, but his confidence that God would provide was never disappointed. MacDonald received very little in royalties for his books, in part because pirated editions appeared on both sides of the Atlantic. Additional income came from occasional lectureships and the amateur family dramatic productions Louisa organized, and in 1877 Queen Victoria—who had given his children's books to her grandchildren—gave MacDonald a small Civil List pension. Despite the family's habitually penniless state, their home was widely known as a place of genial hospitality where anyone, from an orphan child to Alfred Lord Tennyson, the poet laureate, would find welcome. One guest wrote, "In some wonderful way, all classes, nations, and creeds met willingly under that roof."

One of MacDonald's early admirers was Lady Byron, the widow of the poet, who sponsored a family trip of several months to Algiers in 1858 after doctors advised Mediterranean air for MacDonald's tuberculosis. John Ruskin and Lewis Carroll were especially close friends—the MacDonald children were the first to read the manuscript of *Alice's Adventures in Wonderland*, and it was their enthusiastic response that convinced Carroll to publish it. MacDonald enjoyed similar relationships among the American literary establishment: during a lecture tour in the northeast in 1872, his itinerary included visits with Ralph Waldo Emerson, John Greenleaf Whittier, and Henry Wadsworth Longfellow. He and Mark Twain struck up an unlikely friendship and discussed co-authoring a book.

But more important to him than his famous acquaintances was his desire to reach a broad public with the gospel message. Apart from writing, he lectured to crowds of up to eight thousand. According to one newspaper account, "There is something indescribable about the man which holds the audience till the last word. It is not eloquence or poetry, nor is there any straining for effect, but it is the man's soul that captivates. You love the man at once."

George MacDonald suffered from lung trouble throughout most of his life, and several of his children had tuberculosis: the deaths of four of them during his lifetime brought great grief, together with an ever firmer faith in the resurrection. Because English winters aggravated tuberculosis, the family moved in 1879 to Bordighera, Italy, where they lived for about twenty years in a villa they called Casa Coraggio (House of Courage). These years and the years leading up to them were MacDonald's most productive literary period: in the two decades between 1870 and 1890, he wrote twenty-two books, including numerous novels of over four hundred pages, all while participating in a lively home life and corresponding with dozens of friends. One acquaintance of this period was Arthur Hughes, an artist in the Pre-Raphaelite school who identified closely with MacDonald's belief that imagination can promote an understanding of God's purpose by "choosing, gathering, and vitally combining the material of a new revelation." Hughes provided dozens of illustrations for MacDonald's books, some of which have been reproduced in this volume. There was a family connection with Hughes as well: the MacDonald's second daughter, Mary Josephine, was engaged to Hughes's nephew Edward Hughes—another artist, who drew the portrait of MacDonald that is on the cover of this book—for four years until her death from tuberculosis in 1878.

The family returned to England in 1900. MacDonald's last years were spent in a house in Surrey that had been designed for him by a son who was an architect. Here he and Louisa celebrated their fiftieth wedding anniversary in June 1901, and here they parted: Louisa died in January of the next year. From then until his death on September 18, 1905, George MacDonald rarely spoke. He kept what his son Greville called "his long vigil," waiting to be taken into what he had once described as "a life beyond, a larger life, more awake, more earnest, more joyous than this!"

✦ ✦ ✦

That George MacDonald is known at all today is likely due to the influence his writings had on two of the twentieth century's most important Christian apologists, G. K. Chesterton and C. S. Lewis. Both men gladly acknowledged their debt to him, and both were eager that he should be more widely read. Chesterton wrote, "When he comes to be more carefully studied as a mystic, as I think he will be when people discover the possibility of collecting jewels scattered in a rather irregular setting, it will be found, I fancy, that he stands for a rather important turning-point in the history of Christendom." For both men, MacDonald's imaginative stories first provided a new view of the world: Chesterton described *The Princess and the Goblin* as "a book that has made a difference to my whole existence," while C. S. Lewis said that, reading *Phantastes* as a young atheist, "I knew that I had crossed a great frontier." Lewis explained this statement when he looked back later in life:

> The quality which had enchanted me in his imaginative works turned out to be the quality of the real universe, the divine, magical, terrifying, and ecstatic reality in which we all live. I should have been shocked in my teens if anyone had told me that what I learned to love in *Phantastes* was goodness. But now that I know, I see there was no deception. The deception is all the other way round—in that prosaic moralism which confines goodness to the region of Law and Duty, which never lets us feel in our face the sweet air blowing from "the land of righteousness."

Both men came to admire MacDonald's realistic novels and religious writings as well; their appreciations at the end of this book provide perspective on the question of George MacDonald's greatness as a writer. In Chesterton's words, he is "not so much a man of letters, as a man with something to say." And what MacDonald says returns invariably to the heart of the gospel. There is an account of a lecture he gave toward the end of his life that describes how, "Acknowledging a vote of thanks, MacDonald said in the homely Scottish tones so characteristic of him: 'I'm getting an old man, and I don't know how soon I may be away, but I would just like to say to the young men and women present that there's nothing in all the world worth doing except following Jesus Christ.'"

✦ ✦ ✦

My grandfather was found to have advanced incurable cancer in May of 2002. During his final summer, his appreciation for the simple and sublime joys of daily life remained vivid, but he never (that I know) questioned or regretted that his time on earth was ending. During those months he referred us to a passage from one of MacDonald's A+ titles, *What's Mine's Mine*, that could have been written about him: "I do care to live—tremendously—but I don't mind where. He who made this room so well worth living in, may surely be trusted with the next!" It is to my grandfather, Richard Arnold Mommsen, that my work on this book is gratefully dedicated.

Marianne Wright
July 2016

For what is the great glory o' God but that,
tho' no man can comprehen' Him,
He comes doon, an lays his cheek till his man's,
an' says till him,
"Eh, my cratur!"

George MacDonald

Finding God

Ask, and it shall be given you;
seek, and ye shall find;
knock, and it shall be opened unto you:

For every one that asketh receiveth;
and he that seeketh findeth;
and to him that knocketh it shall be opened.

Matthew 7:7–8

1.

Seeking

From a sermon reflecting on Jesus' words, "Whoso shall receive one such little child in my name receiveth me" (Matt. 18:5).

Brothers, have you found our king? There he is, kissing little children and saying they are like God.

From the novel Annals of a Quiet Neighbourhood. *A young man despairs of finding a way to talk to the woman he is in love with, and at last decides to ask God for help.*

How often do we look upon God as our last and feeblest resource! We go to Him because we have nowhere else to go. And then we learn that the storms of life have driven us, not upon the rocks, but into the desired haven; that we have been compelled, as to the last remaining, so to the best, the only, the central help.

From a sermon.

Nor will God force any door to enter in. He may send a tempest about the house; the wind of His admonishment may burst

3

doors and windows, yea, shake the house to its foundations; but not then, not so, will He enter. The door must be opened by the willing hand, ere the foot of Love will cross the threshold. He watches to see the door move from within.

Every tempest is but an assault in the siege of Love. The terror of God is but the other side of His love; it is love outside, that would be inside—love that knows the house is no house, only a place, until it enter.

From the novel Thomas Wingfold, Curate. *A young minister, Thomas Wingfold, is challenged by an atheist to defend his religious convictions, and in trying to do so finds how shallow his own faith is. In time he confides in the deeply believing Mr. Polwarth.*

Of course all this he ought to have gone through long ago! But how can a man go through anything till his hour be come? Saul of Tarsus was sitting at the feet of Gamaliel when our Lord said to his apostles—"Yea, the time cometh, that whosoever killeth you will think that he doeth God service." Wingfold had all this time been skirting the wall of the kingdom of heaven without even knowing that there was a wall there, not to say seeing a gate in it. . . .

It never occurred to him—as how should it?—that he might have commenced undergoing the most marvellous of all changes,—one so marvellous, indeed, that for a man to fore-know its result or understand what he was passing through, would be more strange than that a caterpillar should recognise in the rainbow-winged butterfly hovering over the flower at whose leaf he was gnawing, the perfected idea of his own potential self—I mean the change of being born again. . . .

And all the time, the young man was wrestling, his life in his hand, with his own unbelief; while upon his horizon ever and anon rose the glimmer of a great aurora, or the glimpse of a boundless main—if only he could have been sure they were no mirage of his own parched heart and hungry eye—that they were thoughts in the mind of the Eternal, and *therefore* had appeared in his, even as the Word was said to have become flesh and dwelt with men! The next moment he would be gasping in that malarious exhalation from the marshes of his neglected heart—the counter-fear, namely, that the word under whose potent radiance the world seemed on the verge of budding forth and blossoming as the rose, was *too good to be true.*

"Yes, much too good, if there be no living, self-willing Good," said Polwarth one evening, in answer to the phrase just dropped from his lips. "But if there be such a God as alone could be God, can anything be too good to be true?—too good for such a God as contented Jesus Christ?"

From the novel Robert Falconer. *Robert Falconer is a schoolboy who is being raised in a tiny Scottish village by his loving but strictly Calvinist grandmother. His father has abandoned him and his mother died when he was born. This longer selection follows Robert as he grows up and his search for God leads him, as he strives to find the truth, to question the religious dogma that he has been taught.*

Every evening Robert and his grandmother read Scripture and pray together.

They rose from their knees, and Mrs. Falconer sat down by her fire, with her feet on her little wooden stool, and began, as was her wont in that household twilight, ere the lamp was lighted, to review her past life, and follow her lost son through all conditions and circumstances to her imaginable. And when the world to come arose before her, clad in all the glories which her fancy, chilled by education and years, could supply, it was but to vanish in the gloom of the remembrance of him with whom she dared not hope to share its blessedness. This at least was how Falconer afterwards interpreted the sudden changes from gladness to gloom which he saw at such times on her countenance.

But while such a small portion of the universe of thought was enlightened by the glowworm lamp of the theories she had been taught, she was not limited for light to that feeble source. While she walked on her way, the moon, unseen herself behind the clouds, was illuminating the whole landscape so gently and evenly, that the glowworm being the only visible point of radiance, to it she attributed all the light. But she felt bound to go on believing as she had been taught; for sometimes the most original mind has the strongest sense of law upon it, and will, in default of a better, obey a beggarly one only till the higher law that swallows it up manifests itself. Obedience was as essential an element of her creed as of that of any purest-minded monk; neither being sufficiently impressed with this: that, while obedience is the law of the kingdom, it is of considerable importance that that which is obeyed should be in very truth the will of God. It is one thing, and a good thing, to do for God's sake that which is not his will: it is another thing, and altogether a better thing—how much better, no words can tell—to do for God's sake that which is his will. Mrs. Falconer's submission and obedience led her to accept as the will of God, lest she should be guilty of opposition to him, that which it was anything but giving him honour to accept as such. Therefore her love to God was too like the love of the slave or the dog; too little like the love of the child, with whose obedience the Father cannot be satisfied until he cares for his reason as the highest form of his will.

Later at night, Robert is in his attic room.

So Robert sat in the dark.

But the rain had now ceased. Some upper wind had swept the clouds from the sky, and the whole world of stars was radiant over the earth and its griefs.

"O God, where art thou?" he said in his heart, and went to his own room to look out.

There was no curtain, and the blind had not been drawn down, therefore the earth looked in at the storm-window. The sea neither glimmered nor shone. It lay across the horizon like a low level cloud, out of which came a moaning. Was this moaning all of the earth, or was there trouble in the starry places too? thought Robert, as if already he had begun to suspect the truth from afar—that save in the secret place of the Most High, and in the heart that is hid with the Son of Man in the bosom of the Father, there is trouble—a sacred unrest—everywhere—the moaning of a tide setting homewards, even towards the bosom of that Father.

As he grows older, Robert continues to wonder how it is possible to find God, often walking outdoors as he thinks.

And once more the words arose in his mind, "My peace I give unto you."

Now he fell a-thinking what this peace could be. And it came into his mind as he thought, that Jesus had spoken in another place about giving rest to those that came to him, while here he spoke about "my peace." Could this mean a certain kind of peace that the Lord himself possessed? Perhaps it was in virtue of that peace, whatever it was, that he was the Prince of Peace. Whatever peace he had must be the highest and best peace—therefore the one peace for a man to seek, if indeed, as the words of the Lord seemed to imply, a man was capable of possessing it. He remembered the New Testament in his box, and, resolving to try whether he could not make something more out of it, went back to the inn quieter in heart than since he left his home. In the evening he returned to the brook, and fell to searching the story, seeking after the peace of Jesus.

He found that the whole passage stood thus:—

"Peace I leave with you, my peace I give unto you: not as the world giveth, give I unto you. Let not your heart be troubled, neither let it be afraid."

He did not leave the place for six weeks. Every day he went to the burn, as he called it, with his New Testament; every day tried yet again to make out something more of what the Saviour meant. By the end of the month it had dawned upon him, he hardly knew how, that the peace of Jesus (although, of course, he could not know what it was like till he had it) must have been a peace that came from the doing of the will of his Father. From the account he gave of the discoveries he then made, I venture to represent them in the driest and most exact form that I can find they will admit of. When I use the word discoveries, I need hardly say that I use it with reference to Falconer and his previous knowledge. They were these:—that Jesus taught—

First,—That a man's business is to do the will of God:

Second,—That God takes upon himself the care of the man:

Third,—Therefore, that a man must never be afraid of anything; and so,

---

burn stream

Fourth,—be left free to love God with all his heart, and his neighbour as himself.

But one day, his thoughts having cleared themselves a little upon these points, a new set of questions arose with sudden inundation—comprised in these two:

"How can I tell for certain that there ever was such a man? How am I to be sure that such as he says is the mind of the maker of these glaciers and butterflies?"

All this time he was in the wilderness as much as Moses at the back of Horeb, or St. Paul when he vanishes in Arabia: and he did nothing but read the four gospels and ponder over them. Therefore it is not surprising that he should have already become so familiar with the gospel story, that the moment these questions appeared, the following words should dart to the forefront of his consciousness to meet them:—

"If any man will do his will, he shall know of the doctrine, whether it be of God, or whether I speak of myself."

Here was a word of Jesus himself, announcing the one means of arriving at a conviction of the truth or falsehood of all that he said, namely, the doing of the will of God by the man who would arrive at such conviction.

The next question naturally was: What is this will of God of which Jesus speaks? Here he found himself in difficulty. The theology of his grandmother rushed in upon him, threatening to overwhelm him with demands as to feeling and inward action from which his soul turned with sickness and fainting. That they were repulsive to him, that they appeared unreal, and contradictory to the nature around him, was no proof that they were not of God. But on the other hand, that they demanded what seemed to him unjust,—that these demands were founded on what seemed to him untruth attributed to God, on ways of thinking and feeling which are certainly degrading in a man,—these were reasons of the very highest nature for refusing to act upon them so long as, from whatever defects it might be in himself, they bore to him this aspect. He saw that while they appeared to be such, even though it might turn out that he mistook them, to acknowledge them would be to wrong God. But this conclusion left him in no better position for practice than before.

When at length he did see what the will of God was, he wondered, so simple did it appear, that he had failed to discover it at once. Yet not less than a fortnight had he been brooding and pondering over the question, as he wandered up and down that burnside, or sat at the foot of the heather-crowned stone and the silver-barked birch, when the light began to dawn upon him. It was thus.

In trying to understand the words of Jesus by searching back, as it were, for such thoughts and feelings in him as would account for the words he spoke, the perception awoke that at least he could not have meant by the will of God any such theological utterances as those which troubled him. Next it grew plain that what he came to do, was just to lead his life. That he should do the work, such as recorded, and much besides, that the Father gave him to do—this was the will of God concerning him. With this perception arose the conviction that unto every man whom God had sent into the world, he had given a work to do in that world. He had to lead the life God meant him to lead. The will of God was to be found and done in the world. In seeking a true relation to the world, would he find his relation to God?

The time for action was come.

He rose up from the stone of his meditation, took his staff in his hand, and went down the mountain, not knowing whither he went. And these were some of his thoughts as he went:

"If it was the will of God who made me, my will shall not be set against his. I cannot be happy, but I will bow my head and let his waves and his billows go over me. If there is such a God, he knows what a pain I bear. His will be done. Jesus thought it well that his will should be done to the death. Even if there be no God, it will be grand to be a disciple of such a man, to do as he says, think as he thought—perhaps come to feel as he felt."

My reader may wonder that one so young should have been able to think so practically—to the one point of action. But he was in earnest, and what lay at the root of his character, at the root of all that he did, felt, and became, was childlike simplicity and purity of nature. If the sins of his father were mercifully visited upon him, so likewise were the grace and loveliness of his mother. And between the two, Falconer had fared well.

2.

Repentance

From a sermon in the novel Thomas Wingfold, Curate.

At the root of all human bliss lies repentance.

Come then at the call of the Water, the Healer, the Giver of repentance and light, the Friend of publicans and sinners, all ye on whom lies the weight of a sin, or the gathered heap of a thousand crimes. He came to call such as you, that he might make you clear and clean. He cannot bear that you should live on in such misery, such badness, such blackness of darkness. He would give you again your life, the bliss of your being. He will not speak to you one word of reproach, except indeed you should aim at justifying yourselves by accusing your neighbour. He will leave it to those who cherish the same sins in their hearts to cast stones at you: he who has no sin casts no stone.

Heartily he loves you, heartily he hates the evil in you—so heartily that he will even cast you into the fire to burn you clean. By making you clean he will give you rest. If he upbraid, it will not be for past sin, but for the present little faith, holding out to him an acorn-cup to fill.

The rest of you keep aloof, if you will, until you shall have done some deed that compels you to cry out for deliverance; but you that know yourselves sinners, come to him that he may work in you his perfect work, for he came not to call the righteous, but sinners, us, you and me, to repentance.

From a letter to a friend.

What would be the most dreadful thing, do you think? To me it seemed the other day that it would be for God to let any fault or wrong in me pass; for Him not to mind, not to care about it. Better hell a thousand times than that. Let Him forgive, splendidly, tenderly, but let it be forgiveness, and not "never minding." Let Him make every excuse, every honest excuse for us, for that is but fair; but let not our Father be content that one spot should be passed by, or one shade less than His righteousness satisfy Him in us!

From a sermon.

The Christian life is a constant fighting. . . . You think Jesus Christ came to save you from any suffering and to do you good. He came to save you from your sins, and until you are saved from them He will step between you and no suffering. "As many as I love I rebuke and chasten. Be zealous, therefore, and repent" [Rev. 3:19].

What does repent mean? To weep that you have done something wrong? No; that is all very well, but that is not repentance. Is repentance to be vexed with yourself that you have fallen away from your own ideal . . . ? No; that is not repentance. What is repentance? Turning your back upon the evil thing; pressing on to lay hold of that for which Christ laid hold upon you. To repent is to think better of it, to turn away from the evil. No man is ever condemned for the wicked things that he has done; he is condemned because he won't leave them. . . .

The Eternal Son of the Father speaks of Himself as a suppliant at our door. "Behold, I stand at the door and knock." . . . Do you hear Him knocking at your hearts? He wants to get in. What do I mean by that figure? Well, I mean this, that He wants to get to your inner house, your consciousness, your life, and to clean it out for you, and to turn out that self that you are always worshipping—to turn it out, and put the Eternal Father in its place. . . . It is His Father that He wants to see ruling there. He is to be one with us in a way that there is no power in our hearts to understand the closeness of it, no figure in our language to say how close it is, for except you know how close the relation of Jesus Christ to the Father you cannot know how close the relation of every child of God, every creature that He has made, is to his Father, his origin. . . .

When you are unhappy, restless, dissatisfied, do not know what to do with yourself, it is just because you have not Christ as your friend. To know God by knowing Christ, that is salvation, that is redemption, and nothing else is.

From the novel Robert Falconer. *Robert Falconer, who had played violin since early childhood, has suffered from a paralyzing illness. After recovering, he experienced a conversion.*

The rumour got abroad that he was a "changed character,"—how is not far to seek, for [the minister] Mr. MacCleary fancied himself the honoured instrument of his conversion, whereas paralysis and the New Testament were the chief agents, and even the violin had more share in it than the minister. For the spirit of God lies all about the spirit of man like a mighty sea, ready to rush in at the smallest chink in the walls that shut him out from his own—walls which even the tone of a violin afloat on the wind of that spirit is sometimes enough to rend from battlement to base, as the blast of the rams' horns rent the walls of Jericho.

From the novel The Vicar's Daughter. *A man has spoken unkindly to his wife.*

Doubtless he would have given much to obliterate the fact, but he would not confess that he had been wrong. We are so stupid, that confession seems to us to fix the wrong upon us, instead of throwing it, as it does, into the depths of the eternal sea.

From the youth novel Ranald Bannerman's Boyhood. *The boy Ranald, remorseful over a mean action that injured his friend Elsie and her grandmother, Mrs. Gregson, dreads telling his father about it.*

I woke early on the Sunday morning, and a most dreary morning it was. I could not lie in bed, and, although no one was up yet, rose and dressed myself. The house was as waste as a sepulchre. I opened the front door and went out. The world itself was no better. The day had hardly begun to dawn. The dark dead frost held it in chains of iron. The sky was dull and leaden, and cindery flakes of snow were thinly falling. Everywhere life looked utterly dreary and hopeless. What was there worth living for?

I went out on the road, and the ice in the ruts crackled under my feet like the bones of dead things. I wandered away from the house, and the keen wind cut me to the bone, for I had not put on plaid or cloak. I turned into a field, and stumbled along over its uneven surface, swollen into hard frozen lumps, so that it was like walking upon stones. The summer was gone and the winter was here, and my heart was colder and more miserable than any winter in the world. I found myself at length at the hillock where Turkey [the nickname of a boy who is Ranald's closest friend] and I had lain on that lovely afternoon the year before. The stream below was dumb with frost. The wind blew wearily but sharply across the bare field. There was no Elsie Duff, with head drooping over her knitting, seated in the summer grass on the other side of a singing brook. Her head was aching on her pillow because I had struck her with that vile lump; and instead of the odour of white clover she was breathing the dregs of the hateful smoke with which I had filled the cottage. I sat down, cold as it was, on the frozen hillock, and buried my face in my hands. Then my dream returned upon me. This was how I sat in my dream when my father had turned me out-of-doors. Oh how dreadful it would be! I should just have to lie down and die.

I could not sit long for the cold. Mechanically I rose and paced about. But I grew so wretched in body that it made me forget for a while the trouble of my mind, and I wandered home again. The house was just stirring. I crept to the nursery, undressed, and lay down. . . . But I did not sleep again, although I lay till all the rest had gone to the parlour. I found them seated round a blazing fire waiting for my father. He came in soon after, and we had our breakfast, and Davie gave his crumbs as usual to the robins and sparrows which came hopping on the window-sill. I fancied my father's eyes were often turned in my direction, but I could not lift mine to make sure.

I had never before known what misery was.

Only Tom and I went to church that day: it was so cold. My father preached from the text, "Be sure your sin shall find you out." I thought with myself that he had found out my sin, and was preparing to punish me for it, and I was filled with terror as well as dismay. I could scarcely keep my seat, so wretched was I. But when after many instances in which punishment had come upon evil-doers when they least expected it, and in spite of every precaution to fortify themselves against it, he proceeded to say that a man's sin might find him out long before the punishment of it overtook him, and drew a picture of the misery of the wicked man who fled when none pursued him, and trembled at the rustling of a leaf, then I was certain that he knew what I had done, or had seen through my face into my conscience. When at last we went home, I kept waiting the whole of the day for the storm to break, expecting every moment to be called to his study. I did not enjoy a mouthful of my food, for I felt his eyes upon me, and they tortured me. I was like a shy creature of the woods whose hole had been stopped up: I had no place of refuge—nowhere to hide my head; and I felt so naked!

My very soul was naked. After tea I slunk away to the nursery, and sat staring into the fire. Mrs. Mitchell came in several times and scolded me for sitting there, instead of with Tom and the rest in the parlour, but I was too miserable even to answer her. At length she brought Davie, and put him to bed; and a few minutes after, I heard my father coming down the stair with Allister, who was chatting away to him. I wondered how he could. My father came in with the big Bible under his arm, as was his custom on Sunday nights, drew a chair to the table, rang for candles, and with Allister by his side and me seated opposite to him, began to find a place from which to read to us. To my yet stronger conviction, he began and read through without a word of remark the parable of the Prodigal Son. When he came to the father's delight at having him back, the robe, and the shoes, and the ring, I could not repress my tears. "If I could only go back," I thought, "and set it all right! but then I've never gone away." It was a foolish thought, instantly followed by a longing impulse to tell my father all about it. How could it be that I had not thought of this before? I had been waiting all this time for my sin to find me out; why should I not frustrate my sin, and find my father first?

As soon as he had done reading, and before he had opened his mouth to make any remark, I crept round the table to his side, and whispered in his ear,—

"Papa, I want to speak to you."

"Very well, Ranald," he said, more solemnly, I thought, than usual; "come up to the study."

He rose and led the way, and I followed. A whimper of disappointment came from Davie's bed. My father went and kissed him, and said he would soon be back, whereupon Davie nestled down satisfied.

When we reached the study, he closed the door, sat down by the fire, and drew me towards him.

I burst out crying, and could not speak for sobs. He encouraged me most kindly. He said—

"Have you been doing anything wrong, my boy?"

"Yes, papa, very wrong," I sobbed. "I'm disgusted with myself."

"I am glad to hear it, my dear," he returned. "There is some hope of you, then."

"Oh! I don't know that," I rejoined. "Even Turkey despises me."

"That's very serious," said my father. "He's a fine fellow, Turkey. I should not like him to despise me. But tell me all about it."

It was with great difficulty I could begin, but with the help of questioning me, my father at length understood the whole matter. He paused for a while plunged in thought; then rose, saying,—

"It's a serious affair, my dear boy; but now you have told me, I shall be able to help you."

"But you knew about it before, didn't you, papa? Surely you did!"

"Not a word of it, Ranald. You fancied so because your sin had found you out. I must go and see how the poor woman is. I don't want to reproach you at all, now you are sorry, but I should like you just to think that you have been helping to make that poor old woman wicked. She is naturally of a sour disposition, and you have made it sourer still, and no doubt made her hate everybody more than she was already inclined to do. You have been working against God in this parish."

I burst into fresh tears. It was too dreadful.

"What *am* I to do?" I cried.

"Of course you must beg Mrs. Gregson's pardon, and tell her that you are both sorry and ashamed."

"Yes, yes, papa. Do let me go with you."

"It's too late to find her up, I'm afraid; but we can just go and see. We've done a wrong, a very grievous wrong, my boy, and I cannot rest till I at least know the consequences of it."

He put on his long greatcoat and muffler in haste, and having seen that I too was properly wrapped up, he opened the door and stepped out. But remembering the promise he had made to Davie, he turned and went down to the nursery to speak to him again, while I awaited him on the doorsteps. It would have been quite dark but for the stars, and there was no snow to give back any of their shine. The earth swallowed all their rays, and was no brighter for it. But oh, what a change to me from the frightful morning! When my father returned, I put my hand in his almost as fearlessly as Allister or wee Davie might have done, and away we walked together.

"Papa," I said, "why did you say *we* have done a wrong? You did not do it."

"My dear boy, persons who are so near each other as we are, must not only bear the consequences together of any wrong done by one of them, but must, in a sense, bear each other's iniquities even. If I sin, you must suffer; if you sin, you being my own boy, I must suffer. But this is not all: it lies upon both of us to do what we can to get rid of the wrong done; and thus we have to bear each other's sin. I am accountable to make amends as far as I can; and also to do what I can to get you to be sorry and make amends as far as you can."

"But, papa, isn't that hard?" I asked.

"Do you think I should like to leave you to get out of your sin as you best could, or sink deeper and deeper into it? Should I grudge anything to take the weight of the sin, or the wrong to others, off you? Do you think I should want not to be troubled about it? Or if I were to do anything wrong, would you think it very hard that you had to help me to be good, and set things right? Even if people looked down upon you because of me, would you say it was hard? Would you not rather say, 'I'm glad to bear anything for my father: I'll share with him'?"

"Yes, indeed, papa. I would rather share with you than not, whatever it was."

"Then you see, my boy, how kind God is in tying us up in one bundle that way. It is a grand and beautiful thing that the fathers should suffer for the children, and the children for the fathers. Come along. We must step out, or I fear we shall not be able to make our apology to-night. When we've got over this, Ranald, we must be a good deal more careful what company we keep."

"Oh, papa," I answered, "if Turkey would only forgive me!"

"There's no fear. Turkey is sure to forgive you when you've done what you can to make amends. He's a fine fellow, Turkey. I have a high opinion of Turkey—as you call him."

"If he would, papa, I should not wish for any other company than his."

"A boy wants various kinds of companions, Ranald, but I fear you have been neglecting Turkey. You owe him much."

"Yes, indeed I do, papa," I answered; "and I have been neglecting him. If I had kept with Turkey, I should never have got into such a dreadful scrape as this."

"That is too light a word to use for it, my boy. Don't call a wickedness a scrape; for a wickedness it certainly was, though I am only too willing to believe you had no adequate idea at the time *how* wicked it was."

"I won't again, papa. But I am so relieved already."

"Perhaps poor old Mrs. Gregson is not relieved, though. You ought not to forget her."

Thus talking, we hurried on until we arrived at the cottage. A dim light was visible through the window. My father knocked, and Elsie opened the door.

From the novel Thomas Wingfold, Curate. *The narrator is speaking about a woman who has committed and hidden a heinous crime and has now tried to murder the man who deceived her daughter.*

"I suspect it is the weight of her own crime that makes her so fierce to avenge her daughter. I doubt if anything makes one so unforgiving as guilt unrepented of."

From the novel Robert Falconer. *Two men have been discussing how prison chaplains should approach their work.*

The clergyman has the message of salvation, not of sin, to give. Whatever oppression is on a man, whatever trouble, whatever conscious something that comes between him and the blessedness of life, is his sin; for whatever is not of faith is sin; and from all this He came to save us. Salvation alone can rouse in us a sense of our sinfulness. One must have got on a good way before he can be sorry for his sins. There is no condition of sorrow laid down as necessary to forgiveness. Repentance does not mean sorrow: it means turning away from the sins. Every man can do that, more or less. And that every man must do. The sorrow will come afterwards, all in good time. Jesus offers to take us out of our own hands into his, if we will only obey him.

From the novel The Marquis of Lossie. *The estate manager, or factor, is a hardened, cruel man. He has been confined to his bed by a serious accident.*

Sickness sometimes works marvellous changes, and the most marvellous on persons who to the ordinary observer seem the least liable to change. Much apparent steadfastness of nature, however, is but sluggishness, and comes from incapacity to generate change or contribute towards personal growth; and it follows that those whose nature is such can as little prevent or retard any change that has its initiative beyond them. The men who impress the world as the mightiest are those often who can the least—never those who can the most in their natural kingdom; generally those whose frontiers lie openest to the inroads of temptation, whose atmosphere is most subject to moody changes and passionate convulsions, who, while perhaps they can whisper laws to a hemisphere, can utter no decree of smallest potency as to how things shall be within themselves. . . .

But then first, when the false strength of the self imagined great man is gone, when the want or the sickness has weakened the self assertion which is so often mistaken for strength of individuality, when the occupations in which he formerly found a comfortable consciousness of being have lost their interest, his ambitions their glow, and his consolations their colour, when suffering has wasted away those upper strata of his factitious consciousness, and laid bare the lower, simpler, truer deeps, of which he has never known or has forgotten the existence, then there is a hope of his commencing a new and real life.

Powers then, even powers within himself of which he knew nothing, begin to assert themselves, and the man commonly reported to possess a strong will, is like a wave of the sea driven with the wind and tossed. This factor, this man of business, this despiser of humbug, to whom the scruples of a sensitive conscience were a contempt, would now lie awake in the night and weep.

"Ah!" I hear it answered, "but that was the weakness caused by his illness." True: but what then had become of his strength? And was it all weakness? What if this weakness was itself a sign of returning life, not of advancing death—of the dawn of a new and genuine strength! For he wept because, in the visions of his troubled brain, he saw once more the cottage of his father the shepherd, with all its store of lovely nothings round which the nimbus of sanctity had gathered while he thought not of them; wept over the memory of that moment of delight when his mother kissed him for parting with his willow whistle to the sister who cried for it: he cried now in his turn, after five and fifty years, for not yet had the little fact done with him, not yet had the kiss of his mother lost its power on the man: wept over the sale of the pet lamb, though he had himself sold thousands of lambs, since; wept over even that bush of dusty miller by the door, like the one he trampled under his horse's feet in the little yard at Scaurnose that horrible day. And oh, that nest of wild bees with its combs of honey unspeakable! He used to laugh and sing then: he laughed still sometimes—he could hear how he laughed, and it sounded frightful—but he never sang!

Were the tears that honoured such childish memories all of weakness? Was it cause of regret that he had not been wicked enough to have become impregnable to such foolish trifles? Unable to mount a horse, unable to give an order, not caring even for his toddy, he was left at the mercy of his fundamentals; his childhood came up and claimed him, and he found the childish things he had put away better than the manly things he had adopted. It is one thing for St. Paul and another for Mr. Worldly Wiseman to put away childish things. The ways they do it, and the things they substitute, are both so different. And now first to me, whose weakness it is to love life more than manners, and men more than their portraits, the man begins to grow interesting. Picture the dawn of innocence on a dull, whisky drinking, commonplace soul, stained by self indulgence, and distorted by injustice! Unspeakably more interesting and lovely is to me such a dawn than the honeymoon of the most passionate of lovers, except indeed I know them such lovers that their love will outlast all the moons.

From the novel The Elect Lady. *Alexa has enjoyed arguing about matters of faith with a man she considered her intellectual inferior.*

"When you would not discuss things with me, I thought you were afraid of losing the argument. Now I see that, instead of disputing about opinions, I should have been saying: 'God be merciful to me a sinner!'"

From the novel The Vicar's Daughter. *Mrs. Percivale has just realized that she had misjudged a new acquaintance, and asks her forgiveness for having disparaged her.*

"Have you forgiven me?" I asked.

"How can I say I have, when I never had any thing to forgive?"

"Well, then, I must go unforgiven, for I cannot forgive myself," I said.

"O Mrs. Percivale! if you think how the world is flooded with forgiveness, you will just dip in your cup, and take what you want."

I felt that I was making too much even of my own shame, rose humbled, and took my former seat.

From the novel Alec Forbes of Howglen. *A teacher, remorseful for having mistreated his students, now seeks to make amends.*

Can one ever bring up arrears of duty? Can one ever make up for wrong done? Will not heaven be an endless repentance?

It would need a book to answer the first two of these questions. To the last of them I answer, "Yes—but a glad repentance."

3.

Redemption

From the youth novel Ranald Bannerman's Boyhood. *A father is speaking to his son.*

"Of all things, my boy, keep your face to the Sun. You can't shine of yourself, you can't be good of yourself, but God has made you able to turn to the Sun whence all goodness and all shining comes. God's children may be very naughty, but they must be able to turn towards him. The Father of Lights is the Father of every weakest little baby of a good thought in us, as well as of the highest devotion of martyrdom.

"If you turn your face to the Sun, my boy, your soul will, when you come to die, feel like an autumn, with the golden fruits of the earth hanging in rich clusters ready to be gathered—not like a winter. You may feel ever so worn, but you will not feel withered. You will die in peace, hoping for the spring—and such a spring!"

From the novel David Elginbrod. *Margaret, a servant girl, is nursing another young woman, Lady Emily, who has tuberculosis.*

Mrs. Elton left the room. Lady Emily said:

"Read something to me, Margaret."

"What shall I read?"

"Anything you like."

Margaret got a Bible, and read to her one of her father's favourite chapters, the fortieth of Isaiah.

"I have no right to trust in God, Margaret."

"Why, my lady?"

"Because I do not feel any faith in him; and you know we cannot be accepted without faith."

"That is to make God as changeable as we are, my lady."

"But the Bible says so."

"I don't think it does; but if an angel from heaven said so, I would not believe it."

"Margaret!"

"My lady, I love God with all my heart, and I cannot bear you should think so of him. You might as well say that a mother would go away from her little child, lying moaning in the dark, because it could not see her, and was afraid to put its hand out into the dark to feel for her."

"Then you think he does care for us, even when we are very wicked. But he cannot bear wicked people."

"Who dares to say that?" cried Margaret. "Has he not been making the world go on and on, with all the wickedness that is in it; yes, making new babies to be born of thieves and murderers and sad women and all, for hundreds of years? God help us, Lady Emily! If he cannot bear wicked people, then this world is hell itself, and the Bible is all a lie, and the Saviour did never die for sinners. It is only the holy Pharisees that can't bear wicked people."

"Oh! how happy I should be, if that were true! I should not be afraid now."

"You are not wicked, dear Lady Emily; but if you were, God would bend over you, trying to get you back, like a father over his sick child. Will people never believe about the lost sheep?"

"Oh! yes; I believe that. But then—"

"You can't trust it quite. Trust in God, then, the very father of you—and never mind the words. You have been taught to turn the very words of God against himself."

Lady Emily was weeping.

"Lady Emily," Margaret went on, "if I felt my heart as hard as a stone; if I did not love God, or man, or woman, or little child, I would yet say to God in my heart: 'O God, see how I trust thee, because thou art perfect, and not changeable like me. I do not love thee. I love nobody. I am not even sorry for it. Thou seest how much I need thee to come close to me, to put thy arm round me, to say to me, my child; for the worse my state, the greater my need of my father who loves me. Come to me, and my day will dawn. My beauty and my love will come back; and oh! how I shall love thee, my God! and know that my love is thy love, my blessedness thy being.'"

As Margaret spoke, she seemed to have forgotten Lady Emily's presence, and to be actually praying. Those who cannot receive such words from the lips of a lady's-maid, must be reminded what her father was, and that she had lost him. She had had advantages at least equal to those which David the Shepherd had—and he wrote the Psalms.

She ended with:

"I do not even desire thee to come, yet come thou."

She seemed to pray entirely as Lady Emily, not as Margaret. When she had ceased, Lady Emily said, sobbing:

"You will not leave me, Margaret? I will tell you why another time."

"I will not leave you, my dear lady."

✦ ✦ ✦

"Oh, what a comfort you are to me, Margaret!" Lady Emily said, after a short silence. "Where did you learn such things?"

"From my father, and from Jesus Christ, and from God himself, showing them to me in my heart."

"Ah! that is why, as often as you come into my room, even if I am very troubled, I feel as if the sun shone, and the wind blew, and the birds sang, and the tree-tops went waving in the wind, as they used to do before I was taken ill—I mean before they thought I must go abroad. You seem to make everything clear, and right, and plain. I wish I were you, Margaret."

"If I were you, my lady, I would rather be what God chose to make me, than the most glorious creature that I could think of. For to have been thought about—born in God's thoughts—and then made by God, is the dearest, grandest, most precious thing in all thinking. Is it not, my lady?"

"It is," said Lady Emily, and was silent.

From the novel Robert Falconer. *The narrator has been reflecting on the benefit of growing up in the country rather than a town.*

"But I must stop, for I am getting up to the neck in a bog of discrimination. As if I did not know the nobility of some townspeople, compared with the worldliness of some country folk. I give it up. We are all good and all bad. God mend all.

Nothing will do for Jew or Gentile, Frenchman or Englishman, Negro or Circassian, town boy or country boy, but the kingdom of heaven which is within him, and must come thence to the outside of him."

From a sermon.

The making, the redeeming Father will find plenty of like work for his children to do. Dull are those, little at least can they have of Christian imagination, who think that where all are good, things must be dull. It is because there is so little good yet in them, that they know so little of the power or beauty of merest life divine. . . .

The Lord did not die to provide a man with the wretched heaven he may invent for himself, or accept invented for him by others; he died to give him life, and bring him to the heaven of the Father's peace; the children must share in the essential bliss of the Father and the Son. This is and has been the Father's work from the beginning—to bring us into the home of his heart, where he shares the glories of life with the Living One, in whom was born life to light men back to the original life.

This is our destiny; and however a man may refuse, he will find it hard to fight with God—useless to kick against the goads of his love. For the Father is goading him, or will goad him, if needful, into life by unrest and trouble; hell-fire will have its turn if less will not do: can any need it more than such as will neither enter the kingdom of heaven themselves, nor suffer them to enter it that would? The old race of the Pharisees is by no means extinct; they were St. Paul's great trouble, and are yet to be found in every religious community under the sun.

From the novel Robert Falconer. *Robert Falconer has spent years trying to find his vagrant father who abandoned him when he was a child. Falconer now lives and works in impoverished city neighborhoods; he asks his co-worker De Fleuri to ask around for information about his father.*

[De Fleuri] told the story of Falconer and his father, so that in all that region of London it became known that the man who loved the poor was himself needy, and looked to the poor for their help. Without them he could not be made perfect.

Some of my readers may be inclined to say that it was dishonourable in Falconer to have occasioned the publishing of his father's disgrace. Such may recall to their minds that concealment is no law of the universe; that, on the contrary, the Lord of the Universe said once: "There is nothing covered that shall not be revealed." Was the disgrace of Andrew Falconer greater because a thousand men knew it, instead of forty, who could not help knowing it? Hope lies in light and knowledge. Andrew would be none the worse that honest men knew of his vice: they would be the first to honour him if he should overcome it. If he would not—the disgrace was just, and would fall upon his son only in sorrow, not in dishonour.

The grace of God—the making of humanity by his beautiful hand—no, heart—is such, that disgrace clings to no man after repentance, any more than the feet defiled with the mud of the world come yet defiled from the bath. Even the things that proceed out of the man, and do terribly defile him, can be cast off like the pollution of the leper by a grace that goes deeper than they; and the man who says, "I have sinned: I will sin no more," is even by the voice of his brothers crowned as a conqueror, and by their hearts loved as one who has suffered and overcome.

The narrator is a friend of Robert Falconer's who wants to join his work of helping the destitute of London.

One night I was returning home from some poor attempts of my own. I had now been a pupil of Falconer for a considerable time, but having my own livelihood to make, I could not do so much as I would.

It was late, nearly twelve o'clock, as I passed through the region of Seven Dials. Here and there stood three or four brutal-looking men, and now and then a squalid woman with a starveling baby in her arms, in the light of the gin-shops. The babies were the saddest to see—nursery-plants already in training for the places these men and women now held, then to fill a pauper's grave. . . . Now and then a flaunting woman wavered past—a night-shade, as our old dramatists would have called her. I could hardly keep down an evil disgust that would have conquered my pity, when a scanty white dress would stop beneath a lamp, and the gay dirty bonnet, turning round, reveal a painted face, from which shone little more than an animal intelligence, not brightened by the gin she had been drinking. Vague noises of strife and of drunken wrath flitted around me as I passed an alley, or an opening door let out its evil secret. Once I thought I heard the dull thud of a blow on the head. The noisome vapours were fit for any of Swedenborg's hells. There were few sounds, but the very quiet seemed infernal. The night was hot and sultry. A skinned cat, possibly still alive, fell on the street before me. Under one of the gas-lamps lay something long: it was a tress of dark hair, torn perhaps from some woman's head: she had beautiful hair at least. Once I heard the cry of murder, but where, in that chaos of humanity, right or left, before or behind me, I could not even guess. Home to such regions, from gorgeous stage-scenery and dresses, from splendid, mirror-beladen casinos, from singing-halls, and places of private and prolonged revelry, trail the daughters of men at all hours from midnight till morning. Next day they drink hell-fire that they may forget. Sleep brings an hour or two of oblivion, hardly of peace; but they must wake, worn and miserable, and the waking brings no hope: their only known help lies in the gin-shop. What can be done with them? But the secrets God keeps must be as good as those he tells.

But no sights of the night ever affected me so much as walking through this same St. Giles's on a summer Sunday morning, when church-goers were in church. Oh! the faces that creep out into the sunshine then, and haunt their doors! Some of them but skins drawn over skulls, living Death's-heads, grotesque in their hideousness.

I was not very far from Falconer's abode. My mind was oppressed with sad thoughts and a sense of helplessness. I began to wonder what Falconer might at that moment be about. I had not seen him for a long time—a whole fortnight. He might be at home: I would go and see, and if there were light in his windows I would ring his bell.

I went. There was light in his windows. He opened the door himself, and welcomed me. I went up with him, and we began to talk. I told him of my sad thoughts, and my feelings of helplessness.

"He that believeth shall not make haste," he said. "There is plenty of time. You must not imagine that the result depends on you, or that a single human soul can be lost because you may fail. The question, as far as you are concerned, is, whether you are to be honoured in having a hand in the work that God is doing, and will do, whether you help him or not. Some will be honoured: shall it be me? And this honour gained excludes no one: there is work, as there is bread in his house, enough and to spare. It shows no faith in God to make frantic efforts or frantic lamentations. Besides, we ought to teach ourselves to see, as much as we may, the good that is in the condition of the poor."

"Teach me to see that, then," I said. "Show me something."

"The best thing is their kindness to each other. There is an absolute divinity in their self-denial for those who are poorer than themselves. I know one man and woman, married people, who pawned their very furniture and wearing apparel to procure cod-liver oil for a girl dying in consumption. She was not even a relative, only an acquaintance of former years. They had found her destitute and taken her to their own poor home. There are fathers and mothers who will work hard all the morning, and when dinner-time comes 'don't want any,' that there may be enough for their children—or half enough, more likely. Children will take the bread out of their own mouths to put in that of their sick brother, or to stick in the fist of baby crying for a crust—giving only a queer little helpless grin, half of hungry sympathy, half of pleasure, as they see it disappear. The marvel to me is that the children turn out so well as they do; but that applies to the children in all ranks of life."

From the novel David Elginbrod. *Robert Falconer is with another young coworker, Hugh Sutherland.*

They went on, Hugh accompanying Falconer in one of his midnight walks through London, as he had done repeatedly before. From such companionship and the scenes to which Falconer introduced him, he had gathered this fruit, that he began to believe in God for the sake of the wretched men and women he saw in the world. At first it was his own pain at the sight of such misery that drove him, for consolation, to hope in God; so, at first, it was for his own sake. But as he saw more of them, and grew to love them more, he felt that the only hope for them lay in the love of God; and he hoped in God for them. He saw too that a God not both humanly and absolutely divine, a God less than that God shadowed forth in the Redeemer of men, would not do.

But thinking about God thus, and hoping in him for his brothers and sisters, he began to love God. Then, last of all, that he might see in him one to whom he could abandon everything, that he might see him perfect and all in all and as he must be— for the sake of God himself, he believed in him as the Saviour of these his sinful and suffering kin.

From the novel The Seaboard Parish. *The discovery of a snake during a picnic leads to a discussion about the recently developed theory of evolution, and whether it is possible for a snake to evolve into a bird.*

"The most presumptuous thing in the world is to pronounce on the possible and the impossible. I do not know what is possible and what is impossible. I can only tell a little of what is true and what is untrue. But I do say this, that between the condition of many decent members of society and that for the sake of which God made them, there is a gulf quite as vast as that between a serpent and a bird. I get peeps now and then into the condition of my own heart, which, for the moment, make it seem impossible that I should ever rise into a true state of nature—that is, into the simplicity of God's will concerning me. The only hope for ourselves and for others lies in him—in the power the creating spirit has over the spirits he has made."

From the novel The Vicar's Daughter. *Marion Clare is at the bedside of a dying friend who has recently begun to believe in Jesus.*

"Ah, Miss Clare! to think I might have done something for *Him* by doing it for *them!* Alas! I have led a useless life, and am dying out of this world without having borne any fruit! Ah, me, me!"

"You are doing a good deal for him now," said Marion, "and hard work too!" she added; "harder far than mine."

"I am only dying," she returned—so sadly!

"You are enduring chastisement," said Marion. "The Lord gives one one thing to do, and another another. We have no right to wish for other work than he gives us. It is rebellious and unchildlike, whatever it may seem. Neither have we any right to wish to be better in *our* way: we must wish to be better in *his.*"

"But I *should* like to do something for *him;* bearing is only for myself. Surely I may wish that?"

"No: you may not. Bearing is not only for yourself. You are quite wrong in thinking you do nothing for him in enduring," returned Marion, with that abrupt decision of hers which seemed to some like rudeness. "What is the will of God? Is it not your sanctification? And why did he make the Captain of our salvation perfect through suffering? Was it not that he might in like manner bring many sons into glory? Then, if you are enduring, you are working with God,—for the perfection through suffering of one more: you are working for God in yourself, that the will of God may be done in you; that he may have his very own way with you. It is the only work he requires of you now: do it not only willingly, then, but contentedly. To make people good is all his labor: be good, and you are a fellow-worker with God in the highest region of labor. He does not want you for other people—*yet.*"

✦ ✦ ✦

So long as men do not feel that they are in a bad condition and in danger of worse, the message of deliverance will sound to them as a threat. Yea, the offer of absolute well-being upon the only possible conditions of the well-being itself, must, if heard at all, rouse in them a discomfort whose cause they attribute to the message, not to themselves; and immediately they will endeavor to justify themselves in disregarding it.

There are those doing all they can to strengthen themselves in unbelief, who, if the Lord were to appear plainly before their eyes, would tell Him they could not help it, for He had not until then given them ground enough for faith, and when He left them, would go on just as before, except that they would speculate and pride themselves on the vision. If men say, "We want no such deliverance," then the Maker of them must either destroy them as vile things for whose existence He is to Himself accountable, or compel them to change. If they say, "We choose to be destroyed," He, as their Maker, has a choice in the matter too. Is He not free to say, "You can not even slay yourselves, and I choose that you shall know the death of living without Me; you shall learn to choose to live indeed. I choose that you shall know what I *know* to be good"?

And however much any individual consciousness may rebel, surely the individual consciousness which called that other into being, and is the Father of that being . . . has a right to object that by rebellion His creature should destroy the very power by which it rebels, and from a being capable of a divine freedom by partaking of the divine nature, should make of itself the merest slave incapable of will of any sort!

Is it a wrong to compel His creature to soar aloft into the ether of its origin, and find its deepest, its only true self? It is God's knowing choice of life against man's ignorant choice of death.

From the fantasy novel Lilith. *Mr. Vane finds himself in a mysterious otherworldly place inhabited by a childish people called the Lovers or Little Ones, as well as a race of sinister giants known as the Bags. Mr. Vane's guide, Mara, tells him the history of the country and how it can gain redemption.*

"There is a city in that grassy land," she replied, "where a woman is princess. The city is called Bulika. But certainly the princess is not a girl! She is older than this world, and came to it from yours—with a terrible history, which is not over yet. She is an evil person, and prevails much with the Prince of the Power of the Air. The people of Bulika were formerly simple folk, tilling the ground and pasturing sheep. She came among them, and they received her hospitably. She taught them to dig for diamonds and opals and sell them to strangers, and made them give up tillage and pasturage and build a city.

One day they found a huge snake and killed it; which so enraged her that she declared herself their princess, and became terrible to them. The name of the country at that time was *The Land of Waters;* for the dry channels, of which you have crossed so many, were then overflowing with live torrents; and the valley, where now the Bags and the Lovers have their fruit-trees, was a lake that received a great part of them. But the wicked princess gathered up in her lap what she could of the water over the whole country, closed it in an egg, and carried it away. Her lap, however, would not hold more than half of it; and the instant she was gone, what she had not yet taken fled away underground, leaving the country as dry and dusty as her own heart.

Were it not for the waters under it, every living thing would long ago have perished from it. For where no water is, no rain falls; and where no rain falls, no springs rise. Ever since then, the princess has lived in Bulika, holding the inhabitants in constant

terror, and doing what she can to keep them from multiplying. Yet they boast and believe themselves a prosperous, and
certainly are a self-satisfied, people—good at bargaining and
buying, good at selling and cheating; holding well together for a
common interest, and utterly treacherous where interests clash;
proud of their princess and her power, and despising every one
they get the better of; never doubting themselves the most hon-
ourable of all the nations, and each man counting himself better
than any other. The depth of their worthlessness and height of
their vainglory no one can understand who has not been there
to see, who has not learned to know the miserable misgoverned
and self-deceived creatures."

"I thank you, madam. And now, if you please, will you tell me
something about the Little Ones—the Lovers? I long heartily to
serve them. Who and what are they? and how do they come to
be there? Those children are the greatest wonder I have found in
this world of wonders."

"In Bulika you may, perhaps, get some light on those matters.
There is an ancient poem in the library of the palace, I am told,
which of course no one there can read, but in which it is plainly
written that after the Lovers have gone through great troubles
and learned their own name, they will fill the land, and make
the giants their slaves."

"By that time they will have grown a little, will they not?" I
said.

"Yes, they will have grown; yet I think too they will not have
grown. It is possible to grow and not to grow, to grow less and
to grow bigger, both at once—yes, even to grow by means of not
growing!"

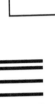

BUSINESS REPLY MAIL
FIRST–CLASS MAIL   PERMIT NO. 332   CONGERS, NY

POSTAGE WILL BE PAID BY ADDRESSEE

PLOUGH QUARTERLY
PO BOX 345
CONGERS NY 10920–9895

"Your words are strange, madam!" I rejoined. "But I have heard it said that some words, because they mean more, appear to mean less!"

"That is true, and such words *have* to be understood. It were well for the princess of Bulika if she heard what the very silence of the land is shouting in her ears all day long! But she is far too clever to understand anything."

"Then I suppose, when the little Lovers are grown, their land will have water again?"

"Not exactly so: when they are thirsty enough, they will have water, and when they have water, they will grow. To grow, they must have water. And, beneath, it is flowing still."

4.

Jesus

From a sermon.

Only one thing I have to say, and that always: and if I did not believe it, why should I trouble myself:

Jesus Christ is the way to God. You cannot get that by any mere theological system. It is no use talking about Jesus Christ, using any set of terms, however systematic and well-fitting. You must know Him. How to do this? By studying His words, His will.

We are all so anxious, naturally, to get comfortable. We lie in bed, tossing about this way and that, thinking to arrange ourselves comfortably. But it's no use. We ought to get out of bed and set about doing our duty. Do His will: then we shall know Him. We cannot get to know Him till we have given up seeking self. In some form or other there must be the new Birth from above. So long as we seek self, we shall not find the Way, the Truth, or the Life.

From a letter to his father, written when he was twenty-nine and at a time when he did not have a dependable income for his growing family.

I am always finding out meaning which I did not see before, and which I now cannot see perfectly—for, of course, till my heart is like [Christ's] great heart, I cannot know fully what he meant. The great thing for understanding what he said is to have a living sense of the reality that a young man of poor birth appeared unexpectedly in Judea and uttered most unwelcome truths, setting at nought all the respectabilities of the time, and calling bad, bad, and good, good, in the face of all religious per-versions and false honourings. The first thing is to know Jesus as a man. . . . The life, thoughts, deeds, aims, beliefs of Jesus have to be fresh expounded for every age, for all the depth of Eternity lies in them. . . .

I can hardly say I have any fear, and but very little anxiety about the future. Did not Jesus say, Consider the lilies? We have only to do our work. . . . Jesus lived a grand, simple life in poverty and love. . . . His spirit is working in the earth—and in my heart too, I trust.

From a sermon in the novel Adela Cathcart.

The winter is the childhood of the year. Into this childhood of the year came the child Jesus; and into this childhood of the year must we all descend. It is as if God spoke to each of us accord-ing to our need: My son, my daughter, you are growing old and cunning; you must grow a child again, with my son, this blessed birth-time. You are growing old and selfish; you must become a child. You are growing old and careful; you must become a child. You are growing old and distrustful; you must become a child. You are growing old and petty, and weak, and foolish; you must become a child—my child, like the baby there, that strong sunrise of faith and hope and love, lying in his mother's arms in the stable.

From the novel The Seaboard Parish. *A man is speaking to his daughters.*

"There was once a baby born in a stable, because his poor mother could get no room in a decent house. Where she lay I can hardly think. They must have made a bed of hay and straw for her in the stall, for we know the baby's cradle was the manger. Had God forsaken them? or would they not have been more *comfortable,* if that was the main thing, somewhere else? Ah! if the disciples, who were being born about the same time of fisher-fathers and cottage-mothers, to get ready for him to call and teach by the time he should be thirty years of age—if they had only been old enough, and had known that he was coming—would they not have got everything ready for him? They would have clubbed their little savings together, and worked day and night, and some rich women would have helped them, and they would have dressed the baby in fine linen, and got him the richest room their money would get, and they would have made the gold that the wise men brought into a crown for his little head, and would have burnt the frankincense before him. And so our little manger-baby would have been taken away from us. No more the stable-born Saviour—no more the poor Son of God born for us all, as strong, as noble, as loving, as worshipful, as beautiful as he was poor!

"And we should not have learned that God does not care for money; that if he does not give more of it it is not that it is scarce with him, or that he is unkind, but that he does not value it himself. And if he sent his own son to be not merely brought up in the house of the carpenter of a little village, but to be born in the stable of a village inn, we need not suppose because a man sleeps under a haystack and is put in prison for it next day, that God does not care for him."

"But why did Jesus come so poor, papa?"

"That he might be just a human baby. That he might not be distinguished by this or by that accident of birth; that he might have nothing but a mother's love to welcome him, and so belong to everybody; that from the first he might show that the kingdom of God and the favour of God lie not in these external things at all—that the poorest little one, born in the meanest dwelling, or in none at all, is as much God's own and God's care as if he came in a royal chamber with colour and shine all about him. Had Jesus come amongst the rich, riches would have been more worshipped than ever."

From a letter to a reader.

Have you really been reading my books, and at this time ask me what I have lost of the old faith? . . . With many of the forms gathered round that faith I have [no sympathy]. At a very early age I had begun to cast them from me, but all the time my faith in Jesus as the Son of the Father of men and the Saviour of us all, has been growing. . . .

Do not suppose that I believe in Jesus because it is said so-and-so in a book. I believe in him because he is himself the vision of him in that book, and, I trust, his own living power in me, having enabled me to understand him, to look him in the face, as it were, to accept him as my Master and Saviour, in following whom I shall come to the rest of the Father's peace. The Bible is to me the most precious *thing* in the world, because it tells me his story; and what good men thought about him who knew him and accepted him. . . .

It is Jesus who is the Revelation of God, not the Bible; that is but a means to a mighty eternal end. The book is indeed sent us by God, but it nowhere claims to be his very word. If it were— and it would be no irreverence to say it—it would have been a good deal better written. Yet even its errors and blunders do not touch the truth, and are the merest trifles—dear as is the little spot of earth on the whiteness of the snowdrop. Jesus alone is The Word of God.

With all sorts of doubts I am familiar, and the result of them is, has been, and will be, a widening of my heart and soul and mind to greater glories of the truth—the truth that is in Jesus—and not in Calvin or Luther or St. Paul or St. John, save as they got it from Him, from whom every simple heart may have it, and can alone get it. You cannot have such proof of the existence of God or the truth of the Gospel story as you can have of a proposition in Euclid or a chemical experiment. But the man who shall order his way by the word of the Master shall partake of his peace, and shall have in himself a growing conviction that in him are hid all the treasures of wisdom and knowledge. . . .

One more thing I must say: though the Bible contains many an utterance of the will of God, we do not need to go there to find how to begin to do his will. In every heart there is a consciousness of some duty or other required of it: that is the will of God. He who would be saved must get up and do that will—if it be but to sweep a room or make an apology, or pay a debt. It was he who had kept the commandments whom Jesus invited to be his follower in poverty and labour. . . .

I cannot say I never doubt, nor until I hold the very heart of good as my very own in Him, can I wish not to doubt. For doubt is the hammer that breaks the windows clouded with human fancies, and lets in the pure life. But I do say that all my hope, all my joy, all my strength are in the Lord Christ and his Father; that all my theories of life and growth are rooted in him; that his truth is gradually clearing up the mysteries of this world. . . .

To Him I belong heart and soul and body, and he may do with me as he will—nay, nay—I pray him to do with me as he wills, for that is my only well-being and freedom.

From a sermon.

We are and remain such creeping Christians, because we look at ourselves and not at Christ; because we gaze at the marks of our own soiled feet, and the trail of our own defiled garments. . . . Or, having committed a petty fault, I mean a fault such as only a petty creature could commit, we mourn over the defilement to ourselves, and the shame of it before our friends, children, or servants, instead of hastening to make the due confession and amends to our fellow, and then, forgetting our own paltry self with its well-earned disgrace, lift up our eyes to the glory which alone will quicken the true man in us, and kill the peddling creature we so wrongly call our *self.* The true self is that which can look Jesus in the face, and say *My Lord.*

From a letter to his oldest son.

That existence is a splendid thing I am more and more con-vinced, while, at the same time, but for my hope in God, I should have no wish for its continuance, and should feel it but a phantasmagoria. But Jesus Christ did come, for no man could have invented him; and he thought our being worth giving himself for; and he was perfectly satisfied with his God and Father. And so I am content in God.

From the novel Donal Grant. *A young woman, Lady Arctura, is confiding her troubles to her younger brother's tutor, a peasant named Donal Grant. She has just told him her discovery that a recent illness was due to being secretly drugged by her uncle, and that in despair she has been tempted to experiment with drugs herself.*

"I am sorely tried with painful thoughts, and feel sometimes as if I would do almost anything to get rid of them."

"There must be a good way of getting rid of them! Think it of God's mercy," said Donal, "that you cannot get rid of them the other way."

"I do; I do!"

"The shield of his presence was over you."

"How glad I should be to think so! But we have no right to think he cares for us till we believe in Christ—and—and—I don't know that I do believe in him!"

"Wherever you learned that, it is a terrible lie," said Donal. "Is not Christ the same always, and is he not of one mind with God? Was it not while we were yet sinners that he poured out his soul for us? It is a fearful thing to say of the perfect Love, that he is not doing all he can, with all the power of a maker over the creature he has made, to help and deliver him!"

"I know he makes his sun to shine and his rain to fall upon the evil and the good; but those good things are only of this world!"

"Are those the good things then that the Lord says the Father will give to those that ask him? How can you worship a God who gives you all the little things he does not care much about, but will not do his best for you?"

"But are there not things he cannot do for us till we believe in Christ?"

"Certainly there are. But what I want you to see is that he does all that can be done. He finds it very hard to teach us, but he is never tired of trying. Anyone who is willing to be taught of God, will by him be taught, and thoroughly taught."

"I am afraid I am doing wrong in listening to you, Mr. Grant—and the more that I cannot help wishing what you say might be true! But are you not in danger—you will pardon me for saying it—of presumption?—How can all the good people be wrong?"

"Because the greater part of their teachers have set themselves to explain God rather than to obey and enforce his will. The gospel is given to convince, not our understandings, but our hearts; that done, and never till then, our understandings will be free. Our Lord said he had many things to tell his disciples, but they were not able to hear them. If the things be true which I have heard from Sunday to Sunday since I came here, the Lord has brought us no salvation at all, but only a change of shape to our miseries. They have not redeemed you, Lady Arctura, and never will.

"Nothing but Christ himself, your lord and friend and brother, not all the doctrines about him, even if every one of them were true, can save you. Poor orphan children, we cannot find our God, and they would have us take instead a shocking caricature of him!"

"But how should sinners know what is or is not like the true God?"

"If a man desires God, he cannot help knowing enough of him to be capable of learning more—else how should he desire him? Made in the image of God, his idea of him cannot be all wrong. That does not make him fit to teach others—only fit to go on learning for himself. But in Jesus Christ I see the very God I want. I want a father like him. He reproaches some of those about him for not knowing him—for, if they had known God, they would have known him: they were to blame for not knowing God. No other than the God exactly like Christ can be the true God. It is a doctrine of devils that Jesus died to save us from our father. There is no safety, no good, no gladness, no purity, but with the Father, his father and our father, his God and our God."

"But God hates sin and punishes it!"

"It would be terrible if he did not. All hatred of sin is love to the sinner. Do you think Jesus came to deliver us from the punishment of our sins? He would not have moved a step for that. The horrible thing is being bad, and all punishment is help to deliver us from that, nor will punishment cease till we have ceased to be bad. God will have us good, and Jesus works out the will of his father. Where is the refuge of the child who fears his father? Is it in the farthest corner of the room? Is it down in the dungeon of the castle, my lady?"

"No, no!" cried Lady Arctura, "in his father's arms!"

"There!" said Donal, and was silent.

"I hold by Jesus!" he added after a pause, and rose as he said it, but stood where he rose.

From a sermon.

Man finds it hard to get what he wants, because he does not want the best; God finds it hard to give, because he would give the best, and man will not take it.

What Jesus did, was what the Father is always doing; the suffering he endured was that of the Father from the foundation of the world, reaching its climax in the person of his Son. God provides the sacrifice; the sacrifice is himself. He is always, and has ever been, sacrificing himself to and for his creatures. It lies in the very essence of his creation of them. The worst heresy, next to that of dividing religion and righteousness, is to divide the Father from the Son—in thought or feeling or action or intent; to represent the Son as doing that which the Father does not himself do. Jesus did nothing but what the Father did and does. If Jesus suffered for men, it was because his Father suffers for men; only he came close to men through his body and their senses, that he might bring their spirits close to his Father and their Father, so giving them life, and losing what could be lost of his own. He is God our Saviour: it is because God is our Saviour that Jesus is our Saviour. The God and Father of Jesus Christ could never possibly be satisfied with less than giving himself to his own!

The unbeliever may easily imagine a better God than the common theology of the country offers him; but not the lovingest heart that ever beat can even reflect the length and breadth and depth and height of that love of God which shows itself in his Son—one, and of one mind, with himself. The whole history is a divine agony to give divine life to creatures. The outcome of that agony, the victory of that creative and again creative energy, will be radiant life, whereof joy unspeakable is the flower. Every child will look in the eyes of the Father, and the eyes of the Father will receive the child with an infinite embrace.

From the novel There and Back. *A worldly man visits a minister and is astonished how everyday events seem transformed by the simple belief that God has entrusted him with something precious.*

Never will it be right with men, until every commonest meal is a glad recognition of the living Saviour who gives himself, always and perfectly, to his brothers and sisters.

From a sermon.

Do you ever think "I could worship God if he was so-and-so?" Do you imagine that God is not as good, as perfect, as absolutely all-in-all as your thoughts can imagine? Aye, you cannot come up to it; do what you will you never will come up to it. Use all the symbols that we have in nature, in human relations, in the family—all our symbols of grace and tenderness, and loving-kindness between man and man, and between man and woman, and between woman and woman, but you can never come up to the thought of what God's ministration is.

When our Lord came he just let us see how his Father was doing this always, he "came to give his life a ransom for many." It was in giving his life a ransom for us that he died; that was the consummation and crown of it all, but it was his life that he gave for us—his whole being, his whole strength, his whole energy—not alone his days of trouble and of toil, but deeper than that, he gave his whole being for us; yea, he even went down to death for us.

From a sermon.

He did not care for government. No such kingdom would serve the ends of his father in heaven, or comfort his own soul. What was perfect empire to the Son of God, while he might teach one human being to love his neighbour, and be good like his father! To be love-helper to one heart, for its joy, and the glory of his father, was the beginning of true kingship! The Lord would rather wash the feet of his weary brothers, than be the only perfect monarch that ever ruled in the world. . . .

Pilate thereupon — as would most Christians nowadays, instead of setting about being true—requests a definition of truth. . . . Neither Pilate nor they ask the one true question, How am I to be a true man? How am I to become a man worth being a man? The Lord is a king because his life, the life of his thoughts, of his imagination, of his will, of every smallest action, is true—true first to God in that he is altogether his, true to himself in that he is himself altogether, and true to his fellows in that he will endure anything they do to him, nor cease declaring himself the son and messenger and likeness of God. They will kill him, but it matters not: the truth is as he says!

From a sermon in the novel Thomas Wingfold, Curate.

Come, then, sore heart, and see whether his heart can not heal thine. He knows what sighs and tears are, and if he knew no sin in himself, the more pitiful must it have been to behold the sighs and tears that guilt wrung from the tortured hearts of his brethren and sisters.

Brothers, sisters, we must get rid of this misery of ours. It is slaying us. It is turning the fair earth into a hell, and our hearts into its fuel. There stands the man who says he knows: take him

at his word. Go to him who says in the might of his eternal tenderness and his human pity, "Come unto me, all ye that labor
and are heavy-laden, and I will give you rest. Take my yoke upon
you, and learn of me; for I am meek and lowly in heart: and
ye shall find rest unto your souls. For my yoke is easy, and my
burden is light."

From a letter written when he was sixty.

Yes, we are growing old; but the Ancient of Days cannot be old;
and Jesus Christ is not old. . . . He is child and man and one
perfect friend. He is accountable for me, else I should not like to
live. . . . He is my life and in the good to come I rejoice—in the
hope of the glory of God. . . .

I believe in nothing but Jesus Christ, in whom are all the mysteries of reality. Less than the story of him could not satisfy me,
though less might give me hope. But if he be such as that story
says, then all is well. If God be indeed such a God as satisfies
Jesus, then hail to the world with all its summers and snow, all
its delight and its aching, all its jubilance and its old age! We
shall come out of it the sons and daughters of life of God himself
the only Father.

5.

God's Glory

From a sermon.

When my being is consciously and willedly in the hands of him who called it to live and think and suffer and be glad—given back to him by a perfect obedience—I thenceforward breathe the breath, share the life of God himself. Then I am free, in that I am true—which means one with the Father. And freedom knows itself to be freedom.

When a man is true, if he were in hell he could not be miserable. He is right with himself because right with him whence he came. To be right with God is to be right with the universe; one with the power, the love, the will of the mighty Father, the cherisher of joy, the lord of laughter, whose are all glories, all hopes, who loves everything, and hates nothing but selfishness, which he will not have in his kingdom.

From the novel Donal Grant. *Donal Grant, a young man who has just left his childhood home to seek employment, is newly arrived as a guest of the cobbler Andrew Comin and his wife. It is Sunday morning.*

Notwithstanding his weariness Donal woke early, for he had slept thoroughly. He rose and dressed himself, drew aside the little curtain that shrouded the window, and looked out. It was a lovely morning. His prospect was the curious old main street of the town. The sun that had shone into it was now shining from the other side, but not a shadow of living creature fell upon the rough stones! Yes—there was a cat shooting across them like the culprit he probably was! If there was a garden to the house, he would go and read in the fresh morning air!

He stole softly through the outer room, and down the stair; found the back-door and a water-butt; then a garden consisting of two or three plots of flowers well cared for; and ended his discoveries with a seat surrounded and almost canopied with honeysuckle, where doubtless the cobbler sometimes smoked his pipe! "Why does he not work here rather than in the archway?" thought Donal. But, dearly as he loved flowers and light and the free air of the garden, the old cobbler loved the faces of his kind better. His prayer for forty years had been to be made like his master; and if that prayer was not answered, how was it that, every year he lived, he found himself loving the faces of his fellows more and more? Ever as they passed, instead of interfering with his contemplations, they gave him more and more to think: were these faces, he asked, the symbols of a celestial language in which God talked to him?

Donal sat down, and took his Greek Testament from his pocket. But all at once, brilliant as was the sun, the light of his life went out, and the vision rose of the gray quarry, and the girl turning from him in the wan moonlight. Then swift as thought followed the vision of the women weeping about the forsaken tomb; and with his risen Lord he rose also—into a region far "above the smoke and stir of this dim spot," a region where life is good even with its sorrow. The man who sees his disappointment beneath him, is more blessed than he who rejoices in fruition. Then prayer awoke, and in the light of that morning of peace he drew nigh the living one, and knew him as the source of his being. Weary with blessedness he leaned against the shadowing honeysuckle, gave a great sigh of content, smiled, wiped his eyes, and was ready for the day and what it should bring. But the bliss went not yet; he sat for a while in the joy of conscious loss in the higher life. With his meditations and feelings mingled now and then a few muffled blows of the cobbler's hammer: he was once more at work on his disabled shoe.

"Here is a true man!" he thought, "a Godlike helper of his fellow!"

When the hammer ceased, the cobbler was stitching; when Donal ceased thinking, he went on feeling. Again and again came a little roll of the cobbler's drum, giving glory to God by doing his will: the sweetest and most acceptable music is that which rises from work a-doing; its incense ascends as from the river in its flowing, from the wind in its blowing, from the grass in its growing. All at once he heard the voices of two women in the next garden, close behind him, talking together.

"Eh," said one, "there's that godless cratur, An'rew Comin, at his wark again upo' the Sawbath mornin'!"

"Ay, lass," answered the other, "I hear him! Eh, but it'll be an ill day for him whan he has to appear afore the jeedge o' a'! He winna hae his comman'ments broken that gait!"

---

that gait that way

"Troth, na!" returned the former; "it'll be a sair sattlin day for him!"

Donal rose, and looking about him, saw two decent, elderly women on the other side of the low stone wall. He was approaching them with the request on his lips to know which of the Lord's commandments they supposed the cobbler to be breaking, when, seeing that he must have overheard them, they turned their backs and walked away.

And now his hostess, having discovered he was in the garden, came to call him to breakfast—the simplest of meals—porridge, with a cup of tea after it because it was Sunday, and there was danger of sleepiness at the kirk.

"Yer shune's waitin' ye, sir," said the cobbler. "Ye'll fin' them a better job nor ye expeckit. They're a better job, onygait, nor I expeckit!"

Donal made haste to put them on, and felt dressed for the Sunday.

"Are ye gaein' to the kirk the day, Anerew?" asked the old woman, adding, as she turned to their guest, "My man's raither pecooliar aboot gaein' to the kirk! Some days he'll gang three times, an' some days he winna gang ance!—He kens himsel' what for!" she added with a smile, whose sweetness confessed that, whatever was the reason, it was to her the best in the world.

"Ay, I'm gaein' the day: I want to gang wi' oor new freen'," he answered.

---

sair sattlin sore settling
kirk church
shune shoes
onygait anyways
the day today
gang go
kens knows

"I'll tak him gien ye dinna care to gang," rejoined his wife.

"Ow, I'll gang!" he persisted. "It'll gie's something to talk aboot, an' sae ken ane anither better, an' maybe come a bit nearer ane anither, an' sae a bit nearer the maister. That's what we're here for—comin' an' gaein'."

"As ye please, Anerew! What's richt to you's aye richt to me. O' my ain sel' I wad be doobtfu' o' sic a rizzon for gaein' to the kirk—to get something to speyk aboot."

"It's a gude rizzon whaur ye haena a better," he answered. "It's aften I get at the kirk naething but what angers me—lees an' lees agen my Lord an' my God. But whan there's ane to talk it ower wi', ane 'at has some care for God as weel's for himsel', there's some guid sure to come oot o' 't—some revelation o' the real richteousness—no what fowk 'at gangs by the ministers ca's richteousness.— Is yer shune comfortable to yer feet, sir?"

"Ay, that they are! an' I thank ye: they're full better nor new."

"Weel, we winna hae worship this mornin'; whan ye gang to the kirk it's like aitin' mair nor's guid for ye."

"Hoots, Anerew! ye dinna think a body can hae ower muckle o' the word!" said his wife, anxious as to the impression he might make on Donal.

"Ow na, gien a body tak it in, an' disgeist it! But it's no a bonny thing to hae the word stickin' about yer moo', an' baggin' oot yer pooches, no to say lyin' cauld upo' yer stamack, an' it for the life o' men. The less ye tak abune what ye put in practice the better;

---

gien if
haena haven't
lees lies
aitin' mair nor's guid eating more than is good
ower muckle too much
moo' mouth
pooches cheeks

an' gien the thing said hae naething to du wi' practice, the less ye heed it the better.—

"Gien ye hae dune yer brakfast, sir, we'll gang—no 'at it's freely kirk-time yet, but the Sabbath's 'maist the only day I get a bit o' a walk, an' gien ye hae nae objection til a turn aboot the Lord's muckle hoose afore we gang intil his little ane—we ca' 't his, but I doobt it—I'll be ready in a meenute."

Donal willingly agreed, and the cobbler, already clothed in part of his Sunday best, a pair of corduroy trousers of a mouse colour, having indued an ancient tail-coat of blue with gilt buttons, they set out together; and for their conversation, it was just the same as it would have been any other day: where every day is not the Lord's, the Sunday is his least of all.

From a sermon.

Friends, I have not said we are not to utter our opinions. I have only said we are not to make those opinions the point of a fresh start, the foundation of a new building, the groundwork of anything. They are not to occupy us in our dealings with our brethren. Opinion is often the very death of love. Love aright, and you will come to think aright; and those who think aright must think the same. In the meantime, it matters nothing. The thing that does matter is, that whereto we have attained, by that we should walk. But, while we are not to insist upon our opinions, which is only one way of insisting upon ourselves, however we may cloak the fact from ourselves in the vain imagination of thereby spreading the truth, we are bound by loftiest duty to spread the truth; for that is the saving of men.

---

muckle hoose large house

Do you ask, How spread it, if we are not to talk about it? Friends, I never said, Do not talk about the truth, although I insist upon a better and the only indispensable way: let your light shine. What I said before, and say again, is, Do not talk about the lantern that holds the lamp, but make haste, uncover the light, and let it shine. Let your light so shine before men that they may see your good works,—I incline to the Vatican reading of *good things*,—and glorify your Father who is in heaven. It is not, Let your good works shine, but, Let your light shine. Let it be the genuine love of your hearts, taking form in true deeds; not the doing of good deeds to prove that your opinions are right. If ye are thus true, your very talk about the truth will be a good work, a shining of the light that is in you.

A true smile is a good work, and may do much to reveal the Father who is in heaven; but the smile that is put on for the sake of looking right, or even for the sake of being right, will hardly reveal him, not being like him. Men say that you are cold: if you fear it may be so, do not think to make yourselves warm by putting on the cloak of this or that fresh opinion; draw nearer to the central heat, the living humanity of the Son of Man, that ye may have life in yourselves, so heat in yourselves, so light in yourselves; understand him, obey him, then your light will shine, and your warmth will warm. There is an infection, as in evil, so in good. The better we are, the more will men glorify God. If we trim our lamps so that we have light in our house, that light will shine through our windows, and give light to those that are not in the house. But remember, love of the light alone can trim the lamp.

From the novel David Elginbrod. *David is speaking to a young man, Hugh Sutherland, about the right way to worship God.*

"But his glory! consistin' in his trowth an' lovin'kindness—(man! that's a bonny word)—an' grand self-forgettin' devotion to his creaters—lord! man, it's unspeakable. I care little for his glory either, gin by that ye mean the praise o' men. A heap o' the anxiety for the spread o' his glory, seems to me to be but a desire for the sempathy o' ither fowk. There's no fear but men'll praise him, a' in guid time—that is, whan they can.

"But, Mr. Sutherlan', for the glory o' God, raither than, if it were possible, one jot or one tittle should fail of his entire perfection of holy beauty, I call God to witness, I would gladly go to hell itsel'; for no evil worth the full name can befall the earth or ony creater in't, as long as God is what he is. For the glory o' God, Mr. Sutherlan', I wad die the deith. For the will o' God, I'm ready for onything he likes. I canna surely be in muckle danger o' lichtlyin' him. I glory in my God."

From the novel Wilfrid Cumbermede. *The narrator, an orphan, is describing how the uncle who raised him taught him reverence.*

He would utter the name of God to a child only at grand moments.

———————————

gin if
lichtlyin' belittling

6.

The Divine Plan

From the novel Wilfrid Cumbermede. *The narrator is reflecting on his best friend, who lived a tragic life and died young.*

And whenever the thought arose that God might have given [my friend] a fairer chance in this world, I was able to reflect that apparently God does not care for this world save as a part of the whole; and on that whole I had yet to discover that he could have given him a fairer chance.

From the novel David Elginbrod. *Hugh Sutherland has recently begun to tutor Harry, a spoiled child who has rarely been outside and thinks he is too ill to walk long distances.*

Hugh read for an hour, and then made Harry put on his cloak, notwithstanding the rain, which fell in a slow thoughtful spring shower. Taking the boy again on his back, he carried him into the woods. There he told him how the drops of wet sank into the ground, and then went running about through it in every direction, looking for seeds: which were all thirsty little things, that wanted to grow, and could not, till a drop came and gave them drink. And he told him how the rain-drops were made up in the

65

skies, and then came down, like millions of angels, to do what they were told in the dark earth. The good drops went into all the cellars and dungeons of the earth, to let out the imprisoned flowers. And he told him how the seeds, when they had drunk the rain-drops, wanted another kind of drink next, which was much thinner and much stronger, but could not do them any good till they had drunk the rain first.

"What is that?" said Harry. "I feel as if you were reading out of the Bible, Mr. Sutherland."

"It is the sunlight," answered his tutor. "When a seed has drunk of the water, and is not thirsty any more, it wants to breathe next; and then the sun sends a long, small finger of fire down into the grave where the seed is lying; and it touches the seed, and something inside the seed begins to move instantly and to grow bigger and bigger, till it sends two green blades out of it into the earth, and through the earth into the air; and then it can breathe. And then it sends roots down into the earth; and the roots keep drinking water, and the leaves keep breathing the air, and the sun keeps them alive and busy; and so a great tree grows up, and God looks at it, and says it is good."

"Then they really are living things?" said Harry.

"Certainly."

"Thank you, Mr. Sutherland. I don't think I shall dislike rain so much any more."

✦ ✦ ✦

The next morning was still rainy; and when Hugh found Harry in the library as usual, he saw that the clouds had again gathered over the boy's spirit. He was pacing about the room in a very odd manner. The carpet was divided diamond-wise in a regular pattern. Harry's steps were, for the most part, planted upon every third diamond, as he slowly crossed the floor in a variety of directions; for, as on previous occasions, he had not perceived the entrance of his tutor. But, every now and then, the boy would make the most sudden and irregular change in his mode of progression, setting his foot on the most unexpected diamond, at one time the nearest to him, at another the farthest within his reach. When he looked up, and saw his tutor watching him, he neither started nor blushed: but, still retaining on his countenance the perplexed, anxious expression which Hugh had remarked, said to him:

"How can God know on which of those diamonds I am going to set my foot next?"

"If you could understand how God knows, Harry, then you would know yourself; but before you have made up your mind, you don't know which you will choose; and even then you only know on which you intend to set your foot; for you have often changed your mind after making it up."

Harry looked as puzzled as before.

"Why, Harry, to understand how God understands, you would need to be as wise as he is; so it is no use trying. You see you can't quite understand me, though I have a real meaning in what I say."

"Ah! I see it is no use; but I can't bear to be puzzled."

"But you need not be puzzled; you have no business to be puzzled. You are trying to get into your little brain what is far too grand and beautiful to get into it. Would you not think it very stupid to puzzle yourself how to put a hundred horses into a stable with twelve stalls?"

Harry laughed, and looked relieved.

"It is more unreasonable a thousand times to try to understand such things. For my part, it would make me miserable to think that there was nothing but what I could understand. I should feel as if I had no room anywhere."

From the novel The Vicar's Daughter. *A minister has been criticized for befriending the child of a single mother rather than rebuking the mother.*

Certain people considered him not eager enough to convert the wicked: whatever apparent indifference he showed in that direction arose from his utter belief in the guiding of God, and his dread of outrunning his designs. He would *follow* the operations of the Spirit.

From the novel Robert Falconer. *Mr. Gordon, the narrator, and his friend Robert Falconer live in a poor part of the city.*

One evening when I called to see them, Falconer said,

"We are going out of town for a few weeks, Gordon: will you go with us?"

"I am afraid I can't."

"Why? You have no teaching at present, and your writing you can do as well in the country as in town."

"That is true; but still I don't see how I can. I am too poor for one thing."

"Between you and me that is nonsense."

"Well, I withdraw that," I said. "But there is so much to be done, specially as you will be away, and Miss St. John is at the Lakes."

"That is all very true; but you need a change. I have seen for some weeks that you are failing. Mind, it is our best work that

He wants, not the dregs of our exhaustion. I hope you are not of the mind of our friend Mr. Watts, the curate of st. Gregory's."

"I thought you had a high opinion of Mr. Watts," I returned.

"So I have. I hope it is not necessary to agree with a man in everything before we can have a high opinion of him."

"Of course not. But what is it you hope I am not of his opinion in?"

"He seems ambitious of killing himself with work—of wearing himself out in the service of his master—and as quickly as possible. A good deal of that kind of thing is a mere holding of the axe to the grindstone, not a lifting of it up against thick trees. Only he won't be convinced till it comes to the helve. I met him the other day; he was looking as white as his surplice. I took upon me to read him a lecture on the holiness of holidays. 'I can't leave my poor,' he said. 'Do you think God can't do without you?' I asked. 'Is he so weak that he cannot spare the help of a weary man?' But I think he must prefer quality to quantity, and for healthy work you must be healthy yourself. How can you be the visible sign of the Christ-present amongst men, if you inhabit an exhausted, irritable brain? Go to God's infirmary and rest a while. Bring back health from the country to those that cannot go to it. If on the way it be transmuted into spiritual forms, so much the better. A little more of God will make up for a good deal less of you."

"What did he say to that?"

"He said our Lord died doing the will of his Father. I told him—'Yes, when his time was come, not sooner. Besides, he often avoided both speech and action.' 'Yes,' he answered, 'but he could tell when, and we cannot.' 'Therefore,' I rejoined, 'you ought to accept your exhaustion as a token that your absence will be the best thing for your people. If there were no God, then perhaps you ought to work till you drop down dead—I don't know.'"

"Is he gone yet?"

"No. He won't go. I couldn't persuade him."

"When do you go?"

"To-morrow."

"I shall be ready, if you really mean it."

From the novel Thomas Wingfold, Curate. *A young man tells his sister, whose life has been serene and shallow, that in a moment of passion he murdered a woman.*

Sometimes a thunderbolt, as men call it, will shoot from a clear sky; and sometimes into the midst of a peaceful family, or a yet quieter individuality, without warning of gathered storm above, or lightest tremble of earthquake beneath, will fall a terrible fact, and from the moment everything is changed. That family or that life is no more what it was—probably never more can be what it was. Better it ought to be, worse it may be—which, depends upon itself. But its spiritual weather is altered. The air is thick with cloud, and cannot weep itself clear. There may come a gorgeous sunset though.

It were a truism for one who believes in God to say that such catastrophes, so rending, so frightful, never come but where they are needed. The Power of Life is not content that they who live in and by him should live poorly and contemptibly. If the presence of low thoughts which he repudiates, yet makes a man miserable, how must it be with him if they who live and move and have their being in him are mean and repulsive, or alienated through self-sufficiency and slowness of heart?

From the novel Malcolm. *Malcolm, a young fisherman from the northern coast of Scotland, is watching at sunset as fishermen put to sea with Lady Florimel, who has recently arrived in his native town of Portlossie.*

Nor did Portlossie alone send out her boats, like huge seabirds warring on the live treasures of the deep; from beyond the headlands east and west, out they glided on slow red wing, from Scaurnose, from Sandend, from Clamrock, from the villages all along the coast, spreading as they came, each to its work apart through all the laborious night, to rejoin its fellows only as home drew them back in the clear gray morning, laden and slow with the harvest of the stars. But the night lay between, into which they were sailing over waters of heaving green that for ever kept tossing up roses—a night whose curtain was a horizon built up of steady blue, but gorgeous with passing purple and crimson, and flashing with molten gold.

Malcolm was not one of those to whom the sea is but a pond for fish, and the sky a storehouse of wind and rain, sunshine and snow: he stood for a moment gazing, lost in pleasure. Then he turned to Lady Florimel: she had thrown her daisies on the sand, appeared to be deep in her book, and certainly caught nothing of the splendour before her beyond the red light on her page.

"Saw ye ever a bonnier sicht, my leddy?" said Malcolm.

She looked up, and saw, and gazed in silence. Her nature was full of poetic possibilities; and now a formless thought foreshadowed itself in a feeling she did not understand: why should such a sight as this make her feel sad? The vital connection between joy and effort had begun from afar to reveal itself with the question she now uttered.

"What is it all for?" she asked dreamily, her eyes gazing out on the calm ecstasy of colour, which seemed to have broken the bonds of law, and ushered in a new chaos, fit matrix of new heavens and new earth.

"To catch herrin'," answered Malcolm, ignorant of the mood that prompted the question, and hence mistaking its purport.

But a falling doubt had troubled the waters of her soul, and through the ripple she could descry it settling into form. She was silent for a moment.

"I want to know," she resumed, "why it looks as if some great thing were going on. Why is all this pomp and show? Something ought to be at hand. All I see is the catching of a few miserable fish! If it were the eve of a glorious battle now, I could understand it if those were the little English boats rushing to attack the Spanish Armada, for instance. But they are only gone to catch fish. Or if they were setting out to discover the Isles of the West, the country beyond the sunset! but this jars."

"I canna answer ye a' at ance, my leddy," said Malcolm; "I maun tak time to think aboot it. But I ken brawly what ye mean." Even as he spoke he withdrew, and, descending the mound, walked away beyond the bored craig, regardless now of the far lessening sails and the sinking sun. The motes of the twilight were multiplying fast as he returned along the shore side of the dune, but Lady Florimel had vanished from its crest. He ran to the top: thence, in the dim of the twilight, he saw her slow retreating form, phantom-like, almost at the grated door of the tunnel, which, like that of a tomb, appeared ready to draw her in, and yield her no more.

"My leddy, my leddy," he cried, "winna ye bide for 't?"

He went bounding after her like a deer. She heard him call, and stood holding the door half open.

maun must
ken brawly know broadly
winna ye bide won't you stay

"It's the battle o' Armageddon, my leddy," he cried, as he came within hearing distance.

"The battle of what?" she exclaimed, bewildered. "I really can't understand your savage Scotch."

"Hoot, my leddy! the battle o' Armageddon 's no ane o' the Scots battles; it's the battle atween the richt and the wrang, 'at ye read aboot i' the buik o' the Revelations."

"What on earth are you talking about?" returned Lady Florimel in dismay, beginning to fear that her squire was losing his senses.

"It's jist what ye was sayin', my leddy: sic a pomp as yon bude to hing abune a gran' battle some gait or ither."

"What has the catching of fish to do with a battle in the Revelations?" said the girl, moving a little within the door.

"Weel, my leddy, gien I took in han' to set it furth to ye, I wad hae to tell ye a' that Mr. Graham has been learnin' me sin ever I can min'. He says 'at the whole economy o' natur is fashiont unco like that o' the kingdom o' haven: its jist a gradation o' services, an' the highest en' o' ony animal is to contreebute to the life o' ane higher than itsel'; sae that it's the gran' preevilege o' the fish we tak, to be aten by human bein's, an' uphaud what's abune them."

"That's a poor consolation to the fish," said Lady Florimel.

"Hoo ken ye that, my leddy? Ye can tell nearhan' as little aboot the hert o' a herrin' sic as it has as the herrin' can tell aboot yer ain, whilk, I'm thinkin', maun be o' the lairgest size."

"How should you know anything about my heart, pray?" she asked, with more amusement than offence.

---

bude to hing abune would be fitting to hang above
gien if
unco uncommonly
en' end, purpose

"Jist by my ain," answered Malcolm.

Lady Florimel began to fear she must have allowed the fisher lad more liberty than was proper, seeing he dared avow that he knew the heart of a lady of her position by his own. But indeed Malcolm was wrong, for in the scale of hearts, Lady Florimel's was far below his. She stepped quite within the door, and was on the point of shutting it, but something about the youth restrained her, exciting at least her curiosity; his eyes glowed with a deep, quiet light, and his face, even grand at the moment, had a greater influence upon her than she knew. Instead therefore of interposing the door between them, she only kept it poised, ready to fall to the moment the sanity of the youth should become a hair's breadth more doubtful than she already considered it.

"It's a' pairt o' ae thing, my leddy," Malcolm resumed. "The herrin' 's like the fowk 'at cairries the mate an' the pooder an' sic like for them 'at does the fechtin'. The hert o' the leevin' man's the place whaur the battle's foucht, an' it's aye gaein' on an' on there atween God an' Sawtan; an' the fish they haud fowk up till 't."

"Do you mean that the herrings help you to fight for God?" said Lady Florimel with a superior smile.

"Aither for God or for the deevil, my leddy, that depen's upo' the fowk themsel's. I say it hauds them up to fecht, an' the thing maun be fouchten oot. Fowk to fecht maun live, an' the herrin' hauds the life i' them, an' sae the catchin' o' the herrin' comes in to be a pairt o' the battle."

"Wouldn't it be more sensible to say that the battle is between the fishermen and the sea, for the sake of their wives and children?" suggested Lady Florimel supremely.

"Na, my leddy, it wadna be half sae sensible, for it wadna justifee the grandur that hings ower the fecht. The battle wi' the sea

---

fecht fight

's no sae muckle o' an affair. An', 'deed, gien it warna that the wives an' the verra weans hae themsel's to fecht i' the same battle o' guid an' ill, I dinna see the muckle differ there wad be atween them an' the fish, nor what for they sudna ate ane anither as the craturs i' the watter du.

"But gien 't be the battle I say, there can be no pomp o' sea or sky ower gran' for 't; an' it's a weel waured gien it but haud the gude anes merry an' strong, an' up to their work. For that, weel may the sun shine a celestial rosy reid, an' weel may the boatie row, an' weel may the stars luik doon, blinkin' an' luikin' again ilk ane duin' its bonny pairt to mak a man a richt hertit guid willed sodger!"

"And, pray, what may be your rank in this wonderful army?" asked Lady Florimel, with the air and tone of one humouring a lunatic.

"I'm naething but a raw recruit, my leddy; but gien I hed my chice, I wad be piper to my reg'ment."

"How do you mean?"

"I wad mak sangs. Dinna lauch at me, my leddy, for they're the best kin' o' wapon for the wark 'at I ken. But I'm no a makar, an' maun content mysel' wi' duin' my wark."

"Then why," said Lady Florimel, with the conscious right of social superiority to administer good counsel, "why don't you work harder, and get a better house, and wear better clothes?"

Malcolm's mind was so full of far other and weightier things that the question bewildered him; but he grappled with the reference to his clothes.

---

sae muckle so great
verra weans very children
waured expended
ilk each
richt hertit guid willed sodger right-hearted good-willed soldier
makar poet

"'Deed, my leddy," he returned, "ye may weel say that, seein'
ye was never aboord a herrin' boat! but gien ye ance saw the
inside o' ane fu' o' fish, whaur a body gangs slidderin' aboot,
maybe up to the middle o' 's leg in wamlin' herrin', an' the neist
meenute, maybe, weet to the skin wi' the splash o' a muckle jaw,
ye micht think the claes guid eneuch for the wark, though ill fit,
I confess wi' shame, to come afore yer leddyship."

"I thought you only fished about close by the shore in a little
boat; I didn't know you went with the rest of the fishermen:
that's very dangerous work, isn't it?"

"No ower dangerous my leddy. There's some gangs doon ilka
sizzon; but it's a' i' the w'y o' yer wark."

"Then how is it you're not gone fishing tonight?"

"She's a new boat, an' there's anither day's wark on her afore
we win oot. Wadna ye like a row the nicht, my leddy?"

"No, certainly; it's much too late."

"It'll be nane mirker nor 'tis; but I reckon ye're richt. I cam
ower by jist to see whether ye wadna like to gang wi' the boats
a bit; but yer leddyship set me aff thinkin' an' that pat it oot o'
my heid."

"It's too late now anyhow. Come tomorrow evening, and I'll
see if I can't go with you."

"I canna, my leddy, that's the fash o' 't! I maun gang wi' Blue
Peter the morn's nicht. It was my last chance, I'm sorry to say."

"It's not of the slightest consequence," Lady Florimel returned;
and, bidding him goodnight, she shut and locked the door.

---

jaw wave
doon ilka sizzon down every season
nane mirker no darker
fash o' 't trouble with it
morn's nicht tomorrow

The same instant she vanished, for the tunnel was now quite dark. Malcolm turned with a sigh, and took his way slowly homeward along the top of the dune. All was dim about him; dim in the heavens, where a thin veil of gray had gathered over the blue; dim on the ocean, where the stars swayed and swung, in faint flashes of dissolving radiance, cast loose like ribbons of seaweed: dim all along the shore, where the white of the breaking wavelet melted into the yellow sand; and dim in his own heart, where the manner and words of the lady had half hidden her starry reflex with a chilling mist.

From a letter to a friend.

Blessed be the Father of our Lord who has given us such lively hope. Even in my worst times I am able to look forward to the glory to be revealed. Be comforted, dear friend. Surely *he* comes nearer to you than ever who alone can comfort. It seems as if he threw a veil of sorrow over us sometimes, in order that in its shadows he might get nearer our hearts. . . .

I cannot be wrong in thinking that we have as yet but the faintest glimmer of the splendour of the future that is at hand for those who shall see God and in him all the lovely and loved ones who have vanished for a time. You must have had a sore time—one after another taken from you! But when we are brought low, he cometh nigh to us. The world seems full of dark and strange things, which drive me more and more to believe that he orders all things in a way that we can but partially understand because of its goodness. For my own part I know that I have needed to be afflicted, and yet need it, but at the last I shall say it was well to be afflicted.

From a letter to a friend, written while MacDonald's daughter Mary was dying of tuberculosis at age twenty-four.

I think my wife will be telling you about Mary. So much is better, but all is not better, and she does not get stronger, I much fear. The perfect will be done. Why should we be like the little child that would snatch her sick kitten out of the lap of her mother? When I look forward and think how I shall look back on my own folly, I want to have some of the wisdom now. If Jesus was born, and said such things, and died, and rose, and lived again, can I trust my God too much? Am I in danger of losing my human tenderness if I say—Let the Lord do as he will: I shall only hope and look forward the more. The present in no way satisfies me, least of all the present in myself. I want to be God's man, not the man of my own idea. I look forward—God grant that I press forward.

From the novel There and Back. *Arthur and Alice's mother is an alcoholic; they are talking with their friend Richard, who is sick.*

"Poor mother!" sighed Arthur; "she's not in her right mind! We're in constant terror lest she drop down dead!"

"She's not a very good mother to you!" said Richard.

"No, but that has nothing to do with loving her," answered Alice.

Later Richard thinks more about her.

"If the woman is drinking herself to death," he said to himself, "I wish she would be quick about it! In this world she is doing no good to herself, and much harm to others!" But it would be the ruin, he said to himself, of all hope in the care and love of God, to believe that she could be allowed to live a moment longer than it was well she should live.

Then he thought how wise must be a God who, to work out his intent, would take all the conduct, good and bad, all the endeavours of all his children, in all their contrarieties, and out of them bring the right thing. If he knew such a God, one to trust in absolutely, he would lie still without one movement of fear, he would go to sleep without one throb of anxiety about any he loved! The perfect Love would not fail because one of his children was sick! He would try to be quiet, if only in the hope that there was a perfect heart of hearts, thinking love to and into and about all its creatures. If there was such a splendour, he would either make him well, and send him out again to do for Alice and Arthur what he could, or he would let him die and go where all he loved would come after him—where he might perhaps help to prepare a place for them!

From an essay.

God makes the man that makes the book, or the picture, or the machine. Would God give us a drama? He makes a Shakespere. Or would he construct a drama more immediately his own? He begins with the building of the stage itself, and that stage is a world—a universe of worlds. He makes the actors, and they do not act,—they *are* their part. He utters them into the visible to work out their life—his drama. When he would have an epic, he sends a thinking hero into his drama, and the epic is the soliloquy of his Hamlet. Instead of writing his lyrics, he sets his birds and his maidens a-singing.

All the processes of the ages are God's science; all the flow of history is his poetry. His sculpture is not in marble, but in living and speech-giving forms, which pass away, not to yield place to those that come after, but to be perfected in a nobler studio.

What he has done remains, although it vanishes; and he never either forgets what he has once done, or does it even once again. As the thoughts move in the mind of a man, so move the worlds of men and women in the mind of God, and make no confusion there, for there they had their birth, the offspring of his imagination. Man is but a thought of God.

From the novel The Elect Lady. *Andrew is visiting Dawtie, a servant girl who has been unjustly imprisoned for theft.*

"Weel, An'rew, gien the Lord hasna appeart in His ain likeness to deliver me, He's done the next best thing."

"Dawtie," answered Andrew, "the Lord never does the next best. The thing He does is always better than the thing He does not."

---

gien if

7*

The Boundlessness of Love

From the novel Weighed and Wanting. *Describing two elderly sisters living in genteel poverty.*

It looked as if God had forgotten them—toiling for so little all day long, while the fact was they forgot God, and were thus miserable and oppressed because they would not have him interfere as he would so gladly have done.

From a sermon.

If we will but let our God and Father work his will with us, there can be no limit to his enlargement of our existence, to the flood of life with which he will overflow our consciousness. We have no conception of what life might be, of how vast the consciousness of which we could be made capable. Many can recall some moment in which life seemed richer and fuller than ever before; to some, such moments arrive mostly in dreams: shall soul, awake or asleep, infold a bliss greater than its life, the living God, can seal, perpetuate, enlarge? Can the human twilight of a dream be capable of generating or holding a fuller life than the morning of divine activity?

81

Surely God could at any moment give to a soul, by a word to that soul, by breathing afresh into the secret caves of its being, a sense of life before which the most exultant ecstasy of earthly triumph would pale to ashes! If ever sunlit, sail-crowded sea, under blue heaven flecked with wind-chased white, filled your soul as with a new gift of life, think what sense of existence must be yours, if he whose thought has but fringed its garment with the outburst of such a show, take his abode with you, and while thinking the gladness of a God inside your being, let you know and feel that he is carrying you as a father in his bosom!

From the novel David Elginbrod. *David Elginbrod is manager of the estate to which Hugh Sutherland has just come to be a tutor to the sons of the owner, a wealthy lady. David is explaining to Hugh why he believes in Jesus.*

The almost passionate earnestness with which David spoke, would alone have made it impossible for Hugh to reply at once. After a few moments, however, he ventured to ask the question:

"Would you do nothing that other people should know God, then, David?"

"Onything 'at he likes. But I would tak' tent o' interferin'. He's at it himsel' frae mornin' to nicht, frae year's en' to year's en'."

"But you seem to me to make out that God is nothing but love!"

"Ay, naething but love. What for no?"

"Because we are told he is just."

"Would he be lang just if he didna lo'e us?"

"But does he not punish sin?"

---

tak' tent stop short
What for no? Why not?

"Would it be ony kin'ness no to punish sin? No to us a' means to pit awa' the ae ill thing frae us? Whatever may be meant by the place o' meesery, depen' upo't, Mr. Sutherlan', it's only anither form o' love, love shinin' through the fogs o' ill, an' sae gart leuk something verra different thereby. Man, raither nor see my Maggy—an' ye'll no doot 'at I lo'e her—raither nor see my Maggy do an ill thing, I'd see her lyin' deid at my feet. But supposin' the ill thing ance dune, it's no at my feet I wad lay her, but upo' my heart, wi' my auld arms aboot her, to hand the further ill aff o' her. An' shall mortal man be more just than God? Shall a man be more pure than his Maker? O my God! my God!"

From the novel The Seaboard Parish. *A father is speaking to his daughters, Connie and Wynnie, while a storm is raging outside. Connie has just said that she is "afraid I delight in it."*

"But tell me, Connie," [the father] said, "why you are *afraid* you enjoy hearing the wind about the house."

"Because it must be so dreadful for those that are out in it."

"Perhaps not quite so bad as we think. You must not suppose that God has forgotten them, or cares less for them than for you because they are out in the wind."

"But if we thought like that, papa," said Wynnie, "shouldn't we come to feel that their sufferings were none of our business?"

"If our benevolence rests on the belief that God is less loving than we, it will come to a bad end somehow before long, Wynnie."

From a sermon on Revelation 2:17.

> To him that overcometh, I will give a white stone, and in the
> stone a new name written, which no man knoweth saving he that
> receiveth it.

As the fir-tree lifts up itself with a far different need from the need of the palm-tree, so does each man stand before God, and lift up a different humanity to the common Father. And for each God has a different response. With every man he has a secret—the secret of the new name. In every man there is a loneliness, an inner chamber of peculiar life into which God only can enter. I say not it is *the innermost chamber*—but a chamber into which no brother, nay, no sister can come.

From this it follows that there is a chamber also—(O God, humble and accept my speech)—a chamber in God himself, into which none can enter but the one, the individual, the peculiar man,—out of which chamber that man has to bring revelation and strength for his brethren. This is that for which he was made—to reveal the secret things of the Father.

By his creation, then, each man is isolated with God; each, in respect of his peculiar making, can say, "*my* God;" each can come to him alone, and speak with him face to face, as a man speaketh with his friend.

From the novel Alec Forbes of Howglen. *Mr. Cowie, who is dying, is the local Church of England minister; Annie Anderson is an orphan child who has stopped going to his church in favor of the local mission chapel, which is presided over by Mr. Turnbull.*

As a Protestant in the Church of England, Mr. Cowie would ordinarily have rejected the idea of departed souls interceding for the living as too Catholic.

Except his own daughters there was no one who mourned so deeply for the loss of Mr. Cowie as Annie Anderson. She had left his church and gone to the missionars, and found more spiritual nourishment than Mr. Cowie's sermons could supply, but she could not forget his gentle words, or his shilling; for by their means, although she did not know it, Mr. Cowie's self had given her a more confiding notion of God, a better feeling of his tenderness, than she could have had from all Mr. Turnbull's sermons together. What equal gift could a man give? Was it not worth bookfuls of sound doctrine? Yet the good man, not knowing this, had often looked back to that interview, and reproached himself bitterly that he, so long a clergyman of that parish, had no help to give the only child who ever came to him to ask such help. So, when he lay on his death-bed, he sent for Annie, the only soul, out of all his parish, over which he felt that he had any pastoral cure.

When, with pale, tearful face, she entered his chamber, she found him supported with pillows in his bed. He stretched out his arms to her feebly and wept.

"I'm going to die, Annie," he said.

"And go to heaven, sir, to the face o' God," said Annie, not sobbing, but with tears streaming silently down her face.

"I don't know, Annie. I've been of no use; and I'm afraid God does not care much for me."

"If God loves you half as much as I do, sir, ye'll be well off in heaven. And I'm thinkin' he maun love ye mair nor me. For, ye see, sir, God's love itsel'."

"I don't know, Annie. But if ever I win there, which'll be more than I deserve, I'll tell him about you, and ask him to give you the help that I couldn't give you."

Love and Death make us all children.— Can Old Age be an evil thing, which does the same?

The old clergyman had thought himself a good Protestant at least, but even his Protestantism was in danger now. Happily Protestantism was nothing to him now. Nothing but God would do now.

From the same novel. Alec Forbes, who had left his country home and the values he was raised with for life at a university, has returned home to recover from a lengthy sickness. He is being nursed by his friend Cupples. Annie, now a young woman who loves Alec but who has been treated badly by him, has been living with his mother while he was away from home.

At length one lovely morning, when the green corn lay soaking in the yellow sunlight, and the sky rose above the earth deep and pure and tender like the thought of God about it, Alec became suddenly aware that life was good, and the world beautiful. He tried to raise himself, but failed. Cupples was by his side in a moment. Alec held out his hand with his old smile so long disused. Cupples propped him up with pillows, and opened the window that the warm waves of the air might break into the cave where he had lain so long deaf to its noises and insensible to its influences. The tide flowed into his chamber like Pactolus, all

---

maun must

golden with sunbeams. He lay with his hands before him and his eyes closed, looking so happy that Cupples gazed with reverent delight, for he thought he was praying. But he was only blessed.

So easily can God make a man happy! The past had dropped from him like a wild but weary and sordid dream. He was reborn, a new child, in a new bright world, with a glowing summer to revel in. One of God's lyric prophets, the larks, was within earshot, pouring down a vocal summer of jubilant melody. The lark thought nobody was listening but his wife; but God heard in heaven, and the young prodigal heard on the earth. He would be a good child henceforth, for one bunch of sun-rays was enough to be happy upon. His mother entered. She saw the beauty upon her boy's worn countenance; she saw the noble watching love on that of his friend; her own filled with light, and she stood trans-fixed and silent. Annie entered, gazed for a moment, fled to her own room, and burst into adoring tears.—For she had seen the face of God, and that face was Love—love like the human, only deeper, deeper—tenderer, lovelier, stronger. She could not recall what she had seen, or how she had known it; but the conviction remained that she had seen His face, and that it was infinitely beautiful.

"He has been wi' me a' the time, my God! . . . He's been wi' me I kenna hoo lang, and He's wi' me noo. And I hae seen His face, and I'll see His face again. And I'll try sair to be a gude bairn. Eh me! It's jist wonnerfu'! And God's jist . . . naething but God Himsel'."

---

kenna hoo lang don't know how long
sair sorely, very hard
gude bairn good child

From a letter to a friend whose husband had died.

Sometimes the change that must come in me seems so immense, it is nothing less than a birth from above. But if there be One who could call us into thought, He is able for this too. We have but a poor glimmering notion of what life means. If we were *one with* the life eternal, the delight of mere consciousness would, I think, be something unspeakable. The greatest bliss is just the one thing we cannot do without. As often as we get a little glimmer of the truth, we are ready to feel as if now we could get on and be at peace a while; whereas it is every moment a breathing of God's breath, a walking with God, a thinking of God's thoughts, a consciousness of His presence as our deepest being: this is what we need, to live other than a broken, half-slavish life. . . .

Have patience, and let your wings grow. There is no food for feathers like patience. I have been learning a little about patience lately. Ah, what lovely quiet we have here! But it only gives room for severer battle. It is in desert places that the real battles of the world have been first gained. And who can tell? nay, I think I can almost tell, that now in your loneliness, now that the noise of the surf of the tide of the world has receded, and will recede yet further from your dwelling, you will find more unexpected doors opening around you, and will learn more clearly than ever that you are all the time in the heart of the Father, where your beautiful husband is also. It cannot be very long. We will go on cheerfully. Our life might be a call to those beyond: "We are coming, friends!"

Christ be with us and teach us. I am generally . . . sooner or later sent back to Him when I get into a hedge. That he knew God and was satisfied is a lovely comfort. If He lived really, all is well, and we will trust even when we cannot get things all right in our thoughts. To what a bliss we are called—to be the heirs of God!

From the novel There and Back. *Richard is a young man recovering from a serious illness. He has loved Barbara long and hopelessly, but just before getting sick had finally received a letter from her saying that she returns his love.*

The morning after the concert, he had taken Barbara's letter from under his pillow, and would not let it out of his hand. His mother, fearing he would wear it to pieces, once and again tried to remove it; but the moment she touched it, he would cry out and strike; and when in his restless turning he dropped it, he showed himself so miserable that she could not but put it in his hand again, when he would lie perfectly quiet for a while. Dreaming of Barbara however, I fancy, he at length forgot her letter, and his mother again put it under his pillow. With the Lord, we shall forget even the gospel of John.

The Way of Discipleship

Jesus answered and said unto him,
"If a man love me, he will keep my words:
and my Father will love him,
and we will come unto him,
and make our abode with him."

John 14:23

8.

Faith

From the novel There and Back, *regarding the futility of arguing about faith with a skeptic.*

"You cannot prove to me that you have a father!" says the blind sage, reasoning with the little child.

"Why should I prove it?" answers the child. "I am sitting on his knee! If I could prove it, that would not make you see him; that would not make you happy like me! You do not care about my father, or you would not stand there disputing; you would feel about until you found him!"

From a lecture on Tennyson's poem, "The Two Voices," in which a soul debates within itself, with one voice urging suicide and the other representing faith and hope.

Since this poem was written there has been a tremendous wave of unbelief over the world, affecting all thinking men and women. Yet one result has been, that there is more real faith abroad now than there has ever been in the world before. But doubt and questioning must now affect every thinking mind, and this in some cases leads to the suggestions of this Tempting

93

Voice. Well, if there be no God, the Tempting Voice is right. All human life would be a sham. Man is befooled.

But yet there is another way. Go and do God's will and you will know. That is the remedy to the gloomy doubts and the terrible depression of this age. And remember what so many forget, the Christian duty of joy. . . . You say: "It is not in my power to rejoice now." Well, I deny it. You have the power, if only you will exert the will. And don't let slip the youthful dreams. Such things will help you against that false self which comes with the Tempting Voice to despair. And don't let gloomy pictures of results keep coming before you. "Tomorrow" has no existence till it actually comes. Let it take care of itself.

From the novel Warlock o' Glenwarlock. *Cosmo is speaking with his tutor Mr. Simon, "a man of peculiar opinions . . . but everything in him is . . . on a grand scale. A man must learn to judge for himself, and he will teach you that." They are discussing the world beyond.*

"Never in my life have I had one whisper from that world."

"You are saying a great deal more than you can possibly know, Cosmo," answered Mr. Simon. "You have had no communication recognized by you as such, I grant. And I, who am so much older than you, must say the same. If there be any special fitness in the night, in its absorbing dimness, and isolating silence, for such communication—and who can well doubt it?—I have put myself in the heart of it a thousand times, when, longing after an open vision, I should have counted but the glimpse of a ghostly garment the mightiest boon, but never therefrom has the shadow of a feather fallen upon me. Yet here I am, hoping no less, and believing no less! The air around me may be full of ghosts—I do not know; I delight to think they may somehow be with us, for all they are so unseen; but so long as I am able to believe and hope in the one great ghost, the Holy Ghost that fills all, it would trouble me little to learn that betwixt me and the visible centre was nothing but what the senses of men may take account of. If there be a God, he is all in all, and filleth all things, and all is well.

"What matter where the region of the dead may be? Nowhere but here are they called the dead. When, of all paths, that to God is alone always open, and alone can lead the wayfarer to the end of his journey, why should I stop to peer through the fence either side of that path? If he does not care to reveal, is it well I should make haste to know? I shall know one day, why should I be eager to know now?"

"But why might not something show itself once—just for once, if only to give one a start in the right direction?" said Cosmo.

"I will tell you one reason," returned Mr. Simon, "the same why everything is as it is, and neither this nor that other way— namely, that it is best for us it should be as it is. But I think I can see a little way into it. Suppose you saw something strange—a sign or a wonder—one of two things, it seems to me likely, would follow:—you would either doubt it the moment it had vanished, or it would grow to you as one of the common things of your daily life—which are indeed in themselves equally wonder- ful. Evidently, if visions would make us sure, God does not care about the kind of sureness they can give, or for our being made sure in that way. A thing that gained in one way, might be of less than no value to us, gained in another, might, as a vital part of the process, be invaluable. God will have us sure of a thing by knowing the heart whence it comes; that is the only worthy assurance. To know, he will have us go in at the great door of obedient faith; and if anybody thinks he has found a backstair, he will find it land him at a doorless wall. It is the assurance that comes of inmost beholding of himself, of seeing what he is, that God cares to produce in us. Nor would he have us think we know him before we do, for thereby thousands walk in a vain show.

"At the same time I am free to imagine if I imagine holily—that is, as his child. And I imagine space full of life invisible; imagine that the young man needed but the opening of his eyes to see the horses and chariots of fire around his master, an inner circle to the horses and chariots that encompassed the city to take him [2 Kings 6:8–23].

"As I came now through the fields, I lost myself for a time in the feeling that I was walking in the midst of lovely people I have known, some in person, some by their books. Perhaps they were with me—are with me—are speaking to me now. For if all our thoughts, from whatever source, whether immediately from God, or through ourselves, seem to enter the chamber of our consciousness by the same door, why may it not be so with some that come to us from other beings? Why may not the dead speak to me, and I be unable to distinguish their words from my thoughts? The moment a thought is given me, my own thought rushes to mingle with it, and I can no more part them. Some stray hints from the world beyond may mingle even with the folly and stupidity of my dreams. . . .

"All is well. The only thing worth a man's care is the will of God, and that will is the same whether in this world or in the next. That will has made this world ours, not the next; for nothing can be ours until God has given it to us. Curiosity is but the contemptible human shadow of the holy thing, wonder.

No, my son, let us make the best we can of this life, that we may become able to make the best of the next also."

"And how make the best of this?" asked Cosmo.

"Simply by falling in with God's design in the making of you. That design must be worked out—cannot be worked out without you. You must walk in the front of things with the will of God—not be dragged in the sweep of his garment that makes the storm behind him! To walk with God is to go hand in hand with him, like a boy with his father. Then, as to the other world, or any world, as to the past sorrow, the vanished joy, the coming fear, all is well; for the design of the making, the loving, the pitiful, the beautiful God, is marching on towards divine completion, that is, a never ending one. Yea, if it please my sire that his infinite be awful to me, yet will I face it, for it is his. Let your prayer, my son, be like this: 'O Maker of me, go on making me, and let me help thee. Come, O Father! here I am; let us go on. I know that my words are those of a child, but it is thy child who prays to thee. It is thy dark I walk in; it is thy hand I hold.'"

From a short story, The Golden Key. *The child Tangle has been traveling through a mysterious land looking for "the country whence the shadows fall." She has already visited the Old Man of the Sea, and is now in the cave of the Old Man of the Earth.*

"Tell me the way to the country whence the shadows fall."

"Ah! That I do not know. I only dream about it myself. I see its shadows sometimes in the mirror. But I think the Old Man of the Fire must know. He is much older than I am. He is the oldest man of all."

"Where does he live?"

"I will show you the way to his place. I never saw him myself." . . .

He led her to the side of the cave, and told her to lay her ear against the wall.

"What do you hear?"

"I hear," said Tangle, "the sound of a great water running inside the rock."

"That river runs down to the dwelling of the oldest man of all—the Old Man of the Fire. . . . The river is the only way to him."

Then the Old Man of the Earth stooped over the floor of the cave, raised a huge stone from it, and left it leaning. It disclosed a great hole that went plumb-down.

"That is the way," he said.

"But there are no stairs."

"You must throw yourself in. There is no other way."

From the novel Robert Falconer. *Robert Falconer is a university student who is searching for meaning in life.*

Robert had not settled at any of the universities, but had moved from one to the other as he saw fit, report guiding him to the men who spoke with authority. The time of doubt and anxious questioning was far from over, but the time was long gone by—if in his case it had ever been—when he could be like a wave of the sea, driven of the wind and tossed. He had ever one anchor of the soul, and he found that it held—the faith of Jesus (I say the faith of Jesus, not his own faith in Jesus), the truth of Jesus, the life of Jesus. However his intellect might be tossed on the waves of speculation and criticism, he found that the word the Lord had spoken remained steadfast; for in doing righteously, in loving mercy, in walking humbly, the conviction increased that Jesus knew the very secret of human life.

Now and then some great vision gleamed across his soul of the working of all things towards a far-off goal of simple obedience to a law of life, which God knew, and which his son had justified through sorrow and pain. Again and again the words of the Master gave him a peep into a region where all was explicable, where all that was crooked might be made straight, where every mountain of wrong might be made low, and every valley of suffering exalted. Ever and again some one of the dark perplexities of humanity began to glimmer with light in its inmost depth. Nor was he without those moments of communion when the creature is lifted into the secret place of the Creator.

Looking back to the time when it seemed that he cried and was not heard, he saw that God had been hearing, had been answering, all the time; had been making him capable of receiving the gift for which he prayed. He saw that intellectual difficulty encompassing the highest operations of harmonizing truth, can no more affect their reality than the dullness of chaos disprove the motions of the wind of God over the face of its waters.

From the novel The Vicar's Daughter. *The narrator has just been speaking to her dying friend about faith.*

For I knew that the confidence in Christ which prevents us from thinking of ourselves, and makes us eager to obey his word, leaving all the care of our feelings to him, is a true and healthy faith.

From the novel Alec Forbes of Howglen. *Annie, an orphan child, comes to the house of the deaf stone-mason Thomas for advice.*

"Lat her come in, than," bawled Thomas.

"He's tellin' ye to come in, Annie," said Jean, as if she had been interpreting his words. But she detained her nevertheless to ask several unimportant questions. At length the voice of Thomas rousing her once more, she hastened to introduce her.

"Gang in there, Annie," she said, throwing open the door of the dark room. The child entered and stood just within it, not knowing even where Thomas sat. But a voice came to her out of the gloom:

"Ye're no feared at the dark, are ye, Annie? Come in."

"I dinna ken whaur I'm gaein'."

"Never min' that. Come straucht foret. I'm watchin' ye."

For Thomas had been sitting in the dark till he could see in it (which, however, is not an invariable result), while out of the little light Annie had come into none at all. But she obeyed the voice, and went straight forward into the dark, evidently much to the satisfaction of Thomas, who seizing her arm with one hand laid the other, horny and heavy, on her head, saying:

"Noo, my lass, ye'll ken what faith means. Whan God tells ye to gang into the mirk, gang!"

"But I dinna like the mirk," said Annie.

"No human sowl *can*," responded Thomas. "Jean, fess a can'le direckly."

---

gang go
dinna ken don't know
straucht foret straight forward
mirk darkness
fess fetch

From the novel The Seaboard Parish. *An elderly man describes an outing in summer.*

I think I must have been the very happiest of the party myself. No doubt I was younger much than I am now, but then I was quite middle-aged, with full confession thereof in gray hairs and wrinkles. Why should not a man be happy when he is growing old, so long as his faith strengthens the feeble knees which chiefly suffer in the process of going down the hill? True, the fever heat is over, and the oil burns more slowly in the lamp of life; but if there is less fervour, there is more pervading warmth; if less of fire, more of sunshine; there is less smoke and more light.

Verily, youth is good, but old age is better—to the man who forsakes not his youth when his youth forsakes him. The sweet visitings of nature do not depend upon youth or romance, but upon that quiet spirit whose meekness inherits the earth. The smell of that field of beans gives me more delight now than ever it could have given me when I was a youth. And if I ask myself why, I find it is simply because I have more faith now than I had then. It came to me then as an accident of nature—a passing pleasure flung to me only as the dogs' share of the crumbs. Now I believe that God *means* that odour of the bean-field; that when Jesus smelled such a scent about Jerusalem or in Galilee, he thought of his Father. And if God means it, it is mine, even if I should never smell it again.

From the same novel. Ethelwyn (Wynnie) is in love with an artist, Mr. Percivale. Her father is not sure he approves.

"Yes," she answered shyly. "He was so kind that somehow I got heart to try again. He's very nice, isn't he?"

My answer was not quite ready.

"Don't you like him, papa?"

"Well—I like him—yes. But we must not be in haste with our judgments, you know. I have had very little opportunity of seeing into him. There is much in him that I like, but—"

"But what? please, papa."

"To tell the truth then, Wynnie, for I can speak my mind to you, my child, there is a certain shyness of approaching the subject of religion; so that I have my fears lest he should belong to any of these new schools of a fragmentary philosophy which acknowledge no source of truth but the testimony of the senses and the deductions made therefrom by the intellect."

"But is not that a hasty conclusion, papa?"

"That is a hasty question, my dear. I have come to no conclusion. I was only speaking confidentially about my fears."

"Perhaps, papa, it's only that he's not sure enough, and is afraid of appearing to profess more than he believes. I'm sure, if that's it, I have the greatest sympathy with him."

I looked at her, and saw the tears gathering fast in her eyes.

"Pray to God on the chance of his hearing you, my darling, and go to sleep," I said. "I will not think hardly of you because you cannot be so sure as I am. How could you be? You have not had my experience. Perhaps you are right about Mr. Percivale too. But it would be an awkward thing to get intimate with him, you know, and then find out that we did not like him after all. You couldn't like a man much, could you, who did not believe in anything greater than himself, anything marvellous, grand, beyond our understanding—who thought that he had come out of the dirt and was going back to the dirt?"

"I could, papa, if he tried to do his duty notwithstanding—for I'm sure I couldn't. I should cry myself to death."

"You are right, my child. I should honour him too. But I should be very sorry for him. For he would be so disappointed in himself."

From the novel Malcolm. *Malcolm, an orphan, has just learned of a terrible deed done by the woman he thinks might be his mother. He talks to his former teacher, Mr. Graham.*

"I wonner what God thinks aboot it a'! It gars a body spier whether he cares or no," said Malcolm gloomily.

"It does," responded Mr. Graham solemnly.

"Div ye alloo that, sir?" returned Malcolm, aghast. "That soon's as gien a'thing war rushin' thegither back to the auld chaos."

"I should not be surprised," continued the master, apparently heedless of Malcolm's consternation, "if the day should come when well meaning men, excellent in the commonplace, but of dwarfed imagination, refused to believe in a God on the ground of apparent injustice in the very frame and constitution of things. Such would argue, that there might be either an omnipotent being who did not care, or a good being who could not help; but that there could not be a being both all good and omnipotent, for such would never have suffered things to be as they are."

"What wad the clergy say to hear ye, sir?" said Malcolm, himself almost trembling at the words of his master. . . .

"The main objection of theologians would be, I presume, that it did not present a God perfect in power as in goodness; but I think it a far more objectionable point that it presents evil as

---

gars a body spier makes a person wonder
div ye alloo do you think
gien if

possessing power in itself. My chief objection, however, would be a far deeper one—namely, that its good being cannot be absolutely good; for, if he knew himself unable to insure the well being of his creatures, if he could not avoid exposing them to such foreign attack, had he a right to create them? Would he have chosen such a doubtful existence for one whom he meant to love absolutely? Either, then, he did not love like a God, or he would not have created."

"He micht ken himsel' sure to win i' the lang rin."

"Grant the same to the God of the Bible, and we come back to where we were before."

"Does that satisfee yersel', Maister Graham?" asked Malcolm, looking deep into the eyes of his teacher.

"Not at all," answered the master.

"Does onything?"

"Yes: but I will not say more on the subject now. The time may come when I shall have to speak that which I have learned, but it is not yet. All I will say now is, that I am at peace concerning the question. Indeed, so utterly do I feel myself the offspring of the One, that it would be enough for my peace now—I don't say it would have been always—to know my mind troubled on a matter: what troubled me would trouble God: my trouble at the seeming wrong must have its being in the right existent in him. In him, supposing I could find none I should yet say there must lie a lucent, harmonious, eternal, not merely consoling, but absolutely satisfying solution."

From the novel Thomas Wingfold, Curate. *Doctor Paul Faber, a determined atheist, is speaking with the local minister, Thomas Wingfold, who had previously struggled to find faith himself.*

"Well," [said Faber,] "all I have to say is, I can't for the life of me see what you want to believe in a God for! It seems to me the world would go rather better without any such fancy. Look here now: there is young Spenser—out there at Harwood—a patient of mine. His wife died yesterday—one of the loveliest young creatures you ever saw. The poor fellow is as bad about it as fellow can be. Well, he's one of your sort, and said to me the other day, just as you would have him, 'It's the will of God,' he said, 'and we must hold our peace.'—'Don't talk to me about God,' I said, for I couldn't stand it. 'Do you mean to tell me that, if there was a God, he would have taken such a lovely creature as that away from her husband and her helpless infant, at the age of two and twenty? I scorn to believe it.'"

"What did he say to that?"

"He turned as white as death, and said never a word."

"Ah, you forgot that you were taking from him his only hope of seeing her again!"

"I certainly did not think of that," said Faber.

"Even then," resumed Wingfold, "I should not say you were wrong, if you were prepared to add that you had searched every possible region of existence, and had found no God; or that you had tried every theory man had invented, or even that you were able to invent yourself, and had found none of them consistent with the being of a God. I do not say that then you would be right in your judgment, for another man, of equal weight, might have had a different experience. I only say, I would not then blame you. But you must allow it a very serious thing to assert as a conviction, without such grounds as the assertor has pretty fully satisfied himself concerning, what *could* only drive the sting of death ten times deeper."

The doctor was silent.

"I doubt not you spoke in a burst of indignation; but it seems to me the indignation of a man unaccustomed to ponder the things concerning which he expresses such a positive conviction."

"You are wrong there," returned Faber; "for I was brought up in the straitest sect of the Pharisees, and know what I am saying."

"The straitest sect of the Pharisees can hardly be the school in which to gather any such idea of a God as one could wish to be a reality."

"They profess to know."

"Is that any argument of weight, they and their opinions being what they are?—If there be a God, do you imagine he would choose any strait sect under the sun to be his interpreters?"

"But the question is not of the idea of a God, but of the existence of any, seeing, if he exists, he must be such as the human heart could never accept as God, inasmuch as he at least permits, if not himself enacts cruelty. My argument to poor Spenser remains—however unwise or indeed cruel it may have been."

"I grant it a certain amount of force—as much exactly as had gone to satisfy the children whom I heard the other day agreeing that Dr. Faber was a very cruel man, for he pulled out nurse's tooth, and gave poor little baby such a nasty, nasty powder!"

"Is that a fair parallel? I must look at it."

"I think it is. What you do is often unpleasant, sometimes most painful, but it does not follow that you are a cruel man, and a hurter instead of a healer of men."

"I think there is a fault in the analogy," said Faber. "For here am I nothing but a slave to laws already existing, and compelled to work according to them. It is not my fault therefore that the remedies I have to use are unpleasant. But if there be a God, he has the matter in his own hands."

"There is weight and justice in your argument, which may well make the analogy appear at first sight false. But is there no theory possible that should make it perfect?"

"I do not see how there should be any. For, if you say God is under any such compulsion as I am under, then surely the house is divided against itself, and God is not God any more."

"For my part," said the curate, "I think I *could* believe in a God who did but his imperfect best: in one all power, and not all goodness, I could not believe.

"But suppose that the design of God involved the perfecting of men as the *children of God*—'I said ye are gods,'—that he would have them partakers of his own blessedness in kind—be as himself;—suppose his grand idea could not be contented with creatures perfect *only* by his gift, so far as that should reach, and having no willing causal share in the perfection, that is, partaking not at all of God's individuality and free-will and choice of good; then suppose that suffering were the only way through which the individual could be set, in separate and self-individuality, so far apart from God, that it might *will*, and so become a partaker of his singleness and freedom;—and suppose that this suffering must be and had been initiated by God's taking his share, and that the infinitely greater share;—suppose next, that God saw the germ of a pure affection, say in your friend and his wife, but saw also that it was a germ so imperfect and weak that it could not encounter the coming frosts and winds of the world without loss and decay, while, if they were parted now for a few years, it would grow and strengthen and expand, to the certainty of an infinitely higher and deeper and keener love through the endless ages to follow—so that by suffering should come, in place of contented decline and death, a troubled birth of joyous result in health and immortality;—suppose all this, and what then?"

Faber was silent a moment, then answered, "Your theory has but one fault: it is too good to be true."

"My theory leaves plenty of difficulty, but has no such fault as that. Why, what sort of a God would content you, Mr. Faber? The one idea is too bad, the other too good to be true. Must you expand and pare until you get one exactly to the measure of yourself ere you can accept it as thinkable or possible? Why, a less God than that would not rest your soul a week. The only possibility of believing in a God seems to me to lie in finding an idea of a God large enough, grand enough, pure enough, lovely enough to be fit to believe in."

"And have you found such—may I ask?"

"I think I am finding such."

"Where?"

"In the man of the New Testament. I have thought a little more about these things, I fancy, than you have, Mr. Faber. I may come to be sure of something; I don't see how a man can ever be sure of *nothing*."

From the novel Paul Faber. *Paul Faber's defense of his atheist convictions disturbs the faith of a young woman, Dorothy Drake, whose father is the minister of a local church.*

[Her father], never doubting the security of his child's faith, had no slightest suspicion into what a sore spot his words had carried torture. He did not know that the genius of doubt—shall I call him angel or demon?—had knocked at her door, had called through her window; that words dropped by Faber, indicating that science was against all idea of a God, and the confidence of their tone, had conjured up in her bosom hollow fears, faint dismays, and stinging questions.

Ready to trust, and incapable of arrogance, it was hard for her to imagine how a man like Mr. Faber, upright and kind and self-denying, could say such things if he did not *know* them true. The very word *science* appeared to carry an awful authority. She did not understand that it was only because science had never come closer to Him than the mere sight of the fringe of the outermost folds of the tabernacle of His presence, that her worshipers dared assert there was no God. She did not perceive that nothing ever science could find, could possibly be the God of men; that science is only the human reflex of truth, and that truth itself can not be measured by what of it is reflected from the mirror of the understanding. She did not see that no incapacity of science to find God, even touched the matter of honest men's belief that He made His dwelling with the humble and contrite.

Nothing she had learned from her father either provided her with reply, or gave hope of finding argument of discomfiture; nothing of all that went on at chapel or church seemed to have any thing to do with the questions that presented themselves. Such a rough shaking of so-called faith has been of endless service to many, chiefly by exposing the insecurity of all foundations of belief, save that which is discovered in digging with the spade of obedience.

Well indeed is it for all honest souls to be thus shaken, who have been building upon doctrines concerning Christ, upon faith, upon experiences, upon any thing but Christ Himself, as revealed by Himself and His spirit to all who obey Him, and so revealing the Father.

From the novel There and Back. *Richard, loving but feeling himself unworthy of Barbara, groundlessly concludes that she is about to marry the odious Mr. Lestrange.*

Then the thought suggested itself that she might have come to London to prepare for her marriage with Mr. Lestrange. She must of course be married some day! He had always taken that for granted, but now, for the first time somehow, the thought came near enough to burn. He did not attempt to analyze his feelings; he was too miserable to care for his feelings. The thought was as terrible as if it had been quite new. It was not a live thought before; now it was alive and until now he had not known misery. . . . His heart sank into a draw-well of misery, out of which the rope of thinking could draw up nothing but suicide. But as often as the bucket rose thus laden, Richard cast its content from him. It was cowardly to hide one's head in the sand of death. So long as he was able to stand, why should he lie down? If a morrow was on the way, why not see what the morrow would bring? why not look the apparition in the face, though for him it brought no dawn!

Once more the loud complaint against life awoke and raged. What an evil, what a wrong was life! Who had dared force the thing upon him? What being, potent in ill, had presumed to call him from the blessed regions of negation, the solemn quiet of being and knowing nothing, and compel him to live without, nay, against his will, in misery such as only an imagination keen to look upon suffering could have embodied or even invented? Alas, there was no help! If he lifted his hand against the life he hated, he might but rush into a region of torture more exquisite! For might not the life-compelling tyrant, offended that he should desire to cease, fix him in eternal beholding of his love and his hate folded in one—to sicken, yet never faint, in aeonian pain, such as life essential only could feel! He rebelled against the highest as if the highest were the lowest—as if the power that *could* create a heart for bliss, might gloat on its sufferings.

Again and again he would take the side of God against himself: but always there was the undeniable, the inexplicable misery! Whence came it? It could not come from himself, for he hated it? and if God did not cause, yet he could prevent it! Then he remembered how blessed he had been but a few days before; how ready to justify God; how willing to believe he had reason in all he did: alas for his nature, for his humanity! clothed in his own joy, he was generous to trust God with the bliss of others; the cold blast of the world once again swept over him, and he stood complaining against him more bitterly than ever.

It is a notable argument, surely, against the existence of God, that they who believe in him, believe in him so wretchedly! So many carry themselves to him like peevish children! Richard half believed in God, only to complain of him altogether! Were it not better to deny him altogether, saying that such things being, he cannot be, than to murmur and rebel as against one high and hard?

But I bethink me: is it not better to complain if one but complain to God himself? Does he not then draw nigh to God with what truth is in him? And will he not then fare as Job, to whom God drew nigh in return, and set his heart at rest?

For him who complains and comes not near, who shall plead?—The Son of the Father, saying, "They know not what they do."

He began to wonder whether even an all-mighty and all-good God would be able to contrive such a world as no somebody in it would ever complain of. What if he had plans too large for the vision of men to take in, and they were uncomfortable to their own blame, because, not seeing them, they would trust him for nothing? He knew unworthy men full of complaint against an economy that would not let them live like demons, and be blessed as seraphs! Why should not a man at least wait and see what the possible being was about to do with him, perhaps for him, before he accused or denied him? At worst he would be no worse for the waiting!

His thinking was stopped by a sudden flood of self-contempt. Was Barbara to live alone that he might think of her in peace! He was a selfish, disgraceful, degraded animal, deserving all he suffered, and ten times more! What did it matter whether *he* was happy or not, if it was well with her! . . . For her sake, he would still seek her God, if haply he might find him! Was there not a possible hope that he would justify to him, even in his heart, his ways with men, and his ways with himself among his fellows? What if there was a way so much higher than ours, as to include all the seeming right and seeming wrong in one radiance of righteousness!

The idea was scarce conceivable; it was not one he could illustrate to himself; but, as a thought transcending flesh and blood, better and truer than what *we* are able to think of as truth, he would try to hold by it! Things that we are right in thinking bad, must be bad to God as well as to us; but may there not be things so far above us, that we cannot take them in, and they seem bad because they are so far above us in goodness that we see them partially and untruly? There must be room in his wisdom for us to mistake! He would try to trust! He would say, "If thou art my father, be my father, and comfort thy child. Perhaps thou hast some way! Perhaps things are not as thou wouldst have them, and thou art doing what can be done to set them right! If thou art indeed true to thy own, it were hard not to be believed—hard that one of thine own should not trust thee, should not give thee time to make things clear, should behave to thee as if thou wouldst not explain, when it is that we are unable to understand!"

From the youth novel Ranald Bannerman's Boyhood. *A father is speaking to his son. They have just come from visiting a dying man.*

"Even the refuge in God does not always secure us from external suffering. The heart may be quite happy and strong when the hands are benumbed with cold. Yes, the heart even may grow cold with coming death, while the man himself retreats the farther into the secret place of the Most High, growing more calm and hopeful as the last cold invades the house of his body. I believe that all troubles come to drive us into that refuge—that secret place where alone we can be safe.

"You will, when you go out into the world, my boy, find that most men not only do not believe this, but do not believe that you believe it. They regard it at best as a fantastic weakness, fit only for sickly people. But watch how the strength of such people, their calmness and common sense, fares when the grasp of suffering lays hold upon them. It was a sad sight—that abject hopeless misery I saw this afternoon. If his mind had been an indication of the reality, one must have said that there was no God—no God at least that would have anything to do with him. The universe as reflected in the tarnished mirror of his soul, was a chill misty void, through which blew the moaning wind of an unknown fate. As near as ever I saw it, that man was without God and without hope in the world. All who have done the mightiest things—I do not mean the showiest things . . . —any other of the cloud of witnesses spoken of in the Epistle to the

Hebrews—all the men I say who have done the mightiest things, have not only believed that there was this refuge in God, but have themselves more or less entered into the secret place of the Most High. There only could they have found strength to do their mighty deeds. They were able to do them because they knew God wanted them to do them, that he was on their side, or rather they were on his side, and therefore safe, surrounded by God on every side. My boy, do the will of God—that is, what you know or believe to be right, and fear nothing."

I never forgot the lesson. But my readers must not think that my father often talked like this. He was not at all favourable to much talk about religion. He used to say that much talk prevented much thought, and talk without thought was bad. Therefore it was for the most part only upon extraordinary occasions, of which this is an example, that he spoke of the deep simplicities of that faith in God which was the very root of his conscious life.

9.

Obedience

From a sermon.

If you do not obey him, you will not know him.

You will tell me some of you, that I am always beating that anvil, that obedience to Christ is Christianity. Let me die insisting upon it. For my Lord insists upon it.

From the fairy tale The Lost Princess. *Describing a naughty child who is pleased with herself for having done what she was told for the first time.*

To do one's duty will make anyone conceited who only does it sometimes. Those who do it always would as soon think of being conceited of eating their dinner as of doing their duty. To be conceited of doing one's duty is, then, a sign of how little one does it, and how little one sees what a contemptible thing it is not to do it.

Describing a sermon in the novel Thomas Wingfold, Curate.

He then proceeded to show that faith and obedience are one and the same spirit, passing as it were from room to room in the same heart: what in the heart we call faith, in the will we call obedience.

From a sermon.

Obedience is the grandest thing in the world to begin with. Yes, and we shall end with it too. . . .

Those parents act most foolishly who wish to explain everything to their children—most foolishly. No; teach your child to obey, and you give him the most precious lesson that can be given to a child. Let him come to that before you have had him long, to do what he is told, and you have given him the plainest, first, and best lesson that you can give him. If he never goes to school at all he had better have that lesson than all the schooling in the world.

Hence, when some people are accustomed to glorify this age of ours as being so much better in everything than those which went before, I look back to the times of chivalry, which we regard now, almost, as a thing to laugh at, or a merry thing to make jokes about; but I find that the one essential of chivalry was obedience. It is recognized in our army still, but in those times it was carried much farther. When a boy was seven years old he was sent into another family, and put with another boy there to do what? To wait with him upon the master and the mistress of the house, and to be taught, as well, what few things they knew in those times in the way of intellectual cultivation. But he also learned stern, strict obedience, such as it was impossible for him to forget. Then, when he had been there seven years, hard at work, standing behind the chair, and ministering, he was advanced a step; and what was that step? He was made an esquire. He had his armour given him; he had to watch his armour in the chapel all night, laying it on the altar in silent devotion to God. I do not say that all these things were carried out afterwards, but this was the idea of them. He was an esquire, and what was the duty of an esquire? More service; more important service. He still had to attend to his master, the knight. He had to watch him; he had to groom his horse for him; he had to see that his horse was sound; he had to clean his armour for him; to see that every bolt, every rivet, every strap, every buckle was sound, for the life of his master was in his hands. The master, having to fight, must not be troubled with these things, and therefore the squire had to attend to them. Then seven years after that a more solemn ceremony is gone through, and the squire is made a knight; but is he free of service then? No; he makes a solemn oath to help everybody who needs help, especially women and children, and so he rides out into the world to do the work of a true man. There was a grand and essential idea of Christianity in that—no doubt wonderfully broken and shattered, but not more so than the Christian church has been; wonderfully broken and shattered, but still the essence of obedience. . . .

So with the Christian man; whatever meets him, obedience is the thing. If he is told by his conscience, which is the candle of God within him, that he must do a thing, why he must do it. He may tremble from head to foot at having to do it, but he will tremble more if he turns his back.

You recollect how our old poet Spenser shows us the Knight of the Red Cross, who is the knight of holiness, ill in body, diseased in mind, without any of his armour on, attacked by a fearful giant. What does he do? Run away? No, he has but time to catch up his sword, and, trembling in every limb, he goes on to meet the giant; and that is the thing that every Christian man must do. I cannot put it too strongly; it is impossible. There is no escape from it. If death itself lies before us, and we know it, there is nothing to be said; it is all to be done, and then there is no loss; everything else is all lost unto God.

Look at our Lord. He gave his life to do the will of his Father, and on he went and did it. Do you think it was easy for him—easier for him than it would have been for us? Ah! the greater the man the more delicate and tender his nature, and the more he shrinks from the opposition even of his fellow-men, because he loves them. It was a terrible thing for Christ. Even now and then, even in the little touches that come to us in the scanty story (though enough) this breaks out. We are told by John that at the Last Supper "He was troubled in spirit, and testified." And then how he tries to comfort himself as soon as Judas has gone out to do the thing which was to finish his great work: "Now is the Son of Man glorified, and God is glorified in him. If God be glorified in him, God shall also glorify him in himself." Then he adds,—just gathering up his strength,—"I shall straightway glorify him." This was said to his disciples, but I seem to see in it that some of it was said for himself. This is the grand obedience! Oh, friends, this is a hard lesson to learn.

From the novel There and Back. *Describing a man of faith.*

Having now for many years cared only for the will of God, he was full of joy. For the will of the Father is the root of all his children's gladness, of all their laughter and merriment. The child that loves the will of the Father, is at the heart of things; his will is *with* the motion of the eternal wheels; the eyes of all those wheels are opened upon him, and he knows whence he came. Happy and fearless and hopeful, he knows himself the child of him from whom he came, and his peace and joy break out in light. He rises and shines. Bliss creative and energetic there is none other, on earth or in heaven, than the will of the Father.

From the novel The Marquis of Lossie. *Clementina, a young woman who has recently met the fisherman Malcolm, wants to know more about him. She asks Mr. Graham, who was Malcolm's teacher for many years.*

"You consider your friend a genius?" suggested Clementina.

"I consider him possessed of a kind of heavenly common sense, equally at home in the truths of divine relation, and the facts of the human struggle with nature and her forces. I should never have discovered my own ignorance in certain points of the mathematics but for the questions that boy put to me before he was twelve years of age. A thing not understood lay in his mind like a fretting foreign body. But there is a far more important factor concerned than this exceptional degree of insight. Understanding is the reward of obedience. Peter says, 'the Holy Ghost, whom God hath given them that obey him.'

"Obedience is the key to every door. I am perplexed at the stupidity of the ordinary religious being. In the most practical of all matters, he will talk, and speculate, and try to feel, but he will not set himself to do. It is different with Malcolm. From the first he has been trying to obey. Nor do I see why it should be strange that even a child should understand these things, if they are the very elements of the region for which we were created and to which our being holds essential relations, as a bird to the air, or a fish to the sea. If a man may not understand the things of God whence he came, what shall he understand?"

"How, then, is it that so few do understand?"

"Because where they know, so few obey. This boy, I say, did. If you had seen, as I have, the almost superhuman struggles of his will to master the fierce temper his ancestors gave him, you would marvel less at what he has so early become. I have seen him, white with passion, cast himself on his face on the shore, and cling with his hands to the earth as if in a paroxysm of bodily suffering; then after a few moments rise and do a service to the man who had wronged him. Were it any wonder if the light should have soon gone up in a soul like that?

"When I was a younger man I used to go out with the fishing boats now and then, drawn chiefly by my love for the boy, who earned his own bread that way before he was in his teens. One night we were caught in a terrible storm, and had to stand out to sea in the pitch dark. He was then not fourteen. 'Can you let a boy like that steer?' I said to the captain of the boat. 'Yes; just a boy like that,' he answered. 'Ma'colm 'ill steer as straucht's a porpus.' When he was relieved, he crept over the thwarts to where I sat. 'Is there any true definition of a straight line, sir?' he said. 'I can't take the one in my Euclid.'—'So you're not afraid, Malcolm?' I returned, heedless of his question, for I wanted to see what he would answer. 'Afraid, sir!' he rejoined with some surprise, 'I wad ill like to hear the Lord say, O thou o' little faith!'—'But,' I persisted, 'God may mean to drown you!'—'An' what for no?' he returned. 'Gien ye war to tell me 'at I micht be droon't ohn him meant it, I wad be fleyt eneuch.'

---

what for no why not
gien if
ohn without

"I see your ladyship does not understand: I will interpret the dark saying: 'And why should he not drown me? If you were to tell me I might be drowned without his meaning it, I should be frightened enough.' Believe me, my lady, the right way is simple to find, though only they that seek it first can find it. But I have allowed myself," concluded the schoolmaster, "to be carried adrift in my laudation of Malcolm. You did not come to hear praises of him, my lady."

"I owe him much," said Clementina. "But tell me then, Mr. Graham, how is it that you know there is a God, and one—one—fit to be trusted as you trust him?"

"In no way that I can bring to bear on the reason of another so as to produce conviction."

"Then what is to become of me?"

"I can do for you what is far better. I can persuade you to look and see whether before your own door stands not a gate—lies not a path to walk in. Entering by that gate, walking in that path, you shall yourself arrive at the conviction, which no man can give you, that there is a living Love and Truth at the heart of your being, and pervading all that surrounds you. The man who seeks the truth in any other manner will never find it.

"Listen to me a moment, my lady. I loved that boy's mother. Naturally she did not love me—how could she? I was very unhappy. I sought comfort from the unknown source of my life. He gave me to understand his Son, and so I understood himself, knew that I came of God, and was comforted."

"But how do you know that it was not all a delusion—the product of your own fervid imagination? Do not mistake me; I want to find it true."

"It is a right and honest question, my lady. I will tell you.

"Not to mention the conviction which a truth beheld must carry with itself and concerning which there can be no argument either with him who does or him who does not see it, this experience goes far with me, and would with you if you had it, as you may—namely, that all my difficulties and confusions have gone on clearing themselves up ever since I set out to walk in that way. My consciousness of life is threefold what it was; my perception of what is lovely around me, and my delight in it, threefold; my power of understanding things and of ordering my way, threefold also; the same with my hope and my courage, my love to my kind, my power of forgiveness. In short, I cannot but believe that my whole being and its whole world are in process of rectification for me. Is not that something to set against the doubt born of the eye and ear, and the questions of an intellect that can neither grasp nor disprove? I say nothing of better things still.

"To the man who receives such as I mean, they are the heart of life; to the man who does not, they exist not. But I say—if I thus find my whole being enlightened and redeemed, and know that therein I fare according to the word of the man of whom the old story tells: if I find that his word, and the result of action founded upon that word, correspond and agree, opening a heaven within and beyond me, in which I see myself delivered from all that now in myself is to myself despicable and unlovely; if I can reasonably—reasonably to myself, not to another—cherish hopes of a glory of conscious being, divinely better than all my imagination when most daring could invent—a glory springing from absolute unity with my creator, and therefore with my neighbour; if the Lord of the ancient tale, I say, has thus held word with me, am I likely to doubt much or long whether there be such a lord or no?"

"What, then, is the way that lies before my own door? Help me to see it."

"It is just the old way—as old as the conscience—that of obedience to any and every law of personal duty. But if you have ever seen the Lord, if only from afar—if you have any vaguest suspicion that the Jew Jesus, who professed to have come from God, was a better man than other men, one of your first duties must be to open your ears to his words, and see whether they commend themselves to you as true; then, if they do, to obey them with your whole strength and might, upheld by the hope of the vision promised in them to the obedient.

"This is the way of life, which will lead a man out of the miseries of the nineteenth century, as it led Paul out of the miseries of the first."

From the novel Home Again. *Molly is a young woman whose schooling has been slight. Her friend Walter has returned from studies at Edinburgh University.*

Molly was one of the wise women of the world—and thus: thoughts grew for her first out of things, and not things out of thoughts. God's things come out of His thoughts; our realities are God's thoughts made manifest in things; and out of them our thoughts must come; then the things that come out of our thoughts will be real. Neither our own fancies, nor the judgments of the world, must be the ground of our theories or behavior. This, at least, was Molly's working theory of life.

She saw plainly that her business, every day, hour, moment, was to order her way as He who had sent her into being would have her order her way; doing God's things, God's thoughts would come to her; God's things were better than man's thoughts;

man's best thoughts the discovery of the thoughts hidden in God's things. Obeying him, perhaps a day would come in which God would think directly into the mind of His child, without the intervention of things!

For Molly had made the one rational, one practical discovery, that life is to be lived, not by helpless assent or aimless drifting, but by active co-operation with the Life that has said "Live." To her everything was part of a whole, which, with its parts, she was learning to know, was finding out, by obedience to what she already knew. There is nothing for developing even the common intellect like obedience, that is, duty done. Those who obey are soon wiser than all their lessons; while from those who do not, will be taken away even what knowledge they started with.

Molly was not prepared to attempt convincing Walter, who was so much more learned and clever than she, that the things that rose in men's minds even in their best moods were not necessarily a valuable commodity, but that their character depended on the soil whence they sprung. . . .

Self-will is weakness; the will to do right is strength; Molly willed the right thing and held to it. Hence it was that she was so gentle. She walked lightly over the carpet, because she could run up a hill like a hare. When she caught selfishness in her, she was down upon it with the knee and grasp of a giant. Strong is man and woman whose eternal life subjects the individual liking to the perfect will. Such man, such woman, is free man, free woman.

From a sermon.

The will is the deepest, the strongest, the divinest thing in man; so, I presume, is it in God, for such we find it in Jesus Christ. Here, and here only, in the relation of the two wills, God's and his own, can a man come into vital contact—on the eternal idea, in no one-sided unity of completest dependence, but in willed harmony of dual oneness with the All-in-all. When a man can and does entirely say, "Not my will, but thine be done"—when he so wills the will of God as to do it, then is he one with God—one, as a true son with a true father. . . .

Obedience is the joining of the links of the eternal round. Obedience is but the other side of the creative will. Will is God's will, obedience is man's will; the two make one. . . . If we do the will of God, eternal life is ours—no mere continuity of existence, for that in itself is worthless as hell, but a being that is one with the essential Life, and so within his.

From the novel A Rough Shaking. *Describing a minister and his wife.*

Mr. Porson was a man about five and forty; his wife was a few years younger. His theories of religion were neither large nor lofty; he accepted those that were handed down to him, and did not trouble himself as to whether they were correct. He did what was better: he tried constantly to obey the law of God, whether he found it in the Bible or in his own heart. Thus he was greater in the kingdom of heaven than thousands that knew more, had better theories about God, and could talk much more fluently concerning religion than he. By obeying God he let God teach him. So his heart was always growing; and where the heart grows, there is no fear of the intellect; there it also grows, and in the best fashion of growth.

From the novel Paul Faber, Surgeon. *Paul Faber is an atheist, but cares diligently for his patients.*

It is better to be an atheist who does the will of God, than a so-called Christian who does not. The atheist will not be dismissed because he said "Lord, Lord," and did not obey [Matt. 7:21]. The thing that God loves is the only lovely thing, and he who does it, does well, and is upon the way to discover that he does it very badly. When he comes to do it as the will of the perfect Good, then is he on the road to do it perfectly—that is, from love of its own inherent self-constituted goodness, born in the heart of the Perfect. The doing of things from duty is but a stage on the road to the kingdom of truth and love. Not the less must the stage be journeyed. . . .

But duty itself is only a stage toward something better. It is but the impulse, God-given I believe, toward a far more vital contact with the truth. We shall one day forget all about duty, and do everything from the love of the loveliness of it, the satisfaction of the rightness of it.

10.

Growth of Character

From the novel Mary Marston. *Describing a young man.*

Like most men, he was so well satisfied with himself, that he saw no occasion to take trouble to be anything better than he was. Never suspecting what a noble creature he was meant to be, he never saw what a poor creature he was.

From a sermon.

When you fear, you do not trust or love. Hope in God, who is not the God of the perfect only, but of the *becoming*. . . . Do not be afraid of letting your imagination work. Invent as glorious an outcome of all the troubles of your life as you can possibly think of: 'for as the Heaven is high above the Earth,' so it is above the most exalted imaginations.

From the novel What's Mine's Mine. *Describing a young woman who narrowly escaped drowning.*

The danger she had been in, and her deliverance through the voluntary sharing of it by Ian, had awaked the simpler, the real nature of the girl, hitherto buried in impressions and their responses. She had lived but as a mirror meant only to reflect the outer world: something of an operative existence was at length beginning to appear in her. She was growing a woman. And the first stage in that growth is to become as a little child.

From the novel David Elginbrod. *Hugh Sutherland, the tutor on the estate David Elginbrod manages, dines every Sunday with David and his wife Janet.*

Many things were spoken by the simple wisdom of David, which would have enlightened Hugh far more than they did, had he been sufficiently advanced to receive them. But their very simplicity was often far beyond the grasp of his thoughts; for the higher we rise, the simpler we become; and David was one of those of whom is the kingdom of Heaven.

There is a childhood into which we have to grow, just as there is a childhood which we must leave behind; a childlikeness which is the highest gain of humanity, and a childishness from which but few of those who are counted the wisest among men, have freed themselves in their imagined progress towards the reality of things.

From the novel Donal Grant. *Donal Grant, who has grown up in a small Scottish village, is now leaving home for the first time, to seek employment.*

It was a lovely morning in the first of summer. Donal Grant was descending a path on a hillside to the valley below—a sheep-track of which he knew every winding as well as any boy his half-mile to and from school. But he had never before gone down the hill with the feeling that he was not about to go up again. He was on his way to pastures very new, and in the distance only negatively inviting. But his heart was too full to be troubled—nor was his a heart to harbour a care, the next thing to an evil spirit, though not quite so bad; for one care may drive out another, while one devil is sure to bring in another.

A great billowy waste of mountains lay beyond him, amongst which played the shadows at their games of hide and seek— graciously merry in the eyes of the happy man, but sadly solemn in the eyes of him in whose heart the dreary thoughts of the past are at a like game. Behind Donal lay a world of dreams into which he dared not turn and look, yet from which he could scarce avert his eyes.

He was nearing the foot of the hill when he stumbled and almost fell, but recovered himself with the agility of a mountaineer, and the unpleasant knowledge that the sole of one of his shoes was all but off. Never had he left home for college that his father had not made personal inspection of his shoes to see that they were fit for the journey, but on this departure they had been forgotten. He sat down and took off the failing equipment. It was too far gone to do anything temporary with it; and of discomforts a loose sole to one's shoe in walking is of the worst. The only thing was to take off the other shoe and both stockings and go barefoot. He tied all together with a piece of string, made them fast to his deerskin knapsack, and resumed his walk. The thing did not trouble him much. To have what we want is riches, but to be able to do without is power. To have shoes is a good thing; to be able to walk without them is a better. But it was long since Donal had walked barefoot, and he found his feet like his shoe, weaker in the sole than was pleasant.

"It's time," he said to himself, when he found he was stepping gingerly, "I ga'e my feet a turn at the auld accomplishment. It's a pity to grow nae so fit for onything suner nor ye need. I wad like to lie doon at last wi' hard soles!"

In every stream he came to he bathed his feet, and often on the way rested them, when otherwise able enough to go on. He had no certain goal, though he knew his direction, and was in no haste. He had confidence in God and in his own powers as the gift of God, and knew that wherever he went he needed not be hungry long, even should the little money in his pocket be spent. It is better to trust in work than in money: God never buys anything, and is for ever at work; but if any one trust in work, he has to learn that he must trust in nothing but strength—the self-existent, original strength only; and Donal Grant had long begun to learn that. The man has begun to be strong who knows that, separated from life essential, he is weakness itself; that, one with his origin, he will be of strength inexhaustible.

Donal was now descending the heights of youth to walk along the king's highroad of manhood: happy he who, as his sun is going down behind the western, is himself ascending the eastern hill, returning through old age to the second and better childhood which shall not be taken from him! He who turns his back on the setting sun goes to meet the rising sun; he who loses his life shall find it. Donal had lost his past—but not so as to be ashamed. There are many ways of losing! His past had but crept, like the dead, back to God who gave it; in better shape it would be his by and by! Already he had begun to foreshadow this truth: God would keep it for him.

Later in the story Donal meets a shoemaker, Andrew Comin, from whom he learns much that is important.

"Did it ever occur to ye, sir," [Comin] said, "'at maybe deith micht be the first waukin' to some fowk?"

"It has occurrt to me," answered Donal; "but mony things come intil a body's heid 'at he's no able to think oot! They maun lie an' bide their time."

"Lat nane o' the lovers o' law an' letter perswaud ye the Lord wadna hae ye think—though nane but him 'at obeys can think wi' safety. We maun do first the thing 'at we ken, an' syne we may think aboot the thing 'at we dinna ken. I fancy 'at whiles the Lord wadna say a thing jist no to stop fowk thinkin' aboot it. He was aye at gettin' them to mak use o' the can'le o' the Lord.

"It's my belief the main obstacles to the growth o' the kingdom are first the oonbelief o' believers, an' syne the w'y 'at they lay doon the law. 'Afore they hae learnt the rudimen's o' the trowth themsel's, they begin to lay the grievous burden o' their dullness an' ill-conceived notions o' holy things upo' the min's an' consciences o' their neebours, fain, ye wad think, to haud them frae growin' ony mair nor themsel's.

"Eh, man, but the Lord's won'erfu'! Ye may daur an' daur, an' no come i' sicht o' 'im!"

---

maun must
ken know
dinna ken do not know
fowk folk
haud hold
mair more
daur dare, risk
sicht sight

From the novel Alec Forbes of Howglen. *An elderly man is speaking to a young woman whom he knew as a child.*

"Eh, lassie!" he said, "ye're grown a wumman! Ye'll hae the bigger hert to love the Lord wi'."

From the children's novel Gutta Percha Willie: the Working Genius. *Regarding the processes of growth.*

Time passed, and Willie grew. Have my readers ever thought what is meant by growing? It is far from meaning only that you get bigger and stronger. It means that you become able both to understand and to wonder at more of the things about you. There are people who the more they understand, wonder the less; but such are not growing straight; they are growing crooked.

There are two ways of growing. You may be growing up, or you may be growing down; and if you are doing both at once, then you are growing crooked. There are people who are growing up in understanding, but down in goodness. It is a beautiful fact, however, that you can't grow up in goodness and down in understanding; while the great probability is, that, if you are not growing better, you will by and by begin to grow stupid. Those who are growing the right way, the more they understand, the more they wonder; and the more they learn to do, the more they want to do. Willie was a boy of this kind. I don't care to write about boys and girls, or men and women, who are not growing the right way. They are not interesting enough to write about.

From the novel Paul Faber, Surgeon. *A young woman who has been abandoned by the father of her child is in despair; choosing to live in solitude, she starts to experience the power of God.*

There is a great power in quiet, for God is in it. Not seldom He seems to lay His hand on one of His children, as a mother lays hers on the restless one in the crib, to still him. Then the child sleeps, but the man begins to live up from the lower depths of his nature. So the winter comes to still the plant whose life had been rushing to blossom and fruit. When the hand of God is laid upon a man, vain moan, and struggle and complaint, it may be indignant outcry follows; but when, outwearied at last, he yields, if it be in dull submission to the inexorable, and is still, then the God at the heart of him, the God that is there or the man could not be, begins to grow.

From the fantasy novel Lilith. *The narrator, a young man, finds himself in a strange world which reflects his own inner indecision.*

"Oblige me by telling me where I am."

"That is impossible. You know nothing about whereness. The only way to come to know where you are is to begin to make yourself at home."

"How am I to begin that where everything is so strange?"

"By doing something."

"What?"

"Anything; and the sooner you begin the better! for until you are at home, you will find it as difficult to get out as it is to get in." . . .

But what mattered *where* while *everywhere* was the same as *nowhere!* I had not yet, by doing something in it, made *anywhere* into a place! I was not yet alive; I was only dreaming I lived! I was but a consciousness with an outlook!

There is only one true way, however, to get out of any position we may be in, and that is to do the work of it so well that we grow fit for a better one.

From the novel The Flight of the Shadow. *An old woman reflects on what she has learned in life.*

Half the misery in the world comes from trying to look, instead of trying to be, what one is not.

From the novel Paul Faber, Surgeon. *A young woman knows she has acted wrongly, but can't pull herself together to set things right.*

How many people would like to be good, if only they might be good without taking trouble about it! They do not like goodness well enough to hunger and thirst after it, or to sell all that they may buy it; they will not batter at the gate of the kingdom of heaven; but they look with pleasure on this or that aerial castle of righteousness, and think it would be rather nice to live in it.

From the novel Home Again. *A young man is confessing a deceitful act to the person he wronged.*

"In confession, a man must use plain words: I was a coward, a false friend, a false man. . . .

"Let us be true, whatever come of it, and look the facts of things in the face! If I am a poor creature, let me be content to know it! for have I not the joy that God can make me great! And is not the first step toward greatness to refuse to call that great which is not great, or to think myself great when I am small? Is it not an essential and impassable bar to greatness for a man to imagine himself great when there is not in him one single element of greatness? Let us confess ourselves that which we can not consent to remain! The confession of not being, is the sole foundation for becoming. Self is a quicksand; God is the only rock. I have been learning a little."

From the novel There and Back. *A young man, Richard, is convalescing from a serious illness.*

One of the benefits of illness is, that either from general weakness, or from the brain's being cast into quiescence, habits are broken for a time, and more simple, childlike, and natural modes of thought and feeling, modes more approximate to primary and original modes, come into action, whereby the right thing has a better chance. A man's self-stereotyped thinking is unfavourable to revelation, whether through his fellows, or direct from the divine. If there be a divine quarter, those must be opener to its influences who are not frozen in their own dullness, cased in their own habits, bound by their own pride to foregone conclusions, or shut up in the completeness of human error, theorizing beyond their knowledge and power.

Having thus in a measure given himself up, Richard began to grow better. It is a joy to think that a man may, while anything but sure about God, yet come into correlation with him! How else should we be saved at all? For God alone is our salvation; to know him is salvation. He is in us all the time, else we could never move to seek him. It is true that only by perfect faith in him can we be saved, for nothing but perfect faith in him is salvation; there is no good but him, and not to be one with that good by perfect obedience, is to be unsaved; but one better thought concerning him, the poorest desire to draw near him, is an approach to him.

Very unsure of him we may be: how should we be sure of what we do not yet know? but the unsureness does not nullify the approach. A man may not be sure that the sun is risen, may not be sure that the sun will ever rise, yet has he the good of what light there is. Richard was fed from the heart of God without knowing that he was indeed partaking of the spirit of God. He had been partaking of the body of God all his life. The world had been feeding him with its beauty and essential truth, with the sweetness of its air, and the vastness of its vault of freedom. But now he had begun, in the words of St. Peter, to be a partaker of the divine nature.

It was a long time before he was strong again—in fact he never would be so strong again in this world. His mother took him to the seaside, where, in a warm secluded bay on the south coast, he was wrapt closer, shall I not say, in the garments of the creating and reviving God. He was again a child, and drew nearer to the heart of his mother than he had ever drawn before. Believing he knew her sad secret, he set himself to meet her every wish—which was always some form of anxiety about himself. He spoke so gently to her, that she felt she had never until now had him her very child. How little men think, alas, of the duty that lies in *tone*!

But Richard was started on a voyage of self-discovery. He had begun to learn that regions he had thought wholesome, productive portions of his world, were a *terra incognita* of swamps and sandy hills, haunted with creeping and stinging things. When a man finds he is not what he thought, that he has been talking fine things, and but imagining he belonged to their world, he is on the way to discover that he is not up to his duty in the smallest thing. When, for very despair, it seems impossible to go on, then he begins to know that he needs more than himself; that there is none good but God; that, if he can gain no help from the perfect source of his being, that being ought not to have been given him; and that, if he does not cry for help to the father of his spirit, the more pleasant existence is, the less he deserves it should continue. Richard was beginning to feel in his deepest nature, where alone it can be felt, his need of God, not merely to comfort him in his sorrows, and so render life possible and worth living, but to make him such that he could bear to regard himself; to make him such that he could righteously consent to be.

The only thing that can reassure a man in respect of the mere fact of his existence, is to know himself started on the way to grow better, with the hope of help from the source of his being: how should he by himself better that which he was powerless to create? All betterment must be radical: of the roots of his being he knows nothing. His existence is God's; his betterment must be God's too!—God's through honest exercise by man of that which is highest in man—his own will, God's best handiwork. By actively willing the will of God, and doing what of it lies to his doing, the man takes the share offered him in his own making, in his own becoming. In willing actively and operatively to be that which he was made in order to be, he becomes creative—so far as a man may. In this kind also he becomes like his Father in heaven.

Letter written to his oldest son when he was twenty-eight.

My dearly Loved Son,
It puzzles me a little that you . . . should be so changeable and troubled by the appearance of things. "In quietness and confidence shall be your strength." "Wait on the Lord." You are so impatient! You hardly give him time to do anything for you! . . . Do not always be speculating about your future and thinking what you shall do. You are not a bit nearer knowing for that; and it is a great waste of brain tissue, to say nothing of spiritual energy. . . .

There is more action in dismissing a useless care than in a month's brooding over the possible or the probable. When the hour for decision arrives, one moment's clear untroubled thought will do what weeks and weeks of brooding beforehand will only make more uncertain and difficult.

From the novel The Marquis of Lossie. *A man is contemplating that "religion is neither more nor less than life."*

Whoever can think of religion as an addition to life, however glorious—a starry crown, say, set upon the head of humanity, is not yet the least in the kingdom of heaven. Whoever thinks of life as a something that could be without religion, is in deathly ignorance of both. Life and religion are one, or neither is anything: I will not say neither is growing to be anything. Religion is no way of life, no show of life, no observance of any sort. It is neither the food nor the medicine of being. It is life essential. To think otherwise is as if a man should pride himself on his honesty, or his parental kindness, or hold up his head amongst men because he never killed one: were he less than honest or kind or free from blood, he would yet think something of himself!

The man to whom virtue is but the ornament of character, something over and above, not essential to it, is not yet a man.

From an essay.

To every man I say, "Do the truth you know, and you shall learn the truth you need to know."

From the children's book The Princess and the Goblin. *The child princess Irene is looking for a mysterious wise woman who lives at the top of one of the towers of the castle where Irene lives.*

This day's adventure, however, did not turn out like yesterday's, although it began like it; and indeed today is very seldom like yesterday, if people would note the differences—even when it rains. The princess ran through passage after passage, and could not find the stair of the tower. My own suspicion is that she had not gone up high enough, and was searching on the second instead of the third floor.

II.

Conscience

From the novel Wilfrid Cumbermede. *Two boys have been talking about what they believe is written in the Bible and why.*

Another pause followed, during which [my friend] searched for a chapter [of the New Testament] to fit the mood. I will not say what chapter he found, for, after all, I doubt if we had any real notion of what it meant. I know, however, that there were words in it which found their way to my conscience; and, let men of science or philosophy say what they will, the rousing of a man's conscience is the greatest event in his existence.

From the novel Robert Falconer. *Robert Falconer is speaking to his friend about women in a boarding house, whom he has tried to help.*

"There are good and bad amongst them as in every class. But one thing is clear to me, that no indulgence of passion destroys the spiritual nature so much as respectable selfishness."

From the novel There and Back. *Regarding the conscience.*

What is called a good conscience is often but a dull one that gives no trouble when it ought to bark loudest.

From a sermon on Ephesians 5:14.

> Awake, thou that sleepest, and arise from the dead, and Christ shall give thee life.

"But I do not know how to awake and arise!"

I will tell you: Get up, and do something the master tells you; so make yourself his disciple at once. Instead of asking yourself whether you believe or not, ask yourself whether you have this day done one thing because he said, Do it, or once abstained because he said, Do not do it.

It is simply absurd to say you believe, or even want to believe in him, if you do not anything he tells you. If you can think of nothing he ever said as having had an atom of influence on your doing or not doing, you have too good ground to consider yourself no disciple of his. Do not, I pray you, worse than waste your time in trying to convince yourself that you are his disciple notwithstanding—that for this reason or that you still have cause to think you believe in him. What though you should succeed in persuading yourself to absolute certainty that you are his disciple, if, after all, he say to you, "Why did you not do the things I told you? Depart from me; I do not know you!" . . .

What have you done this day because it was the will of Christ? Have you dismissed, once dismissed, an anxious thought for the morrow? Have you ministered to any needy soul or body, and kept your right hand from knowing what your left hand did? Have you begun to leave all and follow him? Did you set yourself to judge righteous judgment? Are you being ware of covetousness? Have you forgiven your enemy? Are you seeking the kingdom of God and his righteousness before all other things? Are you hungering and thirsting after righteousness? Have you given to some one that asked of you? Tell me something that you have done, are doing, or are trying to do because he told you. If you do nothing that he says, it is no wonder that you cannot trust in him.

From the novel The Seaboard Parish. *Mr. Turner, a doctor, and Mr. Walton, a minister, are walking near the sea, where Mr. Turner has recommended Mr. Walton bring his family. Their talk turns to the source of the will to do right.*

"A dreary place in winter, Turner," I said. . . . "I think even now there is a certain freshness in the wind that calls up a kind of will in the nerves to meet it."

"That is precisely what I wanted for you all. You observe there is no rasp in its touch, however. There are regions in this island of ours where even in the hottest day in summer you would frequently discover a certain unfriendly edge in the air, that would set you wondering whether the seasons had not changed since you were a boy, and used to lie on the grass half the idle day."

"I often do wonder whether it may not be so, but I always come to the conclusion that even this is but an example of the involuntary tendency of the mind of man towards the ideal. He forgets all that comes between and divides the hints of perfection scattered here and there along the scope of his experience. I especially remember one summer day in my childhood, which has coloured all my ideas of summer and bliss and fulfilment of content. It is made up of only mossy grass, and the scent of the earth and wild flowers, and hot sun, and perfect sky—deep and blue, and traversed by blinding white clouds. I could not have been more than five or six, I think, from the kind of dress I wore, the very pearl buttons of which, encircled on their face with a ring of half-spherical hollows, have their undeniable relation in my memory to the heavens and the earth, to the march of the glorious clouds, and the tender scent of the rooted flowers; and, indeed, when I think of it, must, by the delight they gave me, have opened my mind the more to the enjoyment of the eternal paradise around me. What a thing it is to please a child!"

"I know what you mean perfectly," answered Turner. "It is as I get older that I understand what Wordsworth says about childhood. It is indeed a mercy that we were not born grown men, with what we consider our wits about us. They are blinding things those wits we gather. I fancy that the single thread by which God sometimes keeps hold of a man is such an impression of his childhood as that of which you have been speaking."

"I do not doubt it; for conscience is so near in all those memories to which you refer. The whole surrounding of them is so at variance with sin! A sense of purity, not in himself, for the child is not feeling that he is pure, is all about him; and when afterwards the condition returns upon him,—returns when he is conscious of so much that is evil and so much that is unsatisfied in him,—it brings with it a longing after the high clear air of moral well-being."

"Do you think, then, that it is only by association that nature thus impresses us? that she has no power of meaning these things?"

"Not at all. No doubt there is something in the recollection of the associations of childhood to strengthen the power of nature upon us; but the power is in nature herself, else it would be but a poor weak thing to what it is. There *is* purity and state in that sky. There *is* a peace now in this wide still earth—not so very beautiful, you own—and in that overhanging blue, which my heart cries out that it needs and cannot be well till it gains—gains in the truth, gains in God, who is the power of truth, the living and causing truth. There is indeed a rest that remaineth, a rest pictured out even here this night, to rouse my dull heart to desire it and follow after it, a rest that consists in thinking the thoughts of Him who is the Peace because the Unity, in being filled with that spirit which now pictures itself forth in this repose of the heavens and the earth."

"True," said Turner, after a pause. "I must think more about such things. The science the present day is going wild about will not give us that rest."

"No; but that rest will do much to give you that science. A man with this repose in his heart will do more by far, other capabilities being equal, to find out the laws that govern things. For all law is living rest."

From the fairy tale The Lost Princess. *Rosamond, a selfish young princess, has been taken to the house of the old Wise Woman to be taught to consider others. The Wise Woman has left her with instructions to keep the fire burning.*

People are so ready to think themselves changed when it is only their mood that is changed! Those who are good-tempered because it is a fine day, will be ill-tempered when it rains: their selves are just the same both days; only in the one case, the fine weather has got into them, in the other the rainy. Rosamond, as she sat warming herself by the glow of the peat-fire, turning over in her mind all that had passed, and feeling how pleasant the change in her feelings was, began by degrees to think how very good she had grown, and how very good she was to have grown good, and how extremely good she must always have been that she was able to grow so very good as she now felt she had grown; and she became so absorbed in her self-admiration as never to notice either that the fire was dying, or that a heap of fir-cones lay in a corner near it. Suddenly, a great wind came roaring down the chimney, and scattered the ashes about the floor; a tremendous rain followed, and fell hissing on the embers; the moon was swallowed up, and there was darkness all about her.

Then a flash of lightning, followed by a peal of thunder, so terrified the princess, that she cried aloud for the old woman, but there came no answer to her cry.

Then in her terror the princess grew angry, and saying to herself, "She must be somewhere in the place, else who was there to open the door to me?" began to shout and yell, and call the wise woman all the bad names she had been in the habit of throwing at her nurses. But there came not a single sound in reply.

Strange to say, the princess never thought of telling herself now how naughty she was, though that would surely have been reasonable. On the contrary, she thought she had a perfect right to be angry, for was she not most desperately ill used—and a princess too? But the wind howled on, and the rain kept pouring down the chimney, and every now and then the lightning burst out, and the thunder rushed after it, as if the great lumbering sound could ever think to catch up with the swift light!

At length the princess had again grown so angry, frightened, and miserable, all together, that she jumped up and hurried about the cottage with outstretched arms, trying to find the wise woman. But being in a bad temper always makes people stupid, and presently she struck her forehead such a blow against something. . . . There, worn out with weeping and rage, she soon fell fast asleep.

12.

Work

From the fairy tale The Lost Princess. *Continued from the previous chapter. Princess Rosamond has woken up again.*

Soon [Princess Rosamond] began to grow weary of having nothing to do. Then she remembered that the old woman, as she called her, had told her to keep the house tidy.

"The miserable little pig-sty!" she said: "Where's the use of keeping such a hovel clean?"

But in truth she would have been glad of the employment, only just because she had been told to do it she was unwilling; for there are people—however unlikely it may seem—who object to doing a thing for no other reason than that it is required of them.

"I am a princess," she said, "and it is very improper to ask me to do such a thing."

She might have judged it quite as suitable for a princess to sweep away the dust as to sit the centre of a world of dirt. But just because she ought, she wouldn't. Perhaps she feared that if she gave in to doing her duty once, she might have to do it always—which was true enough—for that was the very thing for which she had been specially born.

From the children's novel Gutta Percha Willie: The Working Genius. *Willie, a seven-year-old boy, has been watching his elderly neighbor, Mrs. Wilson, knitting.*

I must not forget to tell you that Willie did ask his father the question with Mrs. Wilson's answer to which he had not been satisfied—I mean the question whether God worked; and his father's answer, after he had sat pondering for a while in his chair, was something to this effect:—

"Yes, Willie; it seems to me that God works more than anybody—for He works all night and all day, and, if I remember rightly, Jesus tells us somewhere that He works all Sunday too. If He were to stop working, everything would stop being. The sun would stop shining, and the moon and the stars; the corn would stop growing; there would be no more apples or gooseberries; your eyes would stop seeing; your ears would stop hearing; your fingers couldn't move an inch; and, worst of all, your little heart would stop loving."

"No, papa," cried Willie; "I shouldn't stop loving, I'm sure."

"Indeed you would, Willie."

"Not you and mamma."

"Yes; you wouldn't love us any more than if you were dead asleep without dreaming."

"That would be dreadful."

"Yes it would. So you see how good God is to us—to go on working, that we may be able to love each other."

"Then if God works like that all day long, it must be a fine thing to work," said Willie.

"You are right. It is a fine thing to work—the finest thing in the world, if it comes of love, as God's work does."

This conversation made Willie quite determined to learn to knit; for if God worked, he would work too. And although the work he undertook was a very small work, it was like all God's great works, for every loop he made had a little love looped up in it, like an invisible, softest, downiest lining to the stockings. And after those, he went on knitting a pair for his father; and indeed, he learned to work with a needle as well, and to darn the stockings he had made, and even tried his hand at the spinning.

Some time later Willie is in the shop of Hector, a cobbler.

"And what's your business, Hector?" asked Willie, in a half-absent mood.

Some readers may perhaps think this a stupid question, and perhaps so it was; but Willie was not therefore stupid. People sometimes appear stupid because they have more things to think about than they can well manage; while those who think only about one or two things may, on the contrary, appear clever when just those one or two things happen to be talked about.

"What is my business, Willie? Why, to keep people out of the dirt, of course."

"How?" asked Willie again.

"By making and mending their shoes. Mr. Dick, now, when he goes out to look at the stars through his telescope, might get his death of cold if his shoemaker did not know his business. Of the general business, it's a part God keeps to Himself to see that the stars go all right, and that the sun rises and sets at the proper times. For the time's not the same any two mornings running, you see, and he might make a mistake if he wasn't looked after, and that would be serious. But I told you I don't understand about astronomy, because it's not my business. I'm set to keep folk's feet off the cold and wet earth, and stones and broken glass; for however much a man may be an astronomer and look up at the sky, he must touch the earth with some part of him, and generally does so with his feet."

"And God sets you to do it, Hector?"

"Yes. It's the way He looks after people's feet. He's got to look after everything, you know, or everything would go wrong. So He gives me the leather and the tools and the hands—and I must say the head, for it wants no little head to make a good shoe to measure—and it is as if He said to me—'There! you make shoes, while I keep the stars right.' Isn't it a fine thing to have a hand in the general business?"

From the novel There and Back. *Describing the education of a boy who loved to spend time in the bookbinding shop of his father.*

To become able to make something is, I think, necessary to thorough development. I would rather have son of mine a carpenter, a watchmaker, a wood-carver, a shoemaker, a jeweller, a blacksmith, a bookbinder, than I would have him earn his bread as a clerk in a counting-house. Not merely is the cultivation of operant faculty a better education in faculty, but it brings the man nearer to every thing operant; humanity unfolds itself to him the readier; its ways and thoughts and modes of being grow the clearer to both intellect and heart.

The poetry of life, the inner side of that nature which comes from him who, on the Sabbath-days even, "worketh hitherto," rises nearer the surface to meet the eyes of the man who makes. What advantage the carpenter of Nazareth gathered from his bench, is the inheritance of every workman, in proportion as he does divine, that is, honest work.

From the novel Annals of a Quiet Neighbourhood. *A young minister who has recently arrived in the village where he is to live is out walking and getting to know his new home.*

As I went again through the village, I observed a narrow lane striking off to the left, and resolved to explore in that direction. It led up to one side of the large house of which I have already spoken. As I came near, I smelt what has been to me always a delightful smell—that of fresh deals under the hands of the carpenter. In the scent of those boards of pine is enclosed all the idea the tree could gather of the world of forest where it was reared. It speaks of many wild and bright but chiefly clean and rather cold things. If I were idling, it would draw me to it across many fields.

Turning a corner, I heard the sound of a saw. And this sound drew me yet more. For a carpenter's shop was the delight of my boyhood; and after I began to read the history of our Lord with something of that sense of reality with which we read other histories, and which, I am sorry to think, so much of the well-meant instruction we receive in our youth tends to destroy, my feeling about such a workshop grew stronger and stronger, till at last I never could go near enough to see the shavings lying on the floor of one, without a spiritual sensation such as I have in entering an old church; which sensation, ever since having been admitted on the usual conditions to a Mohammedan mosque, urges me to pull off, not only my hat, but my shoes likewise. And the feeling has grown upon me, till now it seems at times as if the only cure in the world for social pride would be to go for five silent minutes into a carpenter's shop. How one can think of himself as above his neighbours, within sight, sound, or smell of one, I fear I am getting almost unable to imagine, and one ought not to get out of sympathy with the wrong. Only as I am growing old now, it does not matter so much, for I daresay my time will not be very long.

So I drew near to the shop, feeling as if the Lord might be at work there at one of the benches. And when I reached the door, there was my pale-faced hearer of the Sunday afternoon, sawing a board for a coffin-lid.

As my shadow fell across and darkened his work, he lifted his head and saw me.

I could not altogether understand the expression of his countenance as he stood upright from his labour and touched his old hat with rather a proud than a courteous gesture. And I could not believe that he was glad to see me, although he laid down his saw and advanced to the door. It was the gentleman in him, not the man, that sought to make me welcome, hardly caring whether I saw through the ceremony or not. True, there was a smile on his lips, but the smile of a man who cherishes a secret grudge; of one who does not altogether dislike you, but who has a claim upon you—say, for an apology, of which claim he doubts whether you know the existence. So the smile seemed tightened, and stopped just when it got half-way to its width, and was about to become hearty and begin to shine.

"May I come in?" I said.

"Come in, sir," he answered.

"I am glad I have happened to come upon you by accident," I said.

He smiled as if he did not quite believe in the accident, and considered it a part of the play between us that I should pretend it. I hastened to add—

"I was wandering about the place, making some acquaintance with it, and with my friends in it, when I came upon you quite unexpectedly. You know I saw you in church on Sunday afternoon."

"I know you saw me, sir," he answered, with a motion as if to return to his work; "but, to tell the truth, I don't go to church very often."

I did not quite know whether to take this as proceeding from an honest fear of being misunderstood, or from a sense of being in general superior to all that sort of thing. But I felt that it would be of no good to pursue the inquiry directly. I looked therefore for something to say.

"Ah! your work is not always a pleasant one," I said, associating the feelings of which I have already spoken with the facts before me, and looking at the coffin, the lower part of which stood nearly finished upon trestles on the floor.

"Well, there are unpleasant things in all trades," he answered. "But it does not matter," he added, with an increase of bitterness in his smile.

"I didn't mean," I said, "that the work was unpleasant—only sad. It must always be painful to make a coffin."

"A joiner gets used to it, sir, as you do to the funeral service. But, for my part, I don't see why it should be considered so unhappy for a man to be buried. This isn't such a good job, after all, this world, sir, you must allow."

"Neither is that coffin," said I, as if by a sudden inspiration.

The man seemed taken aback. . . . He looked at the coffin and then looked at me.

"Well, sir," he said, after a short pause, which no doubt seemed longer both to him and to me than it would have seemed to any third person, "I don't see anything amiss with the coffin. I don't say it'll last till doomsday, as the gravedigger says to Hamlet, because I don't know so much about doomsday as some people pretend to; but you see, sir, it's not finished yet."

"Thank you," I said; "that's just what I meant. You thought I was hasty in my judgment of your coffin; whereas I only said of it knowingly what you said of the world thoughtlessly. How do you know that the world is finished anymore than your coffin? And how dare you then say that it is a bad job?"

The same respectfully scornful smile passed over his face, as much as to say, "Ah! it's your trade to talk that way, so I must not be too hard upon you."

"At any rate, sir," he said, "whoever made it has taken long enough about it, a person would think, to finish anything he ever meant to finish."

"One day is with the Lord as a thousand years, and a thousand years as one day," I said.

"That's supposing," he answered, "that the Lord did make the world. For my part, I am half of a mind that the Lord didn't make it at all."

"I am very glad to hear you say so," I answered.

Hereupon I found that we had changed places a little. He looked up at me. The smile of superiority was no longer there, and a puzzled questioning, which might indicate either "Who would have expected that from you?" or, "What can he mean?" or both at once, had taken its place. I, for my part, knew that on the scale of the man's judgment I had risen nearer to his own level. As he said nothing, however, and I was in danger of being misunderstood, I proceeded at once.

"Of course it seems to me better that you should not believe God had done a thing, than that you should believe He had not done it well!"

"Ah! I see, sir. Then you will allow there is some room for doubting whether He made the world at all?"

"Yes; for I do not think an honest man, as you seem to me to be, would be able to doubt without any room whatever. That would be only for a fool. But it is just possible, as we are not perfectly good ourselves—you'll allow that, won't you?"

"That I will, sir; God knows."

"Well, I say—as we're not quite good ourselves, it's just possible that things may be too good for us to do them the justice of believing in them."

"But there are things, you must allow, so plainly wrong!"

"So much so, both in the world and in myself, that it would be to me torturing despair to believe that God did not make the world; for then, how would it ever be put right? Therefore I prefer the theory that He has not done making it yet."

"But wouldn't you say, sir, that God might have managed it without so many slips in the making as your way would suppose? I should think myself a bad workman if I worked after that fashion."

"I do not believe that there are any slips. You know you are making a coffin; but are you sure you know what God is making of the world?"

"That I can't tell, of course, nor anybody else."

"Then you can't say that what looks like a slip is really a slip, either in the design or in the workmanship. You do not know what end He has in view; and you may find some day that those slips were just the straight road to that very end."

"Ah! maybe. But you can't be sure of it, you see."

"Perhaps not, in the way you mean; but sure enough, for all that, to try it upon life—to order my way by it, and so find that it works well. And I find that it explains everything that comes near it. You know that no engineer would be satisfied with his engine on paper, nor with any proof whatever except seeing how it will go."

He made no reply.

From the novel The Seaboard Parish. *Connie, a young woman who lives at home with her parents, is speaking with her father, a minister.*

"But indeed, papa, I am very full of care sometimes, though not perhaps about to-morrow precisely. But that does not matter, does it?"

"Certainly not. Tell me what you are full of care about, my child, and perhaps I can help you."

"You often say, papa, that half the misery in this world comes from idleness, and that you do not believe that in a world where God is at work every day, Sundays not excepted, it could have been intended that women any more than men should have nothing to do. Now what am I to do? What have I been sent into the world for? I don't see it; and I feel very useless and wrong sometimes."

"I do not think there is very much to complain of you in that respect, Connie. You, and your sister as well, help me very much in my parish. You take much off your mother's hands too. And you do a good deal for the poor. You teach your younger brothers and sister, and meantime you are learning yourselves."

"Yes, but that's not work."

"It is work. And it is the work that is given you to do at present. And you would do it much better if you were to look at it in that light. Not that I have anything to complain of."

"But I don't want to stop at home and lead an easy, comfortable life, when there are so many to help everywhere in the world."

"Is there anything better in doing something where God has not placed you, than in doing it where he has placed you?"

"No, papa. But my sisters are quite enough for all you have for us to do at home. Is nobody ever to go away to find the work meant for her? You won't think, dear papa, that I want to get away from home, will you?"

"No, my dear. I believe that you are really thinking about duty. And now comes the moment for considering the passage to which you began by referring:—What God may hereafter require of you, you must not give yourself the least trouble about. Everything he gives you to do, you must do as well as ever you can, and that is the best possible preparation for what he may want you to do next. If people would but do what they have to do, they would always find themselves ready for what came next. And I do not believe that those who follow this rule are ever left floundering on the sea-deserted sands of inaction, unable to find water enough to swim in."

In the course of the book Connie is paralyzed by an accident. She still lives at home, unable to move from her bed and cared for by her family.

One day she received me with a still happier smile than I had yet seen upon her face, put out her thin white hand, took mine and kissed it, and said, "Papa," with a lingering on the last syllable.

"What is it, my pet?" I asked.

"I am so happy!"

"What makes you so happy?" I asked again.

"I don't know," she answered. "I haven't thought about it yet.

But everything looks so pleasant round me. Is it nearly winter yet, papa? I've forgotten all about how the time has been going."

"It is almost winter, my dear. There is hardly a leaf left on the trees—just two or three disconsolate yellow ones that want to get away down to the rest. They go fluttering and fluttering and trying to break away, but they can't."

"That is just as I felt a little while ago. I wanted to die and get away, papa; for I thought I should never be well again, and I should be in everybody's way.—I am afraid I shall not get well, after all," she added, and the light clouded on her sweet face.

"Well, my darling, we are in God's hands. We shall never get tired of you, and you must not get tired of us. Would you get tired of nursing me, if I were ill?"

"O, papa!" And the tears began to gather in her eyes.

"Then you must think we are not able to love so well as you."

"I know what you mean. I did not think of it that way. I will never think so about it again. I was only thinking how useless I was."

"There you are quite mistaken, my dear. No living creature ever was useless. You've got plenty to do there."

"But what have I got to do? I don't feel able for anything," she said; and again the tears came in her eyes, as if I had been telling her to get up and she could not.

"A great deal of our work," I answered, "we do without knowing what it is. But I'll tell you what you have got to do: you have got to believe in God, and in everybody in this house."

"I do, I do. But that is easy to do," she returned.

"And do you think that the work God gives us to do is never easy? Jesus says his yoke is easy, his burden is light. People sometimes refuse to do God's work just because it is easy. This is, sometimes, because they cannot believe that easy work is his work; but there may be a very bad pride in it: it may be because they think that there is little or no honour to be got in that way; and therefore they despise it. Some again accept it with half a heart, and do it with half a hand. But, however easy any work may be, it cannot be well done without taking thought about it. And such people, instead of taking thought about their work, generally take thought about the morrow, in which no work can be done any more than in yesterday. The Holy Present!—I think I must make one more sermon about it—although you, Connie," I said, meaning it for a little joke, "do think that I have said too much about it already."

From the novel Wilfrid Cumbermede. *A young man, separated from the girl he loves and unable to concentrate on his work, decides he "should have done better to go down to the Moat, and be silent."*

Certainly work is not always required of a man. There is such a thing as a sacred idleness, the cultivation of which is now fearfully neglected. Abraham, seated in his tent door in the heat of the day, would be to the philosophers of the nineteenth century an object for uplifted hands and pointed fingers. They would see in him only the indolent Arab, whom nothing but the foolish fancy that he saw his Maker in the distance, could rouse to run.

13.

Prayer

From the novel Wilfrid Cumbermede. *The narrator finds "the universe . . . but one dreary chasm whence I could not escape."*

I looked up to the blue sky, wept, and for the first time fell on my knees. "O God!" I cried, and that was all. But what are the prayers of the whole universe more than expansions of that one cry? It is not what God can give us, but God that we want.

From a sermon.

Am I going to do a good deed? Then, of all times,—Father, into thy hands; lest the enemy should have me now.

From the novel Robert Falconer. *A young man has returned to the attic bedroom where he lived as a boy; the room holds some of the possessions of his mother, who died when he was very young.*

It was a nothing of a place—with a window that looked only to heaven. There was the empty bedstead against the wall, where he had so often kneeled, sending forth vain prayers to a deaf heaven! Had they indeed been vain prayers, and to a deaf heaven? or had they been prayers which a hearing God must answer not according to the haste of the praying child, but according to the calm course of his own infinite law of love?

Here, somehow or other, the things about him did not seem so much absorbed in the past, notwithstanding those untroubled rows of papers bundled in red tape. True, they looked almost awful in their lack of interest and their non-humanity, for there is scarcely anything that absolutely loses interest save the records of money; but his mother's workbox lay behind them. And, strange to say, the side of that bed drew him to kneel down: he did not yet believe that prayer was in vain. If God had not answered him before, that gave no certainty that he would not answer him now. It was, he found, still as rational as it had ever been to hope that God would answer the man that cried to him.

This came, I think, from the fact that God had been answering him all the time, although he had not recognized his gifts as answers.

From the novel David Elginbrod. *Euphra, a young woman who has been treated shabbily by a highborn admirer, now finds herself lonely, sick, and miserable.*

Some natures will endure an immense amount of misery before they feel compelled to look there for help, whence all help and healing comes. They cannot believe that there is verily an unseen mysterious power, till the world and all that is in it has vanished in the smoke of despair; till cause and effect is nothing to the intellect, and possible glories have faded from the imagination; then, deprived of all that made life pleasant or hopeful, the immortal essence, lonely and wretched and unable to cease, looks up with its now unfettered and wakened instinct, to the source of its own life—to the possible God who, notwithstanding all the improbabilities of his existence, may yet perhaps be, and may yet perhaps hear his wretched creature that calls. In this loneliness of despair, life must find The Life; for joy is gone, and life is all that is left: it is compelled to seek its source, its root, its eternal life. This alone remains as a possible thing.

Strange condition of despair into which the Spirit of God drives a man—a condition in which the Best alone is the Possible!

Other simpler natures look up at once. Even before the first pang has passed away, as by a holy instinct of celestial childhood, they lift their eyes to the heavens whence cometh their aid. Of this class Euphra was not. She belonged to the former. And yet even she had begun to look upward, for the waters had closed above her head. She betook herself to the one man of whom she had heard as knowing about God. She wrote, but no answer came. Days and days passed away, and there was no reply.

"Ah! just so!" she said, in bitterness. "And if I cried to God for ever, I should hear no word of reply. If he be, he sits apart, and leaves the weak to be the prey of the bad. What cares he?"

Yet, as she spoke, she rose, and, by a sudden impulse, threw herself on the floor, and cried for the first time:

"O God, help me!"

Was there voice or hearing?

She rose at least with a little hope, and with the feeling that if she could cry to him, it might be that he could listen to her. It seemed natural to pray; it seemed to come of itself: that could not be except it was first natural for God to hear. The foundation of her own action must be in him who made her; for her call could be only a response after all.

From a letter to a friend.

Winter is needful as spring and summer, for Winter is needful as spring and summer for our poor hearts. . . .

Dearest friend, yours must be the kingdom of heaven, for you are poor in spirit. You feel yourself like the Publican, poor. It is coming to you, and when it arrives you will wonder that you doubted, for you will see that it must have been all the time. . . .

When we cannot climb the ladder of prayer, surely God comes down to the foot of it where we lie.

From the novel Donal Grant. *Donal has just arrived at the castle where he is to work as a tutor. He is shown to his room at the top of a watchtower, where he falls asleep and misses dinner.*

The night descended, and when he came to himself, its silences were deep around him. It was not dark: there was no moon, but the twilight was clear. He could read the face of his watch: it was twelve o'clock! No one had missed him! He was very hungry! But he had been hungrier before and survived it! In his wallet were still some remnants of oat-cake! He took it in his hand, and stepping out on the bartizan, crept with careful steps round to the watchtower. There he seated himself in the stone chair, and ate his dry morsels in the starry presences. Sleep had refreshed him, and he was wide awake, yet there was on him the sense of a strange existence. Never before had he so known himself! Often had he passed the night in the open air, but never before had his night-consciousness been such! Never had he felt the same way alone. He was parted from the whole earth, like the ship-boy on the giddy mast! Nothing was below but a dimness; the earth and all that was in it was massed into a vague shadow. It was as if he had died and gone where existence was independent of solidity and sense.

Above him was domed the vast of the starry heavens; he could neither flee from it nor ascend to it! For a moment he felt it the symbol of life, yet an unattainable hopeless thing. He hung suspended between heaven and earth, an outcast of both, a denizen of neither! The true life seemed ever to retreat, never to await his grasp. Nothing but the beholding of the face of the Son of Man could set him at rest as to its reality; nothing less than the assurance from his own mouth could satisfy him that all was true, all well: life was a thing so essentially divine, that he could not know it in itself till his own essence was pure!

But alas, how dream-like was the old story! Was God indeed to be reached by the prayers, affected by the needs of men? How was he to feel sure of it? Once more, as often heretofore, he found himself crying into the great world to know whether there was an ear to hear. What if there should come to him no answer? How frightful then would be his loneliness! But to seem not to be heard might be part of the discipline of his darkness! It might be for the perfecting of his faith that he must not yet know how near God was to him!

"Lord," he cried, "eternal life is to know thee and thy Father; I do not know thee and thy Father; I have not eternal life; I have but life enough to hunger for more: show me plainly of the Father whom thou alone knowest."

And as he prayed, something like a touch of God seemed to begin and grow in him till it was more than his heart could hold, and the universe about him was not large enough to hold in its hollow the heart that swelled with it.

"God is enough," he said, and sat in peace.

From the novel Wilfrid Cumbermede. *Wilfrid, an orphan, lives with his uncle.*

One afternoon, finding me tolerably comfortable, he said, "Shall I read something to you, Wilfrid?"

"I should like it," I answered.

"What shall I read?" he asked.

"Hadn't you something in your head," I rejoined, "when you proposed it?"

"Well, I had; but I don't know if you would like it."

"What did you think of, then?"

"I thought of a chapter in the New Testament."

"How could you think I should not like that?"

"Because I never saw you say your prayers."

"That is quite true. But you don't think I never say my prayers, although you never see me do it?"

The fact was, my uncle, amongst his other peculiarities, did not approve of teaching children to say their prayers. But he did not therefore leave me without instruction in the matter of praying—either the idlest or the most availing of human actions. He would say, "When you want anything, ask for it, Willie; and if it is worth your having, you will have it. But don't fancy you are doing God any service by praying to him. He likes you to pray to him because he loves you, and wants you to love him. And whatever you do, don't go saying a lot of words you don't mean. If you think you ought to pray, say your Lord's Prayer, and have done with it." I had no theory myself on the matter; but when I was in misery on the wild mountains, I had indeed prayed to God; and had even gone so far as to hope, when I got what I prayed for, that he had heard my prayer.

From the novel Thomas Wingfold, Curate. *Mr. Polwarth, the wise and eccentric gate-keeper of an estate, makes regular visits to a young man dying of tuberculosis.*

"Have you been coughing much to-day?" asked the gate-keeper.

"Yes, a good deal—before I came out. But it does not seem to do much good."

"What good would you have it do?"

"I mean, it doesn't do much to get it over. Oh, Mr. Polwarth, I am so tired!"

"Poor fellow! I suppose it looks to you as if it would never be over. But all the millions of the dead have got through it before you. I don't know that that makes much difference to the one who is going through it. And yet it is a sort of company. Only, the Lord of Life is with you, and that is real company, even in dying, when no one else can be with you."

"If I could only feel he was with me!"

"You may feel his presence without knowing what it is."

"I hope it isn't wrong to wish it over, Mr. Polwarth?"

"I don't think it is wrong to wish anything you can talk to him about and submit to his will. St. Paul says, 'In everything let your requests be made known unto God.'"

"I sometimes feel as if I would not ask him for anything, but just let him give me what he likes."

"We must not want to be better than is required of us, for that is at once to grow worse."

"I don't quite understand you."

"Not to ask may seem to you a more submissive way, but I don't think it is so childlike. It seems to me far better to say, 'O Lord, I should like this or that, but I would rather not have it if thou dost not like it also.' Such prayer brings us into conscious and immediate relations with God. Remember, our thoughts are then, passing to him, sent by our will into his mind. Our Lord taught us to pray always and not get tired of it. God, however poor creatures we may be, would have us talk to him, for then he can speak to us better than when we turn no face to him."

From the novel There and Back. *Sir Wilton is advising Richard to take the example of Mr. Wingfold and become a minister.*

"Richard," he said, "you had better make up your mind to go into the church! You hear Mr. Wingfold! I shouldn't like it myself; I should have to be at my prayers all day!"

"Ah, Sir Wilton, it doesn't take time to thank God! It only takes eternity."

From a sermon.

Never wait for a fitter time or place to talk to Him. To wait till thou go to church or to thy closet is to make Him wait. He will listen as thou walkest.

From a sermon.

Go home and speak to God; nay, hold your tongue, and quietly go to him in the secret recesses of your own heart, and know that God is there.

Say, "God has given me this work to do, and I am doing it;" and that is your joy, that is your refuge, that is your going to heaven.

God in Our Midst

For God so loved the world,
that he gave his only begotten Son,
that whosoever believeth in him should not perish,
but have everlasting life.

For God sent not his Son into the world
to condemn the world;
but that the world through him might be saved.

John 3:16–17

14.

Love of Neighbor

From a sermon.

We shall never be able, I say, to rest in the bosom of the Father, till the fatherhood is fully revealed to us in the love of the brothers. For He cannot be our Father, save as He is their Father; and if we do not see Him and feel Him as their Father, we cannot know him as ours.

Never shall we know him aright until we rejoice and exult for our race that he is the Father. He that loveth not his brother whom he hath seen, how can he love God whom he hath not seen?

From the novel Robert Falconer. *Eric Ericson, a university student who has lost his faith and his health, is being cared for by the orphan Robert Falconer.*

Some people take comfort from the true eyes of a dog—and a precious thing to the loving heart is the love of even a dumb animal. What comfort then must not such a boy as Robert have been to such a man as Ericson! Often and often when

Robert thought he was lying asleep, he was watching the face of his watcher. When the human soul is not yet able to receive the vision of the God-man, God sometimes—might I not say always?—reveals himself, or at least gives himself, in some human being whose face, whose hands are the ministering angels of his unacknowledged presence, to keep alive the fire of love on the altar of the heart, until God hath provided the sacrifice—that is, until the soul is strong enough to draw it from the concealing thicket.

Here were two, each thinking that God had forsaken him, or was not to be found by him, and each the very love of God, commissioned to tend the other's heart. In each was he present to the other. The one thought himself the happiest of mortals in waiting upon his big brother, whose least smile was joy enough for one day; the other wondered at the unconscious goodness of the boy, and while he gazed at his ruddy-brown face, believed in God.

From the fantasy novel Lilith. *The narrator is wandering alone in an unknown country.*

Coming to a spot where the pines stood farther apart and gave room for flowering shrubs, and hoping it a sign of some dwelling near, I took the direction where yet more and more roses grew, for I was hungry after the voice and face of my kind—after any live soul, indeed, human or not, which I might in some measure understand.

What a hell of horror, I thought, to wander alone, a bare existence never going out of itself, never widening its life in another life, but, bound with the cords of its poor peculiarities, lying an eternal prisoner in the dungeon of its own being! I began to learn that it was impossible to live for oneself even, save in the presence of others—then, alas, fearfully possible! evil was only through good!

From a sermon given on Christmas Eve in the novel Annals of a Quiet Neighbourhood.

When God comes to man, man looks round for his neighbour. When man departed from God in the Garden of Eden, the only man in the world ceased to be the friend of the only woman in the world; and, instead of seeking to bear her burden, became her accuser to God, in whom he saw only the Judge, unable to perceive that the Infinite love of the Father had come to punish him in tenderness and grace.

But when God in Jesus comes back to men, brothers and sisters spread forth their arms to embrace each other, and so to embrace Him. This is, when He is born again in our souls. For, dear friends, what we all need is just to become little children like Him; to cease to be careful about many things, and trust in Him, seeking only that He should rule, and that we should be made good like Him. What else is meant by "Seek ye first the kingdom of God and his righteousness, and all these things shall be added unto you?" Instead of doing so, we seek the things God has promised to look after for us, and refuse to seek the thing He wants us to seek—a thing that cannot be given us, except we seek it.

We profess to think Jesus the grandest and most glorious of men, and yet hardly care to be like Him; and so when we are offered His Spirit, that is, His very nature within us, for the asking, we will hardly take the trouble to ask for it. But to-night, at least, let all unkind thoughts, all hard judgments of one another, all selfish desires after our own way, be put from us, that we may welcome the Babe into our very bosoms; that when He comes amongst us—for is He not like a child still, meek and lowly of heart? He may not be troubled to find that we are quarrelsome, and selfish, and unjust.

From the book for children At the Back of the North Wind. *Diamond is a little boy who lives near a London stable where cab-horses are kept.*

A few nights after this, Diamond woke up suddenly, believing he heard North Wind thundering along. But it was something quite different. . . . It was a loud, angry voice, now growling like that of a beast, now raving like that of a madman; and when Diamond came a little wider awake, he knew that it was the voice of the drunken cabman, the wall of whose room was at the head of his bed. It was anything but pleasant to hear, but he could not help hearing it. At length there came a cry from the woman, and then a scream from the baby. Thereupon Diamond thought it time that somebody did something, and as himself was the only somebody at hand, he must go and see whether he could not do something.

So he got up and put on part of his clothes, and went down the stair, for the cabman's room did not open upon their stair, and he had to go out into the yard, and in at the next door. This, fortunately, the cabman, being drunk, had left open. By the time he reached their stair, all was still except the voice of the crying baby, which guided him to the right door. He opened it softly, and peeped in. There, leaning back in a chair, with his arms hanging down by his sides, and his legs stretched out before him and supported on his heels, sat the drunken cabman. His wife lay in her clothes upon the bed, sobbing, and the baby was wailing in the cradle. It was very miserable altogether.

Now the way most people do when they see anything very miserable is to turn away from the sight, and try to forget it. But Diamond began as usual to try to destroy the misery. The little boy was just as much one of God's messengers as if he had been an angel with a flaming sword, going out to fight the devil. The devil he had to fight just then was Misery. And the way he fought him was the very best. Like a wise soldier, he attacked him first in his weakest point—that was the baby; for Misery can never get such a hold of a baby as of a grown person. Diamond was knowing in babies, and he knew he could do something to make the baby happy; for although he had only known one baby as yet, and although not one baby is the same as another, yet they are so very much alike in some things, and he knew that one baby so thoroughly, that he had good reason to believe he could do something for any other.

I have known people who would have begun to fight the devil in a very different and a very stupid way. They would have begun by scolding the idiotic cabman; and next they would make his wife angry by saying it must be her fault as well as his, and by leaving ill-bred though well-meant shabby little books for them to read, which they were sure to hate the sight of; while all the time they would not have put out a finger to touch the wailing baby. But Diamond had him out of the cradle in a moment, set him up on his knee, and told him to look at the light.

Now all the light there was came only from a lamp in the yard, and it was a very dingy and yellow light, for the glass of the lamp was dirty, and the gas was bad; but the light that came from it was, notwithstanding, as certainly light as if it had come from the sun itself, and the baby knew that, and smiled to it;

and although it was indeed a wretched room which that lamp lighted—so dreary, and dirty, and empty, and hopeless!—there in the middle of it sat Diamond on a stool, smiling to the baby, and the baby on his knees smiling to the lamp. The father of him sat staring at nothing, neither asleep nor awake, not quite lost in stupidity either, for through it all he was dimly angry with himself, he did not know why. It was that he had struck his wife. He had forgotten it, but was miserable about it, notwithstanding. And this misery was the voice of the great Love that had made him and his wife and the baby and Diamond, speaking in his heart, and telling him to be good. For that great Love speaks in the most wretched and dirty hearts; only the tone of its voice depends on the echoes of the place in which it sounds. On Mount Sinai, it was thunder; in the cabman's heart it was misery; in the soul of St. John it was perfect blessedness.

By and by he became aware that there was a voice of singing in the room. This, of course, was the voice of Diamond singing to the baby—song after song, every one as foolish as another to the cabman, for he was too tipsy to part one word from another: all the words mixed up in his ear in a gurgle without division or stop; for such was the way he spoke himself, when he was in this horrid condition. But the baby was more than content with Diamond's songs, and Diamond himself was so contented with what the songs were all about, that he did not care a bit about the songs themselves, if only baby liked them. But they did the cabman good as well as the baby and Diamond, for they put him to sleep, and the sleep was busy all the time it lasted, smoothing the wrinkles out of his temper.

At length Diamond grew tired of singing, and began to talk to the baby instead. . . . He went on with [his] chatter till baby was asleep, by which time he was tired, and father and mother were both wide awake—only rather confused—the one from the beer, the other from the blow—and staring, the one from his chair, the other from her bed, at Diamond. But he was quite unaware of their notice, for he sat half-asleep, with his eyes wide open, staring in his turn, though without knowing it, at the cabman, while the cabman could not withdraw his gaze from Diamond's white face and big eyes. For Diamond's face was always rather pale, and now it was paler than usual with sleeplessness, and the light of the street-lamp upon it. At length he found himself nodding, and he knew then it was time to put the baby down, lest he should let him fall. So he rose from the little three-legged stool, and laid the baby in the cradle, and covered him up—it was well it was a warm night, and he did not want much covering—and then he all but staggered out of the door, he was so tipsy himself with sleep.

"Wife," said the cabman, turning towards the bed, "I do somehow believe that wur a angel just gone. Did you see him, wife? He warn't wery big, and he hadn't got none o' them wingses, you know. It wur one o' them baby-angels you sees on the gravestones, you know."

"Nonsense, hubby!" said his wife; "but it's just as good. I might say better, for you can ketch hold of him when you like. That's little Diamond as everybody knows, and a duck o' diamonds he is! No woman could wish for a better child than he be."

"I ha' heerd on him in the stable, but I never see the brat afore. Come, old girl, let bygones be bygones, and gie us a kiss, and we'll go to bed."

The cabman kept his cab in another yard, although he had his room in this. He was often late in coming home, and was not one to take notice of children, especially when he was tipsy, which was oftener than not. Hence, if he had ever seen Diamond, he did not know him. But his wife knew him well enough, as did every one else who lived all day in the yard. She was a good-natured woman. It was she who had got the fire lighted and the tea ready for them when Diamond and his mother came home from Sandwich. And her husband was not an ill-natured man either, and when in the morning he recalled not only Diamond's visit, but how he himself had behaved to his wife, he was very vexed with himself, and gladdened his poor wife's heart by telling her how sorry he was. And for a whole week after, he did not go near the public-house, hard as it was to avoid it, seeing a certain rich brewer had built one, like a trap to catch souls and bodies in, at almost every corner he had to pass on his way home. Indeed, he was never quite so bad after that, though it was some time before he began really to reform.

From the novel Weighed and Wanting. *A family lives in a part of London where they are "closely pressed by poor neighbours" with whom they become friendly "after a simple human manner."*

Those who would do good to the poor must attempt it in the way in which best they could do good to people of their own standing. They must make their acquaintance first. They must know something of the kind of the person they would help, to learn if help be possible from their hands. Only man can help man; money without man can do little or nothing, most likely less than nothing.

As our Lord redeemed the world by being a man, the true Son of the true Father, so the only way for a man to help men is to be a true man to this neighbour and that.

From the novel Robert Falconer. *Robert Falconer lives in the slums and often goes out at night to help his neighbors. On this occasion he takes with him a friend, Mr. Gordon.*

The streets swarmed with human faces gleaming past. It was a night of ghosts.

There stood a man who had lost one arm, earnestly pumping bilge-music out of an accordion with the other, holding it to his body with the stump. There was a woman, pale with hunger and gin, three match-boxes in one extended hand, and the other holding a baby to her breast. As we looked, the poor baby let go its hold, turned its little head, and smiled a wan, shrivelled, old-fashioned smile in our faces.

"Another happy baby, you see, Mr. Gordon," said Falconer. "A child, fresh from God, finds its heaven where no one else would. The devil could drive woman out of Paradise; but the devil himself cannot drive the Paradise out of a woman."

"What can be done for them?" I said, and at the moment, my eye fell upon a row of little children, from two to five years of age, seated upon the curb-stone.

They were chattering fast, and apparently carrying on some game, as happy as if they had been in the fields.

"Wouldn't you like to take all those little grubby things, and put them in a great tub and wash them clean?" I said.

"They'd fight like spiders," rejoined Falconer.

"They're not fighting now."

"Then don't make them. It would be all useless. The probability is that you would only change the forms of the various evils, and possibly for worse. You would buy all that man's glue-lizards, and that man's three-foot rules, and that man's dog-collars and chains, at three times their value, that they might get more drink than usual, and do nothing at all for their living to-morrow.—What a happy London you would make if you were Sultan Haroun!" he added, laughing. "You would put an end to poverty altogether, would you not?"

I did not reply at once.

"But I beg your pardon," he resumed; "I am very rude."

"Not at all," I returned. "I was only thinking how to answer you. They would be no worse after all than those who inherit property and lead idle lives."

"True; but they would be no better. Would you be content that your quondam poor should be no better off than the rich? What would be gained thereby? Is there no truth in the words "Blessed are the poor"? A deeper truth than most Christians dare to see.—Did you ever observe that there is not one word about the vices of the poor in the Bible—from beginning to end?"

"But they have their vices."

"Indubitably. I am only stating a fact. The Bible is full enough of the vices of the rich. I make no comment."

"But don't you care for their sufferings?"

"They are of secondary importance quite. But if you had been as much amongst them as I, perhaps you would be of my opinion, that the poor are not, cannot possibly feel so wretched as they seem to us. They live in a climate, as it were, which is their own, by natural law comply with it, and find it not altogether unfriendly. The Laplander will prefer his wastes to the rich fields of England, not merely from ignorance, but for the sake of certain blessings amongst which he has been born and brought up. The blessedness of life depends far more on its interest than upon its comfort. The need of exertion and the doubt of success, renders life much more interesting to the poor than it is to those who, unblessed with anxiety for the bread that perisheth, waste their poor hearts about rank and reputation."

"I thought such anxiety was represented as an evil in the New Testament."

"Yes. But it is a still greater evil to lose it in any other way than by faith in God. You would remove the anxiety by destroying its cause: God would remove it by lifting them above it, by teaching them to trust in him, and thus making them partakers of the divine nature. Poverty is a blessing when it makes a man look up."

"But you cannot say it does so always."

"I cannot determine when, where, and how much; but I am sure it does. And I am confident that to free those hearts from it by any deed of yours would be to do them the greatest injury you could. Probably their want of foresight would prove the natural remedy, speedily reducing them to their former condition—not however without serious loss."

"But will not this theory prove at last an anæsthetic rather than an anodyne? I mean that, although you may adopt it at first for refuge from the misery the sight of their condition occasions you, there is surely a danger of its rendering you at last indifferent to it."

"Am I indifferent? But you do not know me yet. Pardon my egotism. There may be such danger. Every truth has its own danger or shadow. Assuredly I would have no less labour spent upon them. But there can be no true labour done, save in as far as we are fellow-labourers with God. We must work with him, not against him. Every one who works without believing that God is doing the best, the absolute good for them, is, must be, more or less, thwarting God. He would take the poor out of God's hands. For others, as for ourselves, we must trust him. If we could thoroughly understand anything, that would be enough to prove it undivine; and that which is but one step beyond our understanding must be in some of its relations as mysterious as if it were a hundred. But through all this darkness about the poor, at least I can see wonderful veins and fields of light, and with the help of this partial vision, I trust for the rest. The only and the greatest thing man is capable of is Trust in God."

"What then is a man to do for the poor? How is he to work with God?" I asked.

"He must be a man amongst them—a man breathing the air of a higher life, and therefore in all natural ways fulfilling his endless human relations to them. Whatever you do for them, let your own being, that is you in relation to them, be the background, that so you may be a link between them and God, or rather I should say, between them and the knowledge of God."

While Falconer spoke, his face grew grander and grander, till at last it absolutely shone. I felt that I walked with a man whose faith was his genius.

"Of one thing I am pretty sure," he resumed, "that the same recipe Goethe gave for the enjoyment of life, applies equally to all work: 'Do the thing that lies next you.' That is all our business. Hurried results are worse than none. We must force nothing, but be partakers of the divine patience. How long it took to make the cradle! and we fret that the baby Humanity is not reading Euclid and Plato, even that it is not understanding the Gospel of St. John! If there is one thing evident in the world's history, it is that God hasteneth not. All haste implies weakness. Time is as cheap as space and matter. What they call the church militant is only at drill yet, and a good many of the officers too not out of the awkward squad. I am sure I, for a private, am not. In the drill a man has to conquer himself, and move with the rest by individual attention to his own duty: to what mighty battlefields the recruit may yet be led, he does not know. Meantime he has nearly enough to do with his goose-step, while there is plenty of single combat, skirmish, and light cavalry work generally, to get him ready for whatever is to follow. I beg your pardon: I am preaching."

From the novel Donal Grant. *Donal has rescued and comforted Arctura after she had been imprisoned by her wicked uncle in the cellar of his castle. His conversations have led her to a childlike faith.*

At the first dawn of power in his heart, when he began to make songs in the fields and on the hills, he had felt that to brighten with true light the clouded lives of despondent brothers and sisters was the one thing worthest living for: it was what the Lord came into the world for. . . .

To have helped this lovely creature, whose life had seemed lapt in an ever closer-clasping shroud of perplexity, was a thing to be glad of—not to the day of his death, but to the never-ending end of his life! was an honour conferred upon him by the Father, to last for evermore! For he had helped to open a human door for the Lord to enter! she within heard him knock, but, trying, was unable to open!

To be God's helper with our fellows is the one high calling; the presence of God in the house the one high condition.

From the novel The Elect Lady. *A man has become increasingly absorbed in a hobby which his wealth allows him to pursue.*

Dearly as he loved his daughter, he was, by slow fallings away, growing ever less of a companion, less of a comfort, less of a necessity to her, and requiring less and less of her for the good or ease of his existence. We wrong those near us in being independent of them. God himself would not be happy without His Son. We ought to lean on each other, giving and receiving—not as weaklings, but as lovers.

Love is strength as well as need.

From the novel There and Back. *Describing a man who is selfishly infatuated with his own cleverness.*

All things belong to every man who yields his selfishness, which is his one impoverishment, and draws near to his wealth, which is humanity—not humanity in the abstract, but the humanity of friends and neighbours and all men.

From the novel Salted with Fire. *MacLear the shoemaker ("soutar") lives with his grown daughter Maggie.*

"Whaur are ye aff til this bonny mornin', Maggie, my doo?" said the soutar, looking up from his work, and addressing his daughter as she stood in the doorway with her shoes in her hand.

"Jist ower to Stanecross, wi' yer leave, father, to speir the mistress for a goupin or twa o' chaff: yer bed aneth ye's grown unco hungry-like."

"Hoot, the bed's weel eneuch, lassie!"

"Na, it's onything but weel eneuch! It's my pairt to luik efter my ain father, and see there be nae knots aither in his bed or his parritch."

---

my doo my dear
speir ask
goupin double handful
unco uncommon

"Ye're jist yer mither owre again, my lass!—Weel, I winna miss ye that sair, for the minister 'ill be in this mornin'."

"Hoo ken ye that, father?"

"We didna gree vera weel last nicht."

"I canna bide the minister—argle-barglin body!"

"Toots, bairn! I dinna like to hear ye speyk sae scornfulike o' the gude man that has the care o' oor sowls!"

"It wad be mair to the purpose ye had the care o' his!"

"Sae I hae: hasna ilkabody the care o' ilk ither's?"

"Ay; but he preshumes upo' 't—and ye dinna; there's the differ!"

"Weel, but ye see, lassie, the man has nae insicht—nane to speak o', that is; and it's pleased God to mak him a wee stoopid, and some thrawn. He has nae notion even o' the wark I put intil thae wee bit sheenie o' his—that I'm this moment labourin ower!"

"It's sair wastit upo' him 'at caana see the thoucht intil't!"

"Is God's wark wastit upo' you and me excep' we see intil't, and un'erstan't, Maggie?"

The girl was silent. Her father resumed.

"There's three concernt i' the matter o' the wark I may be at: first, my ain duty to the wark—that's me; syne him I'm working for—that's the minister; and syne him 'at sets me to the wark—ye ken wha that is: whilk o' the three wad ye hae me lea' oot o' the consideration?"

For another moment the girl continued silent; then she said—

"Ye maun be i' the richt, father! I believe 't, though I canna

---

gree agree
bairn child
ilkabody everybody
thrawn twisted
sheenie little shoes

jist *see* 't. A body canna like a'body, and the minister's jist the ae man I canna bide."

"Ay could ye, gi'en ye lo'ed the *ane* as he oucht to be lo'ed, and as ye maun learn to lo'e him."

"Weel I'm no come to that wi' the minister yet!"

"It's a trowth—but a sair pity, my dautie."

"He provokes me the w'y that he speaks to ye, father—him 'at's no fit to tie the thong o' your shee!"

"The Maister would lat him tie his, and say *thank ye!*"

"It aye seems to me he has sic a scrimpit way o' believin'! It's no like believin' at a'! He winna trust him for naething that he hasna his ain word, or some ither body's for! Ca' ye that lippenin' til him?"

It was now the father's turn to be silent for a moment. Then he said,—

"Lea' the judgin' o' him to his ain maister, lassie. I ha'e seen him whiles sair concernt for ither fowk."

"'At they wouldna hand wi' *him*, and war condemnt in consequence—wasna that it?"

"I canna answer ye that, bairn."

"Weel, I ken he doesna like you—no ae wee bit. He's aye girdin at ye to ither fowk!"

"May be: the mair's the need I sud lo'e him."

"But hoo *can* ye, father?"

"There's naething, o' late, I ha'e to be sae gratefu' for to *Him* as that I can. But I confess I had lang to try sair!"

"The mair I was to try, the mair I jist couldna."

"But ye could try; and He could help ye!"

---

a'body everybody
ay could ye yes you could
dautie daughter; darling
sic such
lippenin' listening

"I dinna ken; I only ken that sae ye say, and I maun believe ye. Nane the mair can I see hoo it's ever to be broucht aboot."

"No more can I, though I ken it can be. But just think, my ain Maggie, hoo would onybody ken that ever ane o' 's was his disciple, gien we war aye argle-barglin aboot the holiest things— at least what the minister coonts the holiest, though may be I think I ken better? It's whan twa o' 's strive that what's ca'd a schism begins, and I jist winna, please God—and it does please him! He never said, Ye maun a' think the same gait, but he did say, Ye maun a' loe ane anither, and no strive!"

"Ye dinna aye gang to his kirk, father!"

"Na, for I'm jist feared sometimes lest I should stop loein him. It matters little about gaein to the kirk ilka Sunday, but it matters a heap aboot aye loein ane anither; and whiles he says things aboot the mind o' God, sic that it's a' I can dee to sit still."

"Weel, father, I dinna believe that I can lo'e him ony the day; sae, wi' yer leave, I s' be awa to Stanecross afore he comes."

"Gang yer wa's, lassie, and the Lord gang wi' ye, as ance he did wi' them that gaed to Emmaus."

With her shoes in her hand, the girl was leaving the house when her father called after her—

"Hoo's folk to ken that I provide for my ain, whan my bairn gangs unshod? Tak aff yer shune gin ye like when ye're oot o' the toon."

"Are ye sure there's nae hypocrisy aboot sic a fause show, father?" asked Maggie, laughing, "I maun hide them better!"

As she spoke she put the shoes in the empty bag she carried for the chaff. "There's a hidin' o' what I hae—no a pretendin' to hae

---

dinna ken don't know
o' 's of us
gien if
maun must
kirk church

what I haena!—Is' be hame in guid time for yer tay, father.—I
can gang a heap better withoot them!" she added, as she threw
the bag over her shoulder. "I'll put them on whan I come to the
heather," she concluded.

"Ay, ay; gang yer wa's, and lea' me to the wark ye haena the
grace to adverteeze by weirin' o' 't."

Maggie looked in at the window as she passed it on her way,
to get a last sight of her father. The sun was shining into the little
bare room, and her shadow fell upon him as she passed him; but
his form lingered clear in the close chamber of her mind after
she had left him far. And it was not her shadow she had seen,
but the shadow, rather, of a great peace that rested concentred
upon him as he bowed over his last, his mind fixed indeed upon
his work, but far more occupied with the affairs of quite another
region. Mind and soul were each so absorbed in its accustomed
labour that never did either interfere with that of the other. His
shoemaking lost nothing when he was deepest sunk in some one
or other of the words of his Lord, which he sought eagerly to
understand—nay, I imagine his shoemaking gained thereby.

In his leisure hours, not a great, he was yet an intense reader;
but it was nothing in any book that now occupied him; it was
the live good news, the man Jesus Christ himself. In thought, in
love, in imagination, that man dwelt in him, was alive in him,
and made him alive. This moment He was with him, had come
to visit him—yet was never far from him—was present always
with an individuality that never quenched but was continually
developing his own. For the soutar absolutely believed in the
Lord of Life, was always trying to do the things he said, and
to keep his words abiding in him. Therefore was he what the
parson called a mystic, and was the most practical man in the

neighbourhood; therefore did he make the best shoes, because the Word of the Lord abode in him.

The door opened, and the minister came into the kitchen. The soutar always worked in the kitchen, to be near his daughter, whose presence never interrupted either his work or his thought, or even his prayers—which often seemed as involuntary as a vital automatic impulse.

"It's a grand day!" said the minister. "It aye seems to me that just on such a day will the Lord come, nobody expecting him, and the folk all following their various callings—as when the flood came and astonished them."

The man was but reflecting, without knowing it, what the soutar had been saying the last time they encountered; neither did he think, at the moment, that the Lord himself had said something like it first.

"And I was thinkin, this vera meenute," returned the soutar, "sic a bonny day as it was for the Lord to gang aboot amang his ain fowk. I was thinkin maybe he was come upon Maggie, and was walkin wi' her up the hill to Stanecross—nearer til her, maybe, nor she could hear or see or think!"

"Ye're a deal taen up wi' vain imaiginins, MacLear!" rejoined the minister, tartly. "What scriptur hae ye for sic a wanderin' invention, o' no practical value?"

" 'Deed, sir, what scriptur hed I for takin my brakwast this mornin, or ony mornin? Yet I never luik for a judgment to fa' upon me for that! I'm thinkin we dee mair things in faith than we ken—but no eneuch! no eneuch! I was thankfu' for't, though, I min' that, and maybe that'll stan' for faith. But gien I gang on this gait, we'll be beginnin as we left aff last nicht, and maybe fa' to strife! And we hae to loe ane anither, not accordin to what the ane thinks, or what the ither thinks, but accordin as each kens the Maister loes the ither, for he loes the twa o' us thegither."

"But hoo ken ye that he's pleased wi' ye?"

"I said naething aboot that: I said he loes you and me!"

"For that, he maun be pleast wi' ye!"

"I dinna think nane aboot that; I jist tak my life i' my han', and awa' wi' 't til *Him*;—and he's never turned his face frae me yet.—Eh, sir! think what it would be gien ever he did!"

"But we maunna think o' him ither than he would hae us think."

"That's hoo I'm aye hingin aboot his door, luikin for him."

"Weel, I kenna what to mak o' ye! I maun jist lea' ye to him!"

"Ye couldna dee a kinder thing! I desire naething better frae man or minister than be left to Him."

"Weel, weel, see til yersel."

"I'll see to *him*, and try to loe my neebour—that's you, Mr. Pethrie. I'll hae yer shune ready by Setterday, sir. I trust they'll be worthy o' the feet that God made, and that hae to be shod by me. I trust and believe they'll nowise distress ye, sir, or interfere wi' yer comfort in preachin. I'll fess them hame mysel, gien the Lord wull, and that without fail."

"Na, na; dinna dee that; lat Maggie come wi' them. Ye wad only be puttin me oot o' humour for the Lord's wark wi' yer havers!"

"Weel, I'll sen' Maggie—only ye wad obleege me by no seein her, for ye micht put *her* oot o' humour, sir, and she michtna gie yer sermon fair play the morn!"

The minister closed the door with some sharpness.

---

fess fetch
havers nonsense

From the fantasy novel Phantastes. *The narrator is a young man who has just journeyed through a mysterious land where he "set out to find my Ideal [and] came back rejoicing that I had lost my Shadow."*

I knew now, that it is by loving, and not by being loved, that one can come nearest the soul of another; yea, that, where two love, it is the loving of each other, and not the being loved by each other, that originates and perfects and assures their blessedness.

I knew that love gives to him that loveth, power over any soul beloved, even if that soul know him not, bringing him inwardly close to that spirit; a power that cannot be but for good; for in proportion as selfishness intrudes, the love ceases, and the power which springs therefrom dies.

Yet all love will, one day, meet with its return.

15.

Creation

From the youth novel Ranald Bannerman's Boyhood. *A man looks back on his childhood.*

Oh the summer days, with the hot sun drawing the odours from the feathery larches and the white-stemmed birches, when, getting out of the water, I would lie in the warm soft grass, where now and then the tenderest little breeze would creep over my skin, until the sun baking me more than was pleasant, I would rouse myself with an effort, and running down to the fringe of rushes that bordered the full-brimmed river, plunge again headlong into the quiet brown water, and dabble and swim till I was once more weary! For innocent animal delight, I know of nothing to match those days—so warm, yet so pure-aired—so clean, so glad.

I often think how God must love his little children to have invented for them such delights! For, of course, if he did not love the children and delight in their pleasure, he would not have invented the two and brought them together.

Yes, my child, I know what you would say,—"How many there are who have no such pleasures!" I grant it sorrowfully;

but you must remember that God has not done with them yet; and, besides, that there are more pleasures in the world than you or I know anything about. And if we had it *all* pleasure, I know I should not care so much about what is better, and I would rather be made good than have any other pleasure in the world; and so would you, though perhaps you do not know it yet.

From the novel Robert Falconer. *Two boys, Robert Falconer and his friend Shargar, have just spent a Saturday afternoon swimming and walking in the country near the village they live in.*

[Robert] lay gazing up into the depth of the sky, rendered deeper and bluer by the masses of white cloud that hung almost motionless below it, until he felt a kind of bodily fear lest he should fall off the face of the round earth into the abyss. A gentle wind, laden with pine odours from the sun-heated trees behind him, flapped its light wing in his face: the humanity of the world smote his heart; the great sky towered up over him, and its divinity entered his soul; a strange longing after something 'he knew not nor could name' awoke within him, followed by the pang of a sudden fear that there was no such thing as that which he sought, that it was all a fancy of his own spirit; and then the voice of Shargar broke the spell, calling to him from afar to come and see a great salmon that lay by a stone in the water. . . . But once aroused, the feeling was never stilled; the desire never left him; sometimes growing even to a passion that was relieved only by a flood of tears.

Strange as it may sound to those who have never thought of such things save in connection with Sundays and Bibles and churches and sermons, that which was now working in Falconer's mind was the first dull and faint movement of the greatest need that the human heart possesses—the need of the God-Man. There must be truth in the scent of that pine-wood: some one must mean it. There must be a glory in those heavens that depends not upon our imagination: some power greater than they must dwell in them. Some spirit must move in that wind that haunts us with a kind of human sorrow; some soul must look up to us from the eye of that starry flower. It must be something human, else not to us divine.

Little did Robert think that such was his need—that his soul was searching after One whose form was constantly presented to him, but as constantly obscured and made unlovely by the words without knowledge spoken in the religious assemblies of the land; that he was longing without knowing it on the Saturday for that from which on the Sunday he would be repelled without knowing it. Years passed before he drew nigh to the knowledge of what he sought.

From a sermon.

I believe that every fact in nature is a revelation of God, is there such as it is because God is such as he is; and I suspect that all its facts impress us so that we learn God unconsciously. . . .

How should we imagine what we may of God, without the firmament over our heads, a visible sphere, yet a formless infinitude! What idea could we have of God without the sky? The truth of the sky is what it makes us feel of the God that sent it out to our eyes. If you say the sky could not but be so and such, I grant it—with God at the root of it. There is nothing for us to conceive in its stead—therefore indeed it must be so. In its discovered laws, light seems to me to be such because God is such. Its so-called laws are the waving of his garments, waving so because he is thinking and loving and walking inside them. We are here in a region far above that commonly claimed for science, open only to the heart of the child and the childlike man and woman—a region in which the poet is among his own things, and to which he has often to go to fetch them. For things as they are, not as science deals with them, are the revelation of God to his children. . . .

Ask a man of mere science, what is the truth of a flower: he will pull it to pieces, show you its parts, explain how they operate, how they minister each to the life of the flower; he will tell you what changes are wrought in it by scientific cultivation; where it lives originally, where it can live; the effects upon it of another climate; what part the insects bear in its varieties—and doubtless many more facts about it. . . .

The truth of the flower is, not the facts about it, be they correct as ideal science itself, but the shining, glowing, gladdening, patient thing throned on its stalk—the compeller of smile and tear from child and prophet. . . .

The idea of God, I repeat, is the flower. He thought it; invented its means; sent it, a gift of himself, to the eyes and hearts of his children. When we see how they are loved by the ignorant and degraded, we may well believe the flowers have a place in the history of the world, as written for the archives of heaven, which we are yet a long way from understanding, and which science could not, to all eternity, understand, or enable to understand.

Watch that child! He has found one of his silent and motionless brothers, with God's clothing upon it, God's thought in its face. In what a smile breaks out the divine understanding between them! Watch his mother when he takes it home to her— no nearer understanding it than he! It is no old association that brings those tears to her eyes, powerful in that way as are flowers, and things far inferior to flowers; it is God's thought, unrecognized as such, holding communion with her. She weeps with a delight inexplicable. It is only a daisy! only a primrose! only a pheasanteye-narcissus! only a lily of the field! only a snowdrop! only a sweet-pea! only a brave yellow crocus! But here to her is no mere fact; here is no law of nature; here is a truth of nature, the truth of a flower—a thought from the heart of God—a truth of God! Not an intellectual truth, but a divine fact, a dim revelation, a movement of the creative soul! Who but a father could think the flowers for his little ones? We are nigh the region now in which the Lord's word is at home—"I am the truth." . . .

What, I ask, is the truth of water? Is it that it is formed of hydrogen and oxygen? . . . . There is no water in oxygen, no water in hydrogen: it comes bubbling fresh from the imagination of the living God, rushing from under the great white throne of the glacier. The very thought of it makes one gasp with an elemental joy no metaphysician can analyse.

The water itself, that dances, and sings, and slakes the wonderful thirst—symbol and picture of that draught for which the woman of Samaria made her prayer to Jesus—this lovely thing itself, whose very wetness is a delight to every inch of the human body in its embrace—this live thing which, if I might, I would have running through my room, yea, babbling along my table—this water is its own self its own truth, and is therein a truth of God.

Let him who would know the love of the maker, become sorely athirst and drink of the brook by the way—then lift up his heart—not at that moment to the maker of oxygen and hydrogen, but to the inventor and mediator of thirst and water, that man might foresee a little of what his soul may find in God. If he become not then as a hart panting for the water-brooks, let him go back to his science and its husks: they will at last make him thirsty as the victim in the dust-tower of the Persian. As well may a man think to describe the joy of drinking by giving thirst and water for its analysis, as imagine he has revealed anything about water by resolving it into its scientific elements. Let a man go to the hillside and let the brook sing to him till he loves it, and he will find himself far nearer the fountain of truth than the triumphal car of the chemist will ever lead the shouting crew of his half-comprehending followers. He will draw from the brook the water of joyous tears, "and worship him that made heaven, and earth, and the sea, and the fountain of waters."

From the novel The Elect Lady. *A young man and woman, although reserved and slow to express their feelings, are learning to love each other by sharing their joy in the created world.*

There was a secret between them—a secret proclaimed on the house-tops, a secret hidden, the most precious of pearls, in their hearts—that the earth is the Lord's and the fullness thereof; that its work is the work of the Lord, whether the sowing of the field, the milking of the cow, the giving to the poor, the spending of wages, the reading of the Bible; that God is all in all, and every throb of gladness His gift; that their life came fresh every moment from His heart; that what was lacking to them would arrive the very moment He had got them ready for it. They were God's little ones in God's world—none the less their own that they did not desire to swallow it, or thrust it in their pockets.

Among poverty-stricken Christians, consumed with care to keep a hold of the world and save their souls, they were as two children of the house. By living in the presence of the living

One, they had become themselves His presence—dim lanterns through which His light shone steady. Who obeys, shines.

From the same novel. A young farmer who writes poetry is talking with a woman he has recently met.

"Then what do you write for, if you care nothing for fame? I thought that was what all poets wrote for."

"So the world thinks; and those that do sometimes have their reward."

"Tell me then what you write for?"

"I write because I want to tell something that makes me glad and strong. I want to say it, and so try to say it. Things come to me in gleams and flashes, sometimes in words themselves, and I want to weave them into a melodious, harmonious whole. I was once at an oratorio, and that taught me the shape of a poem. In a pause of the music, I seemed all at once to see Handel's heavy countenance looking out of his great wig, as he sat putting together his notes, ordering about in his mind, and fixing in their places with his pen, his drums, and pipes, and fiddles, and roaring bass, and flageolets, and hautboys—all to open the door for the thing that was plaguing him with the confusion of its beauty. For I suppose even Handel did not hear it all clear and plain at first, but had to build his orchestra into a mental organ for his mind to let itself out by, through the many music holes, lest it should burst with its repressed harmonic delights. He must have felt an agonized need to set the haunting angels of sound in obedient order and range, responsive to the soul of the thing, its one ruling idea! I saw him with his white rapt face, looking like a prophet of the living God sent to speak out of the heart of the mystery of truth! I saw him as he sat staring at the paper before him, scratched all over as with the fury of a holy anger at his own impotence, and his soul communed with heavenliest harmonies! Ma'am, will any man persuade me that Handel at such a moment was athirst for fame? or that the desire to please a house full or world full of such as heard his oratorios, gave him the power to write his music? No, ma'am! he was filled, not with the longing for sympathy, and not even with the good desire to give delight, but with the music itself. It was crying in him to get out, and he heard it crying, and could not rest till he had let it out; and every note that dropped from his pen was a chip struck from the granite wall between the song-birds in their prison-nest, and the air of their liberty. Creation is God's self-wrought freedom. No, ma'am, I do not despise my fellows, but neither do I prize the judgment of more than a few of them. I prize and love themselves, but not their opinion."

From an essay.

This world is not merely a thing which God hath made, subjecting it to laws; but it is an expression of the thought, the feeling, the heart of God himself. And so it must be; because, if man be the child of God, would he not feel to be out of his element if he lived in a world which came, not from the heart of God, but only from his hand? . . .

Let us go further; and, looking at beauty, believe that God is the first of artists; that he has put beauty into nature, knowing how it will affect us, and intending that it should so affect us; that he has embodied his own grand thoughts thus that we might see them and be glad. Then, let us go further still, and believe that whatever we feel in the highest moments of truth shining through beauty, whatever comes to our souls as a power of life, is meant to be seen and felt by us, and to be regarded not as the work of his hand, but as the flowing forth of his heart, the flowing forth of his love of us, making us blessed in the union of his heart and ours.

From the novel Annals of a Quiet Neighbourhood. *A young man is taking a walk near the village which he has just moved to.*

Pondering, speculating, I now set out for the mill, which, I had already learned, was on the village side of the river. Coming to a lane leading down to the river, I followed it, and then walked up a path outside the row of pollards, through a lovely meadow, where brown and white cows were eating and shining all over the thick deep grass. Beyond the meadow, a wood on the side of a rising ground went parallel with the river a long way. The river flowed on my right. That is, I knew that it was flowing, but I could not have told how I knew, it was so slow. Still swollen, it was of a clear brown, in which you could see the browner trouts darting to and fro with such a slippery gliding, that the motion seemed the result of will, without any such intermediate and complicate arrangement as brain and nerves and muscles. The water-beetles went spinning about over the surface; and one glorious dragon-fly made a mist about him with his long wings.

And over all, the sun hung in the sky, pouring down life; shining on the roots of the willows at the bottom of the stream; lighting up the black head of the water-rat as he hurried across to the opposite bank; glorifying the rich green lake of the grass; and giving to the whole an utterance of love and hope and joy, which was, to him who could read it, a more certain and full revelation of God than any display of power in thunder, in avalanche, in stormy sea.

Those with whom the feeling of religion is only occasional, have it most when the awful or grand breaks out of the common; the meek who inherit the earth, find the God of the whole earth more evidently present—I do not say more present, for there is no measuring of His presence—more evidently present in the commonest things. That which is best He gives most plentifully, as is reason with Him. Hence the quiet fulness of ordinary nature; hence the Spirit to them that ask it.

From the novel The Flight of the Shadow. *An old woman reflects on how her perspective has changed since she was young.*

But I am old, therefore dare to say that I expect more and better and higher and lovelier things than I have ever had. I am not going home to God to say—"Father, I have imagined more beautiful things than thou art able to make true! They were so good that thou thyself art either not good enough to will them, or not strong enough to make them. Thou couldst but make thy creature dream of them, because thou canst but dream of them thyself." Nay, nay! In the faith of him to whom the Father shows all things he does, I expect lovelier gifts than I ever have been, ever shall be able to dream of asleep, or imagine awake.

16.

Our Father in Heaven

From the novel The Seaboard Parish. *Mr. Walton, the speaker, and Mr. Turner are on a hill overlooking the sea.*

"What an awful thing to think that here we are on this great round tumbling ball of a world, held by the feet, and lifting up the head into infinite space—without choice or wish of our own—compelled to think and to be, whether we will or not! Just God must know it to be very good, or he would not have taken it in his hands to make individual lives without a possible will of theirs. He must be our Father, or we are wretched creatures— the slaves of a fatal necessity!

"Did it ever strike you, Turner, that each one of us stands on the apex of the world? With a sphere, you know, it must be so. And thus is typified, as it seems to me, that each one of us must look up for himself to find God, and then look abroad to find his fellows."

"I think I know what you mean," was all Turner's reply.

From the novel David Elginbrod. *Margaret, whose father is poor, is explaining her reaction to an event to Lady Euphra.*

"Perhaps I did. But I had no anxiety about it."

"But that you could not leave to a father such as yours even to settle."

"No. But I could to God. I could trust God with what I could not speak to my father about. He is my father's father, you know; and so, more to him and me than we could be to each other. The more we love God, the more we love each other; for we find he makes the very love which sometimes we foolishly fear to do injustice to, by loving him most. I love my father ten times more because he loves God, and because God has secrets with him."

"I wish God were a father to me as he is to you, Margaret."

"But he is your father, whether you wish it or not. He cannot be more your father than he is. You may be more his child than you are, but not more than he meant you to be, nor more than he made you for. You are infinitely more his child than you have grown to yet. He made you altogether his child, but you have not given in to it yet."

"Oh! yes; I know what you mean. I feel it is true."

"The Prodigal Son was his father's child. He knew it, and gave in to it. He did not say: 'I wish my father loved me enough to treat me like a child again.' He did not say that, but—I will arise and go to my father."

Euphra made no answer, but wept. Margaret said no more.

From the novel Warlock o' Glenwarlock. *Lady Joan is a house-guest of the laird of Glenwarlock and becomes friends with his young son Cosmo.*

"Don't you think," [Cosmo] began again, "though life is so very good—to me especially with you here—you would get very tired if you thought you had to live in this world always—for ever and ever and ever, and never, never get out of it?"

"No, I don't," said Joan. "I can't say I find life so nice as you think it, but one keeps hoping it may turn to something better."

She was amused with what she counted childish talk for a boy of his years—so manly too beyond his years!

"That is very curious!" he returned. "Now I am quite happy; but this moment I should feel just in a prison, if I thought I should never get to another world; for what you can never get out of, is your prison—isn't it?"

"Yes—but if you don't want to get out?"

"Ah, that is true! but as soon as that comes to a prisoner, it is a sign that he is worn out, and has not life enough in him to look the world in the face. I was talking about it the other day with [my tutor] Mr. Simon, else I shouldn't have got it so plain. The blue roof so high above us there, is indeed very different from the stone vault of a prison, for there is no stop or end to it. But if you can never get away from under it, never get off the floor at the bottom of it, I feel as if it might almost as well be something solid that held me in. There would be no promise in the stars then: they look now like promises, don't they? I do not believe God would ever show us a thing he did not mean to give us."

"You are a very odd boy, Cosmo. I am almost afraid to listen to you. You say such presumptuous things!"

Cosmo laughed a little gentle laugh.

"How can you love God, Joan, and be afraid to speak before him? I should no more dream of his being angry with me for thinking he made me for great and glad things, and was altogether generous towards me, than I could imagine my father angry with me for wishing to be as wise and as good as he is, when I know it is wise and good he most wants me to be."

"Ah, but he is your father, you know, and that is very different!"

"I know it is very different—God is so much, much more my father than is the laird of Glenwarlock! He is so much more to me, and so much nearer to me, though my father is the best father that ever lived! God, you know, Joan, God is more than anybody knows what to say about. Sometimes, when I am lying in my bed at night, my heart swells and swells in me, that I hardly know how to bear it, with the thought that here I am, come out of God, and yet not *out* of him—close to the very life that said to everything *be*, and it was!—you think it strange that I talk so?"

"Rather, I must confess! I don't believe it can be a good thing at your age to think so much about religion. There is a time for everything. You talk like one of those good little children in books that always die—at least I have heard of such books—I never saw any of them."

Cosmo laughed again.

"Which of us is the merrier—you or me? Which of us is the stronger, Joan? The moment I saw you, I thought you looked like one that hadn't enough of something—as if you weren't happy; but if you knew that the great beautiful person we call God, was always near you, it would be impossible for you to go on being sad."

Joan gave a great sigh: her heart knew its own bitterness, and there was little joy in it for a stranger to intermeddle with. But she said to herself the boy would be a gray-haired man before he was twenty, and began to imagine a mission to help him out of these morbid fancies.

"You must surely understand, Cosmo," she said, "that, while we are in this world, we must live as people of this world, not of another."

"But you can't mean that the people of this world are banished from Him who put them in it! He is all the same, in this world and in every other. If anything makes us happy, it must make us much happier to know it for a bit of frozen love—for the love that gives is to the gift as water is to snow. Ah, you should hear our torrent sing in summer, and shout in the spring! The thought of God fills me so full of life that I want to go and do something for everybody. I am never miserable. I don't think I shall be when my father dies."

"Oh, Cosmo!—with such a good father as yours! I am shocked."

Her words struck a pang into her own heart, for she felt as if she had compared his father and hers, over whom she was not miserable. Cosmo turned, and looked at her. The sun was close upon the horizon, and his level rays shone full on the face of the boy.

"Lady Joan," he said slowly, and with a tremble in his voice, "I should just laugh with delight to have to die for my father. But if he were taken from me now, I should be so proud of him, I should have no room to be miserable. As God makes me glad though I cannot see him, so my father would make me glad though I could not see him. I cannot see him now, and yet I am glad because my father *is*—away down there in the old castle; and when he is gone from me, I shall be glad still, for he will be *somewhere* all the same—with God as he is now. We shall meet again one day, and run at each other."

From the novel The Flight of the Shadow. *A child has transgressed by opening the cabinet where her uncle keeps his collection of precious stones. He responds by taking time to teach her about them.*

My fault had opened a new source of delight: my stone-lesson was now one of the great pleasures of the week. In after years I saw in it the richness of God not content with setting right what is wrong, but making from it a gain: he will not have his children the worse for the wrong they have done! We shall lose nothing by it: he is our father!

From a sermon.

Come to God, then, my brother, my sister, with all thy desires and instincts, all thy lofty ideals, all thy longing for purity and unselfishness, all thy yearning to love and be true, all thy aspiration after self-forgetfulness and child-life in the breath of the Father; come to him with all thy weaknesses, all thy shames, all thy futilities; with all thy helplessness over thy own thoughts; with all thy failure, yea, with the sick sense of having missed the tide of true affairs; come to him with all thy doubts, fears, dishonesties, meannesses, paltrinesses, misjudgments, wearinesses, disappointments, and stalenesses: be sure he will take thee and all thy miserable brood, whether of draggle-winged angels, or covert-seeking snakes, in to his care, the angels for life, the snakes for death, and thee for liberty in his limitless heart! For he is light, and in him is no darkness at all.

If he were a king, a governor; if the name that described him were *The Almighty,* thou mightst well doubt whether there could be light enough in him for thee and thy darkness; but he is thy father, and more thy father than the word can mean in any lips but his who said, "my father and your father, my God and your God;" and such a father is light, an infinite, perfect light.

Love and Marriage

From the novel The Marquis of Lossie. *A man and woman are in love.*

God only knows how grandly, how passionately yet how calmly, how divinely the man and the woman he has made, might, may, shall love each other.

From the novel What's Mine's Mine. *Christina, having lived most of her life in London, is spending a year in a secluded Scottish village. She is falling in love with a young man she has met.*

Happy is the rare fate of the true—to wake and come forth and meet in the majesty of the truth, in the image of God, in their very being, in the power of that love which alone is being. They love, not this and that about each other, but each the very other—a love as essential to reality, to truth, to religion, as the love of the very God. Where such love is, let the differences of taste, the unfitnesses of temperament be what they may, the two must by and by be thoroughly one. . . .

One morning [Christina] woke from a sound and dreamless sleep, and getting out of bed, drew aside the curtains, looked out, and then opened her window. It was a lovely spring-morning. The birds were singing loud in the fast greening shrubbery. A soft wind was blowing. It came to her, and whispered something of which she understood only that it was both lovely and sad. The sun, but a little way up, was shining over hills and cone-shaped peaks, whose shadows, stretching eagerly westward, were yet ever shortening eastward. His light was gentle, warm, and humid, as if a little sorrowful, she thought, over his many dead children, that he must call forth so many more to the new life of the reviving year.

Suddenly as she gazed, the little clump of trees against the hillside stood as she had never seen it stand before—as if the sap in them were no longer colourless, but red with human life; nature was alive with a presence she had never seen before; it was instinct with a meaning, an intent, a soul; the mountains stood against the sky as if reaching upward, knowing something, waiting for something; over all was a glory. The change was far more wondrous than from winter to summer; it was not as if a dead body, but a dead soul had come alive.

What could it mean? Had the new aspect come forth to answer this glow in her heart, or was the glow in her heart the reflection of this new aspect of the world? She was ready to cry aloud, not with joy, not from her feeling of the beauty, but with a *sensation* almost, hitherto unknown, therefore nameless. It was a new and marvellous interest in the world, a new sense of life in herself, of life in everything, a recognition of brother-existence, a life-contact with the universe, a conscious flash of the divine in her soul, a throb of the pure joy of being.

She was nearer God than she had ever been before. But she did not know this—might never in this world know it; she understood nothing of what was going on in her, only felt it go on; it was not love of God that was moving in her. Yet she stood in her white dress like one risen from the grave, looking in sweet bliss on a new heaven and a new earth, made new by the new opening of her eyes. To save man or woman, the next thing to the love of God is the love of man or woman; only let no man or woman mistake the love of love for love!

She started, grew white, stood straight up, grew red as a sunset:—was it—could it be?—"Is this love?" she said to herself, and for minutes she hardly moved.

It was love. Whether love was in her or not, she was in love—and it might get inside her. She hid her face in her hands, and wept.

With what opportunities I have had of studying, I do not say *understanding*, the human heart, I should not have expected such feeling from Christina—and she wondered at it herself. Till a child is awake, how tell his mood?—until a woman is awaked, how tell her nature? Who knows himself?—and how then shall he know his neighbour?

For who can know anything except on the supposition of its remaining the same? and the greatest change of all, next to being born again, is beginning to love. The very faculty of loving had been hitherto repressed in the soul of Christina—by poor education, by low family and social influences, by familiarity with the worship of riches, by vanity, and consequent hunger after the attentions of men; but now at length she was in love. . . .

For who in heaven or on earth has fathomed the marvel betwixt the man and the woman? Least of all the man or the woman who has not learned to regard it with reverence. There is more in this love to uplift us, more to condemn the lie in us, than in any other inborn drift of our being, except the heavenly tide Godward. From it flow all the other redeeming relations of life. It is the hold God has of us with his right hand, while death is the hold he has of us with his left. Love and death are the two marvels, yea the two terrors—but the one goal of our history.

From the novel Mary Marston. *Reflecting on marriage.*

Love and marriage are of the Father's most powerful means for the making of his foolish little ones into sons and daughters. But so unlike (in many cases) are the immediate consequences to those desired and expected, that it is hard for not a few to believe that he is anywhere looking after their fate—caring about them at all. And the doubt would be a reasonable one, if the end of things was marriage. But the end is life—that we become the children of God; after which, all things can and will go their grand, natural course; the heart of the Father will be content for his children, and the hearts of the children will be content in their Father.

From the novel Malcolm. *Malcolm has grown up among fishermen in a Scottish village. He has just fallen in love for the first time.*

Looking at Malcolm's life from the point of his own consciousness, and not from that of the so called world, it was surely pleasant enough. Innocence, devotion to another, health, pleasant labour with an occasional shadow of danger to arouse the energies, leisure, love of reading, a lofty minded friend, and, above all, a supreme presence, visible to his heart in the meeting of vaulted sky and outspread sea, and felt at moments in any waking wind that cooled his glowing cheek and breathed into him anew of the breath of life, lapped in such conditions, bathed in such influences, the youth's heart was swelling like a rosebud ready to burst into blossom.

But he had never yet felt the immediate presence of woman in any of her closer relations. He had never known mother or sister; and, although his voice always assumed a different tone and his manner grew more gentle in the presence of a woman, old or young, he had found little individually attractive amongst the fisher girls. . . .

But he had now arrived at that season when, in the order of things, a man is compelled to have at least a glimmer of the life which consists in sharing life with another. When once, through the thousand unknown paths of creation, the human being is so far divided from God that his individuality is secured, it has become yet more needful that the crust gathered around him in the process should be broken; and the love between man and woman arising from a difference deep in the heart of God, and essential to the very being of each—for by no words can I express my scorn of the evil fancy that the distinction between them is solely or even primarily physical—is one of his most powerful forces for blasting the wall of separation, and first step towards the universal harmony of twain making one. . . . There is no plainer sign of the need of a God, than the possible fate of love. The celestial Cupid may soar aloft on seraph wings that assert his origin, or fall down on the belly of a snake and creep to hell.

But Malcolm was not of the stuff of which coxcombs are made, and had not begun to think even of the abyss that separated the lady and himself—an abyss like that between star and star, across which stretches no mediating air—a blank and blind space. He felt her presence only as that of a being to be worshipped, to be heard with rapture, and yet addressed without fear.

From the novel Donal Grant. *Donal Grant has been the tutor at the home of Lady Arctura for some time, and they have each come to love the other.*

"I have something to tell you," he said; "and then you must speak again."

"Tell me," said Arctura.

"When I came here," said Donal, "I thought my heart so broken that it would never love—that way, I mean—anymore. But I loved God better than ever: and as one I would fain help, I loved you from the very first. But I should have scorned myself had I once fancied you loved me more than just to do anything for me I needed done. When I saw you troubled, I longed to take you up in my arms, and carry you like a lovely bird that had fallen from one of God's nests; but never once, my lady, did I think of your caring for my love: it was yours as a matter of course. I once asked a lady to kiss me—just once, for a good-bye: she would not—and she was quite right; but after that I never spoke to a lady but she seemed to stand far away on the top of a hill against a sky."

He stopped. Her hands on his fluttered a little, as if they would fly.

"Is she still—is she—alive?" she asked.

"Oh yes, my lady."

"Then she may—change—" said Arctura, and stopped, for there was a stone in her heart.

Donal laughed. It was an odd laugh, but it did Arctura good.

"No danger of that, my lady! She has the best husband in the world—a much better than I should have made, much as I loved her."

"That can't be!"

"Why, my lady, her husband's Sir Gibbie! She's Lady Galbraith! I would never have wished her mine if I had known she loved Gibbie. I love her next to him."

"Then—then—"

"What, my lady?"

"Then—then—Oh, do say something!"

"What should I say? What God wills is fast as the roots of the universe, and lovely as its blossom."

Arctura burst into tears.

"Then you do not—care for me!"

Donal began to understand. In some things he went on so fast that he could not hear the cry behind him. She had spoken, and had been listening in vain for response! She thought herself unloved: he had shown her no sign that he loved her!

His heart was so full of love and the joy of love, that they had made him very still: now the delight of love awoke. He took her in his arms like a child, rose, and went walking about the room with her, petting and soothing her. He held her close to his heart; her head was on his shoulder, and his face was turned to hers.

"I love you," he said, "and love you to all eternity! I have love enough now to live upon, if you should die to-night, and I should tarry till he come. O God, thou art too good to me! It is more than my heart can bear! To make men and women, and give them to each other, and not be one moment jealous of the love wherewith they love one another, is to be a God indeed!"

So said Donal—and spoke the high truth.

From the novel The Marquis of Lossie. *A young man and woman have been talking about how it is possible to have faith despite the suffering in the world.*

If something of that sacred mystery, holy in the heart of the Father, which draws together the souls of man and woman, was at work between them, let those scoff at the mingling of love and religion who know nothing of either; but man or woman who, loving woman or man, has never in that love lifted the heart to the Father, and everyone whose divine love has not yet cast at least an arm round the human love, must take heed what they think of themselves, for they are yet but paddlers in the tide of the eternal ocean. Love is a lifting no less than a swelling of the heart. What changes, what metamorphoses, transformations, purifications, glorifications, this or that love must undergo ere it take its eternal place in the kingdom of heaven, through all its changes yet remaining, in its one essential root, the same, let the coming redemption reveal. The hope of all honest lovers will lead them to the vision. Only let them remember that love must dwell in the will as well as in the heart.

From a letter to his wife, written during the final illness of their oldest daughter, Lilia.

This is your birthday, dearest. I hope you are full of hope in it. Though the outer decay, the inner, the thing that trusts in the perfect creative life, grows stronger—does it not? God will be better to us than we think, however expectant we be. . . .

Dearest, my love to you on this your birthday—a good day for me. I thank God for you.

Your loving
Husband

From the novel Sir Gibbie. *The woman whom Gibbie loves has just promised to marry him.*

Pearl-street and the Auld Hoose are in a town; Glashgar is the mountain which is his spiritual home.

Gibbie went home as if Pearl-street had been the stairs of Glashgar, and the Auld Hoose a mansion in the heavens. He seemed to float along the way as one floats in a happy dream, where motion is born at once of the will, without the intermediating mechanics of nerve, muscle, and fulcrum. Love had been gathering and ever storing itself in his heart so many years for this brown dove! now at last the rock was smitten, and its treasure rushed forth to her service. In nothing was it changed as it issued, save as the dark, silent, motionless water of the cavern changes into the sparkling, singing, dancing rivulet.

Gibbie's was love simple, unselfish, undemanding—not merely asking for no return, but asking for no recognition, requiring not even that its existence should be known. He was a rare one, who did not make the common miserable blunder of taking the shadow cast by love—the desire, namely, to be loved—for love itself; his love was a vertical sun, and his own shadow was under his feet. Silly youths and maidens count themselves martyrs of love, when they are but the pining witnesses to a delicious and entrancing selfishness. But do not mistake me through confounding, on the other hand, the desire to be loved—which is neither wrong nor noble, any more than hunger is either wrong or noble—and the delight in being loved, to be devoid of which a man must be lost in an immeasurably deeper, in an evil, ruinous, yea, a fiendish selfishness. Not to care for love is the still worse reaction from the self-foiled and outworn greed of love. Gibbie's love was a diamond among gem-loves. There are men whose love to a friend is less selfish than their love to the dearest woman; but Gibbie's was not a love to be less divine towards a woman than towards a man.

One man's love is as different from another's as the one is himself different from the other. The love that dwells in one man is an angel, the love in another is a bird, that in another a hog. Some would count worthless the love of a man who loved everybody. There would be no distinction in being loved by such a man!—and distinction, as a guarantee of their own great worth, is what such seek. There are women who desire to be the sole object of a man's affection, and are all their lives devoured by unlawful jealousies. A love that had never gone forth upon human being but themselves, would be to them the treasure to sell all that they might buy. And the man who brought such a love might in truth be all-absorbed therein himself: the poorest of creatures may well be absorbed in the poorest of loves. A heart has to be taught to love, and its first lesson, however well learnt, no more makes it perfect in love, than the A B C makes a savant.

The man who loves most will love best. The man who thoroughly loves God and his neighbour is the only man who will love a woman ideally—who can love her with the love God thought of between them when he made man male and female. The man, I repeat, who loves God with his very life, and his neighbour as Christ loves him, is the man who alone is capable of grand, perfect, glorious love to any woman.

18.

Fatherhood and Motherhood

Motherhood

From the novel Sir Gibbie. *A woman has just taken an orphan into her home.*

She was a mother. One who is mother only to her own children is not a mother; she is only a woman who has borne children. But here was one of God's mothers.

From the novel Warlock o' Glenwarlock. *Cosmo's father has been telling him about his mother, Marion, who died when he was very young.*

"You see, Cosmo, when a woman like that condescends to be wife to one of us and mother to the other, the least we can do, when she is taken from us, is to give her the same love and the same obedience after she is gone as when she was with us. She is with her own kind up in heaven now, but she may be looking down and watching us. It may be God lets her do that, that she may see of the travail of her soul and be satisfied—who can tell? She can't be very anxious about me now, for I am getting old, and my warfare is nearly over; but she may be getting things ready to rest me a bit. She knows I have for a long time now been trying to keep the straight path, as far as I could see it, though sometimes the grass and heather has got the better of it, so that it was hard to find.

"But *you* must remember, Cosmo, that it is not enough to be a good boy, as I shall tell her you have always been: you've got to be a good man, and that is a rather different and sometimes a harder thing. For, as soon as a man has to do with other men, he finds they expect him to do things they ought to be ashamed of doing themselves; and then he has got to stand on his own honest legs, and not move an inch for all their pushing and pulling; and especially where a man loves his fellow man and likes to be on good terms with him, that is not easy.

"The thing is just this, Cosmo—when you are a full-grown man, you must be a good boy still—that's the difficulty. For a man to be a boy, and a good boy still, he must be a thorough man. The man that's not manly can never be a good boy to his mother. And you can't keep true to your mother, except you remember Him who is father and mother both to all of us. I wish my Marion were here to teach you as she taught me. She taught me to pray, Cosmo, as I have tried to teach you—when I was in any trouble, just to go into my closet, and shut to the door, and pray to my Father who is in secret—the same Father who loved you so much as to give you my Marion for a mother. But I am getting old and tired, and shall soon go where I hope to learn faster. Oh, my boy! hear your father who loves you, and never do the thing you would be ashamed for your mother or me to know. Remember, nothing drops out; everything hid shall be revealed.

"But of all things, if ever you should fail or fall, don't lie still because you are down: get up again—for God's sake, for your mother's sake, for my sake—get up and try again."

From the novel The Vicar's Daughter. *A recently married woman is speaking.*

My father used often to say that the commonest things in the world were the loveliest,—sky and water and grass and such; now I found that the commonest feelings of humanity—for what feelings could be commoner than those which now made me blessed amongst women?—are those that are fullest of the divine.

Surely this looks as if there were a God of the whole earth,—as if the world existed in the very foundations of its history and continuance by the immediate thought of a causing thought. For simply because the life of the world was moving on towards its unseen goal, and I knew it and had a helpless share in it, I felt as if God was with me.

Fatherhood

From the novel Warlock o' Glenwarlock. *A young man who was raised by his father has left home, but keeps up a frequent and loving correspondence with him.*

Nobody knows what the relation of father and son may yet come to. Those who accept the Christian revelation are bound to recognize that there must be in it depths infinite, ages off being fathomed yet. For is it not a reproduction in small of the loftiest mystery in human ken—that of the infinite Father and infinite Son? If man be made in the image of God, then is the human fatherhood and sonship the image of the eternal relation between God and Jesus.

From the novel The Seaboard Parish. *The narrator's daughter has just recovered from a long illness.*

This brings me to speak again of my lovely child. For surely a father may speak thus of a child of God. He cannot regard his child as his even as a book he has written may be his. A man's child is his because God has said to him, "Take this child and nurse it for me." She is God's making; God's marvellous invention, to be tended and cared for, and ministered unto as one of his precious things; a young angel, let me say, who needs the air of this lower world to make her wings grow.

And while he regards her thus, he will see all other children in the same light, and will not dare to set up his own against others of God's brood with the new-budding wings. The universal heart of truth will thus rectify, while it intensifies, the individual feeling towards one's own; and the man who is most free from poor partisanship in regard to his own family, will feel the most individual tenderness for the lovely human creatures whom God has given into his own especial care and responsibility.

Show me the man who is tender, reverential, gracious towards the children of other men, and I will show you the man who will love and tend his own best, to whose heart his own will flee for their first refuge after God, when they catch sight of the cloud in the wind.

Parents

From the novel Paul Faber, Surgeon. *A young woman's father had died.*

Few griefs can be so paralyzing as, for a time, that of a true daughter upon the departure, which at first she feels as the loss, of a true parent; but through the rifts of such heartbreaks the light of love shines clearer, and where love is, there is eternity: one day He who is the Householder of the universe, will begin to bring out of its treasury all the good old things, as well as the better new ones.

How true must be the bliss up to which the intense realities of such sorrows are needful to force the way for the faithless heart and feeble will! Lord, like Thy people of old, we need yet the background of the thunder-cloud against which to behold Thee.

She reflects on "how hard he had fought with [his imperfections]" and how this increased her love for him.

The marvel is that our children are so tender and so trusting to the slow developing father in us. The truth and faith which the great Father has put in the heart of the child, makes him the nursing father of the fatherhood in his father; and thus in part it is, that the children of men will come at last to know the great Father. The family, with all its powers for the development of society, is a family because it is born and rooted in, and grows out of the very bosom of God. Gabriel told Zacharias that his son John, to make ready a people prepared for the Lord, should turn the hearts of the fathers to the children.

From the book for children The Princess and Curdie. *Curdie is the son of a miner and his wife.*

There must be something wrong when a mother catches herself sighing over the time when her boy was in petticoats, or a father looks sad when he thinks how he used to carry him on his shoulder. The boy should enclose and keep, as his life, the old child at the heart of him, and never let it go. He must still, to be a right man, be his mother's darling, and more, his father's pride, and more. The child is not meant to die, but to be forever fresh born.

✦ ✦ ✦

There was a change upon Curdie, and father and mother felt there must be something to account for it, and therefore were pretty sure he had something to tell them. For when a child's heart is all right, it is not likely he will want to keep anything from his parents.

From the novel Weighed and Wanting. *The son of a devout couple is "[n]aturally kind-hearted, yet, full of self and its poor importance, he had an admiration of certain easy and showy virtues."*

Wise as was the mother, and far-seeing as was the father, they had made the mistake common to all but the wisest parents, of putting off to a period more or less too late the moment of beginning to teach their children obedience. If this be not commenced at the first possible moment, there is no better reason why it should be begun at any other, except that it will be the harder every hour it is postponed. The spiritual loss and injury caused to the child by their waiting till they fancy him fit to reason with, is immense; yet there is nothing in which parents are more stupid and cowardly, if not stiff-necked, than this. I do not speak of those mere animal parents, whose lasting influence over their progeny is not a thing to be greatly desired, but of those who, having a conscience, yet avoid this part of their duty in a manner of which a good motherly cat would be ashamed. To one who has learned of all things to desire deliverance from himself, a nursery in which the children are humored and scolded and punished instead of being taught obedience, looks like a moral slaughter-house.

From the novel David Elginbrod. *David and Janet's only child, Margaret, is about to leave home for the first time.*

Janet could not bear the idea of her lady-bairn leaving them, to encounter the world alone; but David, though he could not help sometimes feeling a similar pang, was able to take to himself hearty comfort from the thought, that if there was any safety for her in her father's house, there could not be less in her heavenly Father's, in any nook of which she was as full in His eye, and as near His heart, as in their own cottage.

He felt that anxiety in this case, as in every other, would just be a lack of confidence in God, to suppose which justifiable would be equivalent to saying that He had not fixed the foundations of the earth that it should not be moved; that He was not the Lord of Life, nor the Father of His children; in short, that a sparrow could fall to the ground without Him, and that the hairs of our head are not numbered. Janet admitted all this, but sighed nevertheless. So did David too, at times; for he knew that the sparrow must fall; that many a divine truth is hard to learn, all-blessed as it is when learned; and that sorrow and suffering must come to Margaret, ere she could be fashioned into the perfection of a child of the kingdom. Still, she was as safe abroad as at home.

From the novel The Seaboard Parish. *A father watches his sleeping child.*

When parents see their children asleep, especially if they have been suffering in any way, they breathe more freely; a load is lifted off their minds; their responsibility seems over; the children have gone back to their Father, and he alone is looking after them for a while.

---

lady-bairn daughter

From the same novel. A young woman's father is considering her relationship to her fiancé, Mr. Percivale.

I had no doubt that she had made some sort of apology to Mr. Percivale; but I did not make the slightest attempt to discover what had passed between them, for though it is of all things desirable that children should be quite open with their parents, I was most anxious to lay upon them no burden of obligation. For such burden lies against the door of utterance, and makes it the more difficult to open. It paralyses the speech of the soul. What I desired was that they should trust me so that faith should overcome all difficulty that might lie in the way of their being open with me. That end is not to be gained by any urging of admonition. Against such, growing years at least, if nothing else, will bring a strong reaction. Nor even, if so gained would the gain be at all of the right sort. The openness would not be faith.

Besides, a parent must respect the spiritual person of his child, and approach it with reverence, for that too looks the Father in the face, and has an audience with him into which no earthly parent can enter even if he dared to desire it. Therefore I trusted my child.

From a letter to his daughter Mary Josephine—"Elfie"—written when she was sixteen, in response to her request for a definition of "love."

My darling Elfie!

. . . I will with all my heart try to answer your question. And in order to make it as plain as I can I will put the answer in separate parts. You think over each of them separately and all of them together.

In order to anyone loving another, three things are necessary.

1st. That the one should be capable of loving the other, or loving in nature.

2nd. That the other should be fit to be loved or loveable.

3rd. That the one should know the other.

Upon each of these three Points respectively I remark:

1st. Now we are capable of loving, but are not capable enough, and the very best, the only thing indeed that we can do to make ourselves more capable is to do our duty. When a person will not do his duty, he gradually becomes incapable of loving, for it is only good people that can love. All who can love are so far good. For if man were to grow quite wicked he could only hate. Therefore to do our duty is the main thing to lead us to the love of God.

2nd. God is so beautiful, and so patient, and so loving, and so generous that he is the heart and soul and rock of every love and every kindness and every gladness in the world. All the beauty in the world and in the hearts of men, all the painting all the poetry all the music, all the architecture comes out of his heart first. He is so loveable that no heart can know how loveable he is—can only know it in part. When the best loves God best, he does not love him nearly as he deserves, or as he will love him in time.

3rd. In order that we should know God, and so see how loveable he is, we must first of all know and understand Jesus Christ. When we understand what he meant when he spoke, and why he did the things he did, when we see into his heart, then we shall understand God, for Jesus is just what God is. To do this we must read and think. We must also ask God to let us know what he is. For he can do more for those who ask than for those who do not ask.

But if it all depended on us, we might well lose heart about it. For we can never do our duty right until we love God. We can only go on trying. Love is the best thing: the Love of God is the highest thing; we cannot be right—I mean thoroughly right—until we love God. But God knows this better than we do, and he is always teaching us to love him. He wants us to love him, not because he loves himself, but because it is the only wise, good, and joyous thing for us to love him who made us and is most lovely.

So you need not be troubled about it darling Elfie. All you have to do and that is plenty is to go on doing what you know to be right, to keep your heart turned to God for him to lead you, and to read and try to understand the story of Jesus. A thousand other things will come in from God to help you if you do thus.

I am very glad you asked me my child. Ask me anything you like, I will try to answer you—if I know the answer. For this is one of the most important things I have to do in the world.

Mama sends her dear love to you.

Your Father

19.

Education

From the novel Robert Falconer. *A boy has few books available to him, but is being taught by "the face and voice of Nature."*

It is good that children of faculty, as distinguished from capacity, should not have too many books to read, or too much of early lessoning. The increase of examinations in our country will increase its capacity and diminish its faculty. We shall have more compilers and reducers and fewer thinkers; more modifiers and completers, and fewer inventors.

From the novel The Vicar's Daughter. *Theodora is a beloved but mischievous child whose mother has left her in the care of another family. The speaker is a grown daughter.*

But to return to Theodora. She was subject to attacks of the most furious passion, especially when any thing occurred to thwart the indulgence of the ephemeral partiality I have just described. Then, wherever she was, she would throw herself down at once,—on the floor, on the walk or lawn, or, as happened on one occasion, in the water,—and kick and scream. At such times she cared nothing even for my father, of whom generally she stood in considerable awe,—a feeling he rather encouraged. "She has plenty of people about her to represent the gospel," he said once. "I will keep the department of the law, without which she will never appreciate the gospel. My part will, I trust, vanish in due time, and the law turn out to have been, after all, only the imperfect gospel, just as the leaf is the imperfect flower. But the gospel is no gospel till it gets into the heart, and it sometimes wants a torpedo to blow the gates of that open."

From the novel Malcolm. *Malcolm has begun to teach alongside his former teacher, Mr. Graham.*

This matter settled, the business of the school, in which, as he did often, Malcolm had come to assist, began. Only a pupil of his own could have worked with Mr. Graham, for his mode was very peculiar. But the strangest fact in it would have been the last to reveal itself to an ordinary observer. This was, that he rarely contradicted anything: he would call up the opposing truth, set it face to face with the error, and leave the two to fight it out.

The human mind and conscience were, he said, the plains of Armageddon, where the battle of good and evil was forever raging; and the one business of a teacher was to rouse and urge this battle by leading fresh forces of the truth into the field—forces composed as little as might be of the hireling troops of the intellect, and as much as possible of the native energies of the heart, imagination, and conscience. In a word, he would oppose error only by teaching the truth.

From the novel Donal Grant. *Davie's older sister, Arctura, joins his lesson with his tutor Donal Grant.*

Towards the close of school, as Donal was beginning to give his lesson in religion, Lady Arctura entered, and sat down beside Davie.

"What would you think of me, Davie," Donal was saying, "if I were angry with you because you did not know something I had never taught you?"

Davie only laughed. It was to him a grotesque, an impossible supposition.

"If," Donal resumed, "I were to show you a proposition of Euclid which you had never seen before, and say to you, 'Now, Davie, this is one of the most beautiful of all Euclid's propositions, and you must immediately admire it, and admire Euclid for constructing it!'—what would you say?"

Davie thought, and looked puzzled.

"But you wouldn't do it, sir!" he said. "I know you wouldn't do it!" he added, after a moment.

"Why should I not?"

"It isn't your way, sir."

"But suppose I were to take that way?"

"You would not then be like yourself, sir!"

"Tell me how I should be unlike myself. Think."

"You would not be reasonable."

"What would you say to me?"

"I should say, 'Please, sir, let me learn the proposition first, and then I shall be able to admire it. I don't know it yet!'"

"Very good!—Now again, suppose, when you tried to learn it, you were not able to do so, and therefore could see no beauty in it—should I blame you?"

"No, sir; I am sure you would not—because I should not be to blame, and it would not be fair; and you never do what is not fair!"

"I am glad you think so: I try to be fair.—That looks as if you believed in me, Davie!"

"Of course I do, sir!"

"Why?"

"Just because you are fair."

"Suppose, Davie, I said to you, 'Here is a very beautiful thing I should like you to learn,' and you, after you had partly learned it, were to say 'I don't see anything beautiful in this: I am afraid I never shall!'—would that be to believe in me?"

"No, surely, sir! for you know best what I am able for."

"Suppose you said, 'I daresay it is all as good as you say, but I don't care to take so much trouble about it,'—what would that be?"

"Not to believe in you, sir. You would not want me to learn a thing that was not worth my trouble, or a thing I should not be glad of knowing when I did know it."

"Suppose you said, 'Sir, I don't doubt what you say, but I am so tired, I don't mean to do anything more you tell me,'—would you then be believing in me?"

"No. That might be to believe your word, but it would not be to trust you. It would be to think my thinks better than your thinks, and that would be no faith at all."

Davie had at times an oddly childish way of putting things.

"Suppose you were to say nothing, but go away and do nothing of what I told you—what would that be?"

"Worse and worse; it would be sneaking."

"One question more: what is faith—the big faith I mean—not the little faith between equals—the big faith we put in one above us?"

"It is to go at once and do the thing he tells us to do."

"If we don't, then we haven't faith in him?"

"No; certainly not."

"But might not that be his fault?"

"Yes—if he was not good—and so I could not trust him. If he said I was to do one kind of thing, and he did another kind of thing himself, then of course I could not have faith in him."

"And yet you might feel you must do what he told you!"

"Yes."

"Would that be faith in him?"

"No."

"Would you always do what he told you?"

"Not if he told me to do what it would be wrong to do."

"Now tell me, Davie, what is the biggest faith of all—the faith to put in the one only altogether good person."

"You mean God, Mr. Grant?"

"Whom else could I mean?"

"You might mean Jesus."

"They are one; they mean always the same thing, do always the same thing, always agree. There is only one thing they don't do the same in—they do not love the same person."

"What do you mean, Mr. Grant?" interrupted Arctura.

She had been listening intently: was the cloven foot of Mr. Grant's heresy now at last about to appear plainly?

"I mean this," answered Donal, with a smile that seemed to Arctura such a light as she had never seen on human face, "that God loves Jesus, not God; and Jesus loves God, not Jesus. We love one another, not ourselves—don't we, Davie?"

"You do, Mr. Grant," answered Davie modestly.

"Now tell me, Davie, what is the great big faith of all—that which we have to put in the Father of us, who is as good not only as thought can think, but as good as heart can wish—infinitely better than anybody but Jesus Christ can think—what is the faith to put in him?"

"Oh, it is everything!" answered Davie.

"But what first?" asked Donal.

"First, it is to do what he tells us."

"Yes, Davie: it is to learn his problems by going and doing his will; not trying to understand things first, but trying first to do things. We must spread out our arms to him as a child does to his mother when he wants her to take him; then when he sets us down, saying, 'Go and do this or that,' we must make all the haste in us to go and do it. And when we get hungry to see him, we must look at his picture."

"Where is that, sir?"

"Ah, Davie, Davie! don't you know that yet? Don't you know that, besides being himself, and just because he is himself, Jesus is the living picture of God?"

"I know, sir! We have to go and read about him in the book."

"May I ask you a question, Mr. Grant?" said Arctura.

"With perfect freedom," answered Donal. "I only hope I may be able to answer it."

"When we read about Jesus, we have to draw for ourselves his likeness from words, and you know what kind of a likeness the best artist would make that way, who had never seen with his own eyes the person whose portrait he had to paint!"

"I understand you quite," returned Donal. "Some go to other men to draw it for them; and some go to others to hear from them what they must draw—thus getting all their blunders in addition to those they must make for themselves. But the nearest likeness you can see of him, is the one drawn by yourself while doing what he tells you. He has promised to come into those who keep his word. He will then be much nearer to them than in bodily presence; and such may well be able to draw for themselves the likeness of God. —But first of all, and before everything else, mind, Davie, *obedience!*"

"Yes, Mr. Grant; I know," said Davie.

"Then off with you! Only think sometimes it is God who gave you your game."

"I'm going to fly my kite, Mr. Grant."

"Do. God likes to see you fly your kite, and it is all in his March wind it flies. It could not go up a foot but for that."

From a letter to his oldest son written when he was thirty-one.

Many good birthdays be yours, as many will surely be, if only we let the Lord have his way for and with us. More and more I see and feel that what the Father is thinking is my whole treasure and well being. To be one with him seems the only common sense, as well as the only peace.

Let him do with you, my beloved son, as he wills. Be hearty with his will.

20.

Money

From the novel Paul Faber, Surgeon. *A man has lost all his wealth:* "The fact is . . . we are very poor—absolutely poor."

A man ought never to feel rich for riches, nor poor for poverty. The perfect man must always feel rich, because God is rich.

From the novel Weighed and Wanting. *Describing a poor household.*

Our Lord never mentions poverty as one of the obstructions to his kingdom, neither has it ever proved such; riches, cares and desires he does mention.

From the novel Warlock o' Glenwarlock. *A poor man has discovered a treasure hidden in the walls of his house; he is considering how to use his new wealth.*

And the way to use money is not so easily discovered as some would think, for it is not one of God's ready means of doing good. The rich man as such has no reason to look upon himself as specially favoured. He has reason to think himself specially tried. Jesus, loving a certain youth, did him the greatest kindness he had in his power, telling him to give his wealth to the poor, and follow him in poverty.

The first question is not how to do good with money, but how to keep from doing harm with it. Whether rich or poor, a man must first of all do justice, love mercy, and walk humbly with his God; then, if he be rich, God will let him know how to spend. There must be ways in which, even now, a man may give the half, or even the whole of his goods to the poor, without helping the devil. . . .

[I]t is not because of God's poverty that the world is so slowly redeemed. Not the most righteous expenditure of money will save it, but that of life and soul and spirit—it may be, to that, of nerve and muscle, blood and brain. All these our Lord spent—but no money. Therefore I say, that of all means for saving the world, or doing good, as it is called, money comes last in order, and far behind.

From the novel What's Mine's Mine. *The chief of a Scottish clan is prepared to sell his ancestral land to protect the tenant farmers who live on it.*

Those who feel as if the land were their own, do fearful wrong to their own souls! What grandest opportunities of growing divine they lose! Instead of being man-nobles, leading a sumptuous life until it no longer looks sumptuous, they might be God-nobles—saviours of men, yielding themselves to and for their brethren! What friends might they not make with the mammon of unrighteousness, instead of passing hence into a region where no doors, no arms will be open to them! Things are ours that we may use them for all—sometimes that we may sacrifice them. God had but one precious thing, and he gave that!

From the novel Wilfrid Cumbermede. *Wilfrid, about to leave home for boarding school, is for some days so pleased with a parting gift that he is inconsiderate of the people he will be leaving.*

But happily for our blessedness, the joy of possession soon palls.

From the novel David Elginbrod. *Hugh's wealthy employer, Mrs. Glasford, has criticized him for having what she considers unsuitable friends. Later in the day, he is interrupted in his reading by one of these friends, David Elginbrod.*

By and by David came in.

"I'm ower sune, I doubt, Mr. Sutherlan'. I'm disturbin' ye."

"Not at all," answered Hugh. "Besides, I am not much in a reading mood this evening: Mrs. Glasford has been annoying me again."

"Poor body! What's she been sayin' noo?"

Thinking to amuse David, Hugh recounted the short passage between them recorded above. David, however, listened with a very different expression of countenance from what Hugh had anticipated; and, when he had finished, took up the conversation in a kind of apologetic tone.

"Weel, but ye see," said he, folding his palms together, "she hasna' jist had a'thegither fair play. She does na come o' a guid breed. Man, it's a fine thing to come o' a guid breed. They hae a hantle to answer for 'at come o' decent forbears."

---

ower sune too early
a hantle much

"I thought she brought the laird a good property," said Hugh, not quite understanding David.

"Ow, ay, she brocht him gowpenfu's o' siller; but hoo was't gotten? An' ye ken it's no riches 'at 'ill mak' a guid breed—'cep' it be o' maggots. The richer cheese the mair maggots, ye ken. Ye maunna speyk o' this; but the mistress's father was weel kent to hae made his siller by fardins and bawbees, in creepin', crafty ways. He was a bit merchan' in Aberdeen, an' aye keepit his thoom weel ahint the peint o' the ellwan', sae 'at he made an inch or twa upo' ilka yard he sauld. Sae he took frae his soul, and pat intill his siller-bag, an' had little to gie his dochter but a guid tocher.

"Mr. Sutherlan', it's a fine thing to come o' dacent fowk. Noo, to luik at yersel': I ken naething aboot yer family; but ye seem at eesicht to come o' a guid breed for the bodily part o' ye. That's a sma' matter; but frae what I ha'e seen—an' I trust in God I'm no' mista'en—ye come o' the richt breed for the min' as weel. I'm no flatterin' ye, Mr. Sutherlan'; but jist layin' it upo' ye, 'at gin ye had an honest father and gran'father, an' especially a guid mither, ye hae a heap to answer for; an' ye ought never to be hard upo' them 'at's sma' creepin' creatures, for they canna help it sae weel as the like o' you and me can."

---

gowpenfu's double-handful
siller silver
ken know
maunna must not
weel kent well known
fardins and bawbees small change
thoom weel ahint the peint o' the ellwan' thumb well behind the point of the elbow
ilka every
guid tocher good dowry
eesicht eyesight

From the novel The Elect Lady. *Alexa is teased about her farmer friend Andrew by George, an aristocratic and wealthy admirer.*

"Of our friend Andrew?" supplemented George, with a spiteful laugh. "The only honest mode of making money he knows is the strain of his muscles—the farmer-way! He wouldn't keep up his corn for a better market—not he!"

"It so happens that I know he would not; for he and my father had a dispute on that very point, and I heard them. He said poor people were not to go hungry that he might get rich. He was not sent into the world to make money, he said, but to grow corn. The corn was grown, and he could get enough for it now to live by, and had no right, and no desire to get more—and would not keep it up! The land was God's, not his, and the poor were God's children, and had their rights from him! He was sent to grow corn for them!"

From a sermon about the rich young man.

Having kept the commandments, the youth needed and was ready for a further lesson: the Lord would not leave him where he was; he had come to seek and to save. He saw him in sore need of perfection—the thing the commonplace Christian thinks he can best do without—the thing the elect hungers after with an eternal hunger. Perfection, the perfection of the Father, is eternal life. 'If thou wouldest be perfect,' said the Lord. What an honour for the youth to be by him supposed desirous of perfection! And what an enormous demand does he, upon the supposition, make of him!

To gain the perfection he desired, the one thing lacking was, that he should sell all that he had, give it to the poor, and follow the Lord! Could this be all that lay between him and entering into life? God only knows what the victory of such an obedience might at once have wrought in him! Much, much more would be necessary before perfection was reached, but certainly the next step, to sell and follow, would have been the step into life: had he taken it, in the very act would have been born in him that whose essence and vitality is eternal life, needing but process to develop it into the glorious consciousness of oneness with The Life.

There was nothing like this in the law: was it not hard?—Hard to let earth go, and take heaven instead? for eternal life, to let dead things drop? to turn his back on Mammon, and follow Jesus? lose his rich friends, and be of the Master's household? Let him say it was hard who does not know the Lord, who has never thirsted after righteousness, never longed for the life eternal!

The youth had got on so far, was so pleasing in the eyes of the Master, that he would show him the highest favour he could; he would take him to be with him—to walk with him, and rest with him, and go from him only to do for him what he did for his Father in heaven—to plead with men, be a mediator between God and men. He would set him free at once, a child of the kingdom, an heir of the life eternal.

I do not suppose that the youth was one whom ordinary people would call a lover of money; I do not believe he was covetous, or desired even the large increase of his possessions; I imagine he was just like most good men of property: he valued his possessions—looked on them as a good. I suspect that in the case of another, he would have regarded such possession almost as a merit, a desert; would value a man more who had *means,* value a man less who had none—like most of my readers. They have not a notion how entirely they will one day have to alter their judgment, or have it altered for them, in this respect: well for them if they alter it for themselves!

From this false way of thinking, and all the folly and unreality that accompany it, the Lord would deliver the young man. As the thing was, he was a slave; for a man is in bondage to whatever he cannot part with that is less than himself. He could have taken his possessions from him by an exercise of his own will, but there would have been little good in that; he wished to do it by the exercise of the young man's will: that would be a victory indeed for both! So would he enter into freedom and life, delivered from the bondage of mammon by the lovely will of the Lord in him, one with his own. By the putting forth of the divine energy in him, he would escape the corruption that is in the world through lust—that is, the desire or pleasure of *having*.

The young man would not.

Was the Lord then premature in his demand on the youth? Was he not ready for it? Was it meant for a test, and not as an actual word of deliverance? Did he show the child a next step on the stair too high for him to set his foot upon? I do not believe it. He gave him the very next lesson in the divine education for which he was ready. It was possible for him to respond, to give birth, by obedience, to the redeemed and redeeming will, and so be free. It was time the demand should be made upon him. Do you say, 'But he would not respond, he would not obey!'? Then it was time, I answer, that he should refuse, that he should know what manner of spirit he was of, and meet the confusions of soul, the sad searchings of heart that must follow. A time comes to every man when he must obey, or make such refusal—*and know it*.

Shall I then be supposed to mean that the refusal of the young man was of necessity final? that he was therefore lost? that because he declined to enter into life the door of life was closed against him? Verily, I have not so learned Christ. And that the lesson was not lost, I see in this, that he went away sorrowful. Was such sorrow, in the mind of an earnest youth, likely to grow less or to grow more? Was all he had gone through in the way of obedience to be of no good to him? Could the nature of one who had kept the commandments be so slight that, after having sought and talked with Jesus, held communion with him who is the Life, he would care less about eternal life than before? Many, alas! have looked upon his face, yet have never seen him, and have turned back; some have kept company with him for years, and denied him; but their weakness is not the measure of the patience or the resources of God.

Perhaps this youth was never one of the Lord's so long as he was on the earth, but perhaps when he saw that the Master himself cared nothing for the wealth he had told him to cast away, that, instead of ascending the throne of his fathers, he let the people do with him what they would, and left the world the poor man he had lived in it, by its meanest door, perhaps then he became one of those who sold all they had, and came and laid the money at the apostles' feet.

In the meantime he had that in his soul which made it heavy: by the gravity of his riches the world held him, and would not let him rise. He counted his weight his strength, and it was his weakness. Moneyless in God's upper air he would have had power indeed. Money is the power of this world—power for defeat and failure to him who holds it—a weakness to be overcome ere a man can be strong; yet many decent people fancy it a power of the world to come! It is indeed a little power, as food and drink, as bodily strength, as the winds and the waves are powers; but it is no mighty thing for the redemption of men; yea, to the redemption of those who have it, it is the saddest obstruction. To make this youth capable of eternal life, clearly—and the more clearly that he went away sorrowful—the first thing was to make a poor man of him! He would doubtless have gladly devoted his wealth to the service of the Master, yea, and gone with him, *as a rich man*, to spend it for him. But part with it to free him for his service—that he could not—*yet*!

And how now would he go on with his keeping of the commandments? Would he not begin to see more plainly his shortcomings, the larger scope of their requirements? Might he not feel the keeping of them more imperative than ever, yet impossible without something he had not? The commandments can never be kept while there is a strife to keep them: the man is overwhelmed in the weight of their broken pieces. It needs a clean heart to have pure hands, all the power of a live soul to keep the law—a power of life, not of struggle; the strength of love, not the effort of duty.

One day the truth of his conduct must dawn upon him with absolute clearness. Bitter must be the discovery. He had refused the life eternal! had turned his back upon The Life! In deepest humility and shame, yet with the profound consolation of repentance, he would return to the Master and bemoan his unteachableness. There are who, like St. Paul, can say, "I did wrong, but I did it in ignorance; my heart was not right, and I did not know it:" the remorse of such must be very different from that of one who, brought to the point of being capable of embracing the truth, turned from it and refused to be set free. To him the time will come, God only knows its hour, when he will see the nature of his deed, *with the knowledge that he was dimly seeing it so even when he did it*: the alternative had been put before him. And all those months, or days, or hours, or

moments, he might have been following the Master, hearing the
words he spoke, through the windows of his eyes looking into
the very gulfs of Godhead!

The sum of the matter in regard to the youth is this:—He had
begun early to climb the eternal stair. He had kept the commandments, and by every keeping had climbed. But because he
was *well to do*—a phrase of unconscious irony—he felt well to
be—quite, but for that lack of eternal life! His possessions gave
him a standing in the world—a position of consequence—of
value in his eyes. He knew himself looked up to; he liked to be
looked up to; he looked up to himself because of his *means*, forgetting that *means* are but tools, and poor tools too. To part with
his wealth would be to sink to the level of his inferiors! Why
should he not keep it? why not use it in the service of the Master?
What wisdom could there be in throwing away such a grand
advantage? He could devote it, but he could not cast it from him!
He could devote it, but he could not devote himself! He could
not make himself naked as a little child and let his Father take
him! To him it was not the word of wisdom the 'Good Master'
spoke. How could precious money be a hindrance to entering
into life! How could a rich man believe he would be of more
value without his money? that the casting of it away would make
him one of God's Anakim? that the battle of God could be better
fought without its impediment? that his work refused as an
obstruction the aid of wealth? But the Master had repudiated
money that he might do the will of his Father; and the disciple
must be as his master. Had he done as the Master told him, he
would soon have come to understand. Obedience is the opener
of eyes.

✦ ✦ ✦

To return to the summing up of the matter:—

The youth, climbing the stair of eternal life, had come to a landing-place where not a step more was visible. On the cloud-swathed platform he stands looking in vain for further ascent. What he thought with himself he wanted, I cannot tell: his idea of eternal life I do not know; I can hardly think it was but the poor idea of living forever, all that commonplace minds grasp at for eternal life—its mere concomitant shadow, in itself not worth thinking about, not for a moment to be disputed, and taken for granted by all devout Jews: when a man has eternal life, that is, when he is one with God, what should he do but live forever? without oneness with God, the continuance of existence would be to me the all but unsurpassable curse—the unsurpassable itself being, a God other than the God I see in Jesus; but whatever his idea, it must have held in it, though perhaps only in solution, all such notions as he had concerning God and man and a common righteousness. While thus he stands, then, alone and helpless, behold the form of the Son of Man! It is God himself come to meet the climbing youth, to take him by the hand, and lead him up his own stair, the only stair by which ascent can be made. He shows him the first step of it through the mist. His feet are heavy; they have golden shoes. To go up that stair he must throw aside his shoes. He must walk bare-footed into life eternal. Rather than so, rather than stride free-limbed up the everlasting stair to the bosom of the Father, he will keep his precious shoes! It is better to drag them about on the earth, than part with them for a world where they are useless!

But how miserable his precious things, his golden vessels, his embroidered garments, his stately house, must have seemed when he went back to them from the face of the Lord! Surely it cannot have been long before in shame and misery he cast all from him, even as Judas cast from him the thirty pieces of silver, in the agony of every one who wakes to the fact that he has preferred money to the Master! For, although never can man be saved without being freed from his possessions, it is yet only hard, not impossible, for a rich man to enter into the kingdom of God.

From a sermon.

But it is not the rich man only who is under the dominion of things; they too are slaves who, having no money, are unhappy from the lack of it.

From a sermon.

One may readily conclude how poorly God thinks of riches when we see the sort of people he sends them to.

21.

Moralism

From the novel What's Mine's Mine. *Describing a mother who abides strictly by church doctrine; she and her grown son have been talking about matters of belief.*

The patience of God must surely be far more tried by those who would interpret Him than by those who deny Him; the latter speak lies against Him, the former speak lies for Him! . . . She did not yet understand that salvation lies in being one with Christ, even as the branch is one with the vine;—that any salvation short of knowing God is no salvation at all. What moment a man feels that he belongs to God utterly, the atonement is there, the son of God is reaping his harvest.

The good mother was not, however, one of those conceited, stiff-necked, power-loving souls who have been the curse and ruin of the church in all ages; she was but one of those in whom reverence for its passing form dulls the perception of unchangeable truth. They shut up God's precious light in the horn lantern of human theory, and the lantern casts such shadows on the path to the kingdom as seem to dim eyes insurmountable obstructions. For the sake of what they count revealed, they refuse all further revelation, and what satisfies them is merest famine to

249

the next generation of the children of the kingdom. Instead of God's truth they offer man's theory, and accuse of rebellion against God such as cannot live on the husks they call food.

But ah, home-hungry soul! thy God is not the elder brother of the parable, but the father with the best robe and the ring—a God high above all thy longing, even as the heavens are high above the earth.

From the novel David Elginbrod. *In MacDonald's day the alternative to the Church of England was nonconformist chapels, whose original founders had sought to return to the fundamentals of Christianity. As time passed, the chapels became as strict in doctrine as the established church.*

Hugh Sutherland has just moved to a new neighborhood in search of work, and been invited to service at Salem Chapel by Mr. Appleditch, a prospective employer.

To the great discomposure of Hugh, Sunday was inevitable, and he had to set out for Salem Chapel. He found it a neat little Noah's Ark of a place, built in the shape of a cathedral, and consequently sharing in the general disadvantages to which dwarfs of all kinds are subjected, absurdity included. He was shown to Mr. Appleditch's pew. That worthy man received him in sleek black clothes, with white neck-cloth, and Sunday face composed of an absurd mixture of stupidity and sanctity. He stood up, and Mrs. Appleditch stood up, and Master Appleditch stood up, and Hugh saw that the ceremony of the place required that he should force his way between the front of the pew and the person of each of the human beings occupying it, till he reached the top, where there was room for him to sit down. No other recognition was taken till after service.

Meantime the minister ascended the pulpit stair, with all the solemnity of one of the self-elect, and a priest besides. He was just old enough for the intermittent attacks of self-importance to which all youth is exposed, to have in his case become chronic. He stood up and worshipped his creator aloud, after a manner which seemed to say in every tone: "Behold I am he that worshippeth Thee! How mighty art Thou!" Then he read the Bible in a quarrelsome sort of way, as if he were a bantam, and every verse were a crow of defiance to the sinner. Then they sang a hymn in a fashion which brought dear old Scotland to Hugh's mind, which has the sweetest songs in its cottages, and the worst singing in its churches, of any country in the world. But it was almost equaled here; the chief cause of its badness being the absence of a modest self-restraint, and consequent tempering of the tones, on the part of the singers; so that the result was what Hugh could describe only as scraichin. . . .

Then came the sermon. The text was the story of the good Samaritan. Some idea, if not of the sermon, yet of the value of it, may be formed from the fact, that the first thing to be considered, or, in other words, the first head was, "The culpable imprudence of the man in going from Jerusalem to Jericho without an escort."

It was in truth a strange, grotesque, and somewhat awful medley—not unlike a dance of death, in which the painter has given here a lovely face, and there a beautiful arm or an exquisite foot, to the wild-prancing and exultant skeletons. But the parts of the sermon corresponding to the beautiful face or arm or foot, were but the fragments of Scripture, shining like gold amidst the worthless ore of the man's own production—worthless, save as gravel or chaff or husks have worth, in a world where dilution, and not always concentration, is necessary for healthfulness.

But there are Indians who eat clay, and thrive on it more or less, I suppose. The power of assimilation which a growing nature must possess is astonishing. It will find its food, its real Sunday dinner, in the midst of a whole cartload of refuse; and it will do the whole week's work on it. On no other supposition would it be possible to account for the earnest face of Miss Talbot, which Hugh espied turned up to the preacher, as if his face were the very star in the east, shining to guide the chosen kings. It was well for Hugh's power of endurance, that he had heard much the same thing in Scotland, and the same thing better dressed, and less grotesque, but more lifeless, and at heart as ill-mannered, in the church of Arnstead.

Just before concluding the service, the pastor made an announcement in the following terms: "After the close of the present service, I shall be found in the adjoining vestry by all persons desirous of communicating with me on the state of their souls, or of being admitted to the privileges of church-fellowship. Brethren, we have this treasure in earthen vessels, and so long as this vessel lasts"—here he struck his chest so that it resounded—"it shall be faithfully and liberally dispensed. Let us pray."

After the prayer, he spread abroad his arms and hands as if he would clasp the world in his embrace, and pronounced the benediction in a style of arrogance that the pope himself would have been ashamed of.

The service being thus concluded, the organ absolutely blasted the congregation out of the chapel, so did it storm and rave with a fervour anything but divine.

My readers must not suppose that I give this chapel as the type of orthodox dissenting chapels. I give it only as an approximate specimen of a large class of them. The religious life which these communities once possessed, still lingers in those of many country districts and small towns, but is, I fear, all but gone from those of the cities and larger towns. What of it remains in these, has its chief manifestation in the fungous growth of such chapels as the one I have described, the congregations themselves taking this for a sure indication of the prosperity of the body. How much even of the kind of prosperity which they ought to indicate, is in reality at the foundation of these appearances, I would recommend those to judge who are versed in the mysteries of chapel-building societies.

As to Hugh, whether it was that the whole was suggestive of Egyptian bondage, or that his own mood was, at the time, of the least comfortable sort, I will not pretend to determine; but he assured me that he felt all the time, as if, instead of being in a chapel built of bricks harmoniously arranged, as by the lyre of Amphion, he were wandering in the waste, wretched field whence these bricks had been dug, of all places on the earth's surface the most miserable, assailed by the nauseous odours, which have not character enough to be described, and only remind one of the colours on a snake's back.

From the novel Guild Court. *Describing a pious woman.*

Can I hope to move my readers to any pitiful sympathy with Mrs. Worboise? That she is not an interesting woman, I admit; but at the same time, I venture to express a doubt whether our use of the word uninteresting really expresses any thing more than our own ignorance. If we could look into the movements of any heart, I doubt very much whether that heart would be any longer uninteresting to us. Come with me, reader, while I endeavor, with some misgiving, I confess, to open a peep into the heart of this mother, which I have tried hard, though with scarcely satisfactory success, to understand.

Her chief faculty lay in negations. Her whole life was a kind of negation—a negation of warmth, a negation of impulse, a negation of beauty, a negation of health. . . . Now, in so far as this idea had laid hold of the boy, it had aroused the instinct of self-preservation mingled with a repellent feeling in regard to God. All that was poor and common and selfish in him was stirred up on the side of religion; all that was noble (and of that there was far more than my reader will yet fancy) was stirred up against it. The latter, however, was put down by degrees, leaving the whole region, when the far outlook of selfishness should be dimmed by the near urgings of impulse, open to the inroads of the enemy, enfeebled and ungarrisoned. Ah: if she could have told the boy, every time his soul was lifted up within him by anything beautiful, or great, or true, "That, my boy, is God—God telling you that you must be beautiful, and great, and true, else you cannot be his child."

If every time he uttered his delight in flower or bird, she had, instead of speaking of sin and shortcoming, spoken of love and aspiration toward the Father of Light, the God of Beauty! If she had been able to show him that what he admired in Byron's heroes, even, was the truth, courage, and honesty, hideously mingled, as it might be, with cruelty, and conceit, and lies! But almost every thing except the Epistles seemed to her of the devil and not of God. She was even jealous of the Gospel of God, lest it should lead him astray from the interpretation she put upon it. She did not understand that nothing can convince of sin but the vision of holiness; that to draw near to the Father is to leave self behind; that the Son of God appeared that by the sight of himself he might convince the world of sin. But then hers was a life that had never broken the shell, while through the shell the worm of suffering had eaten, and was boring in to her soul. Have pity and not contempt, reader, who would not be like her. . . .

If, instead of constantly referring to the hell that lies in the future, she had reminded him of the beginnings of that hell in his own bosom, appealing to himself whether there was not a faintness there that indicated something wrong, a dull pain that might grow to a burning agony, a consciousness of wrong-doing, thinking, and feeling, a sense of a fearful pit and a miry clay within his own being from which he would gladly escape, a failing even from the greatness of such grotesque ideals as he loved in poetry, a meanness, paltriness, and at best insignificance of motive and action,—and then told him that out of this was God stretching forth the hand to take and lift him, that he was waiting to exalt him to a higher ideal of manhood than any thing which it had entered into his heart to conceive, that he would make him clean from the defilement which he was afraid to confess to himself because it lowered him in his own esteem,—then perhaps the words of his mother, convincing him that God was not against him but for him, on the side of his best feelings and against his worst, might have sunk into the heart of the weak youth, and he would straightway have put forth what strength he had, and so begun to be strong. . . .

And although she was none the less a time-server and a worldly-minded woman that she decried worldliness and popery, and gave herself to the saving of her soul, yet the God who makes them loves even such people and knows all about them; and it is well for them that he is their judge and not we.

From the novel Donal Grant. *The minister in the town Donal has just moved to is a small-minded pedant.*

Donal went for a stroll through the town, and met the minister, but he took no notice of him . . . regarded him as one who had taken an unfair advantage of him. But he had little influence at the castle. The earl never by any chance went to church. His niece, Lady Arctura, did, however, and held the minister for an authority at things spiritual—one of whom living water was to be had without money and without price. But what she counted spiritual things were very common earthly stuff, and for the water, it was but stagnant water from the ditches of a sham theology.

Only what was a poor girl to do who did not know how to feed herself, but apply to one who pretended to be able to feed others? How was she to know that he could not even feed himself? Out of many a difficulty she thought he helped her—only the difficulty would presently clasp her again, and she must deal with it as she best could, until a new one made her forget it, and go to the minister, or rather to his daughter, again. She was one of those who feel the need of some help to live—some upholding that is not of themselves, but who, through the stupidity of teachers unconsciously false,—men so unfit that they do not know they are unfit, direct their efforts, first towards having correct notions, then to work up the feelings that belong to those notions. She was an honest girl so far as she had been taught—perhaps not so far as she might have been without having been taught.

How was she to think aright with scarce a glimmer of God's truth? How was she to please God, as she called it, who thought of him in a way repulsive to every loving soul? How was she to be accepted of God, who did not accept her own neighbour, but looked down, without knowing it, upon so many of her fellow-creatures? How should such a one either enjoy or recommend her religion? It would have been the worse for her if she had enjoyed it—the worse for others if she had recommended it!

Religion is simply the way home to the Father. There was little of the path in her religion except the difficulty of it. The true way is difficult enough because of our unchildlikeness—uphill, steep, and difficult, but there is fresh life on every surmounted height, a purer air gained, ever more life for more climbing. But the path that is not the true one is not therefore easy. Up hill is hard walking, but through a bog is worse.

Those who seek God with their faces not even turned towards him, who, instead of beholding the Father in the Son, take the stupidest opinions concerning him and his ways from other men—what should they do but go wandering on dark mountains, spending their strength in avoiding precipices and getting out of bogs, mourning and sighing over their sins instead of leaving them behind and fleeing to the Father, whom to know is eternal life. Did they but set themselves to find out what Christ knew and meant and commanded, and then to do it, they would soon forget their false teachers. But alas! they go on bowing before long-faced, big-worded authority—the more fatally when it is embodied in a good man who, himself a victim to faith in men, sees the Son of God only through the theories of others, and not with the sight of his own spiritual eyes.

From the novel Thomas Wingfold, Curate. *Describing a devout but unloving woman.*

For nothing is so deadening to the divine as an habitual dealing with the outsides of holy things.

Eternal Life

*Jesus saith unto her, Thy brother shall rise again.
Martha saith unto him, I know that he shall rise
again in the resurrection at the last day.*

*Jesus said unto her,
I am the resurrection, and the life:
he that believeth in me, though he were dead,
yet shall he live: And whosoever liveth
and believeth in me shall never die.
Believest thou this?*

John 11:23–26

22.

Death

From a letter to a friend whose husband had just died.

Did you ever think, dearest sister, what kind of mourning is meant where the Lord says "Blessed are they that mourn"? It is simply and specially those that are mourning for the dead. The Greek word means that. Then the Master says you are a blessed woman, for there is comfort coming that will content you. When it comes, perhaps you will say to yourself, "If I had known it was anything like this, it would have made me happy even when I missed and wanted him." Then might not he say, "You might have expected something good when I told you that such a comfort was coming that I congratulated you even in the midst of your sorrow!" "Will they never trust my Father?" I imagine him saying sometimes.

Yes, dear, it is a hard time for you, but he is drawing you nearer to himself. You will have, I think, to consent to be miserable so far as loneliness makes you miserable, and look to him and him only for comfort. But the words that the Lord speaks are spirit and life. We are in a house with windows on all sides. On one side the sweet garden is trampled and torn, the beeches blown down, the fountain broken; you sit and look out, and it is all very miserable. Shut the window. I do not mean forget the garden as it was, but do not brood on it as it is. Open the window on the other side, where the great mountains shoot heavenward, and the stars, rising and setting, crown their peaks. Down those stairs look for the descending feet of the Son of Man coming to comfort you.

This world, if it were alone, would not be worth much—I should be miserable already; but it is the porch to the Father's home, and he does not expect us to be quite happy, and knows we must sometimes be very unhappy till we get there: We are getting nearer.

From the novel David Elginbrod. *Robert Falconer is walking through the slums with a young companion, Hugh Sutherland.*

As Falconer said no more, and as Hugh was afraid of showing anything like vulgar curiosity, this thread of conversation broke. Nothing worth recording passed until they entered a narrow court in Somers Town.

"Are you afraid of infection?" Falconer said.

"Not in the least, if there be any reason for exposing myself to it."

"That is right.—And I need not ask if you are in good health."

"I am in perfect health."

"Then I need not mind asking you to wait for me till I come out of this house. There is typhus in it."

"I will wait with pleasure. I will go with you if I can be of any use."

"There is no occasion. It is not your business this time."

So saying, Falconer opened the door, and walked in.

Said Hugh to himself: "I must tell this man the whole story; and with it all my own."

In a few minutes Falconer rejoined him, looking solemn, but with a kind of relieved expression on his face.

"The poor fellow is gone," said he.

"Ah!"

"What a thing it must be, Mr. Sutherland, for a man to break out of the choke-damp of a typhus fever into the clear air of the life beyond!"

"Yes," said Hugh; adding, after a slight hesitation, "if he be at all prepared for the change."

"Where a change belongs to the natural order of things," said Falconer, "and arrives inevitably at some hour, there must always be more or less preparedness for it. Besides, I think a man is generally prepared for a breath of fresh air."

Hugh did not reply, for he felt that he did not fully comprehend his new acquaintance. But he had a strong suspicion that it was because he moved in a higher region than himself.

"If you will still accompany me," resumed Falconer, who had not yet adverted to Hugh's object in seeking his acquaintance, "you will, I think, be soon compelled to believe that, at whatever time death may arrive, or in whatever condition the man may be at the time, it comes as the best and only good that can at that moment reach him.

"We are, perhaps, too much in the habit of thinking of death as the culmination of disease, which, regarded only in itself, is an evil, and a terrible evil. But I think rather of death as the first pulse of the new strength, shaking itself free from the old mouldy remnants of earth-garments, that it may begin in freedom the new life that grows out of the old. The caterpillar dies into the butterfly. Who knows but disease may be the coming, the keener life, breaking into this, and beginning to destroy like fire the inferior modes or garments of the present? And then disease would be but the sign of the salvation of fire; of the agony of the greater life to lift us to itself, out of that wherein we are failing and sinning. And so we praise the consuming fire of life."

"But surely all cannot fare alike in the new life."

"Far from it. According to the condition. But what would be hell to one, will be quietness, and hope, and progress to another; because he has left worse behind him, and in this the life asserts itself, and is.—But perhaps you are not interested in such subjects, Mr. Sutherland, and I weary you."

"If I have not been interested in them hitherto, I am ready to become so now. Let me go with you."

"With pleasure."

As I have attempted to tell a great deal about Robert Falconer and his pursuits elsewhere, I will not here relate the particulars of their walk through some of the most wretched parts of London. Suffice it to say that, if Hugh, as he walked home, was not yet prepared to receive and understand the half of what Falconer had said about death, and had not yet that faith in God that gives as perfect a peace for the future of our brothers and sisters, who, alas! have as yet been fed with husks, as for that of ourselves, who have eaten bread of the finest of the wheat, and have been but a little thankful,—he yet felt at least that it was a blessed thing that these men and women would all die—must all die. That spectre from which men shrink, as if it would take from them the last shivering remnant of existence, he turned to for some consolation even for them. He was prepared to believe that they could not be going to worse in the end, though some of the rich and respectable and educated might have to receive their evil things first in the other world; and he was ready to understand that great saying of Schiller—full of a faith evident enough to him who can look far enough into the saying:

"Death cannot be an evil, for it is universal."

From the novel Robert Falconer. *Robert Falconer is watching by the bed of a dying friend.*

Hoping that he would sleep and wake yet again, Robert sat still. After an hour, he looked, and saw that, although hitherto much oppressed, he was now breathing like a child. There was no sign save of past suffering: his countenance was peaceful as if he had already entered into his rest. Robert withdrew, and again seated himself. And the great universe became to him as a bird brooding over the breaking shell of the dying man.

On either hand we behold a birth, of which, as of the moon, we see but half. We are outside the one, waiting for a life from the unknown; we are inside the other, watching the departure of a spirit from the womb of the world into the unknown. To the region whither he goes, the man enters newly born. We forget that it is a birth, and call it a death. The body he leaves behind is but the placenta by which he drew his nourishment from his mother Earth. And as the child-bed is watched on earth with anxious expectancy, so the couch of the dying, as we call them, may be surrounded by the birth-watchers of the other world, waiting like anxious servants to open the door to which this world is but the wind-blown porch.

From the novel Malcolm. *Malcolm, a fisherman and groom on the marquis's estate, has urged the marquis, who is dying of gangrene, to talk to the teacher Mr. Graham.*

"Mr. Graham's here, my lord," said Malcolm.

"Where? Not in the room?" returned the marquis.

"Waitin' at the door, my lord."

"Bah! You needn't have been so ready. Have you told the sexton to get a new spade? But you may let him in. And leave him alone with me."

Mr. Graham walked gently up to the bedside.

"Sit down, sir," said the marquis courteously, pleased with the calm, self possessed, unobtrusive bearing of the man. "They tell me I'm dying, Mr. Graham."

"I'm sorry it seems to trouble you, my lord."

"What! wouldn't it trouble you then?"

"I don't think so, my lord."

"Ah! you're one of the elect, no doubt?"

"That's a thing I never did think about, my lord."

"What do you think about then?"

"About God."

"And when you die you'll go straight to heaven of course."

"I don't know, my lord. That's another thing I never trouble my head about."

"Ah! you're like me then! I don't care much about going to heaven! What do you care about?"

"The will of God. I hope your lordship will say the same."

"No I won't. I want my own will."

"Well, that is to be had, my lord."

"How?"

"By taking his for yours, as the better of the two, which it must be every way."

"That's all moonshine."

"It is light, my lord."

"Well, I don't mind confessing, if I am to die, I should prefer heaven to the other place; but I trust I have no chance of either. Do you now honestly believe there are two such places?"

"I don't know, my lord."

"You don't know! And you come here to comfort a dying man!"

"Your lordship must first tell me what you mean by 'two such places.' And as to comfort, going by my notions, I cannot tell which you would be more or less comfortable in; and that, I presume, would be the main point with your lordship."

"And what, pray, sir, would be the main point with you?"

"To get nearer to God."

"Well, I can't say I want to get nearer to God. It's little he's ever done for me."

"It's a good deal he has tried to do for you, my lord."

"Well, who interfered? Who stood in his way, then?"

"Yourself, my lord."

"I wasn't aware of it. When did he ever try to do anything for me, and I stood in his way?"

"When he gave you one of the loveliest of women, my lord," said Mr. Graham, with solemn, faltering voice, "and you left her to die in neglect, and the child to be brought up by strangers."

The marquis gave a cry. The unexpected answer had roused the slowly gnawing death, and made it bite deeper.

"What have you to do," he almost screamed, "with my affairs? It was for me to introduce what I chose of them. You presume."

"Pardon me, my lord: you led me to what I was bound to say. Shall I leave you, my lord?"

The marquis made no answer.

"God knows I loved her," he said after a while, with a sigh.

"You loved her, my lord!"

"I did, by God!"

"Love a woman like that, and come to this?"

"Come to this! We must all come to this, I fancy, sooner or later. Come to what, in the name of Beelzebub?"

"That, having loved a woman like her, you are content to lose her. In the name of God, have you no desire to see her again?"

"It would be an awkward meeting," said the marquis. His was an old love, alas! He had not been capable of the sort that defies change. It had faded from him until it seemed one of the things that are not! Although his being had once glowed in its light, he could now speak of a meeting as awkward!

"Because you wronged her?" suggested the schoolmaster.

"Because they lied to me, by God!"

"Which they dared not have done, had you not lied to them first."

"Sir!" shouted the marquis, with all the voice he had left. "O God, have mercy! I cannot punish the scoundrel."

"The scoundrel is the man who lies, my lord."

"Were I anywhere else—"

"There would be no good in telling you the truth, my lord. You showed her to the world as a woman over whom you had prevailed, and not as the honest wife she was. What kind of a lie was that, my lord? Not a white one, surely?"

"You are a damned coward to speak so to a man who cannot even turn on his side to curse you for a base hound. You would not dare it but that you know I cannot defend myself."

"You are right, my lord; your conduct is indefensible."

"By heaven! if I could but get this cursed leg under me, I would throw you out of the window."

"I shall go by the door, my lord. While you hold by your sins, your sins will hold by you. If you should want me again, I shall be at your lordship's command."

He rose and left the room, but had not reached his cottage before Malcolm overtook him, with a second message from his master. He turned at once, saying only, "I expected it."

"Mr. Graham," said the marquis, looking ghastly, "you must have patience with a dying man. I was very rude to you, but I was in horrible pain."

"Don't mention it, my lord. It would be a poor friendship that gave way for a rough word."

"How can you call yourself my friend?"

"I should be your friend, my lord, if it were only for your wife's sake. She died loving you. I want to send you to her, my lord. You will allow that, as a gentleman, you at least owe her an apology."

"By Jove, you are right, sir! Then you really and positively believe in the place they call heaven?"

"My lord, I believe that those who open their hearts to the truth, shall see the light on their friends' faces again, and be able to set right what was wrong between them."

"It's a week too late to talk of setting right!"

"Go and tell her you are sorry, my lord, that will be enough to her."

"Ah! but there's more than her concerned."

"You are right, my lord. There is another one who cannot be satisfied that the fairest works of his hands, or rather the loveliest children of his heart, should be treated as you have treated women."

"But the Deity you talk of—"

"I beg your pardon, my lord: I talked of no deity; I talked of a living Love that gave us birth and calls us his children. Your deity I know nothing of."

"Call him what you please: he won't be put off so easily!"

"He won't be put off one jot or one tittle. He will forgive anything, but he will pass nothing. Will your wife forgive you?"

"She will—when I explain."

"Then why should you think the forgiveness of God, which created her forgiveness, should be less?"

Whether the marquis could grasp the reasoning, may be doubtful.

"Do you really suppose God cares whether a man comes to good or ill?"

"If he did not, he could not be good himself."

"Then you don't think a good God would care to punish poor wretches like us?"

"Your lordship has not been in the habit of regarding himself as a poor wretch. And, remember, you can't call a child a poor wretch without insulting the father of it."

"That's quite another thing."

"But on the wrong side for your argument—seeing the relation between God and the poorest creature is infinitely closer than that between any father and his child."

"Then he can't be so hard on him as the parsons say."

"He will give him absolute justice, which is the only good thing. He will spare nothing to bring his children back to himself—their sole well being. What would you do, my lord, if you saw your son strike a woman?"

"Knock him down and horsewhip him."

It was Mr. Graham who broke the silence that followed.

"Are you satisfied with yourself, my lord?"

"No, by God!"

"You would like to be better?"

"I would."

"Then you are of the same mind with God."

"Yes but I'm not a fool! It won't do to say I should like to be: I must be it, and that's not so easy. It's damned hard to be good. I would have a fight for it, but there's no time. How is a poor devil to get out of such an infernal scrape?"

"Keep the commandments."

"That's it, of course; but there's no time, I tell you—at least so those cursed doctors will keep telling me."

"If there were but time to draw another breath, there would be time to begin."

"How am I to begin? Which am I to begin with?"

"There is one commandment which includes all the rest."

"Which is that?"

"To believe on the Lord Jesus Christ."

"That's cant."

"After thirty years' trial of it, it is to me the essence of wisdom. It has given me a peace which makes life or death all but indifferent to me, though I would choose the latter."

"What am I to believe about him then?"

"You are to believe in him, not about him."

"I don't understand."

"He is our Lord and Master, Elder Brother, King, Saviour, the divine Man, the human God: to believe in him is to give ourselves up to him in obedience, to search out his will and do it."

"But there's no time, I tell you again," the marquis almost shrieked.

"And I tell you, there is all eternity to do it in. Take him for your master, and he will demand nothing of you which you are not able to perform. This is the open door to bliss. With your last breath you can cry to him, and he will hear you, as he heard the thief on the cross who cried to him dying beside him. 'Lord, remember me when thou comest into thy kingdom.' 'Today shalt thou be with me in paradise.' It makes my heart swell to think of it, my lord! No cross questioning of the poor fellow! No preaching to him! He just took him with him where he was going, to make a man of him."

"Well, you know something of my history: what would you have me do now? At once, I mean. What would the person you speak of have me do?"

"That is not for me to say, my lord."

"You could give me a hint."

"No. God is telling you himself. For me to presume to tell you, would be to interfere with him. What he would have a man do, he lets him know in his mind."

"But what if I had not made up my mind before the last came?"

"Then I fear he would say to you—'Depart from me, thou worker of iniquity.'"

"That would be hard when another minute might have done it."

"If another minute would have done it, you would have had it."

From a letter to a friend the year after the death of George MacDonald's daughter Mary Josephine at age twenty-four, and less than two months after the death of his son Maurice at age fifteen.

How real death makes things look! And how we learn to cleave to the one shining fact in the midst of the darkness of the world's trouble, that Jesus *did* rise radiant! I too have noble brothers to find where the light has hidden them, besides my faithful children, boy and girl. And you, beloved friends, will find your dear ones also, and when your hearts are filled with love and embraces, you will perhaps turn to us to help you to endure your bliss. . . . He alone who invented the nursery and its bonds, can perfect what he began there. I for my part, cry more for a perfecting of my loves than perhaps anything else.

From the novel Weighed and Wanting. *A child has died.*

When such children as he die, we may well imagine them wanted for special work in the world to which they go. If the very hairs of our head are all numbered, and he said so who knew and is true, our children do not drop hap-hazard into the near world, neither are they kept out of it by any care or any power of medicine: all goes by heavenliest will and loveliest ordinance. Some of us will have to be ashamed of our outcry after our dead. Beloved, even for your dear faces we can wait awhile, seeing it is His father, your father and our father to whom you have gone, leaving us with him still. Our day will come, and your joy and ours, and all shall be well.

From a letter to a friend whose oldest son had died.

What can I say to you, for the hand of the Lord is heavy upon you. But it is his hand, and the very heaviness of it is good. . . . There is but one thought that can comfort, and that is that God is immeasurably more the father of our children than we are. It is because he is our father that we are fathers. . . . It is all well— even in the face of such pain as yours—or the world would go to pieces for me.

It is well to say, "The Lord gave and the Lord hath taken away," but it is not enough. We must add, And the Lord will give again. "The gifts of God are without repentance." He takes that he may give more closely—make *more ours*. . . . The bond is henceforth closer between you and your son.

From the novel What's Mine's Mine. *Mercy and Christina, raised in London, are spending a year in a remote Scottish village. There is a flashflood while they are on a walk with their younger sisters; the chief of the local clan, Alister, and his brother Ian rush to help them.*

[Ian] arrived at the opening of the valley . . . and as soon as he entered it, he saw that the cloudy turmoil was among the hills at its head. With that he began to suspect the danger, and almost the same instant heard the merry voices of the children. Running yet faster, he came in sight of them on the other side of the stream,—not a moment too soon. The valley was full of a dull roaring sound. He called to them as he ran, and the children saw and came running down toward him, followed by Mercy. She was not looking much concerned, for she thought it only the grumbling of distant thunder. But Ian saw, far up the valley, what looked like a low brown wall across it, and knew what it was.

"Mercy!" he cried, "run up the side of the hill directly; you will be drowned—swept away if you do not."

She looked incredulous, and glanced up the hill-side, but came on as if to cross the burn and join him.

"Do as I tell you," he cried, in a tone which few would have ventured to disregard, and turning darted across the channel toward her.

Mercy did not wait his coming, but took the children, each by a hand, and went a little way up the hill that immediately bordered the stream.

---

burn stream

"Farther! farther!" cried Ian as he ran. "Where is Christina?"

"At the ruin," she answered.

"Good heavens!" exclaimed Ian, and darted off, crying, "Up the hill with you! up the hill!"

Christina was standing by the birch-tree in the ruin, looking down the burn. She had heard Ian calling, and saw him running, but suspected no danger.

"Come; come directly; for God's sake, come!" he cried. "Look up the burn!" he added, seeing her hesitate bewildered.

She turned, looked, and came running to him, down the channel, white with terror. It was too late. The charging water, whose front rank was turf, and bushes, and stones, was almost upon her. The solid matter had retarded its rush, but it was now on the point of dividing against the rocky mound, to sweep along both sides, and turn it into an island. Ian bounded to her in the middle of the channel, caught her by the arm, and hurried her back to the mound as fast as they could run: it was the highest ground immediately accessible. As they reached it, the water broke with a roar against its rocky base, rose, swelled—and in a moment the island was covered with a brown, seething, swirling flood.

"Where's Mercy and the children?" gasped Christina, as the water rose upon her.

"Safe, safe!" answered Ian. "We must get to the ruin!"

The water was halfway up his leg, and rising fast. Their danger was but beginning. Would the old walls, in greater part built without mortar, stand the rush? If a tree should strike them, they hardly would! If the flood came from a waterspout, it would soon be over—only how high it might first rise, who could tell! Such were his thoughts as they struggled to the ruin, and stood up at the end of a wall parallel with the current.

The water was up to Christina's waist, and very cold. Here out of the rush, however, she recovered her breath in a measure, and showed not a little courage. Ian stood between her and the wall, and held her fast. The torrent came round the end of the wall from both sides, but the encounter and eddy of the two currents rather pushed them up against it. Without it they could not have stood.

The chief danger to Christina, however, was from the cold. With the water so high on her body, and flowing so fast, she could not long resist it! Ian, therefore, took her round the knees, and lifted her almost out of the water.

"Put your arms up," he said, "and lay hold of the wall. Don't mind blinding me; my eyes are of little use at present. There—put your feet in my hands. Don't be frightened; I can hold you."

"I can't help being frightened!" she panted.

"We are in God's arms," returned Ian. "He is holding us."

"Are you sure we shall not be drowned?" she asked.

"No; but I am sure the water cannot take us out of God's arms."

This was not much comfort to Christina. She did not know anything about God—did not believe in him any more than most people. She knew God's arms only as the arms of Ian—and *they* comforted her, for she *felt* them!

How many of us actually believe in any support we do not immediately feel? in any arms we do not see? But every help is from God; Ian's help was God's help; and though to believe in Ian was not to believe in God, it was a step on the road toward believing in God. He that believeth not in the good man whom he hath seen, how shall he believe in the God whom he hath not seen?

She began to feel a little better; the ghastly choking at her heart was almost gone.

"I shall break your arms!" she said.

"You are not very heavy," he answered; "and though I am not so strong as Alister, I am stronger than most men. With the help of the wall I can hold you a long time."

How was it that, now first in danger, self came less to the front with her than usual? It was that now first she was face to face with reality. Until this moment her life had been an affair of unrealities. Her selfishness had thinned, as it were vaporized, every reality that approached her. Solidity is not enough to teach some natures reality; they must hurt themselves against the solid ere they realize its solidity. Small reality, small positivity of existence has water to a dreaming soul, half consciously gazing through half shut eyes at the soft river floating away in the moonlight: Christina was shivering in its grasp on her person, its omnipresence to her skin; its cold made her gasp and choke; the push and tug of it threatened to sweep her away like a whelmed log!

It is when we are most aware of the *factitude* of things, that we are most aware of our need of God, and most able to trust in him; when most aware of their presence, the soul finds it easiest to withdraw from them, and seek its safety with the maker of it and them. The recognition of inexorable reality in any shape, or kind, or way, tends to rouse the soul to the yet more real, to its relations with higher and deeper existence. It is not the hysterical alone for whom the great dash of cold water is good. All who dream life instead of living it, require some similar shock. Of the kind is every disappointment, every reverse, every tragedy of life. The true in even the lowest kind, is of the truth, and to be compelled to feel even that, is to be driven a trifle nearer to the truth of being, of creation, of God. Hence this sharp contact with Nature tended to make Christina less selfish: it made her forget herself so far as to care for her helper as well as herself.

It must be remembered, however, that her selfishness was not the cultivated and ingrained selfishness of a long life, but that of an uneducated, that is undeveloped nature. Her being had not degenerated by sinning against light known as light; it had not been consciously enlightened at all; it had scarcely as yet begun to grow. It was not lying dead, only unawaked. I would not be understood to imply that she was nowise to blame—but that she was by no means so much to blame as one who has but suspected the presence of a truth, and from selfishness or self-admiration has turned from it. She was to blame wherever she had not done as her conscience had feebly told her; and she had not made progress just because she had neglected the little things concerning which she had promptings. There are many who do not enter the kingdom of heaven just because they will not believe the tiny key that is handed them is fit to open its hospitable gate.

"Oh, Mr. Ian, if you should be drowned for my sake!" she faltered with white lips. "You should not have come to me!"

"I would not wish a better death," said Ian.

"How can you talk so coolly about it!" she cried.

"Well," he returned, "what better way of going out of the world is there than by the door of help? No man cares much about what the idiots of the world call life! What is it whether we live in this room or another? The same who sent us here, sends for us out of here!"

"Most men care very much! You are wrong there!"

"I don't call those who do, men! They are only children! I know many men who would no more cleave to this life than a butterfly would fold his wings and creep into his deserted chrysalis-case.

I do care to live—tremendously, but I don't mind where. He who made this room so well worth living in, may surely be trusted with the next!"

"I can't quite follow you," stammered Christina. "I am sorry. Perhaps it is the cold. I can't feel my hands, I am so cold."

"Leave the wall, and put your arms round my neck. The change will rest me, and the water is already falling! It will go as rapidly as it came!"

"How do you know that?"

"It has sunk nearly a foot in the last fifteen minutes: I have been carefully watching it, you may be sure! It must have been a waterspout, and however much that may bring, it pours it out all at once."

"Oh!" said Christina, with a tremulous joyfulness; "I thought it would go on ever so long!"

"We shall get out of it alive!—God's will be done!"

"Why do you say that? Don't you really mean we are going to be saved?"

"Would you want to live, if he wanted you to die?"

"Oh, but you forget, Mr. Ian, I am not ready to die, like you!" sobbed Christina.

"Do you think anything could make it better for you to stop here, after God thought it better for you to go?"

"I dare not think about it."

"Be sure God will not take you away, if it be better for you to live here a little longer. But you will have to go sometime; and if you contrived to live after God wanted you to go, you would find yourself much less ready when the time came that you must. But, my dear Miss Palmer, no one can be living a true life, to whom dying is a terror."

Christina was silent. He spoke the truth! She was not worth anything! How grand it was to look death in the face with a smile!

If she had been no more than the creature she had hitherto shown herself, not all the floods of the deluge could have made her think or feel thus: her real self, her divine nature had begun to wake. True, that nature was as yet no more like the divine, than the drowsy, arm-stretching, yawning child is like the merry elf about to spring from his couch, full of life, of play, of love. She had no faith in God yet, but it was much that she felt she was not worth anything.

You are right: it was odd to hold such a conversation at such a time! But Ian was an odd man. He actually believed that God was nearer to him than his own consciousness, yet desired communion with him! and that Jesus Christ knew what he said when he told his disciples that the Father cared for his sparrows.

✦ ✦ ✦

Beyond the stream lay Mercy on the hillside, with her face in the heather. Frozen with dread, she dared not look up. Had she moved but ten yards, she would have seen her sister in Ian's arms.

The children sat by her, white as death, with great lumps in their throats, and the silent tears rolling down their cheeks. It was the first time death had come near them.

A sound of sweeping steps came through the heather. They looked up: there was the chief striding toward them.

The flood had come upon him at work in his fields, whelming his growing crops. He had but time to unyoke his bulls, and run for his life. The bulls, not quite equal to the occasion, were caught and swept away. They were found a week after on the hills, nothing the worse, and nearly as wild as when first the chief took them in hand. The cottage was in no danger; and Nancy got a horse and the last of the cows from the farm-yard on to the crest of the ridge, against which the burn rushed roaring, just as the water began to invade the cowhouse and stable. The moment he reached the ridge, the chief set out to look for his brother, whom he knew to be somewhere up the valley; and having climbed to get an outlook, saw Mercy and the girls, from whose postures he dreaded that something had befallen them.

The girls uttered a cry of welcome, and the chief answered, but Mercy did not lift her head.

"Mercy," said Alister softly, and kneeling laid his hand on her.

She turned to him such a face of blank misery as filled him with consternation.

"What has happened?" he asked.

She tried to speak, but could not.

"Where is Christina?" he went on.

She succeeded in bringing out the one word "ruin."

"Is anybody with her?"

"Ian."

"Oh!" he returned cheerily, as if then all would be right. But a pang shot through his heart, and it was as much for himself as for Mercy that he went on: "But God is with them, Mercy. If he were not, it would be bad indeed! Where he is, all is well!"

She sat up, and putting out her hand, laid it in his great palm.

"I wish I could believe that!" she said; "but you know people *are* drowned sometimes!"

"Yes, surely! but if God be with them what does it matter!"

"It is cruel to talk like that to me when my sister is drowning!"

She gave a stifled shriek, and threw herself again on her face.

"Mercy," said the chief—and his voice trembled a little, "you do not love your sister more than I love my brother, and if he be drowned I shall weep; but I shall not be miserable as if a mocking devil were at the root of it, and not one who loves them better than we ever shall. But come; I think we shall find them somehow alive yet! Ian knows what to do in an emergency; and though you might not think it, he is a very strong man."

She rose immediately, and taking like a child the hand he offered her, went up the hill with him. . . .

The child, however, did not for some time show her face to any but Ian. In his presence Christina had no longer self-assertion or wile. Without seeking his notice she would yet manifest an almost childish willingness to please him. It was no sudden change. She had, ever since their adventure, been haunted, both awake and asleep, by his presence, and it had helped her to some discoveries regarding herself. And the more she grew real, the nearer, that is, that she came to being a *person*, the more she came under the influence of his truth, his reality. It is only through live relation to others that any individuality crystallizes.

"You saved my life, Ian!" she said one evening for the tenth time.

"It pleased God you should live," answered Ian.

"Then you really think," she returned, "that God interfered to save us?"

"No, I do not; I don't think he ever interferes."

"Mr. Sercombe says everything goes by law, and God never interferes; my father says he does interfere sometimes."

"Would you say a woman interfered in the management of her own house? Can one be said to interfere where he is always at work? He is the necessity of the universe, ever and always doing the best that can be done, and especially for the individual, for whose sake alone the cosmos exists. If we had been drowned, we should have given God thanks for saving us."

"I do not understand you!"

"Should we not have given thanks to find ourselves lifted out of the cold rushing waters, in which we felt our strength slowly sinking?"

"But you said *drowned*! How could we have thanked God for deliverance if we were drowned?"

"What!—not when we found ourselves above the water, safe and well, and more alive than ever? Would it not be a dreadful thing to lie tossed for centuries under the sea-waves to which the torrent had borne us? Ah, how few believe in a life beyond, a larger life, more awake, more earnest, more joyous than this!"

"Oh, *I* do! but that is not what one means by *life*; that is quite a different kind of thing!"

"How do you make out that it is so different? If I am I, and you are you, how can it be very different? The root of things is individuality, unity of idea, and persistence depends on it. God is the one perfect individual; and while this world is his and that world is his, there can be no inconsistency, no violent difference, between there and here."

"Then you must thank God for everything—thank him if you are drowned, or burnt, or anything!"

"Now you understand me! That is precisely what I mean."

"Then I can never be good, for I could never bring myself to that!"

"You cannot bring yourself to it; no one could. But we must come to it. I believe we shall all be brought to it."

"Never me! I should not wish it!"

"You do not wish it; but you may be brought to wish it; and without it the end of your being cannot be reached. No one, of course, could ever give thanks for what he did not know or feel as good. But what *is* good must come to be felt good. Can you suppose that Jesus at any time could not thank his Father for sending him into the world?"

"You speak as if we and he were of the same kind!"

"He and we are so entirely of the same kind, that there is no bliss for him or for you or for me but in being the loving obedient child of the one Father."

"You frighten me! If I cannot get to heaven any other way than that, I shall never get there."

"You will get there, and you will get there that way and no other. If you could get there any other way, it would be to be miserable."

"Something tells me you speak the truth; but it is terrible! I do not like it."

"Naturally."

She was on the point of crying. They were alone in the drawing-room of the cottage, but his mother might enter any moment, and Ian said no more.

From a letter to a friend whose mother had died.

You will be missing your mother more now than when first she went away! As the days go on and the common look gathers again upon the things round you, and the kingdom of heaven seems no nearer, we are apt to feel more a separation. There seems sometimes to be nowhere beyond, because no voice comes back from the beloved. This parting seems so complete at times. Why is all so dumb? Why no personal relation of the world to which they are gone?

God knows and cares, and uses for us a means of education for our hearts and spirits which we do not ourselves understand. It is not needful that we understand the motive power in the processes that go on within us. It is enough to him who believes it that the Lord *did* rise again, although after that he was hidden from their sight.

Yes, I will believe that I shall hold my own in my arms again, their hearts nearer to mine than ever before. It is a blessed thing to be children and to be parents of children. So God binds us all together. You and I have much to thank God for that we came of such parents. And we shall see them again and our hearts shall rejoice. For what is true of the Lord is true of all of his, for they are one with him. . . . We *shall* see them all and love them more and more to all eternity.

23.

Resurrection

From the novel Seaboard Parish. *Two men are watching the sun set over the sea.*

"Did it ever strike you that the whole history of the Christian life is a series of such resurrections? Every time a man bethinks himself that he is not walking in the light, that he has been forgetting himself, and must repent, that he has been asleep and must awake, that he has been letting his garments trail, and must gird up the loins of his mind—every time this takes place, there is a resurrection in the world. . . .

And every time that a man finds that his heart is troubled, that he is not rejoicing in God, a resurrection must follow—a resurrection out of the night of troubled thoughts into the gladness of the truth. For the truth is, and ever was, and ever must be, gladness, however much the souls on which it shines may be obscured by the clouds of sorrow, troubled by the thunders of fear, or shot through with the lightnings of pain."

From the novel Malcolm. *Malcolm is sitting with his teacher Mr. Graham in the church yard.*

"See," said the schoolmaster as the fisherman sat down beside him, "how the shadow from one grave stretches like an arm to embrace another! In this light the churchyard seems the very birthplace of shadows: see them flowing out of the tombs as from fountains, to overflow the world! Does the morning or the evening light suit such a place best, Malcolm?"

The pupil thought for a while.

"The evenin' licht, sir," he answered at length; "for ye see the sun's deem' like, an' deith's like a fa'in asleep, an' the grave's the bed, an' the sod's the bedclaes, an' there's a lang nicht to the fore."

"Are ye sure o' that, Malcolm?"

"It's the wye folk thinks an' says aboot it, sir."

"Or maybe doesna think, an' only says?"

"Maybe, sir; I dinna ken."

"Come here, Malcolm," said Mr. Graham, and took him by the arm, and led him towards the east end of the church, where a few tombstones were crowded against the wall, as if they would press close to a place they might not enter.

"Read that," he said, pointing to a flat stone, where every hollow letter was shown in high relief by the growth in it of a lovely moss. The rest of the stone was rich in gray and green and brown lichens, but only in the letters grew the bright moss; the inscription stood as it were in the hand of nature herself, "He is not here; he is risen."

While Malcolm gazed, trying to think what his master would have him think, the latter resumed.

---

bedclaes bedclothes

"If he is risen, if the sun is up, Malcolm, then the morning and not the evening is the season for the place of tombs; the morning when the shadows are shortening and separating, not the evening when they are growing all into one. I used to love the churchyard best in the evening, when the past was more to me than the future; now I visit it almost every bright summer morning, and only occasionally at night."

"But, sir, isna deith a dreidfu' thing?" said Malcolm.

"That depends on whether a man regards it as his fate, or as the will of a perfect God. Its obscurity is its dread; but if God be light, then death itself must be full of splendour—a splendour probably too keen for our eyes to receive."

"But there's the deein' itsel': isna that fearsome? It's that I wad be fleyed at."

"I don't see why it should be. It's the want of a God that makes it dreadful, and you will be greatly to blame, Malcolm, if you haven't found your God by the time you have to die."

Later they are joined by Duncan MacPhail, a blind bagpiper who Malcolm lives with and cares for and who believes he is his grandfather; Malcolm calls him "daddy." Duncan's speech is one degree more archaic than Malcolm's, and he has the peculiar habit of referring to himself in the third person feminine.

"I wish you had your sight but for a moment, Mr. MacPhail," said the schoolmaster. "How this sunrise would make you leap for joy."

"Ay!" said Malcolm, "it wad gar daddy grip till's pipes in twa hurries."

---

fleyed at afraid of
gar daddy grip till's pipes in twa hurries it would make daddy run to his pipes in two hurries

"And what should she'll pe wanting her pipes for?" asked Duncan.

"To praise God wi'," answered Malcolm.

"Ay; ay;" murmured Duncan thoughtfully. "Tey are tat."

"What are they?" asked Mr. Graham gently.

"For to praise Cod," answered Duncan solemnly.

"I almost envy you," returned Mr. Graham, "when I think how you will praise God one day. What a glorious waking you will have!"

"Ten it'll pe your opinion, Mr. Graham, tat she'll pe sleeping her sound sleep, and not pe lying wite awake in her coffin all ta time?"

"A good deal better than that, Mr. MacPhail!" returned the schoolmaster cheerily. "It's my opinion that you are, as it were, asleep now, and that the moment you die, you will feel as if you had just woke up, and for the first time in your life. For one thing, you will see far better then than any of us do now."

But poor Duncan could not catch the idea; his mind was filled with a preventing fancy.

"Yes; I know; at ta tay of chutchment," he said. "Put what 'll pe ta use of ketting her eyes open pefore she'll pe up? How should she pe seeing with all ta earth apove her and ta crave-stone too tat I know my poy Malcolm will pe laying on ta top of his old cranfather to keep him waarm, and let peoples pe know tat ta plind piper will be lying town pelow wite awake and fery uncomfortable?"

"Excuse me, Mr. MacPhail, but that's all a mistake," said Mr. Graham positively. "The body is but a sort of shell that we cast off when we die, as the corn casts off its husk when it begins to

---

what should she'll pe wanting her pipes for what would I be wanting my pipes for
wite awake

grow. The life of the seed comes up out of the earth in a new body, as St. Paul says."

"Ten," interrupted Duncan, "she'll pe crowing up out of her crave like a seed crowing up to pe a corn or a parley?"

The schoolmaster began to despair of ever conveying to the piper the idea that the living man is the seed sown, and that when the body of this seed dies, then the new body, with the man in it, springs alive out of the old one, that the death of the one is the birth of the other. Far more enlightened people than Duncan never imagine, and would find it hard to believe, that the sowing of the seed spoken of might mean something else than the burying of the body; not perceiving what yet surely is plain enough, that that would be the sowing of a seed already dead, and incapable of giving birth to anything whatever.

"No, no," he said, almost impatiently, "you will never be in the grave: it is only your body that will go there, with nothing like life about it except the smile the glad soul has left on it. The poor body when thus forsaken is so dead that it can't even stop smiling. Get Malcolm to read to you out of the book of the Revelation how there were multitudes even then standing before the throne. They had died in this world, yet there they were, well and happy."

"Oh, yes!" said Duncan, with no small touch of spitefulness in his tone, "twang twanging at teir fine colden herps! She'll not be thinking much of ta herp for a music maker! And peoples tells her she'll not pe hafing her pipes tere! Och hone! Och hone! She'll chust pe lying still and not pe ketting up, and when ta work is ofer, and eferypody cone away, she'll chust pe ketting up, and taking a look apout her, to see if she'll pe finding a stand o' pipes that some coot highlandman has peen left pehint him when he tied lately."

"You'll find it rather lonely won't you?"

"Yes; no toubt, for they'll aal be cone up. Well, she'll haf her pipes; and she could not co where ta pipes was looked town upon by all ta creat people and all ta smaal ones too."

They had now reached the foot of the promontory, and turned northwards, each of his companions taking an arm of the piper to help him over the rocks that lay between them and the mouth of the cave, which soon yawned before them like a section of the mouth of a great fish. Its floor of smooth rock had been swept out clean, and sprinkled with dry sea sand. There were many hollows and projections along its sides rudely fit for serving as seats, to which had been added a number of forms extemporized of planks and thwarts. No one had yet arrived when they entered, and they went at once to the further end of the cave, that Duncan, who was a little hard of hearing, might be close to the speakers. There his companions turned and looked behind them: an exclamation, followed by a full glance at each other, broke from each.

The sun, just clearing the end of the opposite promontory, shone right into the mouth of the cave, from the midst of a tumult of gold, in which all the other colours of his approach had been swallowed up. The triumph strode splendent over sea and shore, subduing waves and rocks to a path for its mighty entrance into that dark cave on the human coast. With his back to the light stood Duncan in the bottom of the cave, his white hair gleaming argentine, as if his poor blind head were the very goal of the heavenly progress. He turned round.

"Will it pe a fire? She feels something warm on her head," he said, rolling his sightless orbs, upon which the splendour broke waveless, casting a grim shadow of him on the jagged rock behind.

"No," answered Mr. Graham; "it is the sun you feel. He's just out of his grave."

The old man gave a grunt.

"I often think," said the schoolmaster to Malcolm, "that possibly the reason why we are told so little about the world we are going to, is, that no description of it would enter our minds any more than a description of that sunrise would carry a notion of its reality into the mind of your grandfather."

"She's obleeched to you, Mr. Graham!" said the piper with offence. "You take her fery stupid. You're so proud of your eyes, you think a plind man cannot see at aall! Chm!"

From the novel Donal Grant. *Donal is Davie's tutor.*

The next day was Sunday, and in the afternoon Donal and Davie were walking in the old avenue together. They had been to church, and had heard a dull sermon on the most stirring fact next to the resurrection of the Lord himself—his raising of Lazarus. The whole aspect of the thing, as presented by the preaching man, was so dull and unreal, that not a word on the subject had passed between them on the way home.

"Mr. Grant, how could anybody make a dead man live again?" said Davie suddenly.

"I don't know, Davie," answered Donal. "If I could know how, I should probably be able to do it myself."

"It is very hard to believe."

"Yes, very hard—that is, if you do not know anything about the person said to have done it, to account for his being able to do it though another could not. But just think of this: if one had never seen or heard about death, it would be as hard, perhaps harder, to believe that anything could bring about that change.

The one seems to us easy to understand, because we are familiar with it; if we had seen the other take place a few times, we should see in it nothing too strange, nothing indeed but what was to be expected in certain circumstances."

"But that is not enough to prove it ever did take place."

"Assuredly not. It cannot even make it look in the least probable."

"Tell me, please, anything that would make it look probable."

"I will not answer your question directly, but I will answer it. Listen, Davie.

"In all ages men have longed to see God—some men in a grand way. At last, according to the story of the gospel, the time came when it was fit that the Father of men should show himself to them in his son, the one perfect man, who was his very image. So Jesus came to them. But many would not believe he was the son of God, for they knew God so little that they did not see how like he was to his Father. Others, who were more like God themselves, and so knew God better, did think him the son of God, though they were not pleased that he did not make more show. His object was, not to rule over them, but to make them know, and trust, and obey his Father, who was everything to him.

"Now when anyone died, his friends were so miserable over him that they hardly thought about God, and took no comfort from him. They said the dead man would rise again at the last day, but that was so far off, the dead was gone to such a distance, that they did not care for that. Jesus wanted to make them know and feel that the dead were alive all the time, and could not be far away, seeing they were all with God in whom we live; that they had not lost them though they could not see them, for they were quite within his reach—as much so as ever; that they were just as safe with, and as well looked after by his father and their father, as they had ever been in all their lives. It was no doubt a dreadful-looking thing to have them put in a hole, and waste away to dust, but they were not therefore gone out—they were only gone in! To teach them all this he did not say much, but just called one or two of them back for a while. Of course Lazarus was going to die again, but can you think his two sisters either loved him less, or wept as much over him the next time he died?"

"No; it would have been foolish."

"Well, if you think about it, you will see that no one who believes that story, and weeps as they did the first time, can escape reproof. Where Jesus called Lazarus from, there are his friends, and there are they waiting for him! Now, I ask you, Davie, was it worth while for Jesus to do this for us? Is not the great misery of our life, that those dear to us die? Was it, I say, a thing worth doing, to let us see that they are alive with God all the time, and can be produced any moment he pleases?"

"Surely it was, sir! It ought to take away all the misery!"

"Then it was a natural thing to do; and it is a reasonable thing to think that it was done. It was natural that God should want to let his children see him; and natural he should let them know that he still saw and cared for those they had lost sight of. The whole thing seems to me reasonable; I can believe it. It implies indeed a world of things of which we know nothing; but that is for, not against it, seeing such a world we need; and if anyone insists on believing nothing but what he has seen something like, I leave him to his misery and the mercy of God."

If the world had been so made that men could easily believe in the maker of it, it would not have been a world worth any man's living in, neither would the God that made such a world, and so revealed himself to such people, be worth believing in. God alone knows what life is enough for us to live—what life is worth his and our while; we may be sure he is labouring to make it ours. He would have it as full, as lovely, as grand, as the sparing of nothing, not even his own son, can render it. If we would only let him have his own way with us! If we do not trust him, will not work with him, are always thwarting his endeavours to make us alive, then we must be miserable; there is no help for it.

As to death, we know next to nothing about it. "Do we not!" say the faithless. "Do we not know the darkness, the emptiness, the tears, the sinkings of heart, the desolation!" Yes, you know those; but those are your things, not death's. About death you know nothing. God has told us only that the dead are alive to him, and that one day they will be alive again to us. The world beyond the gates of death is, I suspect, a far more homelike place to those that enter it, than this world is to us.

"I don't like death," said Davie, after a silence.

"I don't want you to like, what you call death, for that is not the thing itself—it is only your fancy about it. You need not think about it at all. The way to get ready for it is to live, that is, to do what you have to do."

"But I do not want to get ready for it. I don't want to go to it; and to prepare for it is like going straight into it!"

"You have to go to it whether you prepare for it or not. You cannot help going to it. But it must be like this world, seeing the only way to prepare for it is to do the thing God gives us to do."

"Aren't you afraid of death, Mr. Grant?"

"No, I am not. Why should I fear the best thing that, in its time, can come to me? Neither will you be afraid when it comes. It is not the dreadful thing it looks."

"Why should it look dreadful if it is not dreadful?"

"That is a very proper question. It looks dreadful, and must look dreadful, to everyone who cannot see in it that which alone makes life not dreadful. If you saw a great dark cloak coming along the road as if it were round somebody, but nobody inside it, you would be frightened—would you not?"

"Indeed I should. It would be awful!"

"It would. But if you spied inside the cloak, and making it come towards you, the most beautiful loving face you ever saw—of a man carrying in his arms a little child—and saw the child clinging to him, and looking in his face with a blessed smile, would you be frightened at the black cloak?"

"No; that would be silly."

"You have your answer! The thing that makes death look so fearful is that we do not see inside it. Those who see only the black cloak, and think it is moving along of itself, may well be frightened; but those who see the face inside the cloak, would be fools indeed to be frightened! Before Jesus came, people lived in great misery about death; but after he rose again, those who believed in him always talked of dying as falling asleep; and I daresay the story of Lazarus, though it was not such a great thing after the rising of the Lord himself, had a large share in enabling them to think that way about it."

When they went home, Davie, running up to Lady Arctura's room, recounted to her as well as he could the conversation he had just had with Mr. Grant.

"Oh, Arkie!" he said, "to hear him talk, you would think Death hadn't a leg to stand upon!"

Arctura smiled; but it was a smile through a cloud of unshed tears. Lovely as death might be, she would like to get the good of this world before going to the next!—As if God would deny us any good!—At one time she had been willing to go, she thought, but she was not now!—The world had of late grown very beautiful to her!

From the novel Thomas Wingfold, Curate. *Mr. Drew, a cloth merchant, is talking with the minister, Mr. Wingfold, and Mr. Polwarth, the gate-keeper on the local estate.*

"I can't think, for all that," he said, "why, if there be life beyond the grave, and most sincerely I trust there is—I don't see why we should know so little about it. Confess now, Mr. Polwarth!—Mr. Wingfold!" he said appealingly, "does it not seem strange that, if our dearest friends go on living somewhere else, they should, the moment they cease to breathe, pass away from us utterly—so utterly that from that moment neither hint nor trace nor sign of their existence ever reaches us?

"Nature, the Bible, God himself says nothing about how they exist or where they are, or why they are so silent—cruelly silent if it be in their power to speak,—therefore, they cannot; and here we are left not only with aching hearts but wavering faith, not knowing whither to turn to escape the stare of the awful blank, that seems in the very intensity of its silence to shout in our ears that we are but dust and return to the dust!"

The gate-keeper and curate interchanged a pleased look of surprise at the draper's eloquence, but Polwarth instantly took up his answer.

"I grant you it would be strange indeed if there were no good reason for it," he said.

"Then do you say," asked Wingfold, "that until we see, discover, or devise some good reason for the darkness that overhangs it, we are at liberty to remain in doubt as to whether there be any life within the cloud?"

"I would say so," answered Polwarth, "were it not that we have the story of Jesus, which, if we accept it, is surely enough to satisfy us both as to the thing itself, and as to the existence of a good reason, whether we have found one or not, for the mystery that overshadows it."

"Still I presume we are not forbidden to seek such a reason," said the curate.

The draper was glancing from the one to the other with evident anxiety.

"Certainly not," returned the gate-keeper. "For what else is our imagination given us but the discovery of good reasons that are, or the invention of good reasons that may perhaps be?"

"Can you then imagine any good reason," said Drew, "why we should be kept in such absolute ignorance of everything that befalls the parted spirit from the moment it quits its house with us?"

"I think I know one," answered Polwarth. "I have sometimes fancied it might be because no true idea of their condition could possibly be grasped by those who remain in the tabernacle of the body; that to know their state it is necessary that we also should be clothed in our new bodies, which are to the old as a house to a tent. I doubt if we have any words in which the new facts could be imparted to our knowledge, the facts themselves being beyond the reach of any senses whereof we are now in actual possession. I expect to find my new body provided with new, I mean *other* senses beyond what I now possess: many more may be required to bring us into relation with all the facts in himself which God may have shadowed forth in properties, as we say, of what we call matter. The spaces all around us, even to those betwixt star and star, may be the home of the multitudes of the heavenly host, yet seemingly empty to all who have but our provision of senses.

"But I do not care to dwell upon that kind of speculation. It belongs to a lower region, upon which I grudge to expend interest while the far loftier one invites me, where, if I gather not the special barley of which I am in search, I am sure to come upon the finest of wheat.—Well, then, for my reason: There are a thousand individual events in the course of every man's life, by which God takes a hold of him—a thousand breaches by which he would and does enter, little as the man may know it; but there is one universal and unchanging grasp he keeps upon the race, yet not as the race, for the grasp is upon every solitary single individual that has a part in it: that grasp is—death in its mystery. To whom can the man who is about to die in absolute loneliness and go he cannot tell whither, flee for refuge from the doubts and fears that assail him, but to the Father of his being?"

"But," said Drew, "I cannot see what harm would come of letting us know a little—as much at least as might serve to assure us that there was more of *something* on the other side."

"Just this," returned Polwarth, "that, their fears allayed, their hopes encouraged from any lower quarter, men would, as usual, turn away from the fountain to the cistern of life, from the ever fresh original creative Love to that drawn off and shut in. That there are thousands who would forget God if they could but be assured of such a tolerable state of things beyond the grave as even this wherein we now live, is plainly to be anticipated from the fact that the doubts of so many in respect of religion concentrate themselves now-a-days upon the question whether there is any life beyond the grave; a question which, although no doubt nearly associated with religion,—as what question worth asking is not?—does not immediately belong to religion at all. Satisfy such people, if you can, that they shall live, and what have they gained? A little comfort perhaps—but a comfort not from the highest source, and possibly gained too soon for their well-being. Does it bring them any nearer to God than they were before? Is he filling one cranny more of their hearts in conse-quence? Their assurance of immortality has not come from a knowledge of him, and without him it is worse than worthless. Little indeed has been gained, and that with the loss of much. The word applies here which our Lord in his parable puts into the mouth of Abraham: If they hear not Moses and the prophets, neither will they be persuaded though one rose from the dead. He does not say they would not believe in a future state though one rose from the dead—although most likely they would soon persuade themselves that the apparition after all was only an illusion—but that they would not be persuaded to repent, though one rose from the dead; and without that, what great matter whether they believed in a future state or not? It would only be the worse for them if they did.

"No, Mr. Drew! I repeat, it is not a belief in immortality that will deliver a man from the woes of humanity, but faith in the God of life, the father of lights, the God of all consolation and comfort. Believing in him, a man can leave his friends, and their and his own immortality, with everything else—even his and their love and perfection, with utter confidence in his hands. Until we have the life in us, we shall never be at peace. The living God dwelling in the heart he has made, and glorifying it by inmost speech with himself—that is life, assurance, and safety. Nothing less is or can be such."

From a letter to his son Robert; three of MacDonald's children had died over the previous eight years.

Perhaps we may never all meet again together in this world. God knows: but I have all my life been attended . . . by the feeling of a meeting at hand. It must come one day—the hour when our hearts, all of them, will come together as they have never come before—when, knowing God, we shall know each other in a way infinitely beyond any way we have now. But the new way will fold the old way up in it. The Kingdom of Heaven has come near us that we may enter into it, and be all at home together. Kingdom and home are one.

From a letter to a friend.

Yes, I have never known such a time. Friend after friend going— but our hope is in heaven. God comes nearer and nearer. If only we went as fast as he was drawing us. . . . If we would but understand that we are pilgrims and strangers. It is no use trying to nestle down.

From the novel Wilfrid Cumbermede. *An old man wonders whether "when I creep forth into 'that new world which is the old,' I shall be conscious of the birth, and enjoy the whole mighty surprise, or whether I shall become gradually aware that things are changed and stare about me like the new-born baby."*

No wisest chicken, I presume, can recall the first moment when the chalk-oval surrounding it gave way, and instead of the cavern of limestone which its experience might have led it to expect, it found a world of air and movement and freedom and blue sky—with kites in it.

Appreciations

G. K. Chesterton

G. K. Chesterton was born in 1874, when George MacDonald was forty-nine years old and at the height of his popularity as a novelist. Chesterton encountered the "glorious fairyland of George Macdonald" as a child. The allegorical and fairy tale aspects of MacDonald's books—"the clearness of the ethical issue, the unclouded war of light against darkness, with no twilight or skepticism or timidity"—first attracted Chesterton to MacDonald's writings, which he continued to discuss in print up to the year of his death.

In May 1901, Chesterton, who had been publishing occasional reviews and essays in magazines, was commissioned to write a weekly column in *The Daily News*. This event, coinciding with his marriage to Frances Blogg and coming not long after his conversion, marked the beginning of his remarkably prolific career as an essayist, novelist, critic, journalist, philosopher, and Christian apologist. Chesterton's third *Daily News* column, published on June 11, was written to note an inexpensive reprint of *The Marquis of Lossie*, which had been published twenty-three years earlier. Chesterton again devoted his September 23, 1905, *Daily News* column to George MacDonald, this time commemorating his death five days earlier. The third and final selection included here is an introduction to Greville MacDonald's biography of his father written in 1924, the same year that Chesterton served as chairman at the centenary celebration of MacDonald's birth. Edits have been made to all three essays where the exuberance of Chesterton's interests led him to topics other than George MacDonald.

From Chesterton's 1901 column in the The Daily News *on "George Macdonald and His Work" written to mark a new edition of* The Marquis of Lossie.

If to be a great man is to hold the universe in one's head or heart, Dr. MacDonald is great. No man has carried about with him so naturally heroic an atmosphere. At one time he used to give performances of "The Pilgrim's Progress," appearing himself as Great-heart; and the mere possibility of the thing is typical, for it would be possible with no other modern man. The idea of Matthew Arnold in spangled armour, of Professor Huxley waving a sword before the footlights, would not impress us with unmixed gravity. But Dr. MacDonald seemed an elemental figure, a man unconnected with any particular age, a character in one of his own fairy tales, a true mystic to whom the supernatural was natural.

Many religious writers have written allegories and fairy tales, which have gone to creating the universal conviction that there is nothing that shows so little spirituality as an allegory, and nothing that contains so little imagination as a fairy tale. But from all these Dr. MacDonald is separated by an abyss of profound originality of intention. The difference is that the ordinary moral fairy tale is an allegory of real life. Dr. MacDonald's tales of real life are allegories, or disguised versions, of his fairy tales. It is not that he dresses up men and movements as knights and dragons, but that he thinks that knights and dragons, really existing in the eternal world, are dressed up here as men and movements. It is not the crown, the helmet, or the aureole that are to him the fancy dress; it is the top hat and the frock coat that are, as it were, the disguise of the terrestrial stage conspirators. His allegoric tales of gnomes and griffins do not lower a veil, but rend it. In one of those strange half-decipherable books, like the wild books of a prophet, which he has published in his old age, the hero is shown a glorious rose-bush, and told that it is standing in the same place as the piano in his drawing-room. To understand this idea is to understand George MacDonald, so long as we remember that it is not the rose-bush that is the symbol, but the piano. . . . Dr. MacDonald is far too good a poet to be a good novelist in the highest sense; for it is the glory of the novelist to look at humanity from a hundred standpoints: it is the glory of the poet to look at it from one. Dr. MacDonald sees the world bathed in one awful crimson of the divine love; he cannot look through the green spectacles of the cynic even for a moment.

✦ ✦ ✦

The interesting point about *The Marquis of Lossie* is this, and it contains the whole secret of Dr. MacDonald's work: It is the story of a young Scotch fisherman, who, in his impregnable simplicity and honour, goes up to a fashionable house in London, in order to rescue a fashionable lady (whom he knows to be his half-sister) from a disgraceful *mariage de convenance*. The story, as I have said, is not told with anything like the full measure of Dr. MacDonald's art; it is difficult to lay one's finger on a single scene which is quite properly proportioned, which has not too much philosophy and too little psychology. Yet the whole story is as vivid and as tense as a detective story. We read it with a profound sense of something greatly exciting us, and we cannot tell what it is. Then it will all become clear to us if we happen to remember Dr. MacDonald's magnificent fairy tale, "The Princess and Curdie." That tells of a miner-boy, who, under the mysterious commands of a fairy grandmother, goes to save a king and a princess from the plots of a monstrous and evil city. Suddenly we realize that the two stories are the same, that one runs inside the other, and that the realistic novel is the shell and the fairy tale the kernel. All the awkwardness, all the digression, all the abruptness or slowness of incident, merely mean that the hero longs to throw off the black hat and coat of Malcolm McPhail and declare himself as Curdie, the champion of the fairies. All of the excitement of the story lay in the fact that we knew that he was so.

Dr. MacDonald enters fairyland like a citizen returning to his home. But though a genuine mystic and genuine Celt, he has not reappeared in the movement of Celtic mysticism which has taken place in our time, chiefly because of that singular idea which has taken possession of it, that it is the duty of a mystic to be melancholy. It will take them a century or two perhaps to realize the truth that Dr. MacDonald, I fancy, has always known, that melancholy is a frivolous thing compared with the seriousness of joy. Melancholy is negative, and has to do with the trivialities like death: joy is positive and has to answer for the renewal and perpetuation of being. Melancholy is irresponsible; it could watch the universe fall to pieces: joy is responsible and upholds the universe in the void of space. This conception of the vigilance of the universal Power fills all Dr. MacDonald's novels with the unfathomable gravity of complete happiness, the gravity of a child at play. A curious glow pervades his books: the flowers seem like coloured flames broken loose from the flaming heart of the world: every bush of gorse is a burning bush, burning for the same cause as that of Moses. This sense of a perfect secret almost painfully kept by the universe is what shames the weariness of modern mystics. As if anyone who knew a secret could be weary.

There is another artistic matter in which Dr. MacDonald gave a profoundly original lead, and a lead which has never been followed. This was in his realization of the grotesque in the spiritual world. He has written children's poems full of a kind of nocturnal anarchy, like farcical dreams. The Owl says:

> I can see the wind; now who can do that?
> I can see the dreams that he has in his hat.
> Who else can watch the Lady Moon sit
> Hatching the boats and long-legged fowl
> On her nest the sea, all night, but the Owl?

These wild weddings of ideals have no priest that can join them, except the naked imagination. But the point of Dr. MacDonald's originality lies in this: that while other modern authors have written nonsense, he alone has written what may be called celestial nonsense. The world of *Alice in Wonderland* is one of purely intellectual folly: there are times, indeed, which must have come to any imaginative man, when he feels suddenly homeless and horror-stricken in the world of mathematical madness, when he feels unreason to be older and crueler than reason, and when he realizes the deep truth that nothing on earth is so desolate as unlimited levity. But Dr. MacDonald's world of extravagance, where the moon hatches the ships and the oysters gape to sing, is penetrated through and through with a warmth of world-love, the cosmic comradery of the child. Even monsters are pets on that enormous nursery.

From Chesterton's 1905 obituary of George MacDonald in The Daily News.

If we test the matter by strict originality of outlook, George Macdonald was one of the three or four greatest men of 19th century Britain. He does not in the ordinary sense occupy that position, because his art, though highly individual and fanciful, does not reach the level of his thought and passion. . . .

To appreciate properly men like Macdonald, it is necessary to remember a type of man who is a pillar of simple societies, but whom complex societies tend to turn into something else. I mean the sage, the sayer of things. He is not the poet, for he does not sing; he is not the prose writer, for generally he cannot write. The things he produces form an artistic class by themselves; they are logia or great passionate maxims, the proverbs of philosophy. . . .

George Macdonald was in the same way not a born writer; he was a born maker of spontaneous texts. He also would have very much preferred to walk about the streets of some Greek or Eastern village with a long white beard, simply saying what he had to say. But just as Whitman had to label his tracts of truth poetry, Macdonald labelled his novels. There are some exceptions, which we may notice in a moment, but in the main it is true to say that we only remember his novels, as we only remember Whitman's poetry, by certain bursts of an astonishing sagacity often uttered in five words. Anyone who has read Macdonald's novels will remember a sort of celestial wit in some of the dialogues, retorts that seem really like thunderbolts from heaven, such as some of Robert Falconer's answers to those who inquire about his methods or some of the mystical flippancies of the North Wind, or the perfect reply of Mr. Cupples, in *Alec Forbes*, to the man who objected to his carrying a foxglove on the Lord's

Day. "It angert me sae to see the illfaured thing growin' there on the Lord's Day, that I maist pulled it up by the root." . . .

Macdonald was a mystic who was half mad with joy, of a joy all the more violent because it remained mystical. For him the secret of the Cosmos was a secret because it was too good to tell. The stars and all things in his world tingled with the tension of that painful pleasure of the soul. For him the pity of God was so positive as to be a definite passion like thirst; it was a fierce tenderness; he was never tired of saying that his God was a consuming fire.

The Mystic believes that a rose is red with a fixed and sacred redness, and that a cucumber is green by a thundering decree of Heaven. Hence in all the great Christian Mystics, in St. Francis, in Vaughan, in Macdonald, there is a brightness of colour. . . . Actuality is the keynote of Mysticism. And this great man has now gone deeper into a world of dreadful actuality, of a deepening and dreadful joy.

From Chesterton's introduction to a biography of George and Louisa MacDonald by their son Greville MacDonald.

[I]n a certain rather special sense I for one can really testify to a book that has made a difference to my whole existence, which helped me to see things in a certain way from the start; a vision of things which even so real a revolution as a change of religious allegiance has substantially only crowned and confirmed. Of all the stories I have read, including even all the novels of the same novelist, it remains the most real, the most realistic, in the exact sense of the phrase the most like life. It is called *The Princess and the Goblin*, and is by George MacDonald. . . .

When I say it is like life, what I mean is this. It describes a little princess living in a castle in the mountains which is perpetually undermined, so to speak, by subterranean demons who sometimes come up through the cellars. She climbs up the castle stairways to the nursery or the other rooms; but now and again the stairs do not lead to the usual landings, but to a new room she has never seen before, and cannot generally find again. Here a good great-grandmother, who is a sort of fairy godmother, is perpetually spinning and speaking words of understanding and encouragement. When I read it as a child, I felt that the whole thing was happening inside a real human house, not essentially unlike the house I was living in, which also had staircases and rooms and cellars. This is where the fairy-tale differed from many other fairy-tales; above all, this is where the philosophy differed from many other philosophies. I have always felt a certain insufficiency about the ideal of Progress, even of the best sort which is a Pilgrim's Progress. It hardly suggests how near both the best and the worst things are to us from the first; even perhaps especially at the first. And though like every other sane person I value and revere the ordinary fairy-tale of the miller's third son who set out to seek his fortune (a form which MacDonald himself followed in the sequel called *The Princess and Curdie*), the very suggestion of travelling to a far-off fairyland, which is the soul of it, prevents it from achieving this particular purpose of making all the ordinary staircases and doors and windows into magical things. . . .

And the picture of life in this parable is not only truer than the image of a journey like that of the Pilgrim's Progress, it is even truer than the mere image of a siege like that of The Holy War. There is—something not only imaginative but intimately true about the idea of the goblins being below the house and capable of besieging it from the cellars. When the evil things besieging us do appear, they do not appear outside but inside. . . .

All George MacDonald's other stories, interesting and suggestive in their several ways, seem to be illustrations and even disguises of that one. I say disguises, for this is the very important difference between his sort of mystery and mere allegory. The commonplace allegory takes what it regards as the commonplaces or conventions necessary to ordinary men and women, and tries to make them pleasant or picturesque by dressing them up as princesses or goblins or good fairies. But George MacDonald did really believe that people were princesses and goblins and good fairies, and he dressed them up as ordinary men and women. The fairy-tale was the inside of the ordinary story and not the outside. . . .

The originality of George MacDonald has also a historical significance, which perhaps can best be estimated by comparing him with his great countryman Carlyle. . . . Carlyle could never have said anything so subtle and simple as MacDonald's saying that God is easy to please and hard to satisfy. Carlyle was too obviously occupied with insisting that God was hard to satisfy; just as some optimists are doubtless too much occupied with insisting that He is easy to please. In other words, MacDonald had made for himself a sort of spiritual environment, a space and transparency of mystical light, which was quite exceptional in his national and denominational environment. . . .

In his particular type of literary work he did indeed realize the apparent paradox of a St. Francis of Aberdeen, seeing the same sort of halo round every flower and bird. It is not the same thing as any poet's appreciation of the beauty of the flower or bird. A heathen can feel that and remain heathen, or in other words remain sad. It is a certain special sense of significance, which the tradition that most values it calls sacramental. To have got back to it, or forward to it, at one bound of boyhood, out of the black Sabbath of a Calvinist town, was a miracle of imagination.

C.S. Lewis

C. S. Lewis once wrote, "I was brought back . . . [from atheism to Christianity] by the strong influence of two writers, the Presbyterian George MacDonald and the Roman Catholic G. K. Chesterton." He described many times his first experience of reading George MacDonald's *Phantastes* and its effect on his life. One such account is given in *The Great Divorce*, published in 1945, where he recounts an imaginary trip to heaven where George MacDonald is his guide:

> I tried, trembling, to tell this man all that his writing had done for me. I tried to tell how a certain frosty afternoon at Leatherhead Station when I first bought a copy of *Phantastes* (being then about sixteen years old) had been to me what the first sight of Beatrice had been to Dante: *Here begins the New Life.* I tried to confess how long that Life had delayed in the region of imagination merely: how slowly and reluctantly I had come to admit that his Christendom had more than an accidental connection with it, how hard I had tried not to see that the true name of this quality which first met me in his books is Holiness.

Elsewhere, describing his conversion, he wrote, "George Macdonald I had found for myself at the age of sixteen and never wavered in my allegiance, though I tried for a long time to ignore his Christianity." References to MacDonald's books run through C. S. Lewis's correspondence. What starts as literary appreciation—discussed in lengthy exchanges with his childhood friend Arthur Greeves—becomes a spiritual touchstone. After C. S. Lewis's conversion, and as he became increasingly well-known as a Christian apologist, he was frequently asked to recommend books that would help other seekers, and as often recommended George MacDonald. In 1946 he published a collection of 365 short excerpts from MacDonald's works, writing in the preface:

> In making this collection I was discharging a debt of justice. I have never concealed the fact that I regarded him as my master; indeed I fancy I have never written a book in which I did not quote from him. But it has not seemed to me that those who have received my books kindly take even now sufficient notice of the affiliation. Honesty drives me to emphasize it.

The excerpts from the preface included below offer additional biographical information and, taken together with the selections from his letters, show both how much George MacDonald meant to C. S. Lewis and how MacDonald's value to him was as a guide to understanding and following the gospel.

Lewis had converted from atheism to theism in 1929. In a letter to his friend Arthur Greeves written on June 7, 1930, Lewis is discussing Charles Kingsley's 1863 children's novel The Water Babies. *Lewis and Greeves shared an abiding enthusiasm for George MacDonald's writing.*

The book itself seems to me not very good. There is some fancy, and I don't object to the preaching: but after Macdonald it is tasteless. Put the two side by side and see how Imagination differs from mere fancy, and holiness from mere morality.

From a letter to Arthur Greeves, June 15, 1930.

I envy you your shelf of Macdonalds and long to look over them with your guidance. I have read both *The Princess & the Goblin* and *The Princess & Curdie*. In fact I read the former (the other is a sequel to it) for about the third time when I was ill this spring. Read it at once if you have it, it is the better of the two. There is the fine part about the princess discovering her godmother in the attic spinning. . . . Another fine thing in *The Princess & the Goblin* is where Curdie, in a dream, keeps on dreaming that he has waked up and then finding that he is still in bed. This means the same as the passage where Adam says to Lilith 'Unless you unclose your hand you will never die and therefore never wake. *You may think you have died and even that you have risen again:* but both will be a dream.' This has a terrible meaning, specially for imaginative people. We read of spiritual efforts, and our imagination makes us believe that, because we enjoy the idea of doing them, we have done them. I am appalled to see how much of the change wh[ich] I thought I had undergone lately was only imaginary. The real work seems still to be done. It is so fatally easy to confuse an aesthetic appreciation of the spiritual life with the life itself—to dream that you have waked, washed, and dressed, and then to find yourself still in bed.

From a letter to Arthur Greeves, August 31, 1930.

I have had two delightful moments since I last wrote. The first was the arrival of the Macdonalds. Thank you over and over again! Perhaps the best way I can thank you at the moment is by trying to give you a share in my delight.

Imagine me, then, seated in a shady, but even so sweltering, corner of the garden with a shade temperature of 88°, in the middle of the afternoon. Imagine the sound of Mr. Papworth barking and my rising wearily, as at the 100th interruption, to investigate. I took in the bulky parcel carelessly enough and looked at it without hope of interest, till suddenly your hand-writing transformed the whole situation and in a minute I had it opened. Three distinguishable waves of pleasure went over me. The first was a welling up of all that Macdonald himself stands for: the second an added delight as this present, coming so appropriately from you, linked itself up with all our joint life and old times (I begin to see that it is not all rot—tho' it often is—when people say they will value a gift more for the sake of the giver): the third a pleased surprise at finding three, at least, of the books respectably bound, and clean pages of decent type and paper within—for I had always taken it for granted that they would be hideous.

If I followed my inclinations I would have read them all by now: but fortunately work forbids me such a dangerous orgy. I have however finished *Wilfrid Cumbermede*—I took it down with me after tea that same afternoon to Parson's Pleasure and read . . . under the willows. I shall not venture on my next Macdonald, tho' tempted, for some time, for fear of spoiling my own delights.

As you said in one of your letters, his novels have great and almost intolerable faults. . . . Yet the gold is so good that it carries off the dross and I hope to read this book many times again. . . .

Thanks, Arthur, again and again. I know nothing that gives me such a feeling of spiritual healing, of being washed, as to read G. Macdonald.

From a letter to Arthur Greeves, December 24, 1930.

One reason I enjoyed [MacDonald's] *Quiet Neighbourhood* so much was that I read it immediately after Trollope's *Belton Estate*: quite a good book, but all the time one was making excuses for the author on the moral side: saying that this bit of uncharitableness and that bit of unconscious cynicism, and, throughout, the bottomless *worldliness* (not knowing itself for such) belonged to the period. Then you turned to Macdonald, also a Victorian, and after a few pages were ashamed to have spent even an hour in a world so inferior as that of Trollope's.

From a letter to Arthur Greeves, January 17, 1931.

I have read a new Macdonald since I last wrote, which I think the very best of the novels. I would put it immediately below *Phantastes, Lilith,* the *Fairy Tales,* and the *Diary of an Old Soul.* It is called *What's Mine's Mine.* It has very little of the bad plot interest, and quite frankly subordinates story to doctrine. But such doctrine. Some of the conversations in this book I hope to re-read many times. The scene and the characters are Highland Celtic, as opposed to the Lowland Scots of most of the novels: highly idealised. Yet somehow they convince me. Or if they don't quite convince me as real people, they differ from most ideal characters in this, that I wish they *were* real. . . .

Lewis dated his conversion to Christianity to September 1931.

From a letter to Arthur Greeves, February 4, 1933.

And, talking of this sort of thing, would you believe it—I am actually officially supervising a young woman who is writing

a thesis on G. Macdonald. It is very odd—and curiously difficult—to approach as work something so old and intimate. The
girl is, unfortunately, quite unworthy of her subject: apart from
everything else, she is an American.

From a letter to Arthur Greeves, September 1, 1933.

I have just re-read *Lilith* and am much clearer about the
meaning. . . . The main lesson of the book is against secular phi-
lanthropy—against the belief that you can effectively obey the
2nd command about loving your neighbor without first trying
to love God.

*During the 1940s, Lewis began to speak about Christianity on radio
(these talks were collected and published as* Mere Christianity)
and write Christian apologetics.

*From a letter to Professor Eliza Marian Butler on August 18,
1940, in which Lewis discusses the relationship between myth and
allegory.*

The same story may be mythical or symbolical to one person and
allegorical to another. This I have tested in experience. When I
read George Macdonald's stories as a boy I was overwhelmed
with a sense of significance, but couldn't have identified any one
thing in them with any idea, nor got the significance of the whole
conceptually apart from the story. Now, when I re-read them,
they are almost pure allegory to me—because, in the interval, I
have discovered what they are 'about' by quite a different route.

From a letter to Sister Penelope, an Anglican nun, on November 4, 1940.

Isn't [MacDonald's novel] *Phantastes* good? It did a lot for me years before *I* became a Christian, when I had no idea what was behind it. This has always made it easier for me to understand how the better elements in mythology can be a real *praeparatio evangelica* for people who do not yet know whither they are being led.

From a letter to Mr. H. Moreland, August 19, 1942, responding to a request for a reading list.

My own greatest debt is to George Macdonald, specially the 3 vols of *Unspoken Sermons* (out of print but often obtainable 2nd hand).

From a letter to Arthur Greeves, December 10, 1942.

What a series of rediscoveries life is. All the things which one used to regard as simply the nonsense grown-ups talk have one by one come true—draughts, rheumatism, Christianity. The best one of all remains to be verified. I have introduced such a lot of people to Macdonald this year, in nearly every case with success.

From a letter to Edith Gates, May 23 1944.

Certainly I cannot love my neighbour properly till I love God. As George Macdonald says in his *Unspoken Sermons* (long out of print but if you can get a 2nd hand copy by any means short

---

praeparatio evangelica preparation for the gospel

of stealing, do! It is beyond price) "And beginning to try to love his neighbour he finds that this is no more to be reached in itself than the Law was to be reached in itself."

George MacDonald: An Anthology, edited by Lewis and with a preface by him, was published in 1946.

From a letter to Arthur Greeves, May 13, 1946.

The Macdonald anthology, as you see, is not of his verse, wh[ich] I still consider greatly inferior to his prose. In the novels the three things I like are (a) The parts that have something of a fairy tale quality, like the terror of the trees and wind at the beginning of *W. Cumbermede* or the lovely journey "up Gaunside" in *Sir Gibbie*. (b) (Like you) the melodrama. The older critics are v. unjust to melodrama (c) The *direct* preaching. What I can't stand is the indirect preaching—I mean Connie on her sofa in *The Seaboard Parish*. What between him and Scott and an Ulster upbringing I now find no difficulty with the Scotch dialect parts, indeed I like them. They enable him to make characters say strongly and racily things he w[oul]d spoil in English.

Excerpt from Lewis's preface to the volume George MacDonald: An Anthology. *The Preface begins with a summary of George MacDonald's biography.*

[MacDonald's] lungs were diseased and his poverty was very great. Literal starvation was sometimes averted only by those last-moment deliverances which agnostics attribute to chance and Christians to Providence. It is against this background of reiterated failure and incessant peril that some of the following extracts can be most profitably read. His resolute condemnations of anxiety come from one who has a right to speak; nor does their tone encourage the theory that they owe anything to the pathological wishful thinking—the *spes phthisica*—of the consumptive. None of the evidence suggests such a character. His peace of mind came not from building on the future but from resting in what he called "the holy Present." His resignation to poverty . . . was at the opposite pole from that of the stoic. He appears to have been a sunny, playful man, deeply appreciative of all really beautiful and delicious things that money can buy, and no less deeply content to do without them. It is perhaps significant—it is certainly touching—that his chief recorded weakness was a Highland love of finery; and he was all his life hospitable as only the poor can be.

In making these extracts I have been concerned with MacDonald not as a writer but as a Christian teacher. If I were to deal with him as a writer, a man of letters, I should be faced with a difficult critical problem. If we define Literature as an art whose medium is words, then certainly MacDonald has no place in its first rank—perhaps not even in its second. There are indeed passages, many of them in this collection, where the wisdom and (I would dare to call it) the holiness that are in him triumph over and even burn away the baser elements in his style: the expression becomes precise, weighty, economic; acquires a cutting edge. But he does not maintain this level for long. The texture of his writing as a whole is undistinguished, at times fumbling. Bad pulpit traditions cling to it; there is sometimes a nonconformist verbosity, sometimes an old Scotch weakness for florid ornament . . . , sometimes an oversweetness picked up from Novalis. But this does not quite dispose of him even for the

spes phthisica the hope of the consumptive

literary critic. What he does best is fantasy—fantasy that hovers between the allegorical and the mythopoeic. And this, in my opinion, he does better than any man. . . .

Few of his novels are good and none is very good. They are best when they depart most from the canons of novel writing, and that in two directions. Sometimes they depart in order to come nearer to fantasy, as in the whole character of the hero in *Sir Gibbie* or the opening chapters of *Wilfrid Cumbermede*. Sometimes they diverge into direct and prolonged preachments which would be intolerable if a man were reading for the story, but which are in fact welcome because the author, though a poor novelist, is a supreme preacher. Some of his best things are thus hidden in his dullest books. I am speaking so far of the novels as I think they would appear if judged by any reasonably objective standard. But it is, no doubt, true that any reader who loves holiness and loves MacDonald—yet perhaps he will need to love Scotland too—can find even in the worst of them something that disarms criticism and will come to feel a queer, awkward charm in their very faults. (But that, of course, is what happens to us with all favorite authors.) One rare, and all but unique, merit these novels must be allowed. The "good" characters are always the best and most convincing. His saints live; his villains are stagey.

. . . [I]n MacDonald it is always the voice of conscience that speaks. He addresses the will: the demand for obedience, for "something to be neither more nor less nor other than *done*" is incessant. Yet in that very voice of conscience every other faculty somehow speaks as well—intellect, and imagination, and humor, and fancy, and all the affections; and no man in modern times was perhaps more aware of the distinction between Law and Gospel, the inevitable failure of mere morality. The Divine

Sonship is the key conception which unites all the different elements of his thought. . . . Inexorability—but never the inexorability of anything less than love—runs through it like a refrain; "escape is hopeless"—"agree quickly with your adversary"—"compulsion waits behind"—"the uttermost farthing will be exacted." Yet this urgency never becomes shrill. All the sermons are suffused with a spirit of love and wonder which prevents it from doing so. MacDonald shows God threatening, but (as Jeremy Taylor says) "He threatens terrible things if we will not be happy."

. . . It must be more than thirty years ago that I bought—almost unwillingly, for I had looked at the volume on that bookstall and rejected it on a dozen previous occasions—the Everyman edition of *Phantastes*. A few hours later I knew that I had crossed a great frontier. I had already been waist-deep in Romanticism; and likely enough, at any moment, to flounder into its darker and more evil forms, slithering down the steep descent that leads from the love of strangeness to that of eccentricity and thence to that of perversity. Now *Phantastes* was romantic enough in all conscience; but there was a difference. Nothing was at that time further from my thoughts than Christianity and I therefore had no notion what this difference really was. I was only aware that if this new world was strange, it was also homely and humble; that if this was a dream, it was a dream in which one at least felt strangely vigilant; that the whole book had about it a sort of cool, morning innocence, and also, quite unmistakably, a certain quality of Death, *good* Death. What it actually did to me was to convert, even to baptize (that was where the Death came in) my imagination. It did nothing to my intellect nor (at that time) to my conscience. Their turn came far later and with the help of many other books and men. But when the process was complete—by which, of course, I mean "when it had *really* begun"—I found that I was still with MacDonald and that he had accompanied me all the way and that I was now at last ready to hear from him much that he could not have told me at that first meeting. But in a sense, what he was now telling me was the very same that he had told me from the beginning. There was no question of getting through to the kernel and throwing away the shell: no question of a gilded pill. The pill was gold all through.

Notes

Because MacDonald's works are available in numerous editions as well as online, the source of each selection is given by chapter. A helpful resource is the CD-ROM Ever Yours, George MacDonald, *compiled by Robert Trexler, which contains the text of all MacDonald's books. It is available from www.george-macdonald.com.*

Introduction

vii *widely reproduced photograph*   *English Celebrities of the Nineteenth Century.*

     MacDonald has no place   C. S. Lewis, preface to *George MacDonald: An Anthology.*

viii *beyond price*   C. S. Lewis to Edith Gates, May 23, 1944, in *The Collected Letters of C. S. Lewis,* vol. 2, 616.

     I dare not say   C. S. Lewis, preface.

ix *People find great fault*   Reported in Greville MacDonald, *George MacDonald and his Wife.* The biographical information in this note is mostly taken from this biography, which quotes extensively from MacDonald's letters and accounts of his life by his contemporaries.

     In that style   W. H. Auden, foreword to *The Visionary Novels of George MacDonald.*

xi *I begin to suspect*   George MacDonald, *Thomas Wingfold, Curate,* vol. 2, chap. 9.

     I never have   *George MacDonald and his Wife,* 542.

xii *the wrong side*   *George MacDonald and his Wife,* 426.

xiii *In some wonderful*   Kirsten Jeffrey Johnson, "Did You Know," *Christianity Today,* April 1, 2006.

     There is something   *George MacDonald and his Wife,* 436.

xiv *Arthur Hughes*   Carolyn Hares-Stryker, "Slight Channels: Arthur Hughes and the Illustration of Children's Books" in *Haunted Texts,* 94.

xiv *choosing, gathering* George MacDonald, *A Dish of Orts: Chiefly Papers on the Imagination, and on Shakespeare*, 1895, 22.

xv *his long vigil* *George MacDonald and his Wife*, 560.

   a life beyond George MacDonald, *What's Mine's Mine*, vol. 2, chap. 14.

   When he comes G. K. Chesterton, introduction to *George MacDonald and his Wife*, 13.

   a book that has made Ibid.

   I knew that C. S. Lewis, preface.

xvi *Acknowledging a vote* Anonymous, letter to the editor, *The Spectator*, June 6, 1924.

xvii *For what is the great* George MacDonald, *Donal Grant*, 1883, chap. 34.

Chapter 1 Seeking

1 *Brothers* "The Child in the Midst" in *Unspoken Sermons*, series 1.

3 *How often do we look* *Annals of a Quiet Neighborhood*, chap. 28.

   Nor will God "The Cause of Spiritual Stupidity" in *Unspoken Sermons*, series 2.

4 *Of course all* *Thomas Wingfold, Curate*, vol. 1, chap. 12.

5 *They rose* *Robert Falconer*, part 1, chap. 12.
   So Robert sat *Robert Falconer*, part 2, chap. 7.
   And once more *Robert Falconer*, part 3, chap. 1.

Chapter 2 Repentance

13 *At the root* *Thomas Wingfold, Curate*, vol. 2, chap. 34.

14 *What would be* MacDonald to Mrs. Russell Gurney, November 12, 1877, in *An Expression of Character: The Letters of George MacDonald*, 271.

   The Christian life "To the Church of the Laodiceans" in *George MacDonald in the Pulpit*.

15 *The rumour got* *Robert Falconer*, part 2, chap. 3.

16 *Doubtless he would* *The Vicar's Daughter*, chap. 27.

   I woke early *Ranald Bannerman's Boyhood*, chap. 18.

22 *I suspect* *Thomas Wingfold, Curate*, vol. 3, chap. 21.

23 *The clergyman* *Robert Falconer*, part 3, chap. 17.

   Sickness sometimes *The Marquis of Lossie*, chap. 59.

26 *When you would* *The Elect Lady*, chap. 35.

Have you forgiven *The Vicar's Daughter,* chap. 20.

Can one ever *Alec Forbes of Howglen,* chap. 58.

Chapter 3 Redemption

27 *Of all things* *Ranald Bannerman's Boyhood,* chap. 31.

Mrs. Elton left *David Elginbrod,* book 2, chap. 18.

30 *But I must stop* *Robert Falconer,* part 1, chap. 16.

31 *The making* "Self-Denial" in *Unspoken Sermons,* series 2.
The Lord did not die "The Truth in Jesus" in *Unspoken Sermons,* series 2.

32 *[De Fleuri] told the story* *Robert Falconer,* part 3, chap. 11.

33 *One night I was returning* *Robert Falconer,* part 3, chap. 6.

35 *They went on* *David Elginbrod,* book 3, chap. 17.

36 *The most presumptuous* *The Seaboard Parish,* Vol. 3, chap. 8.

39 *Ah, Miss Clare!* *The Vicar's Daughter,* chap. 38.

There is a city *Lilith: A Romance,* chap. 15.

Chapter 4 Jesus

43 *Only one thing* "I am the Way, the Truth, and the Life" sermon given
in Bordighera in 1885 and as reported in a letter to the editor, *The Spectator,*
October 7, 1905.

44 *I am always* MacDonald to his father, May 20, 1853, in *George
MacDonald and his Wife,* 184.

The winter *Adela Cathcart,* vol. 1, chap. 2.

45 *There was once* *The Seaboard Parish,* vol. 1, chap. 4.

46 *Have you really* MacDonald to an unknown woman, 1886, in *George
MacDonald and his Wife,* 373.

48 *We are and remain* "The Eloi" in *Unspoken Sermons,* series 1.

That existence MacDonald to his son Greville MacDonald, January 20,
1889, in *George MacDonald and his Wife,* 535.

49 *I am sorely* *Donal Grant,* chap. 33.

52 *Man finds it* "Life" in *Unspoken Sermons,* series 2.

53 *Never will* *There and Back,* chap. 57.

Do you ever "True Christian Ministering" in *A Dish of Orts.*

54 *He did not* "Kingship" in *Unspoken Sermons,* series 3.

54   *Come, then*   *Thomas Wingfold, Curate*, vol. 2, chap. 13.

55   *Yes, we are*   MacDonald to Charlotte Powell Godwin, December 28, 1884, in *An Expression of Character*, 312.

Chapter 5   God's Glory

57   *When my being*   "The Truth" in *Unspoken Sermons*, series 3.

58   *Notwithstanding his*   *Donal Grant*, chap. 7.

62   *Friends, I have*   "A Sermon" in *A Dish of Orts*.

64   *But his glory!*   *David Elginbrod*, book 1, chap. 13.
     He would utter   *Wilfrid Cumbermede*, chap. 5.

Chapter 6   The Divine Plan

65   *And whenever the thought*   *Wilfrid Cumbermede*, chap. 54.
     Hugh read   *David Elginbrod*, book 2, chap. 4.

68   *Certain people considered*   *The Vicar's Daughter*, chap. 25.
     One evening when   *Robert Falconer*, part 3, chap. 16.

70   *Sometimes a thunderbolt*   *Thomas Wingfold, Curate*, vol. 1, chap. 21.

71   *Nor did Portlossie*   *Malcolm*, chap. 23.

77   *Blessed be*   MacDonald to Susan Scott, June 1, 1894, in *An Expression of Character*, 360.

78   *I think my wife*   MacDonald to Mrs. William Cowper-Temple, February 17, 1878, in *An Expression of Character*, 276.
     Poor mother!   *There and Back*, chap. 46.
     If the woman   *There and Back*, chap. 47.

79   *God makes*   "The Imagination" in *A Dish of Orts*.

80   *Weel, An'rew*   *The Elect Lady*, chap. 34.

Chapter 7   The Boundlessness of Love

81   *It looked as if God*   *Weighed and Wanting*, chap. 7.
     If we will   "Life" in *Unspoken Sermons*, series 2.

82   *The almost passionate*   *David Elginbrod*, book 1, chap. 13.

83   *But tell me*   *The Seaboard Parish*, vol. 1, chap. 4.

84   *To him that*   "The New Name" in *Unspoken Sermons*, series 1.

85   *Except his own*   *Alec Forbes of Howglen*, chap. 53.
     At length one   *Alec Forbes of Howglen*, chap. 79.

88 *Sometimes the change*   MacDonald to Mrs. Russell Gurney, September 1, 1878, in *An Expression of Character*, 286.

89 *The morning after*   *There and Back*, chap. 47.

Chapter 8   Faith

93 *You cannot prove*   *There and Back*, chap. 35.

    Since this poem   W. F. C., "A Reminiscence of George MacDonald at Bordighera." *The Spectator*, October 7, 1905.

94 *Never in my*   *Warlock o' Glenwarlock*, chap. 22.

97 *Tell me the way*   "The Golden Key" in *Dealings with the Fairies*.

98 *Robert had not*   *Robert Falconer*, part 2, chap. 2.

99 *For I knew*   *The Vicar's Daughter*, chap. 37.

100 *Lat her come*   *Alec Forbes of Howglen*, chap. 29.

101 *I think I must*   *The Seaboard Parish*, vol. 1, chap. 12.
    "Yes," she answered   *The Seaboard Parish*, vol. 2, chap. 6.

103 *I wonner*   *Malcolm*, chap. 47.

105 *"Well," [said Faber]*   *Thomas Wingfold, Curate*, vol. 3, chap. 6.

108 *[Her father], never*   *Paul Faber, Surgeon*, chap. 12.

110 *Then the thought*   *There and Back*, chap. 45.

113 *Even the refuge*   *Ranald Bannerman's Boyhood*, chap. 32.

Chapter 9   Obedience

115 *If you do*   "Know Christ" preached in the West Croydon Congregational Church, 1887, in *George MacDonald in the Pulpit*.

    To do one's duty   *The Lost Princess: A Double Story*, chap. 8.

116 *He then proceeded*   *Thomas Wingfold, Curate*, vol. 3, chap. 31.

    Obedience is   "True Greatness" in *A Dish of Orts*.

118 *Having now*   *There and Back*, chap. 56.

119 *You consider*   *The Marquis of Lossie*, chap. 53.

123 *Molly was*   *Home Again: A Tale*, chap. 30.

125 *The will is*   "Life" in *Unspoken Sermons*, series 2.

125 *Mr. Porson was*   *A Rough Shaking*, chap. 6.

126 *It is better*   *Paul Faber, Surgeon*, chap. 5.

Chapter 10   Growth of Character

127 *Like most men*   *Mary Marston,* chap. 18.

When you fear   "Hope" recorded in "Notes from Broadlands Conferences."

The danger she   *What's Mine's Mine,* vol. 2, chap. 14.

128 *Many things were*   David Elginbrod, book 1, chap. 6.

It was a lovely morning   *Donal Grant,* chap. 1.

132 *Eh, lassie!*   *Alec Forbes of Howglen,* chap. 68.

Time passed   *Gutta Percha Willie,* chap. 5.

133 *There is a great power*   *Paul Faber, Surgeon,* chap. 38.

Oblige me   *Lilith: A Romance,* chap. 3.

134 *Half the misery*   *The Flight of the Shadow,* chap. 1.

How many people   *Paul Faber, Surgeon,* chap. 41.

In confession   *Home Again: A Tale,* chap. 26.

135 *One of the benefits*   *There and Back,* chap. 47.

138 *My dearly Loved*   MacDonald to his son Greville, April 6, 1884, in *George MacDonald and his Wife,* 530.

Whoever can think   *The Marquis of Lossie,* chap. 61.

139 *To every man*   "A Sketch of Individual Development" in *A Dish of Orts.*

This day's adventure   *The Princess and the Goblin.*

Chapter 11   Conscience

141 *Another pause*   *Wilfrid Cumbermede.*

There are good   *Robert Falconer,* part 3, chap. 8.

142 *What is called*   *There and Back,* chap. 13.

Awake, thou that sleepest   "The Truth in Jesus" in *Unspoken Sermons,* series 2

143 *A dreary place*   *The Seaboard Parish,* vol. 2, chap. 7.

145 *People are so*   *The Lost Princess,* chap. 3.

Chapter 12   Work

147 *Soon [Princess Rosamond]*   *The Lost Princess,* chap. 3.

148 *I must not*   *Gutta Percha Willie,* chap. 2.
And what's your   *Gutta Percha Willie,* chap. 5.

150 *To become able* *There and Back*, chap. 4.

151 *As I went* *Annals of a Quiet Neighborhood*, chap. 4.

156 *But indeed* *The Seaboard Parish*, vol. 1, chap. 2.

159 *Certainly work* *Wilfrid Cumbermede.*

Chapter 13 Prayer

161 *I looked up* *Wilfrid Cumbermede.*

Am I going "The Hands of the Father" in *Unspoken Sermons*, series 1.

It was a nothing *Robert Falconer*, part 2, chap. 18.

162 *Some natures will* *David Elginbrod*, book 3, chap. 8.

164 *Winter is needful* MacDonald to Mrs. William Cowper-Temple, April 3, 1883, in *An Expression of Character*, 308.

The night descended *Donal Grant*, chap. 12.

166 *One afternoon* *Wilfrid Cumbermede*, chap. 19.

167 *Have you been* *Thomas Wingfold, Curate*, vol. 3, chap. 20.

168 *"Richard," he said* *There and Back*, chap. 58.

Never wait "Righteousness" in *Unspoken Sermons*, series 3.

Go home and speak "True Christian Ministering" in *A Dish of Orts.*

Chapter 14 Love of Neighbor

171 *We shall never* "Hands of the Father" in *Unspoken Sermons*, series 1.

Some people take *Robert Falconer*, part 2, chap. 9.

172 *Coming to a spot* *Lilith: A Romance*, chap. 16.

173 *When God comes* *Annals of a Quiet Neighbourhood*, chap. 10.

174 *A few nights* *At the Back of the North Wind.*

178 *Those who would* *Weighed and Wanting*, chap. 12.

179 *The streets swarmed* *Robert Falconer*, part 3, chap. 8.

183 *At the first* *Donal Grant*, chap. 64.

Dearly as he *The Elect Lady*, chap. 6.

184 *All things belong* *There and Back*, chap. 7.

Whaur are ye *Salted with Fire.*

191 *I knew now* *Phantastes: A Fairie Romance for Men and Women.*

Chapter 15   Creation

193 *Oh the summer*   *Ranald Bannerman's Boyhood*, chap. 15.

194 *[Robert] lay*   *Robert Falconer*, part 1, chap. 18.

195 *I believe that*   "The Truth" in *Unspoken Sermons*, series 3.

198 *There was a*   *The Elect Lady*, chap. 13.
Then what do   *The Elect Lady*, chap. 21.

200 *This world is*   "Wordsworth's Poetry" in *A Dish of Orts*.

201 *Pondering, speculating*   *Annals of a Quiet Neighborhood*, chap. 3.

202 *But I am old*   *The Flight of the Shadow*, chap. 9.

Chapter 16   Our Father in Heaven

203 *What an awful*   *The Seaboard Parish*, vol. 2, chap. 8.

204 *Perhaps I did*   *David Elginbrod*, book 3, chap. 15.

205 *Don't you think*   *Warlock o' Glenwarlock*, chap. 18.

208 *My fault had opened*   *The Flight of the Shadow*, chap. 5.

Come to God   "Light" in *Unspoken Sermons*, series 3.

Chapter 17   Love and Marriage

209 *God only knows*   *The Marquis of Lossie*, chap. 61.

Happy is the rare fate   *What's Mine's Mine*, vol. 2, chap. 9.

212 *Love and marriage*   *Mary Marston*, chap. 49.

212 *Looking at Malcolm's life*   *Malcolm*, chap. 15.

214 *I have something*   *Donal Grant*, chap. 80.

216 *If something of*   *The Marquis of Lossie*, chap. 42.

This is your Birthday   MacDonald to Louisa MacDonald, November 5, 1891, in *George MacDonald and His Wife*, 525.

217 *Gibbie went home*   *Sir Gibbie*, chap. 59.

Chapter 18   Fatherhood and Motherhood

219 *She was a mother*   *Sir Gibbie*, chap. 11.

You see, Cosmo   *Warlock o' Glenwarlock*, chap. 3.

221 *My father used*   *The Vicar's Daughter*, chap. 2.

Nobody knows   *Warlock o' Glenwarlock*, chap. 24.

222 *This brings me*   *The Seaboard Parish,* vol. 1, chap. 2.

Few griefs can   *Paul Faber, Surgeon,* chap. 49.

223 *There must be something*   *The Princess and Curdie,* chap. 2.
There was a change   *The Princess and Curdie,* chap. 4.

224 *Wise as was*   *Weighed and Wanting,* chap. 2.

225 *Janet could not*   *David Elginbrod,* book 1, chap. 15.

When parents see   *The Seaboard Parish,* vol. 1, chap. 13.
I had no doubt   vol. 2, chap. 6.

226 *My Darling Elfie!*   MacDonald to Mary Josephine MacDonald, August 3, 1869, in *An Expression of Character,* 169.

Chapter 19   Education

229 *It is good*   *Robert Falconer,* part 1, chap. 18.

But to return   *The Vicar's Daughter,* chap. 8.

230 *This matter settled*   *Malcolm,* chap. 7.

231 *Towards the close*   *Donal Grant,* chap. 40.

235 *Many good birthdays*   MacDonald to Greville MacDonald, January 19, 1887, in *George MacDonald and His Wife,* 535.

Chapter 20   Money

237 *A man ought*   *Paul Faber, Surgeon,* chap. 21.

Our Lord never   *Weighed and Wanting,* chap. 7.

And the way   *Warlock o' Glenwarlock,* chap. 60.

238 *Those who feel*   *What's Mine's Mine,* vol. 3, chap. 12.

239 *But happily*   *Wilfrid Cumbermede,* chap. 11.

By and by   *David Elginbrod,* book 1, chap. 13.

241 *Of our friend*   *The Elect Lady,* chap. 24.

Having kept   "The Way" in *Unspoken Sermons,* series 2.

248 *But it is*   "The Hardness of the Way" in *Unspoken Sermons,* series 2.

One may readily   Sermon preached to a wealthy congregation in Glasgow, as reported in *George MacDonald and His Wife,* 157.

Chapter 21   Moralism

249 *The patience of*   *What's Mine's Mine,* vol. 1, chap. 14.

250 *To the great*   *David Elginbrod,* book 3, chap. 6.

253 *Can I hope*   *Guild Court: A London Story,* chap. 12.

256 *Donal went for*   *Donal Grant,* chap. 16.

257 *For nothing is*   *Thomas Wingfold, Curate,* vol. 3, chap. 7.

Chapter 22   Death

261 *Did you ever*   MacDonald to Lady Mount-Temple, December 9, 1888, in *An Expression of Character,* 339.

262 *As Falconer said*   *David Elginbrod,* book 3, chap. 7.

265 *Hoping that he*   *Robert Falconer,* part 3, chap. 4.

266 *Mr. Graham's here*   *Malcolm,* chap. 69.

272 *How real death*   MacDonald to William Cowper-Temple, April 9, 1879, in *An Expression of Character,* 293.

273 *When such children*   *Weighed and Wanting,* chap. 50.

  What can I say   MacDonald to Henry Cecil, March 3, 1890, in *George MacDonald and His Wife,* 536.

274 *[Ian] arrived at*   *What's Mine's Mine,* vol. 2, chap. 13.

284 *You will be*   MacDonald to Susan Scott, January 21, 1888, in *An Expression of Character,* 335.

Chapter 23   Resurrection

287 *Did it ever*   *The Seaboard Parish,* vol. 2, chap. 11.

288 *"See," said the schoolmaster*   *Malcolm,* chap. 12.

293 *The next day*   *Donal Grant,* chap. 38.

298 *I can't think*   *Thomas Wingfold, Curate,* vol. 3, chap. 27.

301 *Perhaps we may*   MacDonald to his son Robert Falconer MacDonald, August 29, 1886, in *George MacDonald and His Wife,* 534.

302 *Yes, I have*   MacDonald to W. C. Davies, June 19, 1878, in *George MacDonald and His Wife,* 487.

  No wisest chicken   *Wilfrid Cumbermede,* chap. 1.

Appreciations: G. K. Chesterton

305 *glorious fairyland*   G. K. Chesterton, *Autobiography,* 169.

  the clearness   G. K. Chesterton, "George MacDonald and His Work," *The Daily News,* June 11, 1901.

310 *If we test* "George MacDonald" (obituary), *The Daily News,* September 23, 1905.

311 *[I]n a certain* Introduction to *George MacDonald and His Wife,* 9.

Appreciations: C. S. Lewis

All letters quoted are taken from The Collected Letters of C. S. Lewis, *as edited by Walter Hooper. Copyright © 2004 by C. S. Lewis Pte. Ltd. Extracts reprinted by permission.*

315 *I was brought* C. S. Lewis to N. Fridama, February 15, 1946 in *The Collected Letters of C. S. Lewis,* vol. 2, ed. Walter Hooper, 702.

I tried, trembling C. S. Lewis, *The Great Divorce,* 61.

George Macdonald I had found C. S. Lewis, preface to *The Incarnation of the Word of God* by Athanasius, trans. Sister Penelope Lawson, 1944.

316 *In making this* C. S. Lewis, preface to *George MacDonald: An Anthology,* xxxvii. Copyright © 1946 by C. S. Lewis Pte. Ltd. Extracts reprinted by permission.

Illustrations by Arthur Hughes

Frontispiece *At the Back of the North Wind*

2 *The Princess and the Goblin*

12 *At the Back of the North Wind*

42 *At the Back of the North Wind*

56 *Gutta Percha Willie*

92 *Phantastes: A Faerie Romance*

140 *Gutta Percha Willie*

160 *The Princess and the Goblin*

170 *Gutta Percha Willie*

192 *The Golden Key*

236 *The Princess and the Goblin*

260 *At the Back of the North Wind*

286 *The Light Princess*

Bibliography

An annotated bibliography of all George MacDonald's works is available at www.macdonaldphillips.com.

Anonymous. Two letters to the editor of *The Spectator,* October 7, 1905.

Auden, W. H. Foreword to *The Visionary Novels of George MacDonald.* Edited by Anne Fremantle. New York: Noonday Press, 1954.

Chesterton, G. K. *Autobiography.* San Francisco: Ignatius Press, 2006. First published 1936 by Hutchinson.

———. "George MacDonald" (obituary). *The Daily News,* September 23, 1905.

———. "George MacDonald and His Work." *The Daily News,* June 11, 1901.

———. Introduction to *George MacDonald and His Wife* by Greville MacDonald. London: Allen & Unwin, 1924.

English Celebrities of the Nineteenth Century. London: Hughes and Edmonds, 1876.

Hares-Stryker, Carolyn. "Slight Channels: Arthur Hughes and the Illustration of Children's Books" in *Haunted Texts: Studies in Pre-Raphaelitism.* Edited by David Latham. Toronto: University of Toronto Press, 2003.

Johnson, Kirsten Jeffrey. "Did you Know?" *Christianity Today,* April 1, 2005. Accessed July 21, 2016. www.christianitytoday.com/history/issues/issue-86/did-you-know.html.

Lewis, C. S. Preface to *The Incarnation of the Word of God* by Athanasius. Translated by Sister Penelope Lawson. London: Geoffrey Bles, 1944.

———. *George MacDonald: An Anthology.* Edited and with a preface by C. S. Lewis. Harper Collins, 2015. First published 1946 by Geoffrey Bles.

———. *The Collected Letters of C. S. Lewis.* Edited by Walter Hooper. 3 vols. Harper Collins, 2004.

———. *The Great Divorce.* New York: The MacMillan Company, 1946.

MacDonald, George. *A Dish of Orts: Chiefly Papers on the Imagination and on Shakespeare.* London: Sampson Low Marston & Company, 1893.

_____ . *A Rough Shaking*. London: Blackie & Sons, 1891.

_____ . *Adela Cathcart*. London: Hurst & Blackett, 1864.

_____ . *Alec Forbes of Howglen*. London: Hurst & Blackett, 1865.

_____ . *An Expression of Character: The Letters of George MacDonald*. Edited by Glenn Edward Sadler. Grand Rapids, MI: W. B. Eerdmans Pub. Co., 1994.

_____ . *Annals of a Quiet Neighbourhood*. London: Hurst & Blackett, 1867.

_____ . *At the Back of the North Wind*. London: Strahan & Co., 1871.

_____ . *David Elginbrod*. London: Hurst & Blackett, 1863.

_____ . *Dealings with the Fairies*. London: Strahan & Co., 1867.

_____ . *Donal Grant*. London: George Routledge & Sons, 1883.

_____ . *George MacDonald in the Pulpit: Compilation of Spoken Sermons from 1871–1901*. Edited by J. Flynn & D. Edwards. Whitehorn, CA: Johannesen, 1996.

_____ . *Guild Court*. London: Hurst & Blackett, 1868.

_____ . *Home Again: A Tale*. London: Kegan Paul, Trench & Co., 1887.

_____ . "Hope," a sermon recorded in "Notes from Broadlands Conferences." Quoted by Barbara Amell. "George MacDonald on Psychology." *Inklings Forever*, vol 4., 2004.

_____ . *Lilith: A Romance*. London: Chatto & Windus, 1895.

_____ . *Malcolm*. London: Henry S. King & Co., 1875.

_____ . *Mary Marsten*. London: Sampson Low Marston & Company, 1881.

_____ . *Paul Faber, Surgeon*. London: Hurst & Blackett, 1879.

_____ . *Phantastes: A Fairie Romance for Men and Women*. London: Smith, Elder, 1858.

_____ . *Ranald Bannerman's Boyhood*. London: Blackie & Son, 1886.

_____ . *Robert Falconer*. London: Hurst & Blackett, 1868.

_____ . *Salted with Fire*. London: Hurst & Blackett, 1897.

_____ . *Sir Gibbie*. London: Hurst & Blackett, 1879.

_____ . *The Elect Lady*. London: Kegan, Paul, Trench & Co., 1888.

_____ . *The Flight of the Shadow*. London: Kegan, Paul, Trench & Co., 1891.

_____ . *The History of Gutta Percha Willie: The Working Genius*. London: Henry S. King & Co., 1873.

_____ . *The Lost Princess: A Double Story*. London: Strahan & Co., 1875.

_____ . *The Marquis of Lossie*. London: Hurst & Blackett, 1877.

———. *The Princess and Curdie*. London: Chatto & Windus, 1882.

———. *The Princess and the Goblin*. London: Strahan & Co., 1872.

———. *The Seaboard Parish*. London, Tinsley Bros., 1868.

———. *The Vicar's Daughter*. London: Tinsley Bros., 1872.

———. *There and Back*. London: Kegan, Paul, Trench & Co., 1891.

———. *Thomas Wingfold, Curate*. London: Hurst and Blackett, 1876.

———. *Unspoken Sermons*, series 1. London: Strahan & Co., 1867.

———. *Unspoken Sermons*, series 2. London: Longmans, Green, 1886.

———. *Unspoken Sermons*, series 3. London: Longmans, Green, 1889.

———. *Warlock o'Glenwarlock*. London: Sampson Low Marston & Company, 1881.

———. *Weighed and Wanting*. London: Sampson Low Marston & Company, 1882.

———. *What's Mine's Mine*. London: Kegan, Paul, Trench & Co., 1886.

———. *Wilfrid Cumbermede*. London: Hurst & Blackett, 1871.

———. *George MacDonald and his Wife*. London: Allen & Unwin, 1924.

MacDonald, Greville. *George MacDonald and His Wife*. London: Allen & Unwin, 1924.

Raeper, William. *George MacDonald*. Oxford: Lion Publishing, 1987.

Other Titles from Plough

The Gospel in Dostoyesvky: Selections from His Works. Passages from Dostoyevsky's greatest novels explore the devastating, yet ultimately healing, implications of the Gospels.

The Gospel in Tolstoy: Selections from His Short Stories, Spiritual Writings, and Novels. A rich, accessible introduction to one of the world's greatest novelists, this anthology shows how the life and teachings of Jesus inspired some of Tolstoy's best literary work.

Provocations: The Spiritual Writings of Kierkegaard. Introduces a man whose writings pare away the fluff of modern spirituality to reveal the basics of the Christ-centered life: decisiveness, obedience, and recognition of the truth.

Tidings: A Novel by Ernst Wiechert. A concentration camp survivor's classic novel of guilt and redemption. First published in 1950, it deserves its place among the masterpieces of European literature.

Salt and Light: Living the Sermon on the Mount by Eberhard Arnold. Unlike dozens of other books on the "Great Teaching" of Jesus, this one not only interprets it, but also says that it ought to be put into practice.

My God and My All: The Life of Saint Francis of Assisi by Elizabeth Goudge. The ever-fascinating life of Saint Francis, retold for today's readers by one of the great novelists of our time.

Plough Publishing House
www.plough.com
PO Box 398, Walden, NY 12586, USA
Robertsbridge, East Sussex TN32 5DR, UK
4188 Gwydir Highway, Elsmore, NSW 2360, AU